BLAME IT ON EMERALD ISLE

LUKE YOUNG

Chapter 1

She's Right in the Middle of Something

Even when you're already having a bad day that's progressively getting worse, there are a lot of things you don't expect to find when you return home early on a Friday afternoon. Like a team of IRS agents sitting on your couch, scrutinizing the home-office deduction you wrote off years ago, or you standing ankle deep in water from a pipe bursting, or your dog getting sick all over your bed.

Or, in my case, my mother, Candace—wearing some sort of fuzzy pink mask, dressed in a leather bustier and short shorts—standing over a bald, masked, middle-aged man, clad in nothing but a white T-shirt. He's seated on the floor with one of her bright candy-apple-red high heels sandwiched between his erect penis and large, nearly avocado-sized testicles.

The funny thing is, she doesn't look shocked to see me. She simply raises her head to look my way and says, "Oh, hi, Ally. I didn't expect you home so early."

Well, obviously.

My gaze returns to the spectacle on the floor, and I notice the penis has a rather extreme bend to the right.

Without skipping a beat, I switch into doctor mode,

crooking my index finger, then straightening it for effect. "You know, there are some new nonsurgical treatments for Peyronie's that can really help your situation."

He mumbles, clearly a bit taken aback, "Okay ... thanks."

"I'm a urologist." Reaching into my purse, I pull out a card. "Why don't you ..."

Suddenly, I return to earth, the absurdity of the situation slapping me right in the face. I don't speak or move. I don't know what to do. I glance from her to him. He's grimacing, of course, because, well, she's literally stepping on his balls. I quickly turn away, my hand still clutching the doorknob.

"We had to evacuate the building."

"Oh my. Is everything okay?" she asks.

Um, no, apparently, things are very not okay. My mother is involved in something unspeakable.

"I'll tell you about it later."

I make the mistake of looking back. My mother loses her balance, falling toward him slightly, and he lets out a girlie squeal.

"Sorry." She places a hand on top of his head to steady herself before extracting her heel from him.

I hear a whimper. It's Isabella—or Izzie for short. We call her that and a dozen other nicknames my daughter, Rachel, has given her. She's an adorable Cavalier King Charles spaniel and cocker spaniel mix. Izzie looks distraught and basically traumatized, trapped in a cage across the room.

Switching into dog-mom mode, I rush to her, dropping my purse on a chair along the way. "Oh my God, why is she in her cage?"

"I didn't want to leave her alone," she replies. "We're almost finished so—"

Sliding to the floor, I open the cage, scooping up our precious pup from her prison. "Are you okay, baby girl?"

Izzie bathes my ear in licks as I clutch her, koala bear–style.

"What happened, baby? It's okay, baby."

That's when I notice the iPhone centered in the ring-light thing pointed right at my mother and her, let's call him, friend.

"Oh crap, we're still live." She raises her hand to the phone. "Sorry, folks."

"Live?! Folks?" My eyes widen in utter bewilderment. "Wh-what's going on here?"

"It's my OnlyFans," she says matter-of-factly.

Oh shit! I've heard of this. OnlyFans, one of the bizarre miracles of modern internet technology—or more likely the second sign of the apocalypse. Random people doing all sorts of dirty, naughty, odd fetish things for money online.

I can't even deal with this right now.

Grabbing my purse, I cross the room toward the hall.

"When I finish here, I'll explain," she pleads and then adds in a cheery tone, "Oh, happy birthday!"

I stop in my tracks and turn back.

The man on the floor says, "Happy birthday."

"Thanks." I nod, scowling uncomfortably. "I'll just leave my card on the table." After dropping my business card, I rush down the hall and slip into my room.

I lay my purse on the floor then place Izzie on the bed and hug her. "Izzie, baby, what did you see? Are you gonna be okay?"

She licks my chin, then rolls on her belly and whines.

"I'm sorry, girl." I close my eyes and sigh while petting my fur baby. *What the absolute fuck is going on here?*

I shouldn't call this my room. To be clear, it's not my house. It's my mother's condo. My daughter and I are staying here temporarily while our new house is being built.

Our last house sold after only a weekend on the market in this crazy post-pandemic housing boom. It sold for twenty-five percent over asking with one condition—we had to be out in three weeks. It's been a whirlwind of activity these past few months with getting our house ready for sale, listing it, selling it in days, and packing all our stuff to put in storage while we wait for the new house to be finished. It's been delay after delay with what they are calling "supply-chain issues" for the tiles, cabinets, and appliances.

My husband, John, isn't staying with us here. He's staying at his parents' place, about ten minutes away, because there isn't room for all of us here—or there for that matter. It's just me and my daughter, when she's not with her dad, staying in this one-hundred-square-foot room with Izzie. All three of us, sharing two single beds, with the dog jumping from bed to bed throughout the night.

So, to say my life has been a little chaotic, disastrous, and crowded would be the understatement of the decade. And that was before the unmentionable scene I just stumbled into.

And, yes, it is my birthday—my forty-second birthday.

"I'm so sorry you had to see that." I stroke Izzie behind her ears, and her eyelids flutter, then drift closed. "You're a sleepy girl. You need a nap." I love babying her. She's a sweetheart. "I would take you for a walk, but—"

Suddenly, Izzie pops up, wide awake.

Oh shit, I said the W-word.

You can't say *walk* around her without her going absolutely apeshit. It's her DEFCON 1 trigger word. She loves a walk like you wouldn't believe.

"Sorry, girl. We can't go out there. I promise once the smoke has cleared, we can."

Hell, if we weren't on the third floor, I'd climb out the window with her, run, and never look back.

Izzie moans, then lies back down as I stroke her soft fur.

My phone rings. Spotting my purse on the floor, I pull it out and see it's my father calling.

Oh, don't worry; my parents are divorced, so my mother isn't cheating on him—or whatever the hell that was with geriatric elephant testicles out there.

I answer, "Hi, Dad."

"Happy birthday, sweetheart."

"Thanks."

"How's work?"

"I'm home. There was some sort of suspected gas leak from a lower floor. The fire department evacuated the whole building. I have to check in with the building management company later, but last I heard, we can return tomorrow morning."

"Wow. I hope so. How's the house coming along?"

"Slow. More delays."

"Sorry to hear that. Hey, the reason I'm calling—besides wishing you a happy birthday—is, I'm not sure I told you, but I'm starting up a photography business."

"Good for you. They say the best businesses develop out of hobbies you love. I know you said you were getting a little bored in retirement."

"I am. I miss feeling productive."

"Are you going to do weddings or ..."

"No, I'm specializing in sensual boudoir photography."

"What? Dad, no." I frown. "You're taking naked pictures of women?"

"Not naked. Although there can be some tasteful nudity."

"Uh-huh."

"Boudoir photography has been around for almost a hundred years. I want to capture the beauty of women in a playful, provocative manner with nudity that is implied rather than shown. I want to portray my subject in a sensual, intimate way."

"Why are you telling me this?" Rolling my eyes, I sigh. *It's been a long day, and I don't need this.*

"I'm having a little trouble getting things off the ground. I mean, I've had a couple sessions, but I don't quite have enough pictures to launch my site properly."

"Okay," I mutter, waiting for the other shoe to drop.

"You're an attractive woman. You're in great shape—"

"Oh my God," I cut him off. "Please don't."

"Don't what?"

"Don't ask me what I think you're going to ask me." Clutching the phone to my ear with my shoulder, I place both palms over my eyes.

"It's not what you think it is."

"Oh good." I smile and return to petting Izzie. "So, what is it?"

"Would you pose for me?" he asks.

I nearly drop the phone. "I thought you just said, 'It's not what you think it is.' "

"Oh, um ..."

"What the hell did you think I thought it was?" I'm literally shaking my head now in disbelief.

"Well, I'm not sure. I guess—"

"Dad, look, I'm not posing naked for you. I don't know how else to say it."

"Like I said, the nudity is implied. It's art. I believe Picasso painted his adult daughter nude. It's—"

"First, you're not Picasso. Second, I'm pretty sure you made that up about him. I'm just going to pretend like you didn't ask me this."

"What? Why? You don't even need to show your face if you don't want to."

I sigh, exhausted. "That doesn't make it even remotely more attractive of an ask."

"Will you just think about it, please?"

"Dad ..." I exhale a long, slow breath. "I don't think I'll ever be able to think about anything other than this for as long as I live."

"Great. I appreciate it," he exclaims cheerily.

"No, Dad, you—"

He's just not getting it. Sheesh.

"Oh, and if you have any friends who might—"

"Please stop. I just walked in the door, and after the day I've had, I just can't, okay?"

"Okay. Sorry. Is your mother there?"

"She ... is," I reply hesitantly.

"Is she busy?"

"She's, um ... she's right in the middle of something." Literally her foot is, to be exact. If he only knew.

"Really? What's she doing?"

"Dad, I've got to go."

"Okay. All right. I'll talk to you later."

"Bye."

After ending the call, I drop the phone onto the mattress. Izzie looks up at me with her tongue hanging out, and I rub her behind the ear.

"Your grandma and grandpa are crazy, baby girl."

She tilts her head, and her eyelids slowly close as I curl up next to her.

"I've got to tell Daddy about this." Grinning, I grab my phone and send a text to John.

While waiting for a reply, I fall asleep.

Chapter 2

One Pearl Necklace, Please

I'm awakened by an incoming text message. Checking the screen, I find it's my best friend, Laurie, wishing me a happy birthday and asking if we can push drinks out thirty minutes. I reply back that we can.

Checking the time, I see I've been napping for almost two hours. My daughter will be home from school in about an hour, and I'll surprise her today by meeting her at the bus with Izzie. Usually, my mother meets her, which I'm rethinking now that I've learned of her little hobby. I'll assume she gets her off the bus without her online costar. I make a mental note to follow up on that.

My parents have been divorced for almost fifteen years now. I was so busy with my residency that I don't remember too many of the details. I don't recall if my mother was overly sad or devastated. I'm pretty sure it was as amicable as a divorce can be. Plus, there was some sort of substantial settlement. My mother had worked only a handful of years before she got married, and being a doctor's wife came with a whole host of clout and responsibility that kept her busy. There was raising me, of course, and tennis at the club, along with her charitable work and supporting my father's practice. I think they were happy. The only vivid childhood memories I have of them as a couple is of them sneaking off some middays, claiming they needed to take a shower or discuss ways they might redecorate their bedroom or some other made-up story. They'd be gone for forty minutes to an hour. I'd hear romantic music and other odd noises as I scampered down to the basement to play with my toys.

Once they emerged, they'd seem happier but exhausted. As I got older, their afternoon disappearances seemed to lessen at about the same time as their arguing increased. Then, the fighting stopped, and next, the lawyers were involved.

About eight years ago, my mother met an attractive man about ten years her junior, who she quickly married. It didn't last long. I understand he made some bad investments, some frivolous purchases, and there was some infidelity on his part. This led to another divorce, and her new trophy ex-husband had the audacity to walk away with a settlement of his own.

Ah, love and marriage—it's a truly wonderful thing.

My mother never really talks about her current financial situation, but I imagine it's not great. After the second divorce, she had to sell the house and buy this small but luxurious condominium. I help her out when I can, but with one kid in a pricey college, another in private school, along with the dream house we're building—where cost overruns are a nearly everyday occurrence there isn't much I can do at this time.

I can only surmise that her new venture is the result of her financial situation and has the potential to be lucrative. Although I wish she were exploring a field a tad less ground*breaking, painful,* soul-*crushing,* but maybe she found herself stuck between a few *rocks* and a *hard* place and ...

Sorry, I'm just cracking myself up on the inside with these

little puns. At this point, I feel if I don't laugh about this, I'll just sit here and cry.

It will be a busy rest of the day, as usual. Rachel will do her homework, and John is bringing over some takeout for a small birthday celebration before he drives Rachel to her jiujitsu class. Rachel will then spend the night at his parents' place, as she splits time between where John and I live while we're in this homeowner limbo. Then, later on, I will head out for a drink with my friend, Laurie.

They say it takes a village to raise a child. In our case, it's literally the truth. There is no way I could have gotten my MD, done a residency, and joined my father's practice, while having a baby in my second year of medical school. Not without three sets of grandparents and her father, John, all pitching in to help. In fact, the grandparents were tripping over one another to watch my adorable and perfect baby boy, Dave. His full name is David, but we call him Dave because his father, David, is no longer with us. I guess he's really David Junior, but can he really be a Junior if his father has passed away and he has a different last name? It's a long story, and I'll get to all that later.

You might be wondering why I chose urology, a specialty largely occupied by men—although the number of women are increasing. When I began medical school, women represented approximately five percent of the urologists in the US while, today, it's closer to double that.

Since I was a teenager, my father wanted me to join his urology and OB/GYN practice, and I shared that goal as well. Pleasing him was my desire, along with helping to bring new life into this world. But when my father's practice was forced to drop the obstetrics and focus on the urology side of the business, I had to make a decision if I wanted to go my own way. Malpractice insurance rates for obstetrics are nearly six times what they are for other specialties. The expectation of childbirth is a perfect outcome, which is understandable, but not practical since there are many more inherent risks than in other areas of medical practice. This combined with the increasing litigiousness of society today, leads to more lawsuits and therefore higher premiums.

So, I traded a career of searching for tiny penises on a sonogram image and asking, "Are you interested in finding out the sex of your baby?" to handling adult penises and cupping testicles while saying, "Please turn your head and cough."

Like my father would say, I'm in the same ballpark, just in a different seat.

A smile spreads over my face with the realization that my mother has now joined the family business. She's also in the ballpark, in a manner of speaking, but sitting in what I'll call the lower deck.

Izzie whines softly by the door. She's long overdue for a walk. I change into some stretch pants and a T-shirt and pause a moment before opening the door, hoping that all evidence of my mother's extracurricular activities is gone. When I reach the living room, I'm pleased to see things are back to normal, and I find my mother sitting on the sofa, working on her computer.

"Sorry about earlier," she says.

"Me too. Next time, I'll call if I'm ever going to be that early."

"We always shoot at his place, but they were repaving the parking lot in front of his building, and there was just too much noise today."

"I'm sure it goes without saying that you need to keep all of ... whatever the hell this is away from your granddaughter."

"Oh God, yes." She raises both hands up. "I'm very careful."

I shoot her a withering look.

"Well, normally, I am, and I will be from now on."

"Okay."

"Let me tell you all about what I'm doing."

"Please don't. At least not right now." I close my eyes before kneeling to slip Izzie's harness on.

"Oh, I'll go with you."

She rises to her feet as Izzie makes her way to the condo door, then looks back to us, wearing the cutest expression. She's so patient and adorable.

"Hold on, baby. Grandma is coming with us."

* * *

My mother and I head toward the bus stop, and as Izzie sniffs patches of grass every ten feet, my mother asks, "Do you know what a pearl necklace is?"

"You mean, the jewelry?"

"No, it's some sort of sexual slang term. I heard it on this radio show and couldn't figure out what they were talking about."

I cringe. "Why would you think I'd know that?"

"Well, you *are* a doctor?"

"So, that makes me some sort of an expert on dirty slang?"

"Remember when I asked what the mile-high club was? You knew that one."

"Jeez, everyone knows that."

"Not everyone," she replies.

"You know, they invented this little thing called the internet a few years back, and you can look up all sorts of things. Just google it."

She frowns. "No way. I don't want that on my search history. I saw this thing on the news and—"

"Your search history?! Let me get this straight. You're running a website where total strangers pay to watch you step on men's genitals, and that doesn't concern you at all. Instead, you're worried about the internet surveillance police reviewing your Google searches?" I look at her like she's out of her mind. "If that's even a thing."

"Oh, yeah, I guess you have a point."

Izzie stops to smell a bush, and although I fear I'll regret it, I ask, "Why do you need to know what this is anyway?"

"The way they were referring to it on the radio, it sounded like I might be able to add that as a feature to my page. You know, not too explicit, but it could generate some buzz."

I raise an eyebrow. "You're telling me that the ball-crushing isn't a big enough draw for the pervs out there and you need to up your game to get a bigger slice of the market?"

"Well, I wouldn't put it that way, but in a sense, yes. I need something to set me apart."

Izzie does a spin move in the grass, preparing to poop.

"Wait, there are other people doing what you're doing?" I ask, horrified.

"A few. This one gal dresses up like a—"

"Stop." I hold my hand up. "Please don't. Here, hold Izzie, and I'll look up this necklace thing for you right now." I shoot her a side-eye. "Just keep an eye out for the internet police while I do."

"Ha-ha."

After handing over the leash, I do a quick search on my phone. "Okay, so a *pearl necklace* is slang for a sex act where a man ejaculates semen on or near the neck, chest, or breasts of another person. The term originates from the way the deposited semen resembles a necklace of white pearls."

She cringes. "I don't want to do that."

"I guess it's back to the old drawing board then."

After bagging Izzie's gift to the planet, we continue walking toward the bus stop, and I say, "Before Rachel gets home, I have to ask, why in the hell are you doing this OnlyFans sex thing?"

"To be clear, I'm not having sex with these men. It's simply entertainment."

"Okay." I cringe. "You might be using the term *entertainment* loosely. But why did you choose to explore this particular … talent?"

"Like I said, there's no actual sex, and it's pretty harmless."

"That's easy for you to say," I jeer. "You're not the one getting your genitals mutilated."

"Oh, it's all for show." She waves her hand at me, frowning. "He's not really getting hurt."

"Either that guy earlier was a great actor or you were really hurting him."

"Well, he didn't complain," she offers with a shrug.

"I'll just have to take your word for it."

"This is the first time in a long time I've felt useful. Plus, where else can I make ten thousand dollars a month in about ten hours a week?"

"You're kidding." My jaw nearly hits the sidewalk. "I barely clear that after taxes and malpractice insurance. I can't believe that after spending eight years in college, five years in residency, thirteen years practicing medicine, and working sixty-five hours a week that …" I simply stare off into space, flabbergasted.

"Some people are making half a million a year or more on that site."

"I never should have gone to medical school." I drag my hand over my face. "Half a million … for ball-crushing?"

"No, that's for other stuff."

"Please don't tell me." I raise my hand up once again, shaking my head. "The only logical explanation for all this is that the world is just about to end, and this is God's little joke, so when he comes down here right before he pulls the plug, he can say, *You idiots never should have created that internet thing.*"

"Jeez, you're grumpy today."

"I can't imagine why," I grumble as we reach the bus stop. I kneel down to pet Izzie. "You're such a good girl. We have to wait for Rachel, okay, baby?"

She says, "So, I was thinking you could help me."

"With what?" I look up at her, horrified.

"Martin is moving to Phoenix."

"Who the hell is Martin?" I rise to my feet.

"Duh, you just met him." She widens her eyes. "Martin, with the crooked penis."

"Sorry, but I don't think we were actually formally introduced."

"Well, I need a replacement."

"Okay." I pause a few seconds to muster the courage to ask, "And you want me to help ... how?"

"Well, you know a lot of men."

"I wouldn't say I know them."

Shrugging, she raises her palms skyward and begins timidly, "Well, um, you know things about their ... their physical characteristics that would be conducive for them ... how should I put this? To be successful on my site."

"I know I'm going to regret this, but what exactly are you saying? What are you asking?"

She exhales deeply. "Look, I need a guy with huge balls. You see balls every day, and I'm sure you've seen your share of big ones. Help me find a guy who's willing to—"

"No, absolutely not."

"Why not?" She frowns, insulted.

My eyes bug out of my head. "Do I really need to explain why not?"

"I never ask you for anything. Can't you just do this one little thing for me?"

I burst out laughing, then cover my mouth.

"What is it now?" she asks, sneering.

"It's not just one little thing you're asking me for. It's—it's ..." I struggle to get out the words without cracking up. "It's *two big things.*"

"Funny." She rolls her eyes. "Are you going to help me or not?"

I give her a tired look.

Suddenly, her eyes come to life. "Oh, what about John? How big are his ..." Upon taking in my appalled expression, she backpedals. "I mean, would you say he fits the, um ... require-ments or ..."

The bus turns the corner down our street, and I breathe a sigh of relief.

"Thank God. Saved by the bus." I wag a finger at her. "I don't want to hear any mention of this, and again, I don't think I have to tell you that your granddaughter can know nothing about this."

"What kind of person do you think I am?" She scoffs.

I cock my head, giving her another side-eye. "You know, sometimes, I'm not so sure."

Rachel rushes down the bus steps and runs to meet Izzie, who lets out a cute, almost-silent little whine while she wiggles her backside and wags her tail furiously. "Hi, snuggy bear. I missed you so much."

She scoops Izzie up in her arms, giving her a big koala-bear hug, and the dog goes to town, licking her neck and ear. Rachel giggles like crazy.

"She missed you so much," I say. "She had a rough da—I mean, she hasn't slept much."

Rachel says, "Mommy, what are you doing here?"

"What, not glad to see me?" I grin. "We had a problem at the building, so everything was canceled for the rest of the day."

Rachel places Izzie down carefully and gives me a hug. "Happy birthday."

"Thank you, honey."

"Hi, Grandma."

"Hi, sweetie."

"Is Daddy at Grandma's yet?" Rachel asks, grabbing Izzie's leash as we head toward home.

My mother says, "He wasn't when we left, but he might be there by now."

Chapter 3

Mine Are Plenty Big

When we return to the condo, I hear a rustling in the kitchen. Izzie hears it, too, and goes tearing off, taking her harness with her. John appears from the kitchen, wearing dress pants and a dress shirt with the sleeves rolled up.

He's tall, but not too tall. He keeps in shape for a man his age and is just fit enough to see the suggestion of his defined chest and arms beneath his shirt.

He lights up when he sees his baby girl—I mean, his fur-baby girl. Kneeling down, he scoops her up into his arms and gives her a hug, getting his own tongue bath on his neck and ear.

"Hey, snuggles. I missed you too." He's taken to calling the dog many of the cute nicknames Rachel has come up with for Izzie.

He kisses the dog on the side of the head, returns her to the floor, then sets his sights on his human baby girl, spreading his arms wide to invite her in. "And how are you, Rachel? I missed you too."

"Daddy." Rachel drops her backpack in the living room and

wraps her arms around him. When she pulls back, she looks up at him, beaming. "Did you get everything?"

"I did."

"Good." Rachel rushes away, grabs her backpack, and disappears down the hall.

"What are you guys up to?" I ask with suspicion.

"You'll find out." John smiles. "Just stay out of the kitchen. It's a disaster, but I have everything under control. You too, Candace. I'll take care of everything."

"You don't need to tell me twice." Candace raises her hands in the air, then sits on the sofa, grabbing her MacBook.

John pulls me close to him, motioning with head nods toward my mother while whispering, "I got your texts about you know who. What the hell is going on? Sorry I couldn't respond. I was in meetings all day."

I press my lips together, shaking my head, and mouth the words, *Not here.*

I pull him by the sleeve down the hall, searching for some privacy to share this off-the-wall news about my mother. Rachel is in our room with the dog, so that's no good. I glance in my mother's room and think better of it. Given the day's discovery, who knows what surprises might be waiting for us there?

"I've had to pee for the last half hour anyway." I pull him into the bathroom and close the door, quickly pulling down my pants and underwear and sitting on the toilet.

He's grinning from ear to ear. "So, what the heck is it?"

"Hold on." I lift a finger, moaning with relief, as it's one of those painful yet gloriously satisfying pees. Don't get me started on the inner workings of the urinary system after a few childbirths. God knows what's going on with that. Even an expert in this field, like myself, can't fix the damage caused by two babies stomping around in there.

"Jeez, hearing you now, I need to go too." He bounces on his heels.

I move to the sink. He stands and urinates unabashedly in front of me.

You'd think we were just a normal married couple who occasionally pee in front of one another like any other. You'd probably be shocked to learn that the nicely sized and shaped penis—as you already know, I've seen more than my fair share—which is now out and attached to my rather attractive and in great shape husband, hasn't been inside me in more than ten years. In fact, I haven't seen it erect in that period of time as well, although I know for a fact that it does get that way. Which in and of itself is very odd. More on all that later.

"So, my mother is—"

"Wait." Now, he gives me the index finger as he closes his eyes, basking in his own release.

I look closer at what's going on—a little just to mess with him, but also out of concern for his health. I cock my head to study the mechanics and his facial expression, along with the slowness of his stream.

He waves a hand at me. "Get out of here so I can finish."

"When are you coming in to have your prostate checked?" I ask in a scolding tone. "That stream is really slow, and you look to be straining way too much."

He flushes, then heads to the sink. "Yeah, like I'm really going to let you stick your finger you know where."

"See Dr. Klein instead."

"I'll make an appointment at some point." He exhales deeply, then adds sarcastically, "This was fun. I love being evaluated medically when I pee. We should do it more often."

He's right; this was fun. It's been a while since we've both had our genitals exposed and experienced such a release within a few minutes of each other. With a little more proximity, a tad more blood flow, and an entirely different kind of release, it could be a lot more fun. That is, if it wasn't for all that other stuff.

I ask, "Are you ready now?"

"Yes."

"So, have you heard of this site OnlyFans?"

"I don't think so." He crinkles up his face. "What's that?"

I hear noises outside the door. "Hold on."

Glancing around the tiny bathroom, I look for a solution. After flipping on the loud fan, I pull him into the shower stall, slide the door closed, and proceed to give him the summary version in all its frighteningly explicit detail as we stand mere inches apart. When I'm done, he's shell-shocked and left momentarily silent.

When he finally regains the power of speech, he says, "I don't think I'll ever be able to look her in the eye again. Isn't she worried people will find out?"

"She doesn't show her face. They wear masks."

"Um, that's not at all comforting to me."

"I think she really needs the money." I shrug before grinning. "You'll be happy to know she asked about, um, your *situation*."

"What situation?" His forehead puckers in horror.

I motion with my eyes to his midsection.

"That situation?! What? Why?"

"Oh, I didn't mention that she's losing her costar and she wondered if you could, uh, fill in."

"What'd you tell her?"

I laugh. "What the hell do you think I told her?"

"I hope you told her no."

I fight the urge to smile. "Well, I told her you were looking for some extra income but that your testicles weren't quite big enough for this line of work."

"Mine are plenty big," he says, insulted.

"Look, John, I don't think you quite get the particular requirements that are needed to be a success in this industry. Once we get out of here, I'll show you some pictures."

"No, that's fine." He recoils, glancing at his watch. "Shit, look at the time."

We step out of the shower, and I turn off the fan.

"I've got a little less than two hours to pull off a fabulous meal, followed by cake and birthday gifts, and then get our daughter off to her class, and we're in here, wasting time, talking about the inadequate size of my balls."

We share a smile, and I open the door to find Rachel sitting on the floor of our room with Izzie on her lap.

She meets my gaze, cringing. "Were you guys pooping in there together?"

"What? No!"

"But you told me Daddy only uses the fan when he poops."

"Um, well ..." I look to John, then back to my daughter, nodding. "Yes, that is true, but in this case—"

"While I'd love to stay and help you with this one"—John pats me on the shoulder, shooting me an evil grin—"I've got a birthday party to throw."

"Gee, thanks."

He rushes away, and I return my attention to Rachel. I open my mouth to speak, but cannot find the words.

She looks at me like I'm from another planet. "You guys are so weird."

"We, um, just had something private to discuss. It's a surprise really, and we didn't want you to hear."

Her eyes twinkle. "Oh, is it about my birthday?"

"Um, yes, yes. It is about your birthday. Now, have you washed your hands since you came home?"

"No."

I give her a disappointed look as I move away from the bathroom door.

"All right," she moans.

As she heads to the sink, I scurry away. Locating my phone, I type a text to John.

Ally:
Thanks so much for the help and support.

John:
Anytime :)

Ally:
Oh, and now, we have to buy her an amazing present for her birthday. It's all I could think of when you abandoned me.

John:
That sounds more like a you problem than an us problem.

Ally:
Bastard. :)

John:
That's what you get for sharing my personal bathroom habits with her.

Ally:
Maybe if that damn house was done, I wouldn't have to explain to her about your bathroom habits. :)

John:
_Better get to work on that amazing
present._

About thirty minutes later, we all sit down to John's lovely meal. He prepared Maine-style lobster rolls—that's the kind that are served cold. It's chunks of sweet, succulent lobster meat, coated in a light dressing—made with mayonnaise, seasonings, and celery—and served on a split-top New England–style hot-dog roll. Unlike that other not-so-good Connecticut-style lobster roll, which is served hot and slathered in butter, this is my absolute favorite. As a side, he prepared kale slaw in a creamy garlic-lemon dressing.

My mother, John, and I enjoy the lobster while Rachel chows down on a grill cheese with fries and broccoli. While John didn't boil the lobsters—he had that done at the seafood market to save on time—he did extract the meat and prepare everything else from scratch. He was even able to find those special rolls after going to three different stores. For dessert, he picked up a strawberry shortcake from this great bakery we know, and Rachel even put in a candle for me to blow out.

With our bellies full and running out of time to get Rachel off to her class, I open up my gifts. My mother gives me a beautiful scarf. John gives me a gorgeous Tiffany & Co. bracelet with alternating peridots and diamonds, which just happens to be my two children's birthstones. Of course, thoughtful man that he is, he planned it that way.

I save the best gift of all for last. Grinning from ear to ear, Rachel hands me a box, clearly wrapped by a nine-year-old. I open it to reveal a professionally bound book of poems she wrote in class over the last few years. The poems are about our family, and the book includes pictures of all of us together, just her with Izzie and some super-cute ones of Izzie as a puppy. I read the first poem, which is on the opposite page of an adorable picture of a younger Rachel holding an eight-week-old Izzie, and I'm about to lose it.

With a single tear streaming down my face, I pull Rachel into my arms and don't want to let go.

When she finally frees herself from my embrace, she says, "Daddy helped me with this."

"I love it." My lower lip quivers as my gaze travels from my lovely daughter to my husband of more than twenty years, and I'm suddenly welling up with tears. "You guys are the best. Thank you so much for the most perfect birthday ever!"

John smiles, then looks at his watch. "Wow, we've got to get moving. Rachel, go grab your stuff."

Chapter 4

Don't Open That Here

My best friend, Laurie, and I celebrate each other's birthdays every year with a glass of wine or two at this little place we love, called Bread and Wine Bistro and Bar. This year, as a special treat, she sends an Uber to pick me up. I assume it's some sort of effort to get me to drink too much and let my hair down, but I hate to tell her I have to work tomorrow and I won't be partaking like she will.

She's a mid-level technical manager at a large Fortune 500 company in the area, and she's been working from home since the pandemic. She doesn't expect to return to the office ever. In fact, she says she'll quit if they make her commute. She's divorced and an absolute dog nut. She had one dog before the virus lockdown and has rescued two more since. Izzie is in love with her and all her dogs as well. She loves to go for a visit to her large fenced-in yard.

Her ex-husband was actually a patient of mine more than a decade ago when he was diagnosed with prostate cancer. She would accompany him to many of his appointments, providing moral support during his ordeal, and we became friendly. After I performed a successful nerve-sparing radical prostatectomy, he regained full sexual function and decided with this second chance at life, he would also pursue a second chance at love and promptly filed for divorce. Laurie was, of course, devastated, but then soon embraced her own newfound freedom, embarking on a new career, a close friendship with yours truly, and a string of serial monogamous relationships, which she openly shared with her new best friend.

Walking through the door, I spot Laurie in the back of the bar and head over.

She stands and greets me with a hug and a nicely wrapped present. "Happy birthday!"

"Thank you. You shouldn't have gotten me anything." After sitting down, I tell her all about John's meal and Rachel's gift before I go to work, opening her gift.

She covers my hand with hers. "Um, you probably don't want to open that here."

Frowning, I shake the box, and it's pretty heavy for its size, which is about as long and wide as a tie box, but around three inches high. "Oh jeez, what did you get me that I can't open in public?"

"I'm not telling, but I have one myself, and you're going to love it." Raising an eyebrow, she shoots me a smile.

"Okay," I reply cautiously and place the gift on the table.

"I ordered us a bottle."

"I wish you had asked me first."

"Rachel is with John tonight, right?"

"She is."

"I figured you could have a few glasses, then go home and try out your present. God knows you need it since you and John don't ..." She tilts her head, wearing a suggestive expression.

"No, I have to work."

"You don't have any surgeries tomorrow, do you?"

"No, but I still have to work."

She sighs. "I think you can inspect a couple of dicks and feel around inside some asses with a slight hangover, can't you?"

Seemingly out of nowhere, the waiter appears with the wine. His alarmed expression clearly indicates he heard Laurie's rather explicit and vulgar description of my typical patient appointment.

Laurie waves her hand in the air. "It's okay. She's a urologist."

The waiter nods with an uneasy smile before dropping off the bottle and two glasses.

I wait until he turns on his heel and scurries away before I reply, "I can, but I'd prefer not to."

"Good. It's settled then." Laurie pours the wine, then says softly, "I still don't get how you do that." She contorts her face. "My ex wanted me to touch him back there, and I refused. I wouldn't touch the outside, much less go inside. Yikes!"

"Can we *not* talk about my work?" I sip my wine.

"You're right. You're right." She takes a sip before asking, "So, how's everyone at home?"

"Rachel's fine and cute as can be. Izzie's adorable. My mother and father are each having their own sort of very late, scary midlife crisis, and John is good. Look at what he gave me for my birthday."

I hold up my hand, and she studies the gorgeous bracelet, wearing a bright smile.

"Tell me again why you aren't sleeping with him."

"We sleep together. I mean, before we sold the house, we did, and we will be sharing a bed again once the new house is finished."

"Okay, let me rephrase." Laurie sighs and says in a weary voice, "Tell me again why you aren't fucking him. He's attractive, he's employed, he's a great father, he has great taste in jewelry, he's crazy about you, and—"

"He's not crazy about me." I frown. "You're well aware of the only reason he married me."

"Right, the whole *guilt and tragic history* thing." She nods unenthusiastically, scowling. "I'm not sure I buy your version of events."

I empty my wineglass in one healthy gulp, then look her in the eye. "Can we not tonight? We're supposed to be celebrating my birthday instead of making me feel like crap."

"Yeah, I'm sorry. But can I ask one last semi-related question."

"Maybe. What is it?" I mutter.

"If you aren't going to sleep with him, can I? Because Tony just lost his job again, and he's really not that good in bed, you know. He won't go down on me for more than a minute. Not that I'd want him to because he just seems lost down there. I think we're through." She shoots me a hopeful look. "So, can I?"

"What's the rule?" I put on a *disappointed mother* frown. "You know the rule, and so does John."

"Are you still doing that? Because that's the stupidest rule in your uniquely bizarre marriage."

"It's basically the only rule." I cock my head, raising an eyebrow. "Now, what's the rule?"

Frowning and bobbing her head, she recites the rule slowly, like a reprimanded child, "He can sleep with anyone he wants, except for people that you know."

"Exactly."

"I still think it's stupid. If he's allowed to sleep around, wouldn't you prefer you approved the women, like vetted them to make sure they weren't sleazy or crazy?"

"Sure, I prefer less sleazy and less crazy, but I trust him to scrutinize on his own, and besides, I like my rule. It keeps me sane—or sane-*ish*."

"Who's less sleazy and crazy than me?"

I give her a look.

"Okay, don't answer that."

"There's, like, a million single guys out there. Find one."

"Right." She scoffs, then refills both our glasses. "Have you looked for one lately?"

"Of course not."

"Uh-huh." Laurie takes a sip from her glass.

"Okay." I smile. "Let's change the subject. So, do you want to hear about my insane mom or dad first?"

"You choose."

"Let's start with my dad. It's slightly less horrifying. Wait, it's much less horrifying."

"So, what's sexy Glenn up to?" She sits up straight in her seat, folding her hands in front of her, looking a little too attentive.

I pull back from the table. "I don't think I want to tell you now."

"I think your dad is sexy. I've always had a thing for him."

"You're kidding." I lift my hands up in dismay. "He's an old, old, old man."

"Haven't you heard that dad bods are in?" She takes another sip from her wineglass.

"Sure, dad bods are, but *granddad* bods definitely are not. That's not a thing."

"He's in pretty good shape for a man his age."

"You might want to take this home." I point to the gift box. "The way you're talking, I'm shocked you're not humping the waiter."

"Speaking of ... do you think he's single?" She cranes her neck, looking for him. "He's sorta cute."

"Anyway ..." I sigh, exhausted. "My father is starting a boudoir photo business, and he asked me to ... to"—I struggle to get out the words—"pose for him to help him build his portfolio for his website."

"Well, that is a little creepy." Laurie scrunches up her face, and then her eyes sparkle seemingly with a realization. "You know, maybe it makes sense for him to be doing this."

"Why is that?"

"For the last thirty-five years, he's been spending most of his time looking at flabby, naked, middle-aged men, and now, he wants to make up for it with the fairer sex."

"I didn't think of that." I pause a moment, then have my own mini epiphany. "Oh, you'll like this part. He also asked if I had any friends who might be interested."

"Really?" she exclaims.

I point to the wine bottle. "Is that your second bottle?"

"I might have had a glass or two at home," she admits.

"Uh-huh."

"So, note to self: call Glenn." Laurie shoots me a wink.

"Just don't tell me anything about it." I look to the ceiling, exhaling deeply.

"I'm sorta kidding, but it'd be fun to immortalize on film what's left of my body before it completely falls apart."

"I think you look great."

"Yeah, for the moment, but that could change quickly."

"Tell me about it."

We share a laugh, and then Laurie says, "So, what's this about your mother?"

"Are you sitting down?" I raise an eyebrow before draining what's left in my glass.

Laurie glances down to her stool for effect, then back to me. "I am."

I top off her glass and refill mine. "Okay, so have you heard of this OnlyFans site, where, like, celebrities and regular people have pages? They try to get paid subscribers to watch them do random, normal stuff, like cleaning their house topless—or worse—and even other weird or more explicit stuff."

Laurie grimaces. "I know your mother doesn't like to clean, so is she ..."

"She's ..." I check the immediate area for eavesdroppers and find we're relatively safe, then whisper, "She's on there, and, uh, calls herself the Ball-Busting Granny."

"What the fuck?!" Laurie blurts out loudly, then ducks her head down, glancing around. "Is that ... is that what I think it is?"

I cringe. "It's exactly what you think it is."

"Like, literally stepping on balls with her feet?"

"Uh-huh." I nod, feeling sick before taking a sip.

"Like bare feet?"

"Heels."

"Ouch." Laurie recoils. "I'm not a doctor, but that can't be good for you."

"Well, I can tell you that it is not doctor recommended." I take a healthy sip. "That's not the worst part."

"What could be worse than that?" Laurie tips back her wineglass.

"She, um ..." I swallow hard, then rub my forehead before admitting, "She's losing her big-balled costar and, um, asked if I could find her a replacement." I widen my eyes, waiting for her to get the full gravity of the ask.

Her eyes twinkle. "You mean, since you see a lot of balls each and every day?"

"Exactly."

"She wants you to use your office as a casting couch," she says in horror.

"That's the idea." I widen my eyes.

"So, she wants you to be her wingwoman?"

"In a strange, depraved sense, yes." I drop my head into my hands and exhale.

"So, are you going to do it?"

Lifting up, I give her an exhausted look. "What do you think?"

Laurie turns away, seemingly deep in thought. She takes a sip from her glass, and then her eyes brighten. "Maybe my soon-to-be ex-boyfriend, Tony, could fill in. He's sorta between gigs at the moment. What exactly are the requirements?"

I clear my throat and open my mouth to speak, but I can't seem to form the words. Grabbing the wine bottle, I see it hasn't magically refilled itself.

Then, I stand and lift it up until I get our waiter's attention, mouthing, *One more.*

Plopping down in my seat, I say, "Big balls."

She purses her lips. "So, when you say big, are we talking lemon-sized, tangerine-sized, or ..."

"More like smallish avocado-sized."

"Holy shit!" Laurie's brows knit together. "And these guys can still walk around and everything?"

I give her a knowing nod. "Some come that size, and I have seen them walk."

"Huh. Why do the balls need to be so big?"

I'm not sure which is more soul-crushingly embarrassing— the fact that we're having this conversation in such detail or that I'm pretty damn sure I know the answer to this question.

Pausing, I'm sure my facial expression looks like I'm nauseous, and then I demonstrate with my hands, one atop the other. "I think it's all about the, um, the spread and being able to see them under the shoes. If they disappear, like your average ones most certainly would, um, that's not good for business."

Suddenly, the neurons in her brain fight through the haze of the wine, and her eyes light up. "Oh, that makes sense."

As fast as it came, her light goes out. "No, sorry, Tony's not going to work. Big penis, but only slightly above average-sized balls. I'd say somewhere between a lemon and a smallish tangerine."

"Well, maybe he can find a penis-crushing site to become the star of," I fight to say while keeping a straight face.

"Maybe." She snorts out a laugh, and we crack up.

Chapter 5

Except for That Time You Fucked Him in Key West

After drinking a little more than we both should have, we make our way outside the bar, waiting for our Ubers.

Laurie says, "You got the last good man."

"He is a great guy." I stumble a bit, then put my hand on her shoulder to steady myself.

"I still don't get how you've slept next to him all those nights and you guys don't do it. I mean, no occasional rolling over in the middle of the night, and his parts"—she uses air quotes—" 'accidentally' slip into your parts?"

"He's my best friend. How can you sleep with your best friend? We tell each other everything. Even bathroom stories. We pick each other's pimples. I mean, at some point, we're just too cozy as friends, and it's too late to have sex."

"Except for that time you fucked him in Key West," Laurie blurts out loudly but in her usual, casual tone.

I glance around to see if anyone is staring. "Yes, the one and only time. We were both drunk, and, well, that ... yeah, that was a mistake." I force my tipsy, sleepy eyes open wide and correct my statement. "I mean, we got Rachel, and I wouldn't trade her for the world, so it was a happy mistake."

She chuckles. "Yeah, maybe you should have done IVF to conceive her instead when banging him is so much cheaper, easier, and a hell of a lot more fun."

"You know what I mean."

"I really don't." She shakes her head. "And you don't even remember anything about that night?"

"Not really."

"So, all you remember is waking up naked and sneaking into the bathroom? You know, the old walk of shame away from your husband." She bugs her eyes out to emphasize the absurdity of that statement.

"Okay, okay. I thought we promised to stop trying to make me feel like crap." I motion in my direction with both hands. "Remember, birthday?"

Ignoring my plea, she plows ahead. "No one would believe your relationship. I don't even believe it."

I sigh. "Hey, it works for both of us. He has his life. I have mine."

"You have a life?!" She snorts out a laugh. "Sorry, I didn't mean that." She places a gentle hand on my arm. "Listen, I really think you're wasting a perfect life that's right in front of you."

Tilting my head back, I let out a soft whimper before returning my attention to her. "Maybe if I really believed that he had married me for me, things would be different. But even if I've been wrong all these years, it's too late now. He's moved on, and way too much time has passed and ..." I spot my ride and force a smile. "This is me. We'll have to pick this therapy session up next time."

"Sorry. I didn't mean—"

"Don't worry about it. Get home safe, okay?"

We share a nod and a smile before I slip into the car.

Inside, the driver offers me a water, which I desperately need to hopefully dilute the alcohol. Drinking it helps clear my head a little. I get why Laurie doesn't understand my marriage. It's certainly not traditional. After the big, horrible thing, it's just where we found ourselves. Him feeling guilty and me feeling desperate, halfway through medical school and pregnant. It sorta worked in a sad, twistedly almost-perfect fashion. There was no way I would ever love again—I was sure of it. I didn't want to drop out of school, and I was definitely going to have and keep the baby. There was no way I was going to give up the only remaining connection I had to the love of my life.

We were always great friends, the three of us, before David was so tragically taken away.

John and David had grown up together on the same street, gone to middle and high school together, then ended up at the same college—not exactly a coincidence. I'm not sure which one of them followed the other, not that it matters. At college is where I met them both at a baseball game, of all places, and almost at once, I was invited into their fold. At first, it was all platonic between the three of us. Then, something changed between David and me, and we just knew we were destined to be together forever—or so I thought.

Even while David and I dated and grew inseparable, John was always there, and it just seemed natural. Sometimes, John would have a girlfriend or be between one relationship or another, and we would always hang out. With cell phone texting just becoming popular at that time, we maintained this text chain that kept us laughing and connected, even when we were apart. Maybe from the outside, it looked odd, this super-close threesome, but to us, it seemed natural.

David died about a month before he was to graduate with his master's degree, and with me about to finish my second year of medical school, we found ourselves five months pregnant. He had a great job lined up, and I was barely showing—or maybe simply hiding it well. We were planning a quiet wedding and a well-timed birth that would only minimally disrupt my next year of school. We had it all worked out.

When David lay in that hospital bed, intubated and unable to speak, but with the wherewithal to communicate that he wanted his phone, the three of us stayed in that room, texting each other, until they rushed him to the operating room. Well, it was mostly David telling us things and making requests, as if he knew he would not survive the surgery. And what were we going to do, tell him *no* and argue with him? We simply agreed and answered yes to every question, assuring him none of the worst-case scenarios he was planning for would come true. We assured him that he would make a full recovery.

A few short hours later, David died. John was beyond devastated and feeling guilty for his own reasons while I was an inconsolable, hormonal goddamn train wreck. All we had left of him were those messages. Although we never shared each other's private texts from David, we read and reread our own over and over. Well, at least, I know I did.

After one sleepless night, John asked me to marry him, assuring me he would take care of me and the baby, which I assumed his best friend in the world had asked him to do.

I also did as I had been instructed by David via those texts and stayed in medical school. What else could I do? Maybe I wasn't thinking clearly. Maybe I shouldn't have, but it all happened so fast.

So, here we were—John and I married at twenty-two; me pregnant, getting bigger by the day, sick with either the loss of my love, the pregnancy, or maybe a little bit of both. We certainly were not going to consummate the marriage at that point.

Then, the baby came just as I was to begin classes, and I had to jump right back into hectic med-school mode. John was working long hours himself at this important job he'd only been with for a few months. We were busy, and I was still recovering from the birth. Thank goodness we had those three sets of doting grandparents to pitch in. I also could never have succeeded without my father's practice, affording me the ability to perform my clinical rotations with a flexible schedule. This was critical to my success.

When this perfect little baby boy was born, we named him David, of course, after his biological father. However, we always call him Dave—a nickname his father never used.

We only both got busier from there, so any kind of physical relationship certainly wasn't on my mind and, I assume, not on John's either. And as the months turned into a year and then two with us sharing a bed, exhausted and falling into a rhythm of simply being there to raise my and John's best friend's son together, there was nothing other than sleep going on between the sheets. I worked long hours for years during my residency, sometimes on twenty-four-hour shifts or night shifts. There were times we didn't share the same schedule or bed for months. I know it seems impossible for a couple who doesn't hate each other to live together for over a decade and never once consummate their marriage, but it's true. This was our version of a family. It was our normal.

I was the one who approached John about *the arrangement,* recognizing that he was a guy and that guys needed sex. I didn't —or at least, I thought I didn't. I had turned that part of myself off somehow. Believe me when I tell you, David and I'd had some passion—lots of it. It was the reason we'd found ourselves with an unplanned pregnancy, but those days were now behind me.

John and I agreed to stay married until Dave went off to

college to give him a stable home life. I told John that as long as he was there for us when we needed him, he could do and see whomever he wanted. And as long as he was safe and wasn't doing or seeing someone I knew, he could live his life. It seemed like the perfect compromise, where he did his thing—a sort of *don't ask, don't tell* thing—and we settled into this closeness, where we shared pretty much everything.

We're like middle school best friends who hang together. We like the same foods and television shows. When apart, like at our jobs, we often text, sharing funny stories about our day. We're the best of friends, who figuratively lock their genitals in a safe before climbing under the sheets.

A little over eleven years into this eighteen-year arrangement, John received a promotion at work, and along with it came an invitation to the corporate retreat to a luxurious resort in breathtakingly beautiful Key West. I hadn't been on vacation since starting medical school, so I agreed to accompany him, and that was when it happened. That was how we got our daughter, Rachel. Somewhere between the gorgeous sunset and the sunrise, there was nudity, penetration, and ejaculation. To be clear, we had sex. I remember some of the nudity, but not much of the rest.

That night, one glass of celebratory champagne had turned into one bottle. Somewhere after that, reminiscing about college days and drinking binges with David had turned into barhopping. The next thing I knew, I woke up, naked, next to my husband of eleven years for the first time. Our luck, that one encounter was all it took.

Some couples try for years and struggle to conceive. We drank a bottle of champagne, rolled over, and—*bam*—it was baby time.

Six weeks later, I knew something was going on inside me,

and the seven years left on our marriage agreement now needed some serious renegotiation.

Like a couple of convicted felons nearing parole, we had slipped up from good behavior and were now serving another eighteen-year sentence. Our clock got rolled back, but we had our odd arrangement, and it was still working. Plus, we now had the added bonus of a beautiful baby girl who we both loved with all our hearts.

How many couples who've been married for over twenty years know not only how many times they've had sex with their spouse, but also the exact date and location of said lone encounter? I get that it's as embarrassing to have this knowledge as it is comical and sad, but it works for us. We're happy, building this dream house, and we've resigned ourselves to live there together until our daughter goes off to college.

But now, John's in love with someone else—I'm almost sure of it. He's in love with a woman who's actually alive, and even to this day, I'm in love with and eternally devoted to a man who's no longer with us. I have John, the second-best man ever born, in my life. I have my work, my perfect son, my perfect daughter, and the most adorable and needy dog on the planet to occupy my time. My life is more than full, and I don't need anything else.

I'm not sure if John still feels responsible for David's death. I certainly don't blame him for it and never have. We've never discussed it, but I just get that sense. You see, they both worked at a restaurant together, waiting tables to make extra money while in graduate school. After growing up together, going to school together, being best friends forever, it's no shock that John got David the job at this little restaurant just off campus.

It was no one's fault that John was invited to a concert by this beautiful girl on that fateful day when he was already scheduled to work. A girl he had wanted to date for the entire semester. And it wasn't John's fault that he asked David to fill in for him. And it certainly wasn't John's fault that this newly retired firefighter would have an aneurysm and die while driving near the restaurant. The car subsequently plowed right through the outdoor seating area and into the bar area, killing one person on the patio instantly and mortally wounding the love of my life with a crush injury in the process. John, of course, blamed himself—at least initially—thinking he should have been the one who had died that day, but again, it was no one's fault.

Chapter 6

Stimulate This

When I reach the condo, I'm a little soberer and a little less somber, successfully pushing thoughts of David to the back of my mind. I find the living room empty, as it's almost midnight and my mother must be sleeping. I'm thankful because I'm not in the mood for another mother-daughter chat. She might ask me what a rim job is, and I'm embarrassed that I know.

With Rachel and Izzie staying with John, I've got my whole tiny room to myself. I feel like a teenager again—sneaking home after drinking too much, coming in too late on a school night after chatting about boys and sex with my best friend. However, what distinguishes this night from all those when I was younger is the fact that I'm closing in on middle age. That, and the explicit discussions of my parents' odd activities of the day, which mostly monopolized the night.

I place my still-unopened gift on the bed and pull out my phone. I find a number of text messages—one from Rachel, wishing me happy birthday again, along with a picture of Izzie licking her face. It's so cute, and it almost brings a tear to my eye. There's a second message from my Dave, who's also wishing me a happy birthday, along with a text to FaceTime him if I have a chance since he will be up late, studying.

He's a senior at Penn, studying prelaw with a concentration in communications. His goal is to go to law school and become an entertainment lawyer or sports attorney—he's still deciding between the two.

After changing into sweats, I dial him up. His handsome, smiling face appears on the screen. Sometimes, when I see him, he looks so much like David that it makes me a little sad. Maybe it's the wine or the fact that I'm up past my bedtime, but tonight happens to be one of those nights.

"Hey, Mom. Happy birthday."

"Thank you. How are you doing?"

"Okay, except studying for this Comm 403 final is killing me."

"What's that?"

"Law of Mass Communications."

"Sounds thrilling," I joke.

"Actually, it's pretty interesting."

"Do you have an exam tomorrow?"

"Yep, at ten."

"Should I let you get back to studying?"

"No, I could use a break. Hold on a sec." His screen pauses, and when he returns, he says, "I didn't realize the time. You're up late."

"I know. I met Laurie for a drink, which turned into more than one."

"Did you have fun?"

"It was interesting." I cock my head. "Sometimes, she can be a lot."

We share a chuckle, and then he says, "I spoke to Dad. Let me see the bracelet."

I hold up my wrist to the camera. "I love it."

Although Dave knows John is not his real father, he has always called him Dad and treated him like his father. It's all he's ever known.

"Nice. Dad said something about Grandma and Grandpa driving you a little crazy today, but he didn't go into any detail. What are they up to?"

"Oh, nothing, just the same old stuff." I chuckle. "But they can be a lot to handle too."

"Okay, so you're not going to tell me." He shakes his head, smiling.

"Never." I widen my eyes. "Some things you can't unknow or unsee. Believe me, you're better off, being oblivious. Just promise me if I get to be their age and start to act crazy, you'll set me straight."

"I'll try." He chuckles.

"Are you eating enough? Your face looks thin."

"I am. I'm fine."

"Sleeping enough?" I ask in an overly concerned motherly tone.

"Did you sleep when you were in school?" he replies sarcastically.

"Gotcha."

Loud conversation spills out of my phone, and Dave turns away, his screen pausing once again.

When he returns, he says, "Hey, I've got to go. A bunch of people just walked in."

"All right. Get some sleep."

"I will." He smiles. "Happy birthday."

"Thanks. Love you."

"Love you too, Mom."

The call ends, and I'm overcome with joy, then suddenly sadness. My son is basically all grown up. I wipe away a tear, then spot the gift-wrapped box on the bed. Do I dare open this up tonight?

Tearing off the wrapping paper, I uncover the box, showing a picture of a gold-and-black device about the size of a banana with a little black suction cup on one end, along with buttons on the other. It's called the Womanwonder X Honeylove Pro90 Rechargeable Clitoral Stimulator.

Could it have a longer and more explicit name? I roll my eyes before turning the box over to read more.

This exclusive collaboration between the pleasure experts at Honeylove and Womanwonder combines deliciously gentle suction with pulsations to lavish your sensitive clitoral nerve endings with a featherlight caress.

Using Womanwonder's revolutionary Pleasure Air Technology, this sleek, ergonomic stimulator encircles your clitoris with a silicone head, offering six intensity levels to gradually build sensation. From a soft flutter to an intense pulse, the Pro90 sends you spiraling toward ecstasy with wave upon blissful wave.

Jesus, God, what is this thing? I drop the box on the bed and turn away, shaking my head. Pumping some lotion into my hand, I moisturize. Then, something catches my eye on the box, and I lean over to read it.

Our customers say ...

"My clitoris just arrived at heaven's door."

"I can possibly even say it might be as good or better than oral sex."

"There's no such thing as a perfect sex toy, but this one is pretty damn close."

I chuckle. I don't think my clitoris has ever been anywhere near heaven's door, although I'm not sure exactly what that means. Maybe one day, I'll try it. I retrieve the box from the bed, move to the dresser, and hide it in the bottom of the drawer, covering it with a bunch of clothing.

After getting ready for bed, I slip under the covers, lying back, gazing up at the ceiling when, suddenly, I laugh out loud. My mind is racing with thoughts of clitoris-sucking battery-powered devices, ball-crushing seniors, and dirty old men. Ones taking pictures of aging yet shapely full-figured moms, clad in lingerie or less—maybe looking over their shoulder, wearing a faux startled expression while covering a nipple. If you'd told me this is what was in store for me on my birthday, I wouldn't have believed it, and yet here I am.

Chapter 7

Crushworthy

The next morning, I wake early and head to the office to catch up on some paperwork cut short because of yesterday's issues. When I arrive, I find the office already buzzing and my retired father chatting up the staff at the front desk. I pray he's not soliciting for models, although the gals love him, and for the most part, he's harmless.

"Hey, Dad."

"Ally, how are you?"

"Good, good." I smile to Gale and Betty out front. "Good morning."

"Good morning," Gale replies. "We've got a full day today. I put the mail on your desk."

"I'm sure it will be." Taking hold of my father's arm, I pull him away and whisper, "Please tell me you're not recruiting for your new venture."

"Oh, I didn't think about that. Thanks for reminding me."

He turns away to head back to the desk, but I won't let go.

"That wasn't a reminder so much as a warning. I know you're aware of the sexual harassment laws in this state, right?"

As I walk him to my office, he says, "Oh, that reminds me. Did you hear the one about the guy who walks into a urologist's office and says, 'Doctor, I've been a faithful, doting husband for thirty years'?"

"Tell me you didn't just share this one out front."

"I know better than that."

"Good." I sigh, exhausted.

"Have you heard it?"

"Probably. I think you've told me all of them, but finish. I could use an inappropriate laugh today." I sit down behind the desk. "But please shut the door."

He closes the door, then smiles. "Okay, so he's all depressed, and he says, 'I love my wife, but the fire is gone, and I haven't even been able to get it up for more than a year now. Obviously, my wife is very, very sad about this. Please, can you help me?' "

"I don't think I've heard this one," I reply, holding back a smile.

"So, the doctor says, 'Sure, we can help you. Here are some Viagra samples. Take these, and if it works, come back in a week for the prescription.' So, the guy returns in a week with a bottle of Glenfiddich Thirty-Year-Old Single Malt Scotch, which is, like, a thousand dollars a bottle, along with some Cuban cigars, and he's grinning from ear to ear."

"Wow, it really must have worked well," I grumble sarcastically, contorting my face.

"You're no fun."

"Come on. Finish the joke." I motion with my hand for him to continue.

"No." He turns away, folding his arms over his chest. "I've shut down. I came in here to see you and maybe be a little slice of heaven in your otherwise naked-old-man-filled day, and what do I get? Sarcastic comments and—"

"I promise, I'll behave."

"Will you?" He widens his eyes, waiting.

I nod.

He smiles brightly, then continues, "Okay, so where was I? Oh, I know. He brings the doctor the gifts and is all happy, and he says, 'Doctor, you're a genius. I'm doing it three or four times a day, every single day. I feel like I'm twenty again!' The doctor gets out his prescription pad and gives him a wink as he asks, 'So, I assume the wife is happy now too,' and the man says, 'I'm not sure. I haven't been home yet.' "

A broad smile spreads over my face before a chuckle escapes from my lips. "That's not bad."

He laughs. "I know you're busy, so I'll get out of your way."

"See you, Dad."

He gives me a wink then slips out of my office.

So, this has been my life for most of the last thirteen years, watching my father harmlessly and playfully flirt with the female staff, hearing the occasional risqué joke, and seeing a long line of men pulling down their pants in front of me. How did I get here? Don't get me wrong; I love my job, and I should point out that about ten percent of my patients are female, and that number is increasing. Women need urological care, too, due to a whole host of issues, and more and more of them, thankfully, are realizing that.

Pulling up our scheduling software, I discover I have forty patients to see, approximately four per hour over the next ten hours without even a break for lunch. On a normal day, I see twenty-five to thirty unless I have a surgery or biopsy. Today will undoubtedly be grueling. Suddenly, a career on OnlyFans is starting to sound better and better, except I'm not sure I have the stomach for crushing anything, but maybe there's a less offensive niche I could fill. I enjoy my second laugh of the day, then pull up my first patient's chart.

* * *

After my fifteenth patient of the morning, both my feet and back are aching, and I'm dealing with a slight headache. I can't continue going out on a work night. I'm just getting too old. My next patient canceled, so I slip into my office and close the door. Folding my hands on the desk, I rest my head, breathing in a sigh of relief. I'm really struggling today, and you haven't heard the worst part yet.

I'm ashamed to admit that with each male patient, I find myself performing an evaluation for testicular, let's call it, crushworthiness. I literally can't stop myself. As pants are being dropped and I'm presented with the patient's most personal of areas, I can't erase from my consciousness certain images, knowledge, and that ridiculous task that my mother so casually assigned to me less than twenty-four hours ago. I feel like I might lose it. My mother has singlehandedly ruined my career. I'm tempted to rip up my license and lodge a complaint against myself to the medical board. I'm sure that would be a first.

Maybe it's not her. Maybe it's this whole prostate cancer industry that's getting to me. Ten years ago, the standard of care was to rush men to have a treatment, whether it was radiation or radical surgery, even for early-stage prostate cancers. These are treatments that often lead to urinary, bowel, and erectile side effects, which are serious quality-of-life issues.

Now, the thinking has changed with more and more men simply watching and waiting to see if their slow-growing cancers become more aggressive and require treatment, and this is a good thing.

Sometimes, we have to deliver some devastating news and discuss serious topics. So, maybe having some levity on occasion helps keep us sane.

That reminds me of another doctor joke. Stop me if you've heard it.

This male doctor is preparing his patient for a minor procedure, and he's about to administer the injection sedative. He holds up the needle and says, "You're going to feel a little prick," and the patient says, "Oh, Doctor, we've only just met."

Cue the *ba-dum-tss* drumbeat.

Hey, I don't write 'em. I just retell 'em, so cut me some slack.

I think the Viagra one was better. Next patient, please!

Calling up my scheduling software, I see that my next two are here to go over biopsy results, and then I have a few minutes for a break, where maybe I can squeeze in a lunch. Barring any *while I'm here, I found this thing on my ... would you mind taking a look* questions, I should be nudity and male-genitalia-free for at least the next hour.

Checking my phone, I see an earlier text from John, asking how my day is going. I reply that it's been an adventure and make a recording of my father's Viagra joke and send it along. I'll save the crushworthiness story for the next time I see him.

When the last patient has finally pulled up his pants and I've completed my paperwork, I pack up my bag. I head to the waiting room and find it empty. It's after seven, and I'm exhausted. Stopping at my mail slot, I spot something odd on the front desk counter and take a closer look. It's a business card holder, filled with cards for a certain boudoir photography business. It reads:

Unbuttoned Intimate Photography

Boudoir photographer, offering classic, underwater, couples, cake smash, and cherry-pie smash photography sessions.

My face freezes into an outraged O. I don't often swear, but I blurt out, "What the fuck is a cherry-pie smash session?"

Thank God I'm alone. Opening up my bag, I sweep the card holder and all the cards inside, grumble another obscenity, and shuffle toward the door. I can't believe I need to have another chat with him about this. Another night of drinking is probably needed here, but I don't dare. I'll take a long, hot bath instead.

As I make my way to my car, I find myself wondering if the Womanwonder X Honeylove Pro90 Rechargeable Clitoral Stimulator is waterproof and whether or not it comes precharged.

Chapter 8

Waterproof and Precharged

Arriving at my mother's condo, I hesitantly open the door and am pleasantly surprised to not find I'm interrupting any live streaming. In fact, I have the place to myself. Rachel and Izzie are both staying the night with John and his parents.

After heating up some leftovers, I make a FaceTime call to Rachel. While I eat, we chat about our day. I let her do most of the talking, until I find she still has some unfinished homework, and we end the call.

Stripping out of my clothes, I turn toward the dresser, which contains the naughtier of my four birthday gifts, and press my index finger to my chin. It might be interesting. In fact, it might have some benefit that I could share with my female patients suffering from sexual dysfunction. At least, that's what I tell myself as I pop open the box.

After removing the packaging, I hit the power button, and the little device comes to life with a dull hum. Check! Grabbing the little instruction booklet, I scan it for the magic word —*waterproof*—and there it is. Check number two!

I head to the sink and give the device a thorough scouring,

then quickly rinse out the bathtub and turn on the water. Returning to the instruction booklet, I learn about all the features and functions, including the six levels of intensity, which claim to offer a range of delicious sensations. I turn on the device, adjusting the intensity from highest to lowest, and settle on level one, thinking I should really be taking baby steps.

My phone lights up with a call. It's Kate Davis, my other close female friend, one I've known forever.

After turning off the water in the tub, I answer the call on speakerphone. "Hey there, Kate."

"Ally, I'm so sorry I didn't call yesterday. I meant to, but so much was going on that—"

"Don't worry about it."

"Happy birthday!"

"Thank you," I reply, picking up the device and discovering it comes with two different-sized silicone heads—one labeled M and one XL.

"Did I catch you at a good time?"

"Sure." I move to the bedroom and find the plastic package, containing the two heads.

"What are you up to?"

"Um, I-I ..." I stammer. I don't have the heart to tell her that I'm currently trying to gauge if my clitoris would be considered a medium or fall into the extra-large category. "I was just about to take a bath."

"So sorry. Should I call back?"

"No, no, I'm sorry." *What the hell am I doing? I haven't spoken to her in weeks, and clit stimulator or no clit stimulator, I'm being rude.* I place the contraption and all its parts on the sink and head to my bedroom. "Now, you have my full attention."

"How's Rachel?"

"Oh, she's great. Busy with jiujitsu, school, and her dog. How are the kids?"

She says, "As you know, Kyle's just about to get his master's from Duke, and Morgan is loving UNC, so everyone's good."

"That's great."

"The reason I called was, I was talking to John last week when we played golf, and I'm not sure if he mentioned doing another family vacation at our place in Emerald Isle with you guys."

"No, he didn't."

"Gosh, it's been, like, five years since we did it, and it was so much fun."

"I remember."

"Yeah, with the kids getting older and so busy, this might be our last chance for a while to all get together."

"Sounds great. When were you thinking?"

"The first two weeks in July. July first is a Saturday and through the fifteenth. Stay the whole two weeks or less. Whatever you can do."

"I need to check with Dave and—"

"Invite your parents too. We have all those bedrooms, and it was a blast with them last time."

"Oh, okay," I reply with hesitation after recent events. "Will do."

"Just let me know when you can. I'd better let you go. Enjoy your bath."

"We have a new doctor starting with the practice in the summer, so this could be good timing. I could use a break. Hey, we should do lunch soon."

"I'd like that."

"Great. I'll check my schedule, and we can compare dates."

"Perfect. Bye."

"Bye."

I have two close friends. Kate is the one I've known since high school, the one I didn't meet under professional circumstances, and the one whose husband I never saw naked.

Sadly, we both have something in common. Her husband died about twelve years ago from a congenital heart defect that had led to sudden cardiac death. It's the swift and unexpected ending of all heart activity. Breathing and blood flow stop right away. Within seconds, the person becomes unconscious and dies. They'd been married about ten years when this happened, and the kids were pretty young.

He'd had this high-powered career in finance and a lot of life insurance. That, coupled with the Social Security survivor benefits for minor children, has kept her more than financially secure. It was a horrible tragedy, but at least they got to spend more than a decade together.

Kate and I are somewhat close, although we haven't seen each other all that much lately because she lives about an hour away. John really stepped up to help her after her husband died —performing handyman-type repairs and generally filling the gap left behind. The two of them also started playing golf together years ago and generally play once or twice a week, weather permitting and even on some pretty cold days. They tell me the rates are much better out of season. I don't play. It's not my thing, not that I have a lot of free time.

A few years after mourning the loss of her husband, where she barely left the house or did much, she decided to try to move on with her life. At least somewhat. They purchased this large oceanfront beach house in Emerald Island, North Carolina. It has seven or eight bedrooms and six or more bathrooms, and she got a pretty good deal on it back before beach real estate prices went through the roof. I think we've gone down three times with them over the years, but it's been a while. With the pandemic and the kids getting older, it's been hard to find the time.

Returning to the bathroom, I empty the cold water from the tub, start to refill it, and grab the device again. After studying the silicone heads, I settle on the medium-sized head, clean it thoroughly, and attach it. Once the tub is full, I slip into the hot water and relax. It feels like heaven. I can't remember the last time I took a bath. Lifting my legs up onto the side of this standard-sized tub, I slide down lower until the water is touching my chin.

I exhale deeply, closing my eyes as I luxuriate in the perfect quietness of this room. No patients. No paperwork. No parents. No kids. This is just what I need. I glance over to the sexual device sitting on the tub's edge, just mocking me. Do I dare actually use this ridiculous contraption?

Picking it up, I study it again, flipping on the switch and setting it on the lowest intensity. I press it to my neck, just to test it, and it feels sorta like a little mouth giving a tiny hickey. Sliding it lower, I roll it slowly over my nipple, which quickly stiffens and sends pulses throughout my body. I used to love having my nipples lightly bitten and sucked, and it's been a very long time since they've experienced that attention.

I gasp, pressing it harder into my breast. Then I slide a hand down my belly between my legs where I slip a finger inside.

"Oh God."

I can't remember the last time I touched myself like this, and I don't think I've ever done it in the tub.

I move the device lower and touch it carefully to my clitoris. At once, it seems to grasp it, combining these deliciously gentle suction actions with pulsations, which stimulate my nerve endings with a featherlight caress.

"Oh my ..." I groan.

I press it a little more firmly. My back arches upward, and without warning, I'm reduced to an orgasming, quivering mess as a thunderous climax spreads through my core. With wave after wave pulsing through me, I struggle to hold the toy against me, and during one particularly strong surge, I drop it into the water. My legs, weak from my odd position, give way, and my bottom slides further toward the tub spout, and my head slips fully under the water.

Gasping, I swallow a mouthful, and regaining my position, I lift my head out of the water, choking and panting for air as water splashes from the tub to the floor. Sitting upright now, I'm pulsating, breathless and sated.

"Holy crap."

Retrieving the toy from the water, I power it off and smile, even as I look at the soaked bathroom floor. I've got some cleanup to do, but it was well worth it.

Chapter 9

Could Robots Replace Men in the Bedroom?

I feel like I'm floating on air, lying in bed, basking in the glory of the first orgasm I've had in I don't know how long. Believe me, it was a big one. I know they say robots are going to take over the world. Although I'm not sure what that means, if this device is any indication, I guess they could replace men in the bedroom. All they'd need to do is somehow figure out how to incorporate a mouth, a tongue, and the perfectly shaped, never-tiring male organ, and you might really have something. We'd never leave the bed. If this new robot could grocery shop, cook, and clean, we might never leave the house. On second thought, all that seems like a tall order and will never happen. Don't listen to me. I'm still regaining my faculties from my bath.

My phone chimes with an incoming text.

John:

Hey, Rachel and I found a poem we left
out of the book. The one she wrote
about her big brother.

Ally:

Oh yeah, I remember that one. It's adorable.

John:
I guess we'll need to start working on
Poems by Rachel, Volume 2.

Ally:
Can't wait.

John:
Kate told me she reached out about the
trip. It stinks that the dates fall right
in the middle of David's birthday,
but if you really want to cut the
trip short or go a week
late, that would be fine.

Crap! It hits me all at once. I stare straight ahead, mouth agape. I didn't put two and two together. Every year, I visit David's grave on his birthday, which is July 7th. I've never missed a year. No matter how busy I am or what the weather is, I find the time on that day. How the hell didn't the dates register with me? In my defense, I was preoccupied with that stupid sex toy. I'm the worst widowed fiancée in the world, if that's even a thing.

John:
I was thinking, if you wanted, I could
come with you. We could even drive
back just for the day. It's only, like,
eight hours if we go straight through
and don't hit too much traffic.
It would be a long round trip,
but doable. Are you there?

Ally:
Driving back is a little crazy.
I appreciate the offer.
Let me give it some thought.

Three dots appear on the screen. Then nothing. Then the three dots again. Then nothing. I'm sure he doesn't know how to respond. I'm barely able to think straight now.

John:
Okay. Whatever you need.

Ally:
Thanks.

John:
Oh, I spoke to the builder. The good news
is, the house should be ready to move
in the third week of July. He asked
if we could meet next week to go over
some things.

Ally:
Sounds good. Let me check my schedule.

John:
It could be fun to get away. It's been a while.

Ally:
Yeah. I'm looking forward to it.

John:

Good night.

Ally:
Good night. Kiss Rachel and Izzie for me.

John:
Will do.

After placing the phone on the night table, I curl up with a pillow and close my eyes. My thoughts are a jumble of David and our tragic past and all that I'll need to do to free myself to take this trip.

Chapter 10

A Guy Walks into a Urologist's Office

The next six weeks are a whirlwind of patient appointments, biopsies, surgeries, visiting Rachel's school, Izzie's vet visit, jiujitsu classes, meeting with the builder, and finally having to pick another hardwood floor since our selection is out of stock indefinitely. In other words, your basic, normal, busy life—a complete shit show.

During all of it, the entire two-week Emerald Island trip is magically falling into place. I come to terms with visiting David's grave early, just before we leave. I'm sure the gods and David will forgive me this one transgression after more than two decades of dedicated service.

Laurie, who adores Izzie, is jealous I'm getting away and has agreed to watch her for the entire trip. She's free, which is not surprising since she has three dogs and can never really leave her home for very long or feasibly take them with her. We decided not to take Izzie, as she does not do well on long car rides and can't stand the heat at the beach. She's much better off with her aunt Laurie and Laurie's pack of pups. In fact, she'll be in heaven.

Now, a second wrinkle is Rachel. For the last four years,

John's parents have taken her to Disney, and this year, the trip is scheduled for the first week of July. This will probably be the last year she really wants to go. She's about to turn ten. She's still somewhat immature for her age. Undoubtedly because we coddle her, but also being stuck at home with remote learning for almost two years during the pandemic didn't do any favors for her maturity and social development. So, Rachel will be at Disney the first week of our trip. Then, her grandparents will drop her off in Emerald Isle, where she can spend the second week at the beach. It's a win-win for her.

On the work front, John was able to get the time off, and in terms of my practice, our new physician is confirmed for a June 1 start date. He will have more than enough time to get up to speed and handle my appointments and any emergencies that arise. My office was also able to reschedule two surgeries—one for before and one for after the trip. Like I said, it's all coming together.

It's Thursday, and I have a late dinner planned with Kate to make up for the lunch we promised to schedule nearly two months ago. With only two patients to go, I'm seeing the light at the end of the tunnel. That reminds me of a urologist tunnel joke, but it's a little racy, so I'll save it for another day.

After reviewing the patient's paperwork, I head into exam room number two and find the man sitting on the table.

"Mr. Ballentine, I'm Dr. Larson. Nice to meet you."

"Good to meet you."

Sitting down on my wheeled stool behind the computer, I pull up his chart. "So, you're having trouble with starting to urinate and maintaining a flow. Is that correct?"

"Yes, and sometimes, it feels like I don't go all way, and in, like, ten minutes, I have that same urgency to go."

"Okay. Let's see. So, your primary care had a prostate-specific antigen test done, and your score is very low for a man your age, so I'd be surprised if you have any sort of prostate issue or enlarged prostate. We can check that as well with a simple digital exam, but I think you have what's called urinary hesitancy. You might need a cystoscopy, which is a procedure that allows us to examine the urinary tract. When did the symptoms first begin?"

"About three months ago. This urinary hesitancy—what causes that?"

"It could be a number of things." I wheel out from behind the computer and pull on latex gloves. "Um, scar tissue in the urethra. Scarring can result from surgery or an injury to the region. Also, medications, like antidepressants, might cause urinary hesitancy."

"Well, I did go on an antidepressant about six months ago. You see, I was let go from my company. They outsourced my whole department to some company in India to increase our shareholder value, they said." He adds in a sarcastic tone, "More like increase executive bonuses."

"I saw this *60 Minutes* piece on that. It's horrible." I shake my head. "These companies want to charge more and more for their products, yet they send our jobs overseas, and all their fellow companies are doing the same. It's shortsighted. How do they think their customers will pay for what they're selling if people are out of work? It's not good for the country."

"I know; I know." He runs his hands through his hair. "I've been under a lot of stress. No one wants to hire a fifty-seven-year-old software developer. They want kids right out of school so they can pay them low salaries."

I nod sympathetically. "That's horrible."

He cringes. "If I do need this cystoscopy, do you think we could do it in the next month? My health coverage runs out and—"

"I'm sure that could be arranged if necessary, but first, let's have look. Please step down and lower your pants and under-wear." I slide my chair closer.

After unbuckling his belt, he slides his khakis and under-wear down, revealing the largest set of testicles I've ever seen. My eyes widen in absolute shock, and I try to hide my reaction.

"Oh, sorry. I know," he begins. "I should have warned you. They are a bit, you know ..."

"Oh, no. No, I just, um ... it's fine." I begin the examination of his penis and testicles, struggling to keep my expression blank.

I can honestly say that over the last month or so, I have not thought once about my mother's hobby or request. I'm not sure how I've been able to do this, surrounded by penises and testicles on a daily basis, but I have. I swear that I have not been evaluating patients for their worthiness. That's my story, and I'm sticking to it.

I cup his massive set in my hand, and it's heavy. Really heavy. They must weight three-quarters of a pound. To be clear, not each, but the set—because each would just be ridiculous. The average testicle is approximately one to two ounces with some outliers hovering in the four-ounce range. These are shockingly a bit larger.

A bead of sweat rolls down my forehead, and I wipe it away. I'm ashamed to say my mother and her bizarre OnlyFans site are all I'm thinking about now.

I steady myself and say, "Please turn your head and cough."

He complies, and I don't feel anything of concern. I continue the exam and don't see or feel any nodules or other issues.

I wheel backward and say, "Everything appears to be fine. Would you like the digital rectal exam? I would slip a lubricated finger into your rectum and feel your prostate for any irregularities or nodules, which could indicate an issue. You'll just feel some pressure."

"Okay."

"Please turn around and place your elbows on the table."

He follows my instruction, and as he bends over, his *Guinness World Record*–worthy set squeezes out in the back between his thighs, like two half-inflated balloons. It's reminiscent of a prospector tossing two large bags of gold over his shoulder.

Thank God he cannot see my facial expression.

I take a deep breath and attempt to regain my composure as I lubricate my index finger.

Wheeling behind him, I clear my throat and somehow recover my professional demeanor enough to complete the exam. I dispose of my gloves and wash my hands thoroughly.

"I didn't feel any issues with your prostate. No irregularities or nodules."

"Good. Good."

"I think the antidepressant could be the culprit here. If you think you want to try going off them, then I would recommend that you check with the doctor who prescribed them to get their thoughts. Then, if they agree, they'll instruct you on how to wean off of it. Within a week or two after that, if you still have symptoms, we could schedule the cystoscopy."

"Sounds like a plan." He clears his throat and exhales slowly. "I hate to ask this, but I've been asking everyone. It's embarrassing, but you wouldn't know of anyone hiring software people or ..."

"No, sorry, I don't. Do you have any other skills?"

He chuckles. "Well, I did do a little underwear modeling in college. As you can probably tell, they didn't need to stuff me for the shoots."

"Right."

Grabbing his belly, he makes a face. "But with this gut, those days are behind me." He raises an eyebrow. "I, uh, it's embarrassing to say, but I actually have done a little acting as well in my day. I was in a couple of low-budget Cinemax After Dark movies."

"You don't say." I swallow hard, turning away, unable to look at him. Suddenly, my pulse is racing, and my career is flashing before my eyes.

"But at this point, I'd take anything. I've been working some shifts at this coffee shop, but that is not paying my bills. In a few months, I think we're going to have to sell the house."

"Jesus, you might lose your house?" I ask, my heart literally aching in my chest.

"Well, I guess I could liquidate my retirement account, but with the penalties and all ..." He drops his head in his hands and whimpers softly.

"Holy shit," I mutter under my breath as I head for the door. "Let me get you some water."

I return with a water bottle and find him sitting on the exam table, eyes welling with tears, but forcing a smile.

"Sorry. You're not a therapist. I'm not sure why I'm—"

"No, no. Don't worry about it." I hand over the bottle, then sit. "Look, I might have an opportunity for you."

"Really?" He sits up a little straighter, and his face brightens slightly. "What is it?"

"Um, well, it's a little ... unusual." I grimace, raising my hands up. "And I hope you don't find this inappropriate. If anyone found out about me telling you this, I think I could have my license taken away so—"

"I would never say anything." He shakes his head vigorously. "I promise."

"Okay ..." I exhale deeply, then close my eyes. "Have you, um, heard about this website called OnlyFans?"

"Yeah, I think so."

"Well, my, uh ... my ..." I turn away so I don't have to look him in the eye. "My mother has a page on there, and she is ... she is, um, looking for a man with ... with your particular—how should I say this? Endowments."

"Endowments?" He gives me a quizzical look. "What endowments?"

"Well, your ... your ..." Wearing an excruciatingly painful expression, I wag an uninspired finger in the general direction of his groin.

He looks down at his lap and says softly, "My balls?"

Closing my eyes, I pause. I swear my heart skips a few beats as I picture explaining my conduct to the medical board. When my heart finally begins to thump again, I nod, cringing. He smiles, seemingly intrigued. Then, for the next few minutes, I have the most uncomfortable yet well-received conversation of my life.

Chapter 11

They're Fake, and They're Spectacular

Arriving at the Bluestone Restaurant, I park the car. Out of the corner of my eye, I spot a woman making a striking entrance, heading toward the front door. I turn for a better look. From the back, she's got a Hollywood waves–type hairstyle, and she's wearing a semi-see-through, tea-length silhouette sheath dress with black appliqués on top and a solid ivory bottom. Glancing down at my own outfit—a nice but conservative sleeveless, U-neck wine-colored dress—I feel a bit underdressed. In my defense, this is a nice place, but it's not that nice. She's dressed for the red carpet, and I don't see one of those anywhere.

When the woman turns, I discover it's my Kate. Suddenly, I'm a little self conscious. After I check my face in the rearview, I notice other couples heading inside, who are dressed more casually, and I feel a bit better.

Inside, I'm shown to the table, and Kate is already sitting there. She does look gorgeous. Spotting me, she smiles brightly, gets to her feet, and does one of those side embraces, so as not to disturb her hair or makeup, which all look professionally done.

"Ally, so great to see you."

"Kate, you look amazing." Standing back, I motion from her head to her feet, grinning and shaking my head. "Are you heading to some sort of charity ball later?"

"No, stop." She blushes, then raises her palms, nodding her head as she looks me over. "You look great."

"I don't believe you, but thanks."

As we take our seats, I say, "I came from work. I didn't know we were going to prom."

"Okay, I get it. I'm a little overdressed." She frowns a bit.

"No, no, sorry. It's just been a long day and an even longer week. Sorry, I didn't mean to be catty."

"No, I'm sorry. I should have told you I was going to get dressed up." Leaning closer, she makes a face and whispers, "I mean, this is a nice place, but it's not that nice."

"I know, right? Good food."

"Great food. It's just that I haven't been out in a while, and I felt like pampering myself a bit."

After the waiter takes our drink order, I say, "Well, you look great. Are you working out?"

"You noticed?" She beams. "I'm on this whole detox, cleanse thing. I've cut out sugar and processed foods. I'm simply eating healthy now. Sometimes, I do cheat. You've got to live a little."

She's very thin, and now I notice her bust. It's big. Very big. I find myself staring at it and have to consciously avert my eyes. Either she's wearing a thickly padded bra or she had them done.

"That's great. You do look fabulous. Are you seeing anyone?"

"No. God, no." She contorts her face, as if she smelled something horrible.

The waiter drops off our mineral waters. "Do you need a few more minutes?"

I glance at my menu. "I'm starving."

"Me too."

"Do you know what you want?"

"I always get the same thing," Kate says.

"Me too. I'll have the crab cakes."

The waiter turns to Kate. "And for you, miss?"

"I'll have the Bluestone salad. Hold the bacon, please, and with the dressing on the side."

Suddenly, a bit self-conscious, I say, "Sorry, one thing. I want just the one crab cake, not two. You do that, right?"

"Certainly." The waiter retrieves our menus, smiles, and head off.

We sit in silence for a few moments, looking at one another and nodding.

Finally, I say, "This is great. I'm so glad you called, and we're so looking forward to the trip."

"So are we." Kate's smile fades. "I waited years after Michael died to finally date again. Well, I told you how awful it was."

"I remember."

"Then, I followed in your footsteps. There was only one man for me. It doesn't happen twice. I don't have to tell you that."

"Yeah," I say softly.

"I get why you do what you do." She leans a little closer. "I mean, you're still doing it, right? Or *not* doing it ..." She flashes me a knowing smirk while raising her eyebrows.

"You mean, John and me?"

"Yes, you guys still aren't physical, right?" she asks timidly. "I mean, John and I talk sometimes on the golf course, and, um, you told me years ago and—"

"No." I raise my hand up. "I know; I know. Nothing's changed. He's ... we just ... I just can't."

"I totally get it. You've got your big career and your kids. It's just sex, right? Who needs it?"

I lean in and softly say, "Sometimes, I really miss it though."

"I understand. I learned to live without it a long time ago." She pauses a moment, and then the corners of her lips curl into a smile. "It's like that *Seinfeld* episode. George stopped having sex and became, like, a genius. Remember that? He learned a new language and was giving talks and ..."

"I remember." I chuckle. "Wait, doesn't Elaine stop having sex and she becomes stupid?"

"I don't think so." Kate frowns, then flips her hand dismissively. "Or maybe. I don't know. That's a silly show."

"It is."

We chat about the kids. I tell her about the house John and I are building, and she tells me again about her health regimen. When our food arrives, Kate goes to work, picking the pecans out of her dish before pouring on the slightest amount of salad dressing, as I start in on my crab cake.

She takes a bite. "I love their dressing."

"This crab cake is fabulous."

She sips from her glass. "So, for the trip, I bought a couple of new games. I remember last time, we played games, and we had so much fun. Your father is a hoot."

"He's really something." I place my fork down. "Can I ask you something?"

"Anything."

After checking that no one is listening, I motion to my chest quickly. "Did you, um ... did you have them done?"

"You noticed?" She glows. "I just love them."

"You look great. So thin and just amazing."

"Yeah, I was always, like, a small B. I just felt like I looked like I had the body of an eleven-year-old boy, you know? And now, I'm, like, a large C."

"So, you're really not seeing anyone?" I narrow my eyes. "I mean, why go to all this trouble and not date?"

"They're for me." She motions with her hands toward her chest. "This is all for me. I don't waste this on a man. I have more confidence, and it just makes me feel better about myself."

"That's, uh, really healthy. I totally get it," I say, although I'm not sure I do or if she's telling me the truth.

When we finish our dinner, we chat for another half hour or so before saying our goodbyes.

Chapter 12

You Didn't Ruin My Life

The Emerald Isle trip is coming up fast, and I'm getting excited. I bought a few new bathing suits. One is even a pretty small bikini—the type of thing I haven't dared to wear in more than two decades. Following Kate's lead, I've been eating healthier, exercising more, and I've been happy with the results. I might actually wear this silly little thing in front of people.

I step into the office waiting room and spot a large, beautiful bunch of red roses on the counter.

"Wow, is it someone's birthday?" I head toward the display and don't see anyone behind the desk. Leaning forward, I breathe in the scent and smile. "These are gorgeous." Searching for the card, I say louder, "Whose are they? Is anyone here?"

Gale appears from the back. "Nice, huh?"

"They are. Who are they for?"

"They're for you, from Mr. Ballentine." Raising her eyebrows, she shoots me a cunning smile. "Evidently, he was really, really satisfied with his appointment."

He must be working with my mother now. I told her not to tell me anything, and she hasn't. I don't want to know a thing.

Hopefully, it works out long-term for them both because I'm officially out of the wingwoman business for good.

"I guess." I shrug, staring at the flowers.

"We've never gotten flowers before." Gale giggles. "What'd you do, put the lead back in his pencil?"

"No, he was looking for work, and I guess the tip I gave him panned out."

"Wow. So you're a career counselor now too."

"I guess so."

I head to my office, wearing a satisfied smile. On the way, I crack myself up. *Tip I gave him ... that's what she said.* I feel like Michael Scott from *The Office.* Like he's giving her the tip now—get it? Wait, that doesn't make much sense. It's more the balls than the tip that he's giving her. I frown, thinking. But then again, *the tip* is also being displayed, so I would think ...

I shake my head, trying to push stupid, dirty urology puns from my brain and actually get control of my thoughts. I so wish my father's sense of humor hadn't rubbed off on me. It's early, and I really need coffee.

After a morning full of patient appointments, I've been able to clear the remainder of the day to tour the house John and I are having built. When I pull into the circular driveway of the twenty-seven-hundred-square-foot modern farmhouse–style ranch, I'm already smiling. I've always wanted a circular drive-way, and this ranch—with its open concept, large bedrooms, custom kitchen, luxurious master bath, and high ceilings—is the dream home John and I have been talking about building for more than ten years. We've been tightening our belts, acceler-ating paying off my student loans, skipping vacations, and having modest Christmases for longer than I care to remember in order to make this a reality.

John pulls his car in behind mine, and I join him, standing in the driveway as we admire the front facade.

"I'm glad we went with the lighter blue," I say.

"It does look good."

The exterior features a twenty-foot-wide porch with a black metal roof and many windows with modern black frames. There is a gable roof centered over the door with three single windows accenting the two-story foyer. On either side of the porch, there are matching gable roof dormers with small black metal shed roofs over the double windows.

John unlocks the eight-foot-tall glass-accented front door, and we step into the large foyer. The scent of fresh paint fills my nose, triggering a vivid memory of John and me shortly after David's death. The time we toured the newly painted apartment David and I had leased. Turning to look at John, I close my eyes for a moment, and then suddenly, I'm back in 2002.

I stood in the living room of the two-bedroom apartment, staring out the window and wondering exactly how I had gotten there. A month earlier, David and I had signed the lease. Just a few weeks prior, we had booked the movers to first retrieve the items from his apartment before heading to mine. We were all set to start our lives together. He had asked me to marry him at our favorite restaurant, and we had been making plans for a small wedding in the summer.

Placing my hands on my growing belly, I turned toward the kitchen and found John on one knee. "Will you marry me?"

I stared at him, unable to speak.

"Just think about it. You don't have to answer now." He rose to his feet and walked to me.

"Okay." I forced a smile and turned back toward the window, staring down to the parking lot.

He said, "I know you were having trouble getting out of this lease, and it's a great location—nice neighborhood and very close to my work. I want to take care of you and love this baby like it's my own. I promise that I will always be there for you both."

"Okay," I repeated.

"I don't ever want to try to replace David. He was like a brother to me, and I don't think I'll ever—"

"Okay," I say softly.

"So, just think about it and let me know when you can."

Turning to look at him, I placed my hand on his arm. "No, you don't understand. I'm saying yes."

"You are?" He looked at me like he didn't believe me or hadn't wanted me to say yes. In that moment, I wasn't sure.

"Yes." I nodded, and a tear fell from my eye.

We stood together, my hand still on his arm, both of us now looking down at the carpet without saying a word. We locked eyes. I could see his lip quivering as he opened his arms, and I stepped inside his embrace. I felt him shaking as we held each other, each expressing our sorrow in our own ways. I fell apart and let it all out while John held me, keeping his sadness and guilt bottled inside. The only outward indication was the hardly perceptible trembling of his body.

"Ally, I'm back here." John tries again. "Ally."

"What?" I open my eyes, and I hear John's voice calling me, but I cannot see him. "Where are you?"

"The laundry room," he calls out.

"Be right there," I say, my voice cracking.

I wipe the tears from my eyes and take a deep, calming breath. I make my way through the large great room with its coffered ceiling, past what will be the kitchen once the cabinets and appliances are installed, to the laundry room.

"Do you think it's big enough? If you want a cabinet with a

counter, we could put it right ..." He stops speaking when he notices my face. "What's wrong?"

"It's nothing."

"You like the house, right?"

"I do." I close my eyes and fight to hold back my emotions. When I open them again, the tears flow.

"What is it?" Moving to me, he places a hand on my shoulder. "What's going on?"

"I just ..." A tear slips over my lips, and I catch it in my mouth, then wipe my eyes with my fingers. "The paint smell ... it's ..."

"Does it bother you? I can open a window."

"No, it's not that. It just brought back this memory. After David died, we went to the apartment, and it had just been painted."

"Had it?"

"Yeah, and you asked me to marry you, and I-I ..." I sniffle, then pinch my nose with my fingers. "I didn't ruin your life, did I?"

"What?" His eyes narrow. "What do you mean?"

"Marrying me. It's not what you wanted. It's what David—"

"Shh." He presses a finger to my lips. "You didn't ruin my life. I've always wanted to take care of you."

"But ..."

I can't find the words, or maybe I simply don't want to ask the question, for fear of the answer, so instead, I just exhale slowly. He pulls me into his arms and holds me tight. I feel like we're right back where we started in that apartment so long ago.

Chapter 13

You've Ruined High Heels for Me Forever

I wake in bed, still fully dressed in my clothes from the day before. I learned long ago that when I feel sad about David, it's much better to not push it down, but instead go with it and let my feelings out. I cry. I cry a lot, but it's only sometimes. It happens much less now that so much time has passed, which, in some ways, is good, but also makes me feel worse, like I've forgotten him. When the sadness overtakes me at inopportune times, I slip away and take a few minutes to let my emotions out. I was a mess at the new house and worse when I came home.

Tomorrow, we leave for Emerald Isle. I have an easy day at the practice with only a handful of patient appointments—my first not until ten o'clock, and I should be out of there by noon. I'm heading to the cemetery this morning to visit David.

After eating a light breakfast, showering, and dressing, I walk to the living room and spot my mother's internet video equipment already set up.

I step back, covering my eyes. "Is everyone decent?"

"No one else is here." My mother appears from the kitchen, dressed in shorts and a pair of bright neon-yellow pumps.

"They're new," she boasts. "They're the Kate pumps from Christian Louboutin."

"Nice."

"Only eight hundred forty-five dollars."

"Mom, that's a lot for a pair of shoes."

"You haven't heard the best part. They're a business expense." Pointing to her toe, she gazes down at the shoes. "What other career could you get a write-off like this?"

I sigh. "First, I'm not sure I'd call what you're doing a career, and second, I think you really need to check with an accountant to be sure you can write off a pair of eight-hundred-dollar heels. Especially ones you use solely for the purpose of stepping on testicles. I think the IRS might have a problem with that."

"You think?" She grimaces, then shrugs. "Well, even if I can't write them off, I still like them, and I have so many new subscribers, thanks to you finding the most perfect—"

"Mom, I told you, I don't want to hear any details."

"Okay, okay. Jeez. Can I ask you one unrelated question though?"

"I guess," I reply cautiously.

"Do you know what I can use to get semen stains out of patent leather? Because—"

"That's your unrelated question? Because that seems totally related."

"Well, you don't know how the semen got there." She raises her shoulders. "It could have happened when I was walking to meet Rachel's bus."

I give her a pointed look. "Did it happen when you were walking to the bus?"

"Well, no, but—"

I put my hands on my hips. "And why would you think I have this knowledge?"

"Your office collects semen samples, doesn't it?"

"Well, yes, but ... look, this is the last time I'm going to tell you to google things like this."

She sighs. "Again, I don't want that on my search history."

With that, my jaw drops open, and I give her a fatigued look. "I just can't do this today."

"Can't do what?" She raises her palms up.

"I have to go." I head toward the door, open it, then turn back. "Just know that you've ruined high heels for me forever."

"What? Why?"

"Because when I look at a nice pair or heels, I will picture"—I scrunch my face up—"*something* under them."

"That's fair." She concedes the point with a nod.

* * *

I park my car at the cemetery and make the short walk to David's grave. I've been here so many times that I could probably make the walk blindfolded. It's pretty easy to find, as it's just to the left of one of the largest and most hideous headstones I've ever seen—some sort of six-foot-tall etched-butterfly monstrosity with a jet-black base that sticks out like a sore thumb.

Every year, I do two things. First, I tell David how his beloved Orioles are doing. The baseball team he idolized and dreamed of playing for since he was a boy. The team that let him down year after year since winning the World Series when he was only a few years old and not yet even a fan. I remember David being especially depressed about his team the year he died since his favorite player, Cal Ripken Jr., had just retired. He did so at the end of the previous year after the team had their worst season in more than thirteen years, almost losing one hundred games.

Second, I read through—or more accurately, perform, as

some sort of melancholy play—the twenty-plus-year-old stored text messages David sent to me from his hospital bed. The ones I still surprisingly have on my current phone. It's the main reason why I've never changed phone carriers in all these years. I'm probably on my eighth phone in that time, but with each new device, I've made sure the messages were transferred. I never let the store take my old phone back from me until they prove the messages are there.

It's probably not a healthy thing to do, but here I am, doing it once again.

Standing before his headstone, I close my eyes and sigh. "David, I'm here early, as you know. I mean, I'm sure you know when your birthday is, and you didn't expect me today, but we're heading on this trip, and although I want to go, I'm sad that I cannot be here to visit you on your birthday."

Tears stream out of my eyes, and I feel weak, so I kneel down in the grass. Pulling out my phone, I google the baseball standings. Sniffling, I wipe my eyes and clear my throat. "The Orioles are seventeen games over five hundred, so it looks like they might actually be good this season. You know I don't follow baseball for obvious reasons, but I did hear they have some decent pitching and have a good chance to make the playoffs. Fingers crossed."

I exhale deeply. "Dave is doing well and about to graduate. John is fine. So is Rachel.

"Oh, my mother and father are losing it. She's, uh ..." A smile spreads over my face, and I scan my surroundings to be sure no one is around. "She's doing this crazy internet thing, where she crushes guys' testicles with her feet and other stuff I definitely don't want to know about. Somehow, she's making money off this, and since that jerk blew through most of her money, she needs it. So, there's a little silver lining there. It's nuts—no pun intended."

I laugh out loud, then shrug. "But what can you do? And my father is taking pictures of women in lingerie. It's this thing called boudoir photography. I'm not sure which of them is the bigger embarrassment right now."

Looking directly at his name on the headstone, I say, "Are you ready?"

After taking another deep, calming breath, I lift my phone and scroll down my text messages to get to David's, then scroll up to the start of his messages from the day of the accident. I look at the headstone. "Remember the first thing you wrote was, *I'm sorry*, and I wrote back, *Don't be. It's not your fault?*"

A tear slips down my cheek. "That was really smart of you to think of using your phone. You were always so quick. If I didn't have these messages from you or could not have communicated with you before … before … I'm not sure what I would have … done."

I fall forward onto my elbows. My eyes are puddles, and my heart is beating out of my chest. I'm absolutely losing it.

"Shit," I mutter before wiping my face and clearing my throat. I feel like I might throw up. I exhale deeply, then push up from the ground. "Sorry. I'm not sure I can …"

Instead of reading the messages out loud, I'm a big, slobbering mess, and all I can do is read them to myself as tears stream down my face and into the grass.

David:

I love you

Ally:

I love you too. They have the best doctors here, and you're going to be fine. They fly people from all over the country to this hospital, and we're so lucky we live right here.

David:
I want you to be happy.

Ally:
Don't say that.

David:
What? Why?

Ally:
Because it sounds like you're saying
goodbye, and you're right here.

David:
Promise me you'll be happy.
Promise me you'll become a doctor
and you'll make a life for yourself
and our baby.

Ally:
Don't you dare do that. Don't give up.
You're going to be fine.

David:
Promise me!

Ally:
No!

David:
Promise me!!!
Promise me!!!

Ally:
I promise.

After reading our last words, I close my eyes. The phone tumbles out of my hand to the grass, and I'm gasping for breath.

Chapter 14

Heading to Emerald Isle

I'm awakened by the alarm blaring at four in the morning. If we have any hope of beating the Saturday summer traffic around Washington DC and through heavily populated Virginia, we've got to get on the road by five. Izzie was dropped off yesterday with Laurie, at what now should be known as her mini dog kennel, and Rachel is packed and ready to leave tomorrow with John's parents for Disney.

John and I are driving alone. We invited my parents to ride with us, but they declined. They are coming down tomorrow, both saying they had a busy day planned. Given their behavior as of late, I didn't dare question it, for fear of any possible details. My son, Dave, is driving separately, picking up Kate's daughter, Morgan, on the way, and they plan to arrive on Sunday as well.

I was a complete mess as I drove home from the cemetery, but was able to pull myself together enough to tie up loose ends at work, then spend most of the rest of the day with Rachel and Izzie before saying our own tearful goodbyes. But once I returned home, I fell apart again, and I don't remember when I finally fell asleep. I'm emotionally and physically exhausted, and I'll probably sleep on the long drive.

John picks me up in his large SUV, bringing me a cup of decaf and an old-fashioned doughnut. He's thoughtful that way, always doing little things for me. He knows I don't travel well and don't want the caffeine to possibly keep me awake on the drive. He'll be fine, as he's a good driver, and he doesn't need me to keep him entertained as we head south.

As we pull out of the parking lot in the darkness, he places a hand on my arm. "How was yesterday at the cemetery?"

"It was sad, but okay. How was your last day at work?"

"I was able to wrap up a few things. I'm pretty sure they won't bother me while we're gone. I debated on leaving my computer at home, but brought it just in case."

"That's smart." I blow on my cup and take a sip.

"How about you? You think they'll survive without you for so long?"

"Dr. Johnson's settled in nicely, and he's covering. It's perfect timing. We'd better take advantage of this. It could be five years before we're both free again for two solid weeks."

We share a smile. I nibble on my doughnut and take a few more sips of coffee before I recline my seat and fall asleep.

I wake to bright sunshine warming my face and look at the clock. It's already after eleven. I slept through most of the ride, and it appears we're making good time since I just saw the Welcome to North Carolina sign.

John says, "Wow, you slept a long time."

"I had a rough night."

"We've hit very little traffic, and we're less than two hours away. Do you need to stop to use the bathroom or anything?"

"No, I can make it. Let's just get there."

He flips on his satellite radio, and a baseball game is on. I don't watch or listen to baseball because most of time, it makes me sad. Although I have some happy memories, too, since that is where I first laid eyes on David.

He was playing for our college team, and a group of us went to the game. College baseball isn't exactly a big draw for fans, like college football or basketball, but we had a decent team. We'd go to a game here and there to lay out in the sun and tan on warm spring days. Sometimes, we'd even go nuts and watch, but mostly, it was a social thing.

I later found out that John had spotted me first in the stands on that day. He was evidently sitting behind me—at least, that was what David told me.

Our team was down two runs with one out in the ninth inning when David came up to bat with two men on base. I was leaning back with my sunglasses on, letting the sun warm my face, when my friend Mary nudged me.

"I've seen him in the dining hall. He's hot."

Sitting up straight in my seat, I checked him out. He walked with a confident gait to the plate as his teammates cheered him on. He was gorgeous and looked so sexy in his uniform.

I lowered my sunglasses for a better look. "He is cute."

I remember every second of that at bat.

He swung hard at the first pitch and nearly lost his balance, using the bat for support to keep from falling over. The next pitch was inside and nearly hit him, as the pitcher was evidently trying to brush him back from the plate. Stepping out of the batter's box, he adjusted his gloves and glared at the pitcher before looking to the dugout at his fired-up teammates.

He connected solidly on the next pitch, sending a towering drive toward left field. It easily cleared the fence but landed just five feet outside the foul pole. He smashed his bat into the dirt, then adjusted his crotch, the way players do, before stepping back into the box. The next pitch was high and evidently right in his sweet spot because David crushed it out to left field again, but this time, it was fair for a walk-off, three-run, game-winning home run.

"Oh, sorry. Do you want me to switch it from the game?" John asks, pulling me from my memory. "I know that can be triggering—"

"No, it's okay." I give him a gentle smile. "I was just thinking about that home run he hit. Do you remember it?"

"Of course I do." He chuckles. "Not that he would ever let anyone forget it. Well, me anyway. It was certainly the highlight of his college career, so it's understandable."

"It was?"

"Yeah, I think he hit two home runs that year. And that was his last year because he had that ankle injury."

"Oh yeah."

John says, "He never fully recovered or got back in the lineup."

"Well, if you're going to go out, that's the way to do it."

"Yeah," he replies softly, and we share a smile.

We don't say another word for a while, but instead listen to the game. In my case and maybe even John's, we're not so much listening as we are trapped in memories of the friend we loved and lost.

Chapter 15

That Incredible House

Emerald Isle is located in the southern Outer Banks on North Carolina's Crystal Coast. The pristine shoreline stretches for twelve miles with its soft white sands and sparkling turquoise waters. We pull into the driveway of the beach house, and I forgot how truly big it is. It's got to be close to six thousand square feet, and it's directly ocean front, meaning there are no houses between it and the ocean. To be clear, it's quite a hike to the water since all the houses in this area are set back past the dunes, and the distance from the dunes to the ocean is probably a good five football fields or more. I recall that making the trek through the heavy sand is not easy on foot. Luckily, they have two heavy-duty beach golf carts they use to get there and transport all the beach gear.

I've been squirming in my seat for the last half hour. I should have taken John up on his offer for a restroom stop.

It must be obvious to him, as he says, "You have to pee, don't you?"

"Uh, yeah."

"I'll grab some stuff. Just run in."

I already have the car door partially open before he brings

us to a full stop. I rush up the stairs and ring the bell. It feels like I'm waiting forever until Kate opens the door. When she does, she gives me a quick hug, and upon seeing my facial expression and my wriggling around, she chuckles and moves aside so I can head to the powder room, which is thankfully just steps away.

When I return, we're given a tour of the recently renovated beach mansion. The home has five king-size bed suites, each with private baths. There are two additional bedrooms with twin bunks in each room, connected by a Jack and Jill bathroom.

We start with the first floor, which features a large carport breezeway—housing the two golf carts, an outdoor shower, and what appears to be spacious parking for three large SUVs. We walk to the backyard area to see the good-sized pool, hot tub, and wooden walkway, which ends on a sandy path through the dunes to the ocean. To the right of the breezeway, we enter the house to discover a large game room, and next to that is the first of the five king-size bed suites. This one has a view of the pool and hot tub. Kate mentions that this is Kyle's room. She tells us that he's generally out late and he can come and go from down here without disturbing anyone.

The second floor has the large open kitchen, great room and laundry room combination, along with two of the bedroom suites. Our host tells us she plans to offer my parents these bedrooms. There is also a screened-in porch and large open-air deck with panoramic views of where the Atlantic Ocean meets the Bogue Sound. From there, you can take the steps down to the pool and hot tub.

There's a loft area on the third floor. It's equipped with a wet bar and large couch to soak in the incredible backyard views of the water. In addition, the third floor is the location of the two remaining king suites with private porches, as well as the two bunk-bed rooms with their shared bath.

Kate explains that her daughter and my son can take the

bunk rooms, and John and I will take one of the suites while she occupies the other.

After the tour, we unload the car, unpack our bags, and follow Kate down to the breezeway to climb in a golf cart and ride to the beach. To get there, we pull out onto the road and head north one block to the cart access.

Tilting my head back, I let the sun soak into my face. "The house is gorgeous."

"I'm happy with how the renovation came out."

I ask, "Kate, when did you arrive?"

"Yesterday afternoon. I had to turn the water back on and get the company to open up the pool and hot tub. And I went grocery shopping."

John says, "We want to buy all the groceries while we're here and pay for any restaurant or takeout meals."

"That's not necessary." Kate turns onto the sand entrance to the beach access.

It's a gorgeous day but hot now that it's just after two o'clock. The July sun is at its peak. A nice breeze is blowing, but it's not doing much to cool me down, and I'm sweating through my shirt.

"We insist on taking everyone to a restaurant. You let us know what's the best place on the island."

"That will be nice." Kate parks the cart ten yards or so from where the waves are breaking.

We slip off our beach slides, and the sand is hot, but not so hot that you can't walk on it. It's a soft, heavy white sand that slopes gently into the emerald-green-and-blue waters of the Atlantic Ocean.

I head down to the water. A wave breaks just ahead of me, sending cold spray and foam over my toes. It's shocking at first, then feels refreshing after having my feet trapped in hot shoes for the long car ride. Standing at the edge of the water, I curl my toes into the sand and gaze out at the perfect ocean. I feel a calm wash over me.

I'm not on call for the first time in probably five years. I can turn my phone off if I choose. I can get drunk. I can do whatever I want.

Chapter 16

Are You a Pothead, Ally?

Kate, John, and I sit at the large dining table, enjoying a chicken and strawberry summer salad that Kate prepared. After we clean up from our meal, we sit out on the back deck, watching the gorgeous sunset, drinking wine, and reminiscing.

Kate leans back in her chair, gazing up at the stars. "We should make the most of our only night alone."

"What do you mean?" John asks.

"There's no one under forty or over fifty here at the moment. Tomorrow will be a little more like a zoo." She flashes us a grin. "I've got a little prescription medicinal marijuana that we could try out. It's supposed to be for beginners."

"Won't Kyle be home tonight?" I ask.

"Not for a while. He's got baseball practice. The regional College World Series tournament is coming up, and we're all invited to the game."

"He's still playing college ball. Isn't he in grad school?" I ask.

Kate says, "This is his last year of eligibility. With the COVID lockdowns, seasons were canceled, and exceptions were made on the five-year eligibility rule. After practice, he's going out with friends."

"God, I haven't smoked since college." I give her a skeptical look. "Plus, I've already had some wine."

"Neither have I," John adds.

"It's a an indica, and like I said, it's recommended for newbies." Kate raises an eyebrow suggestively. "I might have tried a little last night, and it was *amaaazing*."

"Did you?" I lean forward in my seat.

Nodding, she gives me a wicked smile. "It's a strain called Plushberry. It's not too strong, and last night, I also had a glass of wine before I smoked. I was in heaven. We could try a puff or two and get in the hot tub or even go for a swim."

John turns to me and cocks his head. "I'm down if you are."

"Down?" I scoff. "Is that your new cool word?"

"Isn't that how the happening kids say it these days?" He laughs, then puts on a super-deep, mature tone. "Sorry, I meant, I will partake in the legal drug if you will partake."

"Okay, nerd." I roll my eyes.

"It sounds like we're all *down*." Kate rises to her feet with a smile.

John and I decide we should wash off our sweaty day of traveling prior to our little Plushberry adventure because we might be too tired after. Plus, it gives us a chance to let the effects of the wine wear off and FaceTime with Rachel before she goes to bed. Tomorrow is her big travel day. I don't envy her. Her drive to Orlando will be about twice what ours was.

About an hour later, the three of us are in swimsuits, sitting with our legs in the hot tub, while Kate rolls the joint. She's in a fairly skimpy bikini, which is doing a pretty poor job of concealing her newly enhanced breasts. I'm wearing a much more conservative yet flattering one-piece.

I grab the package and read out loud, "*Plushberry is an*

indica-dominant strain that provides a fantastic sense of relaxation for both the mind and body. This strain contains seventeen percent THC, but does not cause excessive drowsiness, making it a good choice for beginners who want to take it easy and relax. The strain has a pleasant berry aroma, as the name implies."

Placing his arms behind him, John leans back. "I could go for a little mind and body relaxation."

"Me too."

Kate lights the joint and takes a quick pull, then lets the smoke out quickly.

"I thought you were supposed to hold your breath," I say.

Kate shakes her head. "No, a lot of people think that. I read you're just supposed to take a two-second inhale and let it out. Holding your breath actually just deprives your brain of oxygen and makes you cough."

"Good to know."

Kate extends the joint to me, and I point to my left. "John first."

"Sissy," John says.

"You just do it first."

He flashes me a grin, then takes a hit off the joint. He takes a deep breath, then hands it to me. With his eyes watering, he says, "That's pretty good."

Holding the joint, I look to John. "Here goes."

I take a quick hit, and already forgetting my instruction, I hold it for a few seconds, then cough it out. John and Kate share a laugh.

"You'll get the hang of it." Kate reaches out, and I hand it over.

She stretches her neck from side to side, then takes a puff. Closing her eyes, she sighs as she hands it to John. He takes a long hit and passes it to me. After taking a quick hit, I exhale deeply without coughing. I feel a slight warmth in my body, like it's melting. I feel my muscles loosening, and a deep calm washes over me.

Kate reaches for the joint, but I pull it back.

"Hold on." I take another longer hit, followed by a deep breath. "Oh, wow."

"She's getting it," Kate quips before taking a hit.

"Hook me up." John snaps his fingers at Kate.

She giggles and hands it over. John takes a long pull. He exhales deeply and cocks his head from side to side, extending it to me.

"No thanks." I wave him away at first, then motion for him to hand it over. "Maybe just one more."

He passes it to me, and I take one last hit.

"Oh shit, so this is what it feels like to relax. I've been missing out." I lazily kick my feet back and forth in the hot tub.

"Are you a pothead, Ally." John shakes his head. "Sorry, I mean, Focker?"

"What?" I look at him like he's out of his mind.

"It's a joke. It's from that movie, um ... what's it—"

"I think your brain is already fried." I laugh.

"*Meet the Parents*. Yeah, that's it." John points at me. "Remember?"

"I guess." I shrug sleepily. "I don't remember movie quotes."

Our host takes another hit, then holds it up. "Anybody else?"

"Not for me," John replies.

"I should have been done two hit ... puffs ago." I laugh out loud. "Hit puffs—sounds like a new cereal for potheads."

We all crack up like idiots at the stupid joke.

Kate points to the house. "There's another bottle of chardonnay right through that door if anyone would care to join me in a glass."

"No way." I shake my head.

"John, are you *down?*" Kate asks, wearing a goofy expression.

"I could be *down* in a few. Let's open it and let it breathe." Rising to his feet, he heads inside.

"Can we please get him to stop saying *down?*"

I roll my eyes, and we gaze at each other, on the verge of laughter.

I lean back and look up to the stars, exhaling deeply. "I'm so glad we did this."

"Me too."

I straighten up to look at her. "Can I ask you a question?"

"Sure. Anything."

I point to her chest. "Were you in a lot of pain when they ..."

"Not really." She beams. "Do you want to see them?"

"No." I shake my head vigorously. "No thanks."

"I don't mind at all."

I look to the house and don't yet see John, so I return my attention to Kate and shrug. "Yeah, sure. Okay."

I swear, before I get the last syllable out of my mouth, she already has her bikini top flipped up over them, and they are staring me right in the face.

My mouth drops open, and I gasp. "Jeez, those are, uh ... those are nice."

"I know. Thanks."

"I mean, really, they did a great job." I point in the general direction of her chest. "They're round and full and perfect, and each nipple is, like, in the right place and in good proportion to the whole breast, you know ..."

"My doctor's in New York, and he does a lot of celebrities. I could get you his name if you're—"

"Oh, no. No thanks."

She leaves her enhancements out in the open as she closes her eyes and leans back. My gaze flips between the door and her implants, and I take this opportunity to study them a little closer. They do look a little odd. They are too big, and the nipples just don't look right. I'm not sure if I'm being catty and a little jealous or simply honest.

I look again to the door, then say, "Maybe you should, you know, put those away."

"Oh, sorry," she says casually before grasping her bikini top and making a show of struggling to cover them.

Even high, I'm annoyed by this. I'm relaxed, but not that relaxed. I grumble some obscenity under my breath before slipping down into the hot tub. Placing my arms on the edge of the tub, I close my eyes and sigh. My work, my past, along with her breasts are all just a faint memory as I let the Plushberry and these hot bubbles work their magic over me.

John appears with the bottle and three glasses. "Sorry I was gone so long. I had to pee."

Kate slips into the hot tub. John places the bottle and glasses near the edge as he sits with his feet in the tub.

He pours a glass for Kate and hands it to her. "Ally, do you want some?"

"I'm fine as is," I mutter softly as I slip a bit further down into the water with the bubbles tickling my chin.

John pours himself a glass and slides into the hot tub, then takes a sip. "This is good."

The three of us sit in silence, luxuriating in the restorative heat and massaging jets of the hot tub for what must be fifteen or twenty minutes.

I take a deep breath and open my eyes to see John refilling his glass. "You'd better not overdo it. I don't think I can lift you out of this water."

"I'm fine." John holds the bottle up. "Kate, do you want a refill?"

Kate opens her eyes. "Just half a glass."

John tops her off.

I rise up out of the water and sit on the edge. "That was just what I needed."

Kate joins me on the edge and sips from her wineglass. "Yeah, John, we're not going to be able to haul your big body out of there. Plus, the water's hot. You shouldn't be in there for very long, especially when you're drinking."

"Yes, Mom." John laughs out loud.

"We're serious," I say.

"Okay, okay. You guys are no fun." He sits on the edge and takes a deep breath. His eyes are glazing over. "Wow, this is, like, the most awesome, super-relaxing, you know, day ever."

Kate and I share a wide-eyed look, and I grab his glass.

"I think you've had enough, big guy."

"What?" He takes in our scolding looks and adds, "You guys suck."

"Don't make me turn this hot tub around," I quip.

"What? That doesn't make any sense." John wrinkles his nose.

"Isn't that from a movie?" I ask.

John says, "You're high."

"No, you are," I retort with a sneer.

"Hey, kids, behave." Kate chuckles, and we all share a laugh. "Why don't we go in and watch a movie?"

"That sounds good. I'm a little cold." I grab a towel and wrap it around my shoulders.

We dry off, and once inside the house, Kate goes to her room and John and I head to ours to change. I slip into a pair of stretch pants and a long-sleeved shirt, then meet them in the loft area, where John turns on the television. It's just after midnight as he searches the guide for movies to watch. We finally settle on some movie on Netflix. Within ten minutes, both of them are nodding off to sleep. I oddly feel wide awake. Maybe because I didn't drink more wine, or it very well could be because I slept for six hours on the ride up.

Kate is stretched out on one side of the big L-shaped sofa, curled up with a pillow, and John is on the opposite side, sitting up with his head at a severely odd angle, resting on his chest.

I turn off the television and tap Kate on the shoulder. "Hey, you fell asleep."

"Did I?" She slowly sits up. "Yeah, I ..."

"Maybe you should go to your room."

"I'm so sleepy," she says in a childlike voice.

I have to laugh as I help her to her feet and guide her to her bedroom door. "Don't forget to say your prayers."

"I won't," she mutters.

I watch as she climbs safely under her comforter before I close the door.

This is your brain on drugs. I recall that old commercial with the eggs frying in the pan.

Turning around, I spot John still in the same position. I tap him on the shoulder and guide my sleepy second toddler to his side of the bed before climbing in next to him.

I feel weird and a little wired. Although John and I have slept in the same bed for more than twenty years, we haven't in the last four months with us living apart while the house is being built. I've found I've gotten used to having my own twin bed all to myself. Not having anyone steal my covers or smack me in the face when they turn is a refreshing change. I crack myself up, picturing our new master bedroom with two twin beds in it, like some 1950s sitcom couple. That would look so odd.

He's always been a heavy sleeper. Nothing like me. He goes out quickly when he hits the pillow and sleeps late. I usually surf Facebook or watch a show on my iPad while sitting up in bed as he snores softly next to me. Eventually, I nod off and don't remember putting my device aside before lying flat. On nights I can't fall asleep, I go out to the living room and read a book or watch TV. I usually only sleep about six hours, and then I'm up and doing things.

Grabbing the iPad from my nightstand, I find it out of power. I have no idea where my charger is or where an outlet might be. I don't feel like rooting around tonight, so I slip out of bed and head to the loft area. The house is eerily quiet and so large. I'm not used to having this much space, but the new house we're building will give us a similar feel with its larger rooms and higher ceilings. I take this opportunity to snoop a little and give myself the behind-the-scenes tour downstairs in the other two king bedrooms before heading to the first floor and ending up sitting out by the pool.

It's a warm night, and a slight breeze is blowing as I curl up on a cushioned lounge chair and stare out at the crystal-blue pool water. I take in a deep breath of the salty air while gazing up at the starry sky. Looking toward the hot tub, I spot the wine bottle, glasses, and ashtray. I can't stand leaving a mess, so I head over, retrieve the bottle and glasses, and deposit them in the sink inside the house. Returning outside, I pick up the ashtray and lighter. There's still half of the joint left unsmoked, and I pause, thinking.

What the hell? Why not? It did feel pretty damn good before, and I wouldn't mind sleeping like a toddler too. I return to the lounge chair and fire it up. After a few hits, I'm right back where I was earlier. Muscles super relaxed. My brain swimming in a delicious fusion of calm and euphoria. I stub the joint out and rest my head back as my eyelids feel heavy. I spot a figure walking toward me. It looks like David in his baseball uniform. I attempt to sit upright, and that's the last thing I remember.

Chapter 17

Previously on Life with Ally

That night, I dream of David and John.

As I sleep, my Plushberry-altered subconscious plays a little game of Previously on *Life with Ally*. I see little clips and highlights from when we all first met. Me sitting at that table in the dining hall with John when David walks over. The day David asked me out for the first time, sitting out under a tree, studying on a gorgeous spring day in the quad. Our first date at the movies. We saw *What Women Want*. I picture Mel Gibson wearing those pantyhose and David and I cracking up uncontrollably, our eyes filling with tears. David reaching over to take my hand.

Then, our second date to Annapolis, Maryland, where we ate at this little restaurant, sitting outside, watching the boats cruise by. David walking me to my dorm room and our first kiss at my door. He really knew how to kiss.

Thinking about it still gives me shivers.

Finally, our third date.

The plan was to get dressed up and eat at one of the nicest restaurants on the water in Baltimore, then have sex after. We didn't speak about it, but I sensed that was where we were headed. I could tell we were both anticipating it. David had a baseball game that day near his parents' house, and I went with him and watched the game. I had my dress with me and was going to freshen up and get changed while he showered. His parents were out of town, and we had the place to ourselves.

His uniform was a little dirty, and he smelled sweaty, but it was a good smell. He just smelled like David. A mixture of his soap and deodorant with a little earthy grass and dirt thrown in. As he was giving me a tour of the downstairs, he inadvertently brushed up against my back. He placed his hands on my shoulders, and I could feel his warm breath on my neck. I turned slowly, and we gazed into each other's eyes.

He said, "We have that reservation."

"I know," I replied breathlessly.

Our bodies and our lips were only inches apart. He wrapped his arms around me and pulled me close. I felt his hard, thick chest pressing into my breasts, and lower, something else was getting hard. I pressed my lips to his neck and breathed in the scent of him. We kissed, and it grew more passionate right there, next to the kitchen. He swept me into his arms and carried me up the steps to his room. We quickly stripped out of our clothes and made love. It was hard and fast at first. We desperately wanted each other. Then, he settled into a gentle rhythm over me, holding my hands over my head as he gazed into my eyes.

When I wake up, I can't remember right away if I'm twenty-one or forty-two. Then, I look over to John and this big, beautiful bedroom, and I realize where I am. Who I am. That it was all just a dream.

I slip out of bed. It's just after eight, and I head down to the kitchen, putting on the kettle for tea. Outside, I curl up on the deck in another cushioned lounge chair, blowing on my mug while taking in what's left of the sunrise and listening to the soft sounds of the crashing waves.

I hear the door open behind me.

"You really shouldn't smoke that stuff alone."

"What's that?"

I turn to find Kate's son, Kyle, staring down at his phone. He's tall, muscular, and lean, wearing shorts and a tight gray T-shirt that accents his thick biceps.

"One sec." He chuckles as he types before slipping the phone into his pocket. He moves to the railing. "I said, you shouldn't smoke that stuff alone. I found you sleeping by the pool."

"I wasn't smoking," I lie, then suddenly, it comes back to me. "That was you?"

"Yep." Grinning, he sits down on the chair next to me.

"I was just, um, cleaning up."

"Really? Just cleaning up, huh?"

"The three of us might have smoked a little a few hours earlier. Just a little." I demonstrate, for no reason, by placing my thumb and index finger about an inch apart.

"Uh-huh." He chuckles. "The roach was still burning a little."

"The what?" I sip from my mug.

"Your joint was still smoldering. So, you're telling me it was burning that way for hours?"

Smiling, I raise a shoulder. "Um, would you buy that?"

"Not for a minute."

"I wouldn't either." I laugh. "Honestly, we were all smoking earlier, and then I couldn't sleep, so I came down and got ... curious."

"Famous last words." He raises one brow, and we share a laugh.

Leaning back, I take a good look at him. "Jeez, you're all

grown up. Last time I saw you, you were, what, like, maybe five eight and—"

"I was a late bloomer," he grumbles. "The curse of my life. But I sprouted."

"I hear you're in grad school and playing ball."

"Yes, and yes. I can't wait to get out of school."

"That bad, huh?"

He shakes his head. "No, just ready for whatever's next."

"And what's next for you?"

"I have no clue." He shrugs.

Gazing at him, I scoff. "Jeez, how tall are you now?"

"Six-three."

"No way." I get to my feet. "Let's see."

He rises up and we stand about a foot apart. I crane my neck to look up to him. He's tall all right. "How much do you weigh?"

"Two twenty maybe." He looks me over and grins. "But you're pretty light."

"What?"

"You don't weigh much. I was a little shocked."

"What are you talking about?" I slip back down to the chair and grab my mug.

"I carried you up to bed. Two full flights."

"I didn't walk up myself?"

"Nope. I carried you."

I ask hesitantly, "You weren't wearing your baseball uniform, were you?"

"I was."

"Oh, I thought I only dreamed that." I pause, then say, "I didn't do anything ... stupid while you were carrying me or—"

"Like what?"

"I don't know ... just in general, I didn't say anything off or ..."

"No, you were cool. Well, I've got to run." He turns toward the door and takes a step, then turns back to me. "There might have been some inadvertent nuzzling."

"Nuzzling?" My eyes widen.

"Inadvertent though." He shrugs. "And you sorta smelled me ... like my neck."

"I'm so sorry. I—"

"Don't worry about it." He waves a hand at me dismissively. "You weren't the first drunk or high girl I deposited safely in her bed."

That statement makes me cackle like a schoolgirl. "You do that a lot, huh?"

"Sometimes. I can say that it was the first time I ever dropped one off into her husband's bed."

"Well, I would hope so." My smile fades. "Oh, but what does that say about me?"

"Just that you overdid it. I think they tell you to always have a drug buddy."

"I'll, uh, try to remember that."

"Oh"—he waves a finger at me, grinning—"there was *one* sorta weird thing."

"What's that?" Placing my mug on the table, I swing my legs around and stare up at him, waiting for the other shoe to drop. *Oh shit, what did I do? Grab his ass or something else? Jesus.*

It seems like he's pausing forever before he tells me what the hell I did or said or—

"You said something like ... 'I'm glad we're not waiting.'" He narrows his eyes. "What did that mean?"

Oh fuckity, fuck, fuck!

I swing my legs back on the chair, clutching my cup near my chest. "Huh. I have no idea. Maybe I was anxious to get to sleep."

He shrugs. "Okay, got to run. It was good seeing you again."
"Um ... you too," I say, my voice cracking.
I watch, mortified, as he heads into the house.

Chapter 18

You Actually Brought Furniture

J ohn stumbles out of the bedroom first at just after eleven thirty. He asks for strong coffee, and I make some. Kate emerges from her bedroom just as the pot is ready. They both look a bit rough around the edges.

John says, "I don't remember even going to bed."

Kate says, "Neither do I."

"We made it a few minutes into some lame movie, and I put you both to bed," I say.

"You did?" John takes a sip of coffee, then runs his hands through his bed hair. "I really wanted to get a round of golf in today, but I don't know."

"Oh, I wanted to also." Kate turns to him. "Maybe just nine holes. What do you think?"

"Yeah, why not? Ally, are you interested in playing? You could rent a set of cl—"

"You hate golf, right?" Kate interrupts. "I mean, you don't play much."

"I don't hate it, but ... you guys go without me. I want to stick around, get some sun, and wait for my parents."

John and Kate eat, shower, then head out on the links as I'm making my way down to the pool in my one-piece. I bake in the sun for twenty minutes or so before slipping under the umbrella and falling asleep. I wake to loud voices and arguing coming from the breezeway. It's my parents, Glenn and Candace, the *very late midlife crisis* duo. Rising to my feet, I slip on my cover-up and meet them at some sort of large, what looks like a twenty-plus-year-old white conversion van, which I've never seen before.

"Hey, guys. How was the trip?"

"Oh, fine," she replies.

"What's with the van?" I ask with trepidation.

"You like it?" he asks.

"Uh, it's big."

"I got a great deal on it." He beams. "Need it for the new business."

"Do you need any help with your luggage?"

"That would be wonderful." He opens up the side door and hands me a large leather bag. "Grab my camera bag. I don't want to leave it out here in the heat."

"Tell me this is for taking picture of the sunset and not something else."

"Well, it's for that and for—"

"Don't you dare say it," I warn.

He says in a cool, calm voice, "I figure if someone wants their boudoir pictures done while I'm here, I want to be ready."

"Jesus, Dad. Do I need to remind you that we're guests here?"

"I won't bother anyone. You're overreacting."

I plead, "Just promise me that—"

"Glenn, do you want all the props now, or can they stay in the van?"

"Props? What props?" My jaw nearly hits the concrete. "What the hell is she talking about?"

He's so composed. He never raises his voice or gets upset. And it really, really pisses me off.

He shrugs and explains once again in that annoyingly soothing voice, "I just brought a few props in case I need them."

Placing the camera bag down, I fold my arms over my chest. "Show me!"

"I don't think you're in the right mood to—"

"I said, show me!"

"Jeez, okay. Calm down and come over here."

I follow him to the back of the van, and he opens both doors. Inside is a large wicker egg chair, a fur-covered stool, and a few bins filled with what looks like fuzzy wraps, lingerie, and other props. My mouth opens wider as my gaze moves from one ridiculous item to the next.

"Holy crap."

"It was already in the van, so ..."

"You brought furniture." I scoff. "You actually brought furniture. I'll say it again—we're guests here." I motion to the house. "This is not our house."

"None of it has to leave the van." He lifts his palms.

"It'd *better not* leave the van."

He wraps his arms around a huge, fluffy white fur blanket. "Can I at least bring this in? It's one of the best boudoir props. It's so versatile. You can lie on it or drape it around your body or hang it off the bed as you're leaning against it. Plus, it's warm if your mother gets cold at night."

I sigh, exhausted while pressing my thumbs into my eyebrows. "Okay, just the blanket."

She says, "Hey, Glenn, do you want this?"

I take a step to the right to see my mother holding up a real, actual, goddamn firefighter jacket and boots. I lose the power of speech for what seems like an eternity. I think I might have suffered a stroke.

"What is it, Candy?" Glenn steps around the back of the van.

She says, "Oh, here are the suspenders and pants."

Finally, I stammer, "Um, I, uh, you ..."

"It's one of my most popular items." Upon taking in my horrified expression, he says softly, "Candace, um, might be best to just leave all that in the van."

Taking a step back, I point an index finger at each of them. "Promise me you'll both behave."

"We promise," they reply almost in unison.

Turning to my mother, I shake my head, incensed. "And if you brought that stupid internet-camera light-ring thing, just march your ass right back in this van and head north. I'm not having that—"

"Jeez!" She raises her hands in the air defensively. "I would never."

"Uh-huh."

He heads for the door, carrying the blanket, along with a backpack and another thinner, longer black bag over his shoulder.

"Wait," She rushes to him, slips the black bag off his shoulder, and heads back to the van, wearing a guilty expression. "I don't need my vitamins right now."

"Yeah, you just keep all your *vitamins* away from everyone. I mean it."

"Okay, okay." She shoots me a snooty look.

I raise my hands in the air. "Anyone purely listening to this conversation would think I'm the parent here and not the other way around. They most certainly would not believe that you guys are almost seventy!"

He turns back to me and stamps his foot and says in a falsetto, "You're so mean!"

"I hate you! I hate you!" my mother adds in a childlike tone.

I turn to them and click my teeth as I shake my head. My anger melts away just enough that I break a smile. "Okay, I get it. I'll lighten up, but promise me that you'll both just dial the crazy back a notch."

They both nod, holding back smiles.

"All right." I chuckle, rolling my eyes. "Now, get upstairs, you two."

Chapter 19

The Male-Genitalia-Drawing, Movie-Title Savant

Around four in the afternoon, Dave and Morgan arrive at the house. With John and Kate back from golfing, Kyle returning from baseball practice, and my parents settled into their respective bedrooms, the entire group is now here.

Hanging out in the great room, we discuss dinner plans and kicking off this vacation with a multigenerational, multifamily game night. After some discussion, we settle on takeout pizza. John runs out to pick up four large pies.

My parents are acting strange. I mean, with each other and more than their normal, everyday strange. I haven't seen them together like this in a while, and it's a little off-putting, to say the least. They're getting along a bit too well. The bad blood between them was resolved long ago, and they have come together and been civil with one another for birthday parties and holidays since then. But something seems off, and I haven't put my finger on it yet. I'm keeping my eye on them, just to be safe.

After the pizza, we head out to the deck to watch the sunset. Morgan is the youngest in the group at nineteen, but her mother, Kate, is a realist and is allowing her to drink in her presence during this trip as long as she doesn't overdo it. One example of overdoing it would be what Kate, John, and I did the night before, and thankfully, Morgan wasn't here to see the wonderful example we all set. I'm sure that the three of us are mature enough to learn from our mistake—at least, that's what I keep telling myself.

Kate has this game night planned as we try to re-create the fun we had playing Pictionary the last time we were all together years ago. This time, the theme is movie titles. One large whiteboard sits on an easel in the center of the room. We split into two teams. Kyle, Kate, John, and I are on one team against my parents, Dave, and Morgan.

Morgan turns to her mother. "Hey, wait. How can you play? You picked the movies and know what they are. You'll have an advantage."

"I didn't." Kate holds up an envelope. "I hold in my hand a hermitically sealed envelope and—"

"What the hell does *hermitically sealed* mean? Does anyone know what that is?" John asks with a smile.

"Okay, it's just a regular, old, sealed envelope and I don't know what's inside. I had a friend back home choose from a list of two hundred random movie titles and put them inside. The rules are, we alternate between teams, and each team has one person drawing while the other three try to guess the title. The timer starts once the pen hits the board, and you get thirty seconds."

I ask, "Is the person drawing allowed to make any hand gestures or facial expressions to confirm that their teammates are on the right track?"

"Yes, those are fine. So, first, the drawer reads the slip and holds up fingers to display how many words are in the title. The drawer is not permitted to speak or write any letters or numbers on the board. And that's basically it. Each team will get one point for a correct guess. We'll keep playing until we either run out of titles, get bored, or try to kill each other," Kate adds with a smile.

"All right. Let's go," Kyle says.

Our team gets to go first, and we decide to go alphabetically by first name, so I draw first. Sliding my hand into the envelope, I pick out a slip, which is *The Sixth Sense*.

I frown at the group as I walk to the board. "Crap."

"Remember, no speaking," Kate scolds.

"Sorry." Pressing my lips together, I hold up three fingers.

"Okay, three words." Kyle moves to the edge of the sofa.

Morgan readies her phone to start the timer.

Holding the pen, I look at the ceiling, figure out a plan, then get started. I quickly draw six dots on the board, then draw a crude outline of my take on a nose with my limited artistic skills.

"*A Bug's Life*," John calls out, and I give him an odd look. He adds defensively, "What? Those look like bugs."

I point to the dots with the pen and make a face.

Kate says, "Um, *Pokémon*."

"You're kidding, right?" Kyle scoffs. "Three words!"

"Well, she was poking at it." Kate slumps back in her seat self-consciously.

I point once again at the dots, then draw some lines coming out of my awful representation of a nose.

Kyle's eyes brighten. "Six ... six noses. Six smells. Oh, *The Sixth Sense*."

"Yes," I shout.

"How the hell did he get that?" Morgan grumbles. "In, like, only ten seconds."

"She's a good drawer," Kyle says.

"What the heck?" Dave complains. "That nose looks like a breast with two nipples."

I give my son a good-natured sneer as I waltz back to my team. "Your turn."

Candace grabs her slip and heads to the board. After holding up three fingers, she draws two circles with dots in the middle, then a stick with other sticks coming out of it with a box on top of it.

Dave calls out, "Breasts, um, striptease."

She shakes her head.

"Not everything is a breast, perv!" Morgan punches him in the arm.

She draws more circles under her other circle, then points to the other stick thing.

My father shouts out, "Tree."

Her eyes light up.

"Okay, *Under the Yum Yum Tree.*"

"What the hell is that?" Dave scoffs. "That can't be a real movie."

"It is a real movie ... with Jack Lemmon."

"She said *three* words!" Morgan grumbles, then calls out, "*The Wishing Tree.*"

Candace frowns, then draws more random crap until John announces, "Time!"

She meanders to her seat, dejected.

"Grandma?" Dave gives her a look.

"Oh, sorry. It was *The Breakfast Club.*" She points at the board and adds sheepishly, "Those are eggs, and that's a tree house. Get it? *Breakfast and a club house* sort of thing."

"We'll get the next one." Dave claps his hands together.

Candace adds sarcastically, "I forgot how much fun this is."

John is up next, and he draws something that no one can identify, which was supposed to convey *Grease.* Next up is Dave, who draws a flag and a circle with a pie shape cut out of it. Morgan gets that it's *American Pie* just before time runs out. The score is tied at one.

Kate goes next and can't draw to save her life. And as luck would have it, she gets a tough one—*The Man with the Golden Gun*—and we can't make heads or tails of anything she has on the board.

My father draws next. His skills rival Kate's, and his team can't come up with *101 Dalmatians*.

Kyle saunters up to the board and turns to the other team. "Oh, it's on now. I took a drawing elective junior year."

"No trash-talking." Dave waves a hand at him.

He pulls a slip from the envelope, smiles, then holds up his index finger. He draws a perfect, artsy female backside, then turns cockily to us.

John says, "Something butt."

Kyle nods and motions with his hand that we're on the right track.

Kate says, "*Butterfly Effect.*"

Kyle shakes his head, turns back, and duplicates his work almost exactly, then points between the two.

I shout out, "*Assassins.*"

"Yes." Kyle pumps his fist and heads toward me with his hand down low, and I slap it.

"How the hell did you get that?" Dave asks, dumfounded.

"It's clearly two asses," I begin. "So, I put two asses together to get ass-ass-ins."

Glenn says, "My friend, you definitely know how to draw an ass."

"Thank you. Thank you." Kyle takes a bow.

The score is now two to one. Morgan goes next and gets *Step Brothers*, and her team guesses *Stepmom* just as time runs out.

I head to the board and pull my slip out of the envelope. I

frown at first, and then a smile spreads over my face. I hold up two fingers, then draw a near-flawless penis and testicles and a pan next to it.

Within two seconds, Kyle calls out, *"Peter Pan."*

"Yes!" I do some sort of locomotive train motion that I swear I've never done before and plop down next to my partner in crime and pat him on the back.

Kyle says, "I believe that's three to one. Do you guys want to call it a game, or do you want the humiliation to continue?"

"It's a long game, *ass boy*," Dave fires back.

Candace heads up to the board. She draws some pretty good-looking breasts, and her team shouts out guesses like, *Showgirls*, *Boogie Nights*, and *Indecent Proposal*, which are all wrong.

She returns to her seat, frowning and once again not divulging what it was supposed to be.

She folds her arms. "I don't want to play anymore."

"Don't be a baby. At least tell us what it is," Morgan says.

Candace sighs. "It was *Titanic*. They were all drawing asses and penises, so I figured a pair of breasts would get you to *Tit-anic*."

"That's one way to go," Dave says slowly, sarcastically. "Another might be a ... I don't know ... a sinking ship."

Candace says, "Oh, I didn't think of that."

It's John's turn, and we guess his correctly just before time runs out, followed by another great performance from my son, whose team quickly gets another point. Then, Kate has another subpar performance, but our team is still up four to two. After Glenn misses his, it's the ass-master Kyle's turn. After holding up four fingers, he draws two simple arrows, one left and one right, and simply stares at me, wearing a bored expression.

My eyes brighten. *"Back to the Future!"*

He just drops the pen and heads back to the sofa without saying a word.

"What the hell?" Dave grumbles. "He must be communicating something to her with his eyes. I call bullshit."

"Communicating with his eyes?!" I scoff. "What the hell does that even mean?"

"I don't know, but you two are up to something."

"Yeah, we're up to kicking one hundred percent of your ass." Kyle holds his fist up, and I bump it.

John says, "That's five to two."

Dave says, "Come on, guys. We're better than this."

Morgan heads to the board and gets her slip. She holds up one finger, then draws an up arrow and a balloon.

Dave calls out, "*Up*."

Those two do some sort of weird happy dance as she returns to her seat with the score now five to three.

I return to the board, review my slip, and frown. I pause to think, then shrug, holding up five fingers. I sketch a smiling mouth and return to my signature penis drawing, then top it off with what looks like a stick figure swinging on a vine, wearing what I hope passes for a loincloth, before reaching for another vine. I turn to my teammates, wearing a tentative yet hopeful expression.

I can see the wheels turning in Kyle's brain, and he starts to work it out softly. "Smile ... penis ... Tarzan ... smile ... cock ... Tarzan ... smile, dick, Jane. I've got it! *Fun with Dick and Jane!*"

"Yes." I raise my arms in triumph, then saunter back to my seat.

"Jesus Christ." Dave rises to his feet. "That's it. I'm done. There is no way you got that from a shitty picture of a smile, another goddamn dick drawing, and a stick figure wearing a bathing suit."

"Um, that's a loincloth." I lift a finger up with my eyebrows raised.

"It's clearly a loincloth," Kyle agrees.

"Jeez, she's getting all the penis ones, and she's a freaking urologist," Glenn begins. "This game is rigged. The game is being stolen from us."

"Rigged?!" I scoff. "Explain how this is rigged. The envelope was sealed." I point to Kyle. "He's just some sort of male-genitalia-drawing, movie-title savant. This is a witch hunt. Our team won fair and square."

"Whatever," Dave mutters and heads away.

Our winning team watches as the rest of the sore losers do their walk of shame.

"You guys were on fire," John says.

Kyle and I lean back on the sofa, hands folded behind our necks, and share a smile, basking in the glory of our sweet, sweet victory.

Chapter 20

Meet Brady and Gronk

It's still early when we wrap up the game, so John and I FaceTime with Rachel and his parents. We catch them when they return from dinner. They tell us they plan on spending the next day at Animal Kingdom. Rachel tells us that she wants to ride the Expedition Everest steel roller coaster, but she's a little scared. She also tells us her grandfather promised to go on it with her, but the look on his face says otherwise. Rachel is clearly exhausted from the drive, so we keep the call short.

I think we all had a little too much family fun for the night. When Kate suggests we all watch a movie, everyone declines. So, we all go our separate ways, and John and I are in bed just before eleven. I'm still riding this exhilarating high from our team's Pictionary win—or more accurately, my and Kyle's victory. It's hard to dispute that we most certainly carried the entire team.

John says, "You two were amazing tonight. I don't think I've ever seen anything like it. You were like Brady and Gronk out there."

"Who?"

"Brady and Gronk!"

"I don't know what that is."

"You know, Brady and Gronk." He looks at me like I should know what the hell he's talking about. "Brady and Gronk." He raises his palms.

"You keep saying that, but I don't know what you're saying. Is that an ice cream brand, like Ben & Jerry's?"

"No. Tom Brady and—"

"Oh, Brady and Rob Gronkowski." I shake my head and swat my hand in the air. "Sure, I've heard of them."

"Exactly."

"Why didn't you just say that?"

"I did."

"No, you didn't." I scrunch my face up. "They really call him Gronk?"

"It's short for Gronkowski."

"Ah, gotcha."

John says, "Yeah, they combined for, like, ten thousand yards and one hundred touchdowns. I think it's, like, the most ever for a quarterback-and-receiver duo."

"Huh. Yeah, we were having some sort of mind meld or something."

"It was freaky."

"What's the plan for tomorrow?" I ask. "I'd really like to get to the beach early."

"I was hoping to get in an early round, then go to the beach later."

"That's fine. Just meet us down there."

Minutes later, John is already asleep. I'm on my iPad, getting sucked down a rabbit hole of one silly Facebook video after another until I finally find my head bobbing. Placing my screen down, I curl up with my pillow.

When my eyes open in the morning, I head out to the kitchen, brew a pot of coffee, and begin preparing breakfast for everyone. I make two pounds of bacon, and a double batch of pancake batter.

John and Kate wake first, and I fire up the griddle. After breakfast, they head out to play golf. As the rest of the vacationers begin to trickle to the second floor, I serve them as well. With Kyle still sleeping, I cook what's left of the batter and leave it on the stove warmer, wrapped in some foil, along with a note that we're heading to the beach.

Kate's already given me the lay of the land, so I know where all the beach gear is stored and how to work the golf cart. It's not a small production, getting all four of us, plus the chairs, tent, towels, and cooler filled with drinks to the beach, but we somehow pull it off.

After about an hour of baking in the sun in my one-piece, I head to the ocean and stand ankle deep in the cold water as the waves break over my legs. A large wave splashes halfway up my body and sends me squealing like a little girl, sprinting back to the shore, where I nearly collide with Kyle.

Reaching out, he keeps me from taking a tumble with one hand as he holds a boogie board with the other. "That one gotcha, huh?"

"It did."

"A little cold, is it?"

"Yep."

"It's not bad once you get used to it. It actually feels warm when you get in."

It's the first time I've seen him without a shirt, and, wow, is he built. The muscles ripple across his broad chest and tight abs, and I'm happy I'm wearing sunglasses so he can't tell that I'm staring. My eyes travel lower to his strong thighs and defined calves, and I feel a little weak in the knees.

I pull myself out of this male model beach runway show and finally reply, "I never really go in over my waist."

"Why not?"

"I'm not a great swimmer, and I don't feel comfortable in the waves."

"They aren't so bad today." He kneels down, scoops some water up in his hand, and looks up at me. "Hey, last night, we really kicked their ass."

"I know. How the hell did we do that?"

"I have no idea." Rising up, he smiles. "Here, let's try this. You think of something, and I'll try to guess what it is."

"No way." I chuckle.

"I'm serious."

"All right."

Placing two fingers to his head, he looks intently at me. "Now, think of something. Go ahead."

All I can think of at this moment is seeing him out of that bathing suit. All of him.

Stop picturing your friend's son naked. Stop it! Stop it, you pervert!

"Okay, do you have it?"

"Um, no—I mean, yes." I cringe.

God, look at those abs and those arms. No, don't look. Stop it! Stop.

He closes his eyes. "Okay, you're thinking about me teaching you how to catch waves with this boogie board."

"Um, that's not it." *Oh, thank God.*

Lowering his hand, he says, "So, what were you thinking?"

"How I'm freezing," I lie.

"Don't be such a sissy." He steps to me, capturing me with one arm around my waist, then carrying me like a package into the deeper water.

"Put me down," I half-heartedly protest, slapping him on the shoulder.

"Nope. You're going to get over this fear."

He drags me farther out until I can just barely touch the bottom with my tiptoes.

"I don't like this." I grit my teeth.

"I've got you. Here, hold the board." He guides me onto the boogie board.

I put a white-knuckle grip on it, and as my body acclimates to the water, it starts to actually feel somewhat warm. It's a fairly large board with space for me to clutch it on one side and him on the other, and we're not directly face-to-face.

"See, this isn't scary, is it?"

"No, not really," I reply timidly.

We're out past where the waves break, and it feels really relaxing to be here with the sun warming my skin, along with the gentle motion of the ocean.

Placing my head on my arms, I relax and let my legs rise up and float near the surface of the water behind me. "This is kinda nice."

"I knew you'd like it. Sometimes, I just float out here for a while."

"It's relaxing." I moan and close my eyes. Suddenly, it hits me, and I lift my head, bringing my legs down in a panic. "How far out are we? I can't touch the bottom!"

"Relax. Relax. I've got you." He snickers. "I'm not going to let you drown or anything."

"Promise?"

He rests his head on his arms, and I do the same, letting my legs rise once again. We're both now floating, looking straight ahead with our elbows barely touching.

I say, "John said something funny about us yesterday."

"What's that?"

"About the game. The way we played. He called us Brady and Gronk."

"I can see that." He laughs. "We were in sync, like the dynamic duo."

"Yeah, but who's who?" I turn to look at him.

"Well, I'm definitely Brady," he says adamantly.

"But I want to be Brady," I whine. "Why do you get to be?"

"Because I was the one who correctly got three of your titles."

I protest, "But wait, I was drawing, and that's the hard part."

"Maybe, but I'm still Brady."

"All right, I'll give it to you." I narrow my eyes, struggling to suppress a smile.

"Cool, Gronky. Can I call you Gronky? You look a little more like a Gronky."

"Knock yourself out, Brady."

"I'm going to teach you how to ride a wave."

"I don't think so." I scoff. "No way."

"Um, do you see where we are?" He points toward the shore.

"What?" When I crane my neck back, I discover we've floated pretty far out. I've been facing away from the coastline this whole time, and I didn't notice that we're now a couple hundred feet out. "Holy crap. We're going to die!"

"We're not going to die," he says in a tired voice. "But if you don't agree to let me teach you, I'm going to leave you out here with the board, and you can figure out how to get back on your own." He lets go of the board and treads water next to me.

"Don't let go! Don't you dare!" I clutch the board now like my life depends on it—because it does!

"I'm serious." Raising an eyebrow, he moves farther away.

"Get back here!"

"Not until you say yes."

"Yes! All right, yes! Just get your ass back here."

He laughs and swims to my side of the board, grabbing hold and turning us toward the shore. "Now, kick."

"Brady, you're a jerk." I start to kick my feet.

We're kicking and kicking, and it takes a good three minutes to fight the current to get back to where the waves are breaking. I'm exhausted. He's now standing with the water at his shoulder level.

He says, "Ready?"

"For what?"

"To ride a wave."

"Not now. I'm tired. I said I would let you teach me, but didn't say when." I push away from the board and try to swim toward the shore, calling back, "I'll pencil you in for next week."

"Absolutely not." He dives after me, grabbing me around the middle, but instead his hand slides up to my breast. He quickly pulls his hand away and lets me go. "Sorry about that."

We're eye to eye—him standing and me struggling to stay above water on my tiptoes.

"Help me!"

He places a hand under my armpit for support, but that doesn't seem to do it for me. Scared, I somehow maneuver behind him until I'm clutching on to his back with my head on his shoulder and my arms curled under his. It must look like he's wearing me as a backpack.

He chuckles. "Don't you feel silly? It's not that deep."

"No! I don't feel silly, and you're mean." I wrap my legs around him and squeeze—partly because I'm scared and a little because I just want to.

Don't judge me. It feels good, and let's just leave it at that.

He says, "Are we doing this or not?"

"Okay. Jeez. Let's get it over with."

He secures the board with one hand, reaching back with the other to disentangle the lunatic—me—from his back.

"This will work a little better if you aren't hanging on me like a chimp."

"How deep is it?"

"It's not. Now, here, grab the board."

I release my death grip on his body, and he guides me onto the boogie board sideways. Placing his strong arms on either side of my body, he directs us in line with the beach and kicks his feet.

"How in the world is this going to work?" I ask, terrified.

"I'll get you in the right position, and you just kick your feet and let the wave do all the work."

"You're not going to let me go, are you?"

"I have to."

"Why?"

"That's just how it has to work. Trust me."

His body is draped all over mine. I feel his strong chest on my back, and I swear I feel other *parts* inadvertently bumping against my backside once or twice. Shivers go down my spine, and I don't think it's from the cold water.

"Okay," I say, clutching the board as a wave lifts us up about five feet and breaks just in front of us. "Wow, that was a big one."

"I know. We'll find a small one to start."

Or maybe we could just float here like this forever with you sort of bumping into me from behind. That seems like it would be kinda nice for an hour or two.

"Okay, here's one. Ready?"

"Not really."

"Just hold on, and I'll be right behind you if something happens."

"What could happ—"

Suddenly, he shoves me forward—hard—and the wave breaks just behind me. I catch it, and it drops me a few feet. Then, I pick up speed, heading toward the shore, smiling and screaming like a child. I end up on my knees, then turn back to him, grinning.

"Now, wasn't that fun?" he says.

"Can I go again?"

Chapter 21

The Note

I reach the second-floor great room, and Kyle is lying on the sofa, wearing just shorts, while video-chatting on his phone. He can't see me from my angle, so I simply stand there, taking in the sight of him. He's laughing and talking loudly. I flash back to our wet bodies draped all over each other —both times, that is—the time I was wrapped around him followed by the time he was wrapped around me. It's sort of one big sexy blur. I'm unsure of what's going on with me and this involuntary reaction I have to being near him.

He's gorgeous, for sure, and that body is just perfect. But he's young enough to be my son, if I had gotten pregnant as a teenager. Not to mention, he's one of my oldest friend's sons. I can't even comprehend the games my mind is playing on me. I'm edgy. I don't feel like eating. It's like I'm in high school again, pining away over some boy.

Does he remind me that much of my David and the way we were together so long ago, or am I just projecting some crazy fantasy on him? Who knows?

Suddenly, he spots me, and I find myself holding my breath.

I give him a nod and what I'm sure is an awkward smile. He's got to think something's wrong with me.

"Dude, hold on," he says into the phone, then smiles. "Hey, Gronk."

"Hey, um, Tom. I mean, Brady." *Jeez, could I be more of a spaz?*

He motions toward the kitchen table. "We're getting takeout from this place called The Village Market. My mother wants everyone to look at the menu. It's over there with all the others. Just text her what you want before five, okay?"

I give him an awkward thumbs-up before heading into the kitchen. Spotting the group of menus on the table, I sit and look though them until I find the right one. When I open it up, a handwritten note slides out and onto the floor. A word catches my eye, and my jaw drops open. I pick it up and read it.

Since the first time I saw you, I've been infatuated. I'm so attracted to you that I can't sleep. Just sleeping in the same house with you again is literally killing me. I ache for you. You've never looked sexier. Come to my room tonight at 2 a.m. when everyone is asleep. I want you so much that it hurts. I don't want her to find out. She'd never understand. Please come. I'll be waiting for you.

I read it again slowly with my heart beating out of my chest. I crane my neck to see the back of his head as he continues his phone chat. I read it once more, then rise to my feet and slowly make my way to the great room. I stand there, mouth agape, about ten feet from him, clutching the note in my clammy hand.

"Dude, I've got to go. Later." He raises his gaze to me. "Did you see something you want?"

"I, uh ..." I narrow my eyebrows in utter confusion. "Huh?"

"For dinner."

I point in some spastic motion toward the kitchen and reply, my voice cracking, "Oh, yeah, sure."

"Are you okay?" He sits up, grabs the TV remote, then studies my face, wearing a curious look.

I say through a thick throat, "No—I mean, yes. I'm good."

He smiles brightly. "You were really killing it out there in the water. You'll be catching waves on your own in no time."

"Really? You think?"

"Definitely."

I look nervously around the room, still holding the paper.

He switches on the TV and begins flipping channels. "Did you see my note?"

"Note?"

"In the kitchen."

"Um, yes, I saw your note."

Without tearing his eyes from the screen, he says, "I hope you can come."

I can't look at him, so I turn toward the screen and mutter, "Um, yeah, I have to check my, uh ... but, yeah, I think I can. I will."

"Great. I will see you there." He gives me a devilish smile. "I don't want to brag, but I'm awesome. You'll see."

He returns his attention to the screen, and I slip back toward the kitchen, where my knees literally buckle. Placing my hand on the nearest wall, I steady myself.

Holy crap! He sure has a high opinion of himself. Could he be more inappropriate and sexy and cocky and gorgeous and I don't know what the hell else, all at the same time?

I'm thankful he can't see me falling apart. I hear people climbing the steps and voices growing louder. Looking down the stairs, I see John.

"There you are," he calls up to me.

"Hi." I shove the note quickly in my pocket and try to remember to breathe.

Chapter 22

Are You Out of Your Freaking Mind?

The eight of us sit at the large table, eating fried chicken. All through dinner, I'm understandably a little preoccupied and picking at my meal. After frolicking in the water all day with this *slightly*—and I use that word loosely—younger gentleman, I've found that he's declared in writing that he's so attracted to me that he cannot sleep. On top of that, he's invited me to his room later for what I can only assume is an *awesome*—his word, not mine—sexual encounter.

How can I, in good conscious, deny him the simple gesture of a night of passion that might just help him get some shut-eye? A night of passion, I might add, that yours truly desperately needs. Sleep is of the utmost importance for someone his age. I'm a doctor, so I know these things.

That was the lamest, most self-serving justification load of crap I've ever spouted. Using my logic, I should fuck his brains out because he's mildly sleep-deprived. Yeah, I'll keep telling myself this.

I rise from the table and announce awkwardly, "Sorry, everyone, I think I'm getting a migraine, so I'm going to go lie down for a little while."

John reaches for my hand. "Do you need anything?"

I shield my eyes from the sun blaring through the wall of windows. Heading toward the stairs, I call back, "No, I just need to get into a darker room."

Once inside our room, I close the blinds, grab my iPad, and hop into bed.

I FaceTime Laurie, and when she answers, she says, "Hi. I can barely see you. Why is it so dark?"

I whisper, "Because I'm hiding."

She holds back a smile. "And why are you whispering?"

"I don't want them to hear me."

"Have you been kidnapped? Who's them?"

"Hold on." I head into the bathroom and lock the door. I climb into the tub and return my attention to the screen. "How's this?"

"Oh, there you are," she says.

"First, how's Izzie?"

"She's got a lot of energy. Here, see for yourself."

Laurie turns her camera to show the four dogs in her backyard, running around like lunatics. Izzie jumps on one of the dog's backs, then runs away, wagging her little tail before she circles back and does it all over again.

"She seems happy. That's one worry off my plate."

Laurie's face returns to the screen. "So, what's up with the covert op?"

"Well, um ... this is sorta embarrassing." I sigh. "I'm not sure how to say this."

"Just say it. You can tell me anything."

"Do you know who Kate's son is?"

"Sort of, I think."

"Well, he and I ... I mean, we've sorta been flirting and—"

"Isn't he, like, sixteen?" Laurie cringes.

"What? No! Like, ten years ago maybe."

She raises an eyebrow, cocking her head. "Ten?"

I groan. "Okay, more like eight. What are you, a cop?"

"And ... and what?"

"And today, he wrote me this note." Pulling it from my pocket, I read it verbatim. When I finish, I ask, "What do you think?"

"I think he wants to fuck you." Laurie nods with her eyes wide.

"Duh, I know that. I'm not an idiot. What do you think I should do?"

"Are you sure the note is for you? Does it have a name on it?"

I look at the paper again, then return to the screen. "Well, no, but he asked me if I read his note, and then he said, 'I hope you can *come.*' Come—get it?" I widen my eyes.

"I'll bet he comes first." She cracks herself up. "You know how guys can be—well, maybe you don't know since you don't ever ..."

I give her a deadly look. "Can you please be serious for once and just tell me what to do?"

"Yeah, sure, I can tell you what to do," she begins in a soft, casual tone. Then, she lets me have it. "Are you out of your freaking mind?! You want to go sneaking around in the middle of the night and have sex with your friend's young son. I say that's the most idiotic thing I've ever heard."

I recline in the tub, the air completely let out of my sails. "Yeah, I guess you're right."

Laurie's eyes brighten. "Wait, didn't I see some pictures posted today on your page of you all at the beach? Which one was he?"

"The tall guy in the red bathing suit."

"Hold on." Laurie's screen displays that it's paused. She's gone for at least ten seconds. When she returns, her mouth is hanging open, and her eyes are sparkling, like she's drunk or something.

"So?"

"Are you out of your freaking mind? If you don't go to his room tonight, I'm going to come over and do it for you." She holds up a finger. "Hold on. Let me see how long of a drive it is. Do you think he'd allow a pinch hitter?" She flashes me a grin. "Get it? He plays baseball, right?"

"He does, but are you serious?"

"About coming out there? No."

"I know that!" I roll my eyes.

"About you fucking him? I'm dead serious. If he wrote you that letter and those pictures aren't airbrushed, I'd be riding those waves until high tide."

Grabbing my phone, I pull a picture up. "Actually, I think he looks better in person."

"Well then, I'd definitely be getting caught in his rip current."

"Do you really think I should just go for it?"

"I'd be letting him come down my channel anytime."

"Okay." I groan.

"Hey, why aren't you reacting to any of my beach puns?"

"Because with each one, I'm wishing you're done and this is serious." I glare at the screen.

"Some of these are gold."

"The channel one was clever." I cock my head. "I'll give you that."

"I like that one too." Laurie smiles. "Is this house big enough that you won't get caught?"

"Yep, he's got the whole first floor to himself."

"Good. Is he single?"

"As far as I know."

"And he's definitely over eighteen, right?"

"Much, much over, like hundreds and hundreds of days over."

She chokes out a laugh. "So, you're counting how many *days* over the legal age of consent he is, not—I don't know—*years*, like a normal person."

"It helps me feel better about it," I say sheepishly. "Should I have gone with months instead?"

She shrugs. "No, days works for me."

Guilt clouds my face as I ask, "So, you really think I should?"

Laurie holds a hand up and counts off on her fingers, one by one. "He's old enough. He wants you. You obviously want him. He's single ... and you're ... you're whatever the fuck you are ... single-ish or single-adjacent." She shrugs.

"Okay, I guess you've convinced me," I say with lukewarm conviction.

"Hey now, don't you go and chicken out on me." She points at the screen, delivering a passionate pregame pep talk, rivaling that of an NFL coach. "You get your sweet ass down there, and you have sex with him! You show him ..." Her passion dissipates with each additional word. "You show him, you know ... whatever the hell it is you know how to do ... with your, um, limited recent experience." She pauses a moment, cringing. "You're not concerned about being out of practice, are you?"

"Well, I wasn't until you just said that!" I recoil from the screen. "Is it still pretty much the same stuff people were doing before?"

"I don't want to scare you, so I'll just say, things haven't changed *much*."

"Much? Oh, crap!"

"I mean, there are some communities where anal is the new oral, and getting tied up and flogged in his sex dungeon is a walk in the park compared to what comes after."

"Wait! What?"

Upon seeing my horrified expression, she lifts her hands. "Sorry. Sorry. I'm not sure where I was going with that. He's a young guy with a dick. It doesn't take much to get him moaning and excited and keeping him that way."

"Okay, good." I exhale.

"Don't worry." Laurie flips her hand at the screen. "Just watch some porn. It's educational. I'll email you some links. Oh shit!"

"Oh shit what?"

"I've got to run. The dogs are throwing themselves on something dead, I think. Good luck! And I want details."

The call ends, and I lean back in the tub with my head resting on the edge, staring at the ceiling.

Chapter 23

Blocked

When I finally return to the second floor, I discover everyone, except Kyle, hanging out on the deck. They ask if I'm feeling better and if I want to go with them to get ice cream. I am, and I do, so we head out and return pretty late. John and Kate plan another morning golf outing and retire to bed.

It's around midnight, and I head to the bathroom to prepare for my clandestine invitation. After shaving my legs, armpits, and bikini area, I indulge in the Jacuzzi tub before switching over to the shower to properly wash my hair. Then, I pluck my eyebrows, paint my fingernails and toenails, and dry my hair, putting it up in a ponytail. Finally, I apply just a little makeup. Nothing too crazy. Just your standard ninety-minute pre-sex-primping process. Which I hope I didn't just slog through for what might amount to two minutes of fun for him and a disappointment for me. I push those negative thoughts from my brain.

I return to the bedroom to find John, as usual, sleeping soundly. Using the flashlight on my phone, I search my drawer for my sexiest bra and panties. Given my recent sexual history, my lingerie collection is not only nothing to brag about; it's nonexistent. However, I do locate some items I don't believe will result in any complaints.

I slip into bed at just after one thirty and open my iPad to find the email from Laurie, containing three links. When I click the first, I'm not surprised to find a ball-crushing video—of course, sent as a joke. I laugh at first. Then, I'm quickly horrified, and I make a mental note to give her hell about this the next time we speak and maybe, just maybe, revisit the topic with my mother. I watch a few minutes of the remaining two links, skipping around when I'm either a little taken aback by the extreme close-ups of genitalia or a tad bored by the action.

I come to the conclusion that basic sex things haven't changed much in two decades since David and I were sneaking around his parents' basement and having all manner of fun. Oh, I'm sure people are doing some really bizarre stuff, but I'm thankful what Laurie considers basic, vanilla yet sexy bedroom fun isn't scaring the hell out of me.

I hear a car pull up outside and rush to the window in time to spot Kyle in the driveway. It's now one forty-five, and I smile with anticipation. The next fifteen minutes seem to take forever as I watch the clock. When it reaches one fifty-nine, I can no longer wait, and I tiptoe to the door and press my ear to it. Since I don't hear a thing, I quietly slip out to the hall. I make my way to the steps, and I can hear the faint sounds of something and see the warm glow of light coming from below. I frown and slowly descend the stairs, one by one, bending down with each step to attempt to spot the source.

Before I can locate it, I hear a female voice whisper, "Ally, is that you?"

Shit! Son of a bitch!

"Ally?"

I sigh, then continue down the steps at a normal pace until I spot my date's mother.

Oh fuck!

I force a smile. "Oh, hi, Kate. What are you doing up?"

"I couldn't sleep."

"Same," I lie as I walk toward her, taking a wide path to surreptitiously glance down the stairs to the first floor.

"Is anything on?" I ask with as much enthusiasm as I can.

I hear a door open behind me and spot my mother coming out of her room. "Mom, are we making too much noise?"

"Oh, no," my mother replies, looking a bit startled. "I thought I left something out here, but I just remembered where I put it. Good night." She backpedals into her room.

"What are you watching?" I ask.

"Just this renovation show." Suddenly, Kate's eyes light up. "Why didn't you tell me your father was doing boudoir photography?"

Because I'm traumatized, horrified, embarrassed, and some other adjectives I'm too keyed up to recall at the moment.

I reply, "Um, I, uh, it must have slipped my mind."

"You just missed him. He was telling me all about it. A good friend of mine had it done, and she was really happy with the pictures."

"Interesting." I nod.

"I'm thinking about having him take some pictures of me."

"Why?" I ask, grimacing, my words dripping with judgment. I try to repair the damage by adding in a softer, genuinely curious tone, "I mean, why now?"

"You know, with this cleanse I'm doing—well, doing before I got down here anyway—I feel like I'm in the best shape of my life, and I want to capture how I look now before my body completely falls apart." She snorts out a laugh.

"That's a good idea," I lie.

I turn my attention to the television, and it's some HGTV renovation show I'm sure I've seen at least twice. We sit in silence for a while, watching the screen, and then I check the clock on the wall. It's a quarter after two. Maybe if I grab a drink and head back to my room, she'll go to bed herself. Then, I can wait ten minutes and maybe salvage the night.

"Well, I just came down for a bottle of water." I rise to my feet. "You should get some sleep, especially if you're getting up early to go golfing." *Like exactly right now would be nice.*

"I probably will after this show is over. I'm sorta interested in how this reno turns out."

Damn!

"All right." I force a smile as I head toward the staircase.

"Aren't you forgetting something?"

"What?"

"Your water bottle."

I tap myself on the forehead a couple of times, rolling my eyes. "Right. Right."

After grabbing the bottle, I slip into bed next to John. I surf the internet for nothing in particular as I repeatedly check the clock. At two thirty, I tiptoe to the door and see the glow from the television still coming from the second floor. I mutter another four-letter word and return to bed, continuing to check the clock as my eyes grow heavy.

Chapter 24

Is That Suntan Lotion in Your Pocket?

I wake alone to find it's after ten, and I can't remember the last time I slept this late. I had planned on trying to slip down to Kyle's room around three last night but fell asleep. I should have set an alarm, but didn't want to risk the chance of waking John. After getting dressed, I go to the second floor to find my parents, Dave, and Morgan watching television in the great room.

"Morning."

"Hey, Mom. You slept late."

"I didn't mean to."

I ask, "Did you guys eat?"

Dave says, "There are doughnuts over there."

"Great," I mutter, meandering toward the landing to the stairs, then finally heading down when I think no one is looking.

Why am I sneaking down like I'm running from a crime scene? I'm allowed to walk down the stairs. Play it cool, doofus. I need to get a grip on myself.

I rush down and find Kyle's door open and his room empty, then step outside to see that his car is gone. Frowning, I head up to the kitchen and pour a cup of coffee, then spot a note on the counter which reads:

Ally, if you get a chance to go to the grocery store, could you pick up a few things? If not, I'll go when we get back from golf.

That note is followed by a full page-and-a-half list of items written in at least four different handwriting styles, ranging from a barely legible scrawl to a neat block print. I check the time again. I really wanted to catch Kyle this morning, but I don't want to give anything away. I have an idea.

Holding up the note, I ask, "Did anyone see Kyle to find out if he put what he wanted on this list?"

"He already saw it," Morgan replies.

"Did he already head down to the beach?"

Morgan says, "No, he was grumpy this morning and took off about an hour ago. Didn't say where."

Crap, he's angry.

I grab the list, then remember John's car was also missing from the driveway. "Dave, can I borrow your car?"

"Sure, the keys are in my room."

After retrieving my keys and purse, I drive to the grocery store, where, as luck would have it, it's pretty crowded. I'm not familiar with the layout, so that burns even more time as I look for the forty-some items on my list. When I finally get out of there, it's going on one o'clock.

When I return to the house, I discover John's car is still missing, Kyle's car is in the driveway, but both golf carts are gone. Grabbing the bags I can carry, I poke my head in Kyle's room and find it empty. I haul the bags up to the second floor, placing them on the counter. I search that floor, then the third floor and find that I'm alone. I let a couple of expletives fly, realizing everyone, including Kyle, is probably at the beach. I rush back down to the car, then up to the kitchen three more times with all the groceries. My heart is racing, and I have to sit for a moment to catch my breath. This place could really use an elevator.

I hurriedly put away all the groceries, run upstairs to put on a bikini and cover-up, grab a water bottle, then head back outside. Spotting the walkway over the dunes, I walk quickly over the boards in the searing July heat. It's a long, long walk, and it takes about three minutes to clear the dunes and spot the ocean. Once I do, I see our beach tent set up and one golf cart parked there. Something catches my eye to the left. It's the other golf cart racing by, heading to the road.

It's Kyle. He's alone.

I'm already exhausted, and now, I have to retrace my steps through this heat and heavy sand back to the house. I pause a moment to catch my breath, then guzzle half the bottle of water before starting the trek.

Midway back, I have to stop again to rest. I haven't done this much cardio in, like, forever. Glancing at my Fitbit, I discover my heart is beating at one hundred forty. I clutch my chest. I'm losing it. This house and beach are gorgeous, but does it need to be half a mile from the damn water? I mean, really, whose idea was it to set the houses so far back? I really would like to have a chat with this person. It's going to kill me. That is, if not sleeping, eating, and pining over him don't already do me in. I mumble some mild obscenities and continue on.

Finally, when I reach the house, I'm about to collapse. I head into the shade of the breezeway. Flopping down on the bench, I drain the rest of the water bottle and pull off my beach cover-up. I sit there as I struggle to catch my breath, trying to summon the courage to go in and apologize for last night.

Suddenly, I hear the outdoor shower turn on to the right of me, and I'm momentarily startled. Craning my neck down, I see feet and ankles. It must be Kyle since John's car is not here, and

I spotted everyone else on the beach. I close my eyes and take a deep, calming breath.

I reach the shower door and push it open. The shower is large enough for two with a bench seat on one side. Kyle's standing, facing away from me, with his head under the water. His body looks even hotter in the fucking shower. He's tan, and he's wet. The muscles in his back are so defined. His shoulders are broad, and his waist is so thin. His bathing suit is hanging low off his hips to where I can see the crack of his sexy ass. He's just perfect. I take in the sight of him with the spray of the shower hitting me slightly. It's cool, and it feels so good.

Pulling his head out of the water, he says, "I'll be right out."

My heart stops! He must have heard me, but he has no idea I'm right behind him. I stand, frozen, and when he finally turns to me, he looks a bit shocked, but not exactly unhappy to see me.

"Hey there. Did you need—"

Leaning forward quickly, I press my lips to his. It's a long, deep kiss. I place my hands on his solid chest, then slide them up to his shoulders. The kiss keeps going and going, our tongues meeting in his mouth and then mine. What feels like minutes later, we pull back from each other.

He looks down at me with his eyes wide and his lips curling up in a smile. "Is this your way of thanking me for the boogie board lessons?"

"What? No." I force a laugh. "I wanted to apologize for yesterday."

"I forgive you. I definitely forgive you." Placing a hand gently behind my head, he coaxes my lips back to his and kisses me. When he finally pulls away, he says, "You're so hot."

"You ain't so bad yourself," I say, trying to sound young and hip, but failing pretty badly.

"What, uh, am I forgiving you for again?" he asks with his eyes roaming over my sweaty bikini-clad body.

"I couldn't come to your room last night."

"Oh, okay." He reaches out and touches one of my breasts through the fabric of my bathing suit.

My nipple stiffens, and I gasp. "I hope you were able to sleep last night."

"What?"

Kissing his chest, I slowly slide my finger down to his sexy belly button to just inside the waistband of his trunks.

"Oh fuck," he groans, now pinching my taut nipple.

"I got your note about how sexy you think I am and how you want me. I feel the same way too." I look into his eyes. "I can't sleep. I don't feel like eating. I don't know what to do. I just know that I have to have you."

"What note?" He pulls back, perplexed.

"Ha-ha!" I click my tongue, shaking my head. "What note? You're hilarious."

He lifts his shoulders, wearing a blank stare. "I, um ..."

"You're not messing with me, are you? Because I can't ..."

"No, I mean, I'm really enjoying this *making out in the shower* business, but I don't know what you're talking about."

"Yesterday, you told me to look at the menus." I widen my eyes as I wave my hands around nervously. "And inside the menu was a note from you to me. Tell me you wrote the note, and I'm not just some lunatic, attacking you in the shower."

He looks to be on the verge of cracking up, and then his gaze takes another trip down my body, then back up. His smile fades, and our eyes lock.

"You are so fucking sexy. I've had a crush on you since I was in high school. I can't even tell you how many times I've ... I've ... you know, to you ... fuck it."

He grabs my head and pulls my lips to his. The kiss is somehow even hotter, sexier, bikini-melting, and more powerful than the last one. His hands slide down my back to my ass, pulling me to him. I feel his erection poking into me. I want him. I've never used the words before, but now, I will. I want his hard cock in my pussy. I need to feel him inside me. I'm tingling all over down there as I push my hips forward, rising up on my tiptoes to center his cock at my spot. Damn these swimsuits, or we'd be doing it already.

I feel him slide his hand under my bikini bottom. He slips a finger inside me, and I gasp, pressing my lips to his neck and sucking at his skin.

"You're so fucking wet."

Cupping the cheeks of my ass, he lifts me up, and I wrap my legs around him. Leaning back, I grind my core into his erection. Now, I grab his head and kiss him, curling my arms around him, pressing my breasts into his chest as I hang on him. I feel his hardness under me, his hot breath on my neck, and his lips on my skin.

Suddenly, it hits me. "Wait."

"What?" he moans.

I pull back with my legs still wrapped around his waist and his hands still cupping my backside. "You're serious? You didn't write the note?"

He shakes his head and gives me a sheepish smile. "I mean, I'm not, like, seventy. It's not 1990. People don't write notes anymore. If I was trying to flirt, I would have sent a sexy text or maybe even a dick pic."

"Shit. Put me down."

"What? Why?"

"Put me down, please. I'm going to be sick."

Releasing his grip on my ass, he gently returns my feet to the wood floor of the shower. He turns off the spray. I sit down on the shower bench and cover my head with my hands, struggling to breathe. When I finally uncover my face, I narrow my eyes, looking up to him.

"Wait. Yesterday, you told me to look at the menus, and when I came back in the room, you asked me if I saw the note. You asked me that, right, or am I completely crazy?"

"Did I?" He pauses, then finally nods. "Oh yeah. I did, but I was talking about the note on the fridge about my baseball game Wednesday. The note about the location and the time."

"Baseball game. Shit. I'm an idiot." I look up to him, grinning oddly and feeling like a fool. I tilt my head back, sigh then level my gaze with his. My body begins to involuntarily shake, and my lips quiver as I fight back tears. "I'm sorry. I—"

"Don't worry about it." He places a hand on my shoulder.

"Jeez, I feel stupid." I break into a chuckle, then clutch my stomach with both hands as this laughing-crying sound spills out of my lips. Suddenly, it hits me, and my jaw drops open. "Oh my God!"

"What is it now?"

"My father is having an affair with my mother."

"Aren't they divorced?"

"Uh, yeah, that's what's so screwed up about it." I scoff. "He must have written the note for her, and it just somehow got mixed in with the menus."

"You think?"

"Last night, she came out of her room around two. And when she saw your mother and me, she slunk back in her room, making up some story about looking for something. She was looking for something all right. She was looking for—"

"Cock." He nods.

"Exactly." I'm eye-level with his midsection, and I notice that he's still sporting a huge bulge in his swimsuit. My gaze is glued to it, and I can't look away. I motion toward his problem area. "Speaking of ..."

"Uh-huh."

"Why are you still hard?"

"Uh, I'm, like, twenty-four. I think it's pretty much a given that when some sexy woman in a bathing suit is kissing me, I'm going to get this way. And I'll mention again that you are so fucking hot, and I've thought about this—"

"Stop." I rise to my feet. "This was all some big misunderstanding. Let's just pretend none of this happened."

"You mean, pretend that you didn't shove your tongue down my throat and grind your"—he points at my midsection, then to his still ridiculously tented trunks—"your parts all up and down my—"

"Yep, let's forget it."

"Okay." He chuckles. "Yeah, let's forget that you were coming to my room to bang me last night."

The engine sound of a car pulling into the breezeway echoes around us. We stand still, and my heart nearly jumps out of my chest.

"Shit."

He steps onto the bench and pokes his head slightly over the top of the wood enclosure and whispers, "It's John and my mother."

"They're back from golf already?" I place my hands on each side of my head and gasp. "How do we get out of here?"

"Hopefully, they won't come back here." He shrugs. "I mean, who takes a shower outside after golf?"

He pokes his head back over the top. "Huh."

"What is it?"

"Oh, nothing." He looks down at me. "How often do they play golf?"

"Every week back home. Here, it's been, like, almost every day so far."

"I didn't realize she liked it that much." He shrugs, then steps down off the bench, smiling. "This is sorta fun, hiding in here. I feel like we're in a movie."

We hear the muffled laughter and talking of the golfing pair as they remain in the car. Placing my finger to my mouth, I give him a deadly serious look. He purses his lips closed while the corners curl up into a smile. I shake my head, scowling as I fight back my own urge to laugh.

We hear the car doors open and then close as John says, "That was a lot of fun."

"It was," Kate replies.

"You think they're still at the beach?" John says.

"Probably. Let's get our suits on and meet them down there."

We hear their footsteps as they climb the wooden steps. I lose my balance and place my hand on Kyle's shoulder to steady myself. He gives me a steamy look, then reaches out to cup my breast outside my swimsuit once again.

"What the hell are you doing?" I whisper.

"Um, touching you." Without removing his hand, he raises his eyebrows and gives me a sheepish look. "Not good?"

"No." I shake my head in disapproval.

His hand falls from my body, and he nods his head downward a couple of times. "Do you see?"

"See what?"

He gives me an evil smile while cocking his head and motioning his eyes down.

"What are you—" I shut my mouth when I spot his still-sizable bulge tenting his swimsuit.

"It's still about a three-quarter chub at this point."

"What's wrong with you?"

"Nothing. Again, I'm young. Look it up; it's a thing." He shrugs his shoulders. "And I'll say it again—you're fucking smoking hot."

"Yeah, yeah." Frowning, I dismiss his comment with a wave of my hand.

"I'm serious."

"Thank you," I grumble. "You stay in here. I'll go upstairs and tell them we just got back and you are rinsing off chairs."

"You know"—he turns his head, refusing to look at me—"Gronk would never leave Brady hanging like this."

"Are you saying that they ..." I wrinkle my nose.

"Not necessarily ... but there *is* an awful lot of naked men in those locker rooms, so you never know."

"Huh." I turn away slowly.

"What I'm saying is, when Brady needs a touchdown to win a game, he throws it up, and Gronk comes down with it, no matter what."

"I get it, but I'm pretty sure Brady can take care of some *things* all by himself." I put on a distasteful frown. "Just do that thing that young men do, like, three, four times a day. I have a son, so I know about this stuff."

"Funny." Placing a hand on my shoulder, he says, "We're not done talking about this."

"Okay. Yes. Later." I slip outside the shower, and now, unfortunately, I'm picturing a locker room full of sexy, naked football players, which is not helping me walk away from this sexy, nearly naked baseball player. I release the door, and it slams closed with a loud thump.

"Ally, is that you?" John calls out, and I hear him descending the stairs.

My eyes bug out of my head. "John, don't come down. I'll be right up."

"What?" he replies.

"No," I yell as I rush toward the steps. I reach the second tread, feel something sharp pierce the bottom of my foot, and then lose my balance, landing hard on my knee. "Ouch! Shit!"

"Are you okay?" John rushes down to me.

"I'm fine." Grimacing, I grasp the handrail and pull myself to my feet.

"What happened?"

"I fell!" I snap. "And I think I have a splinter."

"Let me help you."

Wrapping his arm around me, he walks me up the stairs, and I keep my injured foot raised as we go.

Chapter 25

Isn't That Uncomfortable?

John guides me to the bathroom and helps me to sit on the edge of the tub. With my knees together, I keep my right heel off the floor, still grimacing in pain.

Kate appears in the doorway. "What happened?"

"She fell and maybe has something in her foot," John replies. "Do you have a first aid kit?"

"Be right back," she says as she scurries away.

Grabbing a towel, he spreads it out on the floor. "Maybe you should lie down."

He assists me onto the towel with my head toward the doorway, then sits on the floor in front of me. "Your knee is just bruised, I think. No permanent damage."

"You think?"

Kate returns and hands over the kit. "Do you need anything else?"

"Maybe ice for her knee."

She heads away. I'm lying down with my head on the towel and my left knee bent as John cradles my right foot.

"I see it," he says.

"Is it big?"

"No."

"Get it out, please." Craning my neck up, I look at him. I notice he's taken his eyes off my foot and he's staring between my legs. "What is it?"

"Um, your swimsuit is completely, you know, inside of your ..." He makes a swirly motion with his index finger. "Isn't that uncomfortable?"

"What?" Raising my bottom off the towel, I quickly pull the wet fabric from its hiding place and reply defensively, "Must have happened when I fell." Closing my eyes, I lay my head back down and hold my breath.

"Here's the ice pack." Kate hands it to John as she gives me a sympathetic look. "Does it hurt?"

"A little."

Kyle appears at the door. "Wow, are you okay?"

"I'm fine." I'm looking at him upside down, and as my gaze travels up his body, I'm relieved to find everything in his midsection has returned to an unexcited state.

"What happened?" he asks.

"I fell."

"Oh no. Do you guys need anything?"

"We're good," John replies.

Kate says, "If you guys are okay here, then I think I'm going to head down to the beach for about an hour. Then, we'll talk about dinner."

"You don't need to worry about me. I'm eating with some friends," Kyle says.

Kate asks, "You sure you guys don't need anything else?"

"No. Thanks." Holding my foot, John grabs the tweezer, and as she heads away, he says, "It doesn't look like it's in there too deep, so it should be easy to get out."

"It feels like it's really in there." I frown in pain.

"All right, hold on." Squinting, he positions the tweezer. "Almost ..."

"Ouch." I scowl, sucking air in through my teeth.

"Got it." He holds the tweezer up, displaying the tiny splinter. He pauses, then looks me in the eye, pointing between my legs. "I, um, couldn't help but notice that you're completely shaved again."

"Oh, yeah." I shrug. "Bikini line. It was just to, you know, get in the bathing suit. It had been ignored for a little too long." I force a laugh. "Didn't want to scare anyone at the beach."

He chuckles. "Well, it looks nice." After wiping my wound with alcohol, he applies some antibacterial ointment and a bandage.

"Thanks." I narrow my eyes. "What do you mean, *again?*"

"Oh, it just reminded me of our trip to Key West. What was that, like, nine years ago? Do you remember that?" He cradles my injured foot in his hands and gently rubs my toes.

"How could I forget? We came back with a little unexpected surprise. She's turning ten, so ..."

Looking away toward the window, he continues massaging my foot and says with his voice cracking slightly, "Wow, so going on eleven years. That was some weekend. We drank way, way too much."

"That *is* how we got her."

"I know. I know." His eyes meet mine, and he sighs as a melancholy expression spreads over his face.

"You actually remember the look of my, my ..." I motion toward my midsection with a head nod. "How is that even possible?"

"I mean, not specifically, but it just triggered a memory, you know?" His eyes glaze over as he rubs the ball of my foot more sensually—almost sexually. "We did some pretty crazy things that night, and if memory serves, it was, uh"—he lifts his hand up near his face to demonstrate—"right there for a long time. It was something."

I chuckle. "Wow, I don't remember all that."

"Well, you were a little more drunk than I was."

"Probably," I say as his strong fingers continue to work my foot. "That feels really good."

"Whew." He shivers slightly, then bugs his eyes out as he appears to return from somewhere far away. He pats my foot, and my sensual rub is over. "Anyway, you have the prettiest feet."

"Thanks."

"Do you think you're ready to stand on those pretty feet?"

"I think so."

Gently returning my heel to the floor, he extends his hands to help me up. We stand a few inches from one another, and an awkward silence comes over us. I glance into his eyes, and for a moment, I think he just might kiss me. After another breath, the opportunity evaporates, and he turns his attention to repacking the first aid kit.

"Hey, thanks for patching me up."

"Anytime."

* * *

Moving under the shower spray, I stand for a few moments, just letting the warm water flow down my body. I find myself thinking of our time in Key West and when I came back pregnant. He was right. We'd drunk way too much before falling into bed. We let the beautiful beach and the alcohol, along with the gorgeous hotel, steal our inhibitions. When we had returned home, I believe John might have thought that was a sort of rebirth of our relationship, but I just couldn't do it. I don't know why I could never shake how he reminded me of David—or more specifically, the bad memories I had of what had tran-spired. I know David would have wanted me to move on, espe-cially after so much time, but this was the best I could do.

I pull myself from those thoughts and slump down on the shower seat. Suddenly, I'm thinking of Kyle. He, too, reminds me of David, but in a completely different way. Maybe it makes no sense, but when I see John, all I can think of is how David was so badly injured and suffered at the end and how we both cried his last few days. John was at his bedside almost as much as I was.

When I think of Kyle, he reminds me of David being healthy and full of life and the amazing times we had together. I'm taken back to the times we walked hand in hand around campus, lounged in the quad, had sex in his dorm room or in the car that time in the rain. It's simply different. The images of Kyle's fingers cupping my ass before sliding inside me and his bulging swimsuit fill my brain. My hand slides over my erect nipple, gently circling it before heading down my belly.

"Oh God," I moan.

I really need to come. It's been far too long. Closing my eyes, I picture reaching into Kyle's swimsuit to free his hard cock as he effortlessly suspends my body over his. He moves my suit aside, and all at once, he fills me with his thickness. I slip a finger inside my pussy, and with my palm resting on my clit, it doesn't take long before I'm surrendering to a huge climax.

Chapter 26

Permission to Treat the Witness as Hostile?

Throughout dinner, I find myself thinking about Kyle. That kiss. That long, sexy kiss. The way he scooped me up in his arms effortlessly. His erection pressing into me. I fight to push my thoughts far away from him to something, anything else.

Picking up my phone, I fire up my eReader app and search through my list of unread titles I've been trying to get to for longer than I can remember. It's nearly midnight, and John and Kate retired to their rooms an hour ago, both saying they were wiped out from hitting on the driving range and then playing eighteen holes of golf in the ninety-five-degree midday heat.

Sitting in the great room, I'm on my second glass of dry Riesling. It's absolutely delicious, and not surprisingly, it's making me very tipsy. I'm hoping it helps me get to sleep, although it probably won't keep me asleep all night.

After reading two pages and not recalling a word of the text, I close the app, turning my attention to the half-full wine bottle on the counter. Do I dare go for a third glass? I turn on the television, and after flipping through a few channels, I shut it off, toss the remote to the sofa, and head toward the kitchen for a refill.

Kyle appears, placing his keys on the counter and giving me a smile. "Hey, Gronk."

I chuckle. "I didn't realize we were still doing that."

"It is getting kinda old, isn't it?"

"Maybe just a tad."

"How was your night? What are you up to?"

Holding up the bottle, I say, "You want a glass?"

"Sorry, no, not a big fan." He opens the refrigerator and pulls out a beer.

"We made spaghetti. There are some leftovers. Your mother made her sauce. I'd forgotten how good it was."

"Yeah, it's the best. I already ate. Where is everyone?"

"Morgan and Dave went to a movie, and everyone else is sleeping."

"Really?" He gives me a naughty smile, then takes a pull off his beer.

"Don't." I sigh wearily as I head toward the sofa with my wine.

"It's a nice night. Want to sit out by the pool?"

"Um, I don't know."

"Come on," he pleads, then whispers, "I promise I won't kiss you."

"Okay."

"Much." He moves closer and stands just inches from me.

I look up to him with my lips slightly parted and my pulse quickening. "Kyle, I thought we already sorted this out."

"You mean, when you had your legs wrapped around me in the shower with your tongue down my throat while you wet-humped me?"

"Shh." Motioning with my hand for him to keep it down, I give him an angry look. "Can we not do this here?"

"That's why I asked if you wanted to go outside." Without waiting for my reply, he heads out, leaving the door open behind him.

After taking a couple of deep breaths, I take a healthy sip from my wineglass, then follow him out onto the deck, then down the stairs to the pool area. I find him reclining in one of the chaise lounges.

I slip onto the chair next to him and focus on the white noise of the water feature spilling over the decorative rocks and into the pool.

"Did you really think we weren't going to talk more about ... about ..." He motions with his head toward the outdoor shower. "You know ..."

"I guess not." Closing my eyes for a moment, I sigh before taking another sip. "But what more is there to say?"

"You see, while I was out with my friends, I was thinking a lot about this, and let me see if I have all this straight. Just bear with me here."

"All right."

He takes a sip of his beer, then places it on the table between us before turning to sit sideways on his chair, facing me. "You read a note, which you thought was written by me to you, and purely based on this note, you were on your way to have hot, steamy sex with me in the middle of the night, right?"

"Well, I, um—"

"It's a simple yes or no question," he cuts me off, wearing a tired look.

"But it's really not."

"Yes or no?" He mock glares at me while holding back a smile.

After sipping from my wineglass, I place it on the table, then fold my arms in defiance and give him a sneer.

"Your Honor"—he rises to his feet, then paces back and

forth in front of my chair while holding his head awkwardly high—"permission to treat the witness as hostile?"

"What the hell are you doing?"

"I'll remind the witness that you are under oath."

"Okay." I roll my eyes. "I didn't know you were studying to be a lawyer."

"I'm not. I've just seen a lot of legal thrillers."

"Oh, okay." I chuckle. "So, I'm on trial here?"

Turning to me, he shoots me a serious look. "Only if you don't answer all my questions honestly."

"All right, I'll answer honestly," I say in a tired voice.

"I'm serious." Returning to his seat, he tips back his beer, then adds, "You promise?"

"I promise." I stare up at the stars. "What was the first question again?"

"Were you on your way to my room last night to have sex with me? Yes or no?"

I sigh, then reply, "Yes."

"Okay, now, we're getting somewhere." He sits back in his chair, peeling at the label on his beer. "And only because you ran into my mother and got scared, you did not come to my room."

"That's correct."

"In other words, had you not run into my mother, you would have come to my room, and we would have had sex for somewhere between three to four hours last night. Isn't that correct?"

"Turning my head, I find him grinning at me, and I laugh. "Three to four hours. Really?"

"I'm young and in great shape. I have a lot of stamina." He sneers. "Please answer the question."

I smile defiantly. "Well, I sincerely doubt the *three to four hours* part, but ... wait, I've seen some legal thrillers, too, so I'll say ... asked and answered!" I press my lips together and glare, side-eyeing him.

"What?" He exhales, frowning.

"I mean, stop rephrasing questions I've already answered."

"All right, I'll give you that one. Oh, okay. Where were we? I know. So, you were heading to my room to bang me ... and only didn't because you got scared. Then, earlier today, you burst into my shower, apologized for *not* sleeping with me, then kissed and wet-humped me. Is that correct?"

"You mentioned that before. What the hell is this wet-humping thing?"

"You've heard of dry-humping, right?"

I nod.

"It's like that, but since our bathing suits were wet, it's"—he lifts his palms skyward and shoots me a look—"you know, wet."

"Gotcha."

"And in that shower, we were mere seconds from doing it. Like my, um, junk—for lack of a better term—was, like, I mean, right up against your ... your ..."

"Pussy," I offer in a confident tone.

"Yes, pussy. Thank you."

"Don't mention it."

"I was going to say vagina, but that sounds too formal."

"I agree."

He rubs his chin. "And this is the important part, and I want to make sure I'm crystal clear on this. Isn't it true that the only reason we didn't do it in there is because you learned that I hadn't written the note?"

"I guess. I mean, no." I look at him, puzzled. "Wait, you're confusing me."

"You guess, or is that a yes?"

I pause a few seconds, then mutter softly, "Yes."

Rising to his feet, he puts his hand to his ear, cocking his head in my direction. "I'm sorry, I didn't get that. Could you please repeat your answer more clearly so the jury can hear?"

"Yes! Jeez."

"Thank you."

"Um, I have a question. Should you really be representing yourself in this case? I think they say that a man who is his own lawyer has a fool for a client."

"I've never heard that. Plus, I'm the one asking the questions here." He glares at me before breaking into a smile. "So, my point is, I told you that I don't write notes to women. Why am I being penalized for that?"

"Penalized? What are you talking about?"

"Yes, I'm being punished because I don't put my feelings in writing. When we showered together, I told you"—he flashes his eyes at me suggestively—"that I've had a crush on you for a very long time, and I pretty much feel exactly about you as the person who wrote that note feels about the person they wrote that note to—to express how they feel ... I think." He shakes his head, flabbergasted, pausing and wearing a confused expression. "If you know what I mean."

"What?" I look at him like he's nuts.

"I think you know what I'm trying to say."

"Not really." I chuckle. "Am I still on the witness stand or ..."

He sighs, exhausted. "Let's drop this thing we're doing and just have a real conversation, okay?"

"Well, you started with the jokes." I smile. "Plus, I've had quite a bit of wine."

"I'm serious. Can you be?"

"Okay, yes." I exhale deeply, then turn to meet his gaze. "Look, yes, I'm attracted to you, but I can't have sex with you because I'm married."

"That's not true." He folds his arms across his chest and shakes his head.

"I am married. Go ask my husband."

"No, I'm saying that it's not true that you can't because you're married."

"What do you mean?"

"I overheard my mother on the phone, talking to someone, and she said you and John have some sort of understanding. That you were trapped or it was like a marriage of convenience and that you both saw other people."

"Well, that ... that's not exactly true." I brush my hair off my face. "John and I do have an understanding, and it's a long, long, complicated story. He can see other people, but I don't."

"You don't?"

"No."

"Do you and John have sex?"

"Not in more than ten years," I say. "Wait, how does your mother know about this arrangement? I never told her."

He shrugs. "Maybe John did. They're good friends, aren't they?"

"Yes, but I didn't think he ... well, whatever." I blow out a lengthy, slow breath, then tip back my wineglass.

"Okay, so you haven't been with anyone in a decade. You're attracted to me, and I'm attracted to you. I mean, note writing aside, I've told you how I feel. I'll go write you a note right now if—"

"Okay." Placing my hand on his arm, I continue, "It's not about the note exactly. I don't know what I was doing yesterday. We were in the water together the other day, playing around, and you ... you sorta reminded me of someone from my past, and, yes, the stupid note played a part. I wasn't thinking when I barged in on you in the shower like a lunatic. I was dehydrated and overheated from being out in the sun and—"

"Dehydrated?" He chokes out a laugh.

"Yes. Dehydrated. Hydration is very important."

"Uh-huh." He shakes his head.

"It was wrong. You're my friend's young, young, young, young son."

"I'm not that young."

"You're only a few years older than my son!" I widen my eyes. "I mean, *coo, coo, ca-whatever, Mrs. Robinson.*" I chortle. "Mrs. Robinson called, and she wants her affair back." I literally crack myself up at this joke.

Maybe it's the wine or the situation, or I'm just losing it, but this is so The Graduate—Emerald Isle Edition*!*

"What?" He looks at me like I'm nuts.

"The movie." I motion with my hands. "You know, *The Graduate.*"

"Never saw it." After a few seconds, his expression brightens. "Wait, Dustin Hoffman, right?"

"Yes."

"I haven't seen it, but I've heard of it."

"Well, it's a cautionary tale. Believe me."

We sit in awkward silence for a few moments until he moves closer to me and places a hand on my knee.

"That's just some stupid movie."

The heat from his touch is sending chills up my spine and making me dizzy. I clutch the armrest of the chaise to steady myself and turn to look at him. My gaze starts at his hand, which is still sensually touching my knee, and it travels up his muscular arm to his thick chest, then lands on his gorgeous light-brown eyes.

He stares deeply into my eyes as he says, "All I can tell you is that my heart beats faster when I see you."

We're leaning closer together. Our faces mere inches apart.

My breathing quickens as he continues, "When I was with

you in the ocean and again in that shower, I ... I thought I might ... I don't know ... explode or ... when I was kissing you—"

The sound of the sliding door stops us in our tracks. Quickly, I lean back in my chair, pulling my legs onto the chaise, successfully separating us.

"Mom?" Dave calls from above.

"Yes," I reply as Kyle sits back in his own chair, closing his eyes and frowning. I stand and look up to discover Dave and Morgan peering down at us. "Just having a glass of wine."

For some bizarre reason, I pick up my wineglass to prove it, and like the complete spaz that I am, I lose my balance, falling toward Kyle until he steadies me by grabbing my arm.

"You okay?" Kyle whispers to me before rising to his feet.

"Jeez, Mom." Dave turns to Morgan and shakes his head, laughing.

"I guess she's had enough." Kyle chuckles, looking up at the pair. "How was the movie?"

"It stunk," Morgan replies, and the two moviegoers share a laugh.

"That bad, huh?" I ask.

Dave shrugs. "It was okay."

"Do you guys want to join us?" I ask.

Dave says, "No, I think we're going to crash."

I say, "I'm heading to bed myself in a few minutes."

"Cool. See ya tomorrow," Dave replies, and then they head into the house.

I turn to Kyle, shaking my head with my jaw hanging open. "You see? I can't do this."

"What?" He takes half a step closer.

"They know!"

"They don't know anything." He places a hand on my shoulder.

"I'm flattered. I really am." I exhale deeply. "I just can't. It wouldn't be right. I couldn't live with myself."

"Okay. I understand. I get it. It's never going to happen." He tilts his beer back and drains it, then returns his attention to me. "We'll always have the outdoor shower."

Avoiding his gaze, I return to stare at the water feature. "Yeah."

"At least I don't have to wonder anymore."

I turn to him. "Wonder about what?"

He leans into my ear and whispers, "What your pussy tastes like." He pulls back and looks me in the eye.

I have to remind myself to breathe. "What are you, um, talking about?"

"When you left me in the shower ..." He nods slowly but doesn't say anything for a few seconds.

Instead, he examines me, and under that scrutiny, I feel naked, as if we were still in that shower together in that damp heat.

"I brought my fingers to my lips. You were so wet, and, oh my God, your pussy was so sweet."

"Uh-huh."

"I wanted to slide that bathing suit down your legs and lift you high up against that wall." Wearing a smoldering expression, he holds his hands up near his face, as if he's supporting me. "And slide my tongue deep inside of you."

Wow ... that's very detailed and specific.

He closes his eyes. "Yeah, that's the vision that keeps playing in my head."

"Oh, I, uh ..." I swallow hard.

He closes his eyes. My gaze locks on his tongue, which swipes slowly over his lips, as if he were still there. Still tasting me.

Good Lord.

When he finally opens his eyes, he shrugs and gives me a soft yet cocky smile. "I guess I'll just have to be happy with that little sample rather than getting the full experience."

"I guess," I whisper breathlessly.

He places a hand on my shoulder. "But I do understand. I do."

He turns away and heads into the house, leaving me a tipsy, horny, guilty mess, trapped in a lukewarm pool of my own thoughts and fantasies.

Chapter 27

The Bet

I struggle to get to sleep that night and mostly toss and turn. The last thing I remember is the clock showing three thirty-seven when I finally went down for good. I wake alone, and it's after ten thirty. Grabbing my phone, I see a text message from a number I don't recognize. Upon looking at it, I know exactly who it is.

Unknown:
Watched The Graduate *last night.*
We need to talk.
Everyone else at beach.
Come down to breakfast when your sleepy ass gets up. ;)

The *sleepy ass* comment elicits a chuckle, and I promptly delete the text. I get dressed in some old sweatpants and a long-sleeved sweatshirt because they've got the air-conditioning turned down to just slightly above the meat-locker setting. While it feels good at night under the covers, I've been freezing around here during the day.

I discover a shirtless Kyle in the kitchen, standing by the stove, frying up an egg. I have to admit, he looks good enough to eat with those defined muscles and rippling abs.

I roll my eyes. "If you have that shirt off on my account, you can just put it back on."

He grins. "Or you could just take yours off and see where that leads us."

"Funny. I'm freezing, and I think I'll keep mine on."

"I'm hot, so I'm leaving it off, and you'll just have to deal with it," he teases.

"I think I can somehow control myself," I say, and we share a laugh.

"You want a fried egg sandwich? Someone went out to get fresh bakery bagels this morning. We've got bacon left over from yesterday and some of that sharp cheese. I make a killer one when I just have crappy grocery-store bagels, so this should be something special."

"I'd love one."

"Cool. Do you want your yellow a little runny or not runny at all?"

"A little. Thanks." After pouring a cup of coffee, I sit at the kitchen island, watching him cook. I could get used to this. "So, you watched *The Graduate?*"

"Oh, yeah, I did."

"And ..."

He turns to me, waving the spatula between us, frowning. "I don't know how you could say that if we, you know ... that we would be anything like what happened in that movie."

"What do you mean?"

"First, you don't have a daughter old enough for me to date."

Suddenly, the realization smacks me in the face. "Wow."

"Wow, what?"

"I just realized that my very young daughter is closer in age to you than you are to me." I grimace. "Crap, there is something wrong with me."

"Okay," he groans sarcastically as he flips the eggs. "That is completely different. We're both adults, and the police wouldn't be breaking down the door if we got together."

"True, but it doesn't make it any less cringeworthy."

"You're just trying to talk yourself out of it." He cranes his neck to me and asks, "You want just one egg, right?"

"Yes, one."

"Second, Dustin Hoffman was, like, tiny compared to Mrs. Robinson and she wasn't even attracted to him. She was just trying to get back at her husband, and that doesn't seem to be the case at all between us."

He flips his eggs back over, then places a piece of cheese on each before covering the pan with foil. My mouth is watering as I watch him cook these eggs. I'm starving, but I'm not sure that's the sole reason.

"Okay, maybe that's true," I say.

"Oh, it's true." He brings the skillet over to the island, placing it on a potholder, and then goes to work, assembling his bacon, egg, and cheese masterpieces.

He slides my plate in front of me, then takes the seat next to mine. I take a bite, and it's good. The yellow drips down my hand, and I feel like a slob.

Turning away from him, I bring a hand to my lips to quickly clean it off. "Mmm, that's good."

He takes a bite, then nods. "You've got to love the bagels from this place. They're almost New York–style."

I take another bite, and this time, I get some bacon, and the taste combination is nothing short of amazing. I wish I weren't trying to be all graceful around him because I really want to shovel the rest of this in my mouth.

We sit in silence, enjoying our breakfast sandwiches—him

looking incredible, shirtless with his perfect body and pristine gym shorts, and me, old, a little out of shape and shivering, covered from head to toe in aging, ragged fleece. Instead of Brady and Gronk, this feels a lot more like Brady and Belichick, his middle-aged coach, always dressed like he's cleaning out his gutters in a ratty cutoff sweatshirt.

When we finish, he takes my plate, and I say, "I'll do the dishes. It's the least I can do. It was the best breakfast sandwich I've ever had."

"The secret is, you butter the bagel a little and grill it first."

"I'll have to try that."

After placing the plates in the sink, he turns back to me.

Using a salesperson's voice, he fights to maintain a straight face. "So, what do I have to do to put you in a relationship with me today?" His lips quiver until he finally breaks into a laugh. "Sorry. Sorry."

"Cute." I chuckle, leaning back in my chair.

"I stole that from some TV show, although I can't remember which one."

"It did sound familiar, and it worked well."

"Really? Did it?" he asks with a hopeful smile.

"No, I mean, in the situation ... as a joke."

"Oh." His shoulders slump, and he exhales. "But I'm serious. What do I need to do?"

"Kyle, we've already been through this. I'm flattered, and I'd be lying if I said I wasn't attracted to you."

"So, really, what's the problem then?" he asks, arms spread.

I grip the back of my neck. "You mean, besides all the obvious ones."

"There are no obvious ones." He studies me, his nose scrunches, and he says, "Would the world really stop spinning if this happened? No one has to know. My mother owns a rental property about a mile from here. It's not booked for this week or next."

"So, we just disappear for a couple of hours in the middle of the day." I shrug. "And that doesn't look suspicious at all, right?"

"I'm sure we could figure out some way to pull it off." His eyes twinkle as he adds, "You only live once, right?"

"I'm a lot closer to the end than you are, so I don't think so."

"You're no fun—you know that?" He sighs.

"You probably wouldn't be surprised to learn that you're not the first person to tell me that."

"It's never too late to change." He pauses to think, then asks, "Are you coming to my game tonight?"

"I am."

"How about this? If I hit a home run, we explore this. If I don't, I'll never mention this again. We'll let the gods and fate decide."

"A home run, huh? Is the team you're playing any good?"

"Yeah, they're good. We're better."

"Do you hit many home runs?"

"Some." He gives me a cocky smile. "But not a ton."

"What's the most you've hit in one game?"

"Two."

I move to him and stand within a few inches of his sexy body. So close that I can feel the heat coming off his skin. "Okay, if you hit two home runs, we'll explore the hell out of this."

"Jesus! How about I have to pitch a no-hitter, plus the two home runs, and steal a base too?" He scoffs. "Let's add all that to this sexual bet."

"No, the two home runs will do it." I shrug. "That's my final offer. Take it or leave it."

He cocks his head. "I'm not sure what *explore the hell out of this* means exactly, but it sounds like a lot of fun. I'm in. Deal."

"Deal."

"Let's shake on it." He extends his hand, and we shake.

I turn on my heel and scamper away. *What the hell did I just do?*

Chapter 28

Batter Up

Paranoid and overthinking things, as usual, I force Kyle to walk to the beach first, and I follow about twenty minutes later. For the next four hours or so, I hang with the entire multifamily brood as we enjoy a day of overdoing it in the sun and heat along with some mild *it's five o'clock somewhere* day drinking. Kyle takes a pass on the alcohol, and I can only assume it's to perform at his best in tonight's game.

Maybe it's not fair that he needs to hit two home runs tonight to be able to get around the bases with me, but what the hell? I drive a hard bargain.

That's what she said.

Wait, that doesn't make much sense as a sex pun. Even so, I'm cracking myself up on the beach, but that's probably because I'm tipsy, slightly sunburned, mildly wind-burned, extremely dehydrated, very horny, and tired.

Kyle leaves the beach early, and he's already gone before the rest of us return home to shower and change for our first out-at-a-restaurant meal at this famous place near the stadium. Dinner is a little chaotic and clearly taxing on our waiter, as both my mother and father should not be allowed out in public. Between her food-allergy restrictions and his inability to properly read a menu, I'd be shocked if it wasn't our server's last night working there. I could swear I saw him run, screaming out to the parking lot, just after we paid our check.

As we settle into our uncomfortable ballpark seats, I spot Kyle stretching at his center field position. He looks very good in that uniform, and I try to push down any thoughts or comparisons to my David and just enjoy the game. I figure there is very little chance he could hit two home runs and I'd have to make good on the bet, but I feel this odd excitement. I'm not sure if it's because I've wagered something important on the game or just because I'm here with all these friends on this beautiful, warm night. For tonight, at least, I don't have this sense of tragic history hanging over me. For the first time in a long time, I feel very much alive and not just a spectator in someone else's story.

I nominate myself as the designated driver, and the rest of them start consuming overpriced beer. With the game scoreless, Kyle heads to the plate to lead off the second inning, and we all cheer for him. He strikes out on a full count, taking a massive swing, clearly trying to knock it out of the park. As he heads back to the dugout, our eyes meet, and he shoots me a knowing smile.

In the fourth inning, Kyle's team is down by two runs. He comes up to the plate with a man on third and one out. He takes another big swing, this time getting all of it and sending a deep shot to center field. The outfielder backpedals, takes a few steps on the warning track, then catches the ball with only a few feet to spare. The man on third tags and scores easily. He's credited with a run batted in. Although his teammates congratulate him in the dugout, he is making no progress on his parlay with nearly half the game played.

In the sixth inning, with the bases loaded, he takes the first pitch deep to left field, and the outfielder doesn't even attempt to go for the ball, as it's ten rows deep into the stands. The crowd rises to their feet, erupting in cheers. As he rounds second base, beaming, he lifts a single finger into the air and points it to our screaming group. I'm sure I'm the only one aware that the gesture is for me and me alone.

Kyle leads off in the ninth inning with his team up by one run. With the count full, he smacks the ball hard, sending it deep toward the foul pole in left field. An eerie silence falls over the crowd as we all watch it keep going and going, finally landing in the stands, but sadly a few feet outside the foul pole.

He turns to look at our group and grins, shaking his head. After adjusting his gloves, he returns to the batter's box. He takes another huge swing, driving the next pitch deep to left field. The outfielder goes back and back and back. I rise to my feet, mouth open, eyes wide. It's almost like it's happening in slow motion as the ball continues to lift higher and higher. The crowd joins me on their feet, watching and gasping as the outfielder reaches the warning track. With one hand, he feels for the wall. Then, timing his jump perfectly, he leaps, extending his glove over the wall, and somehow catches the ball. He tumbles down and onto the dirt, lifting his glove to display he caught the ball.

The crowd groans in unison, and I slump down, dejected. Kyle's already rounding second when he sees this, and the smile immediately evaporates from his face. He stops in his tracks, crouches over, catching his breath, then heads to the dugout without even looking up at us.

And it is in that moment that I decide I'm still going to *explore the hell out of this* when we get back home.

Chapter 29

What Are You Doing Here?

Driving home, all I could think about was Kyle. I didn't say a word. I wanted him. I had to have him. I don't know what I was thinking these last few days, wasting valuable time and not simply surrendering to my long-overdue desire. He was robbed of that home run, but I'm not going to rob him of what he deserves—or me of what I deserve.

It's now after midnight, and he still hasn't returned from the game. Everyone else retired to their bedrooms more than an hour ago, including John and me. John lay next to me and fell asleep quickly as I, unable to sleep once again, stared at some random movie on my iPad without really watching it.

I hear a car pull up outside and the door shut. Sliding off the bed, I quietly crawl to the window and peer under the blinds. It's Kyle, returning home, and my pulse quickens. I turn away from the window and lean with my back against the wall, closing my eyes. Pulling my legs up, I wrap my arms around them, rocking slightly back and forth as I summon the courage to go to him.

Am I really going to do this? Sighing, I realize I should have opened a bottle of wine when we returned, but there is no time now.

After taking a deep breath, I get to my feet and head for the door, then silently make my way to the first floor. I haven't even considered what sort of story I might tell if I run into someone. Maybe I'll just pretend to be sleepwalking. At this point, I don't care. I've got a mission, and nothing is going to stop me. Crap, that's not true. If someone catches me, I'll probably jump out the window. Why is my mind even going to these places? Jeez, I really should talk to a therapist about this.

I reach Kyle's door, look back to the empty hall, breathe a sigh of relief, and slip inside. Hearing the sound of the shower running, I turn and lock the door. That doesn't feel secure enough, so I locate a chair and slide it under the knob for an extra layer of protection. As I pass the entrance to the bathroom, I can see his upper body as he washes his hair. The rest of him is covered with the towel draped over the bar. As I stand there, frozen, my eyes roam over his muscular body with my lips parted. For a moment, I consider running away, but instead, I continue watching him as I pull off my T-shirt and slip out of my shorts and underwear.

Standing there with nothing on, I run my fingers over my nipples, feeling them stiffen with excitement. It's been too long since anyone has really touched me. I slide my hand down over my stomach and between my legs. Kyle reaches to turn off the water, and I slip away from the doorway before he can see me.

After pulling down the comforter on his bed, I prop up the pillows and sit up, waiting for him. I don't know what to do with my hands or my legs. Should I spread my legs wide? No, that's a little too slutty. Should I close them and cover up with my hands? Probably not. That's a little too immature. I feel awkward, nervous, exposed, and excited, all at once. I settle on laying my legs flat and together with my hands placed palms down on the sheet on either side of me. Maybe I'm overthinking this just a tad.

Suddenly, he steps out from the bathroom, naked and drying his hair with a towel. I take the whole of him in. His thick, strong thighs to his good-looking cock, flat stomach, and perfect upper body. God, he looks good.

I've seen a lot of penises in my day, mostly in a nonsexual, clinical way. I've sorta become desensitized to seeing them. You know, you've seen one, you've seen a thousand, and believe me, I've seen a thousand. Without question, this is in the top one percent.

"Hi," I mutter weakly.

"Shit!" he exclaims loudly. He steps back, dropping the towel with his eyes bugging out of his head. "You scared the shit out of me."

"Sorry," I whisper, then hold a finger to my lips to remind him we're not alone in this house.

"What are you doing here?"

"What do you think I'm doing here?"

"But I didn't hit that second home run."

Cocking my head, I pat the bed. "Something tells me you'll hit another one right here."

"That's good." He smiles. "Did you just come up with that?"

"No." I raise a shoulder. "I've been waiting to say that."

"Still, it's a good line."

"Thanks."

His eyes connect with mine. "You look so good in my bed."

"I'm nervous."

"Don't be. It's just sex."

"Are you planning on coming over anytime soon?" I tilt my head to the side, putting on an innocent expression.

"I just want to enjoy the view for another few seconds."

"I'm not sure I can wait that long."

Slipping out of bed, I go to him. I rise up on my toes and gaze into his eyes. "Hey."

"Hey there. I guess this is really happening?"

"It's either that or we get dressed and—"

He presses his lips to mine and kisses me softly. I place my hands on his chest. He wraps his arms around me, pulling me close to him, smashing my body to his as our tongues find each other. *Oh God, he's a good kisser.*

I slide my hands down. With one hand, I'm cupping and massaging his large balls, and with the other, I'm carefully tracing my fingers over his growing cock.

He tilts his head back and moans, "Oh fuck, that feels good."

Slipping to my knees, I'm now eye-level with his manhood, and I circle it with both hands cupped together, moving over him. I look up to his face. "You were so amazing out there tonight. I was so impressed. When I saw you hit that grand slam, I knew I had to have you."

He smiles. "So, you're saying if the bases hadn't been loaded, you wouldn't be doing this right now?"

"Shut up." I roll my eyes and return my attention to his cock, placing a tiny kiss on the thick head. Spotting a drip of pre-cum on the tip, I extend my tongue and take it into my mouth.

"Oh, Ally," he groans.

I look up to him. "You taste so good."

He simply nods with his jaw hanging open.

Returning my attention lower, I cover him with my mouth, struggling to fit his thickness inside. He groans in pleasure, raking his hands through my hair as I slowly lick and suck his delicious cock.

After a few minutes of working him over with skills I

haven't tapped into in over two decades—skills I didn't think I still possessed—he gently guides me back and stammers breathlessly, "Holy fuck. Where did you ... I mean, how do you ... I know you work with, um, male, um, but, wow ..."

"I'm a urologist, not a prostitute." I break into a chuckle while still slowly running my fingers over his length.

He tilts his head back and groans. "I know; I know. But you said that you hadn't been with anyone in, like, forever. Don't get me wrong; it's not like I've gotten a ton of blow jobs, but you ... you are, like, a world-class Olympic medalist in this."

I shrug. "Well, I might have stumbled onto some porn and picked up a tip or two."

"Got to love the internet." Stepping back, he reaches his hand out, and I stand. He effortlessly scoops me up in his arms, depositing me on the edge of the bed. "I need to taste you again."

Kneeling on the floor, he parts my legs, settling in between them. Bringing his lips to mine, he gives me a soft kiss before sliding his tongue into my mouth. I'm still tasting his sweet precum as he lays a trail of kisses over my neck and between my breasts until moving to the left one and sucking my pebbled nipple into his mouth. I rake my hands through his dark hair as he teases me with his mouth, lips, and gentle bites.

Rising upright, he stands with his huge erection jutting out before me. My eyes are drawn to it, as are my mouth and the rest of me. I want him so fucking badly that I can feel it. I want to touch it again. I reach for it, and he puts his hands out to stop me.

"I told you, I need to taste your pussy again."

He slips his hands under my backside and guides me slightly further back on the mattress. I place my heels on the edge of the bed. Leaning over, he kisses me again, and I feel his hard cock pressing firmly on my clit. I groan in ecstasy, pushing my hips out desperately, trying to maneuver him inside. When I fail, I whine in disappointment.

"Just wait," he whispers. "Not yet."

"I want you now."

He shakes his head and stands tall with his cock perfectly positioned and hovering just above my pussy. Moving forward slowly, he pushes my knees apart and teases me with his weighty cock as the tip slides over my clit.

"You're so wet."

I moan, "You're killing me."

He pulls back, teasing me again until he positions himself right at my slick entrance. His eyes meet mine, and I part my lips, begging him to push forward, but he instead slips back down to his knees. He places soft kisses on each of my thighs as he works down to my core. He breathes in the scent of me and purrs with his eyes narrowing. I feel his hot breath on my sensitive skin, and it's obliterating me.

Lifting up, he drags his fingers just above my pelvic bone before sliding his hand over my pussy. He gently smooths his thumb over my clit. I exhale slowly as he applies more pressure and makes tiny, circular motions. He slides a finger inside me, and I cry out in pleasure, arching my back and lifting my rear off the bed.

Slowly, he places soft kisses on either side of my pussy, then moves below and above and does the same, teasing me, torturing me with a slow agony of wanting him. I need his tongue inside me. I need his cock inside me. I want to kiss him and suck him.

Suddenly, he presses his full mouth on me and slips his tongue inside. I crane my neck to watch him with one hand in his hair. I pull him closer, feeling his tongue probe deeper. My eyes go black.

His tongue moves over my clit, swirling over it, and I groan. Slipping lower again, he presses his flat tongue at my core and works it up to my clit, then back down over and over, dizzying me with pleasure.

Moving my hands to either side of me, I grip the sheets and whisper, "Oh fuck, Kyle. Yes. Yes."

Placing his palms under each of my knees, he gently curls my legs back, opening me up wide to his oral skills. He slides lower, reaching pleasure zones I didn't know needed attention. I just don't want him to stop—ever. Swiping up and back down, he bathes me with his strong, wide tongue, sending my head spinning. All sense of time, who we are, and where we are, are the furthest things from my mind.

He's expertly bringing me to the edge of climax, then back. Each time closer and closer. This goes on and on until he pulls up from me and wipes his lips.

"You taste so fucking good."

Gasping for breath, I simply stare at him as I slide back and center myself on the bed. He follows me, taking hold of his hard cock and placing it on my entrance.

"Do I need a condom?"

I shake my head and mouth the word *no*.

He presses ever so slightly forward, his bulbous head spreading my soaking wet lips. My eyes roll back in my head, and I gasp loudly, forgetting for a moment that I need to keep my voice down.

He holds a finger to his lips, and I take it into my mouth, sucking on it as he thrusts slowly and shallowly inside me. I nod, as if to urge him on, and reaching out with my fingertips, I brush them against his taut stomach.

I claw at his sides, digging my nails lightly into his skin and pulling him closer. He presses deeper, and his cock fills me fully. He's staring into my eyes now as he rises up on his toes with his arms on either side of me, pounding into me harder and faster.

"Oh God," I whisper.

He's breathing harder now, and his cock is pulsating and thickening inside me. I adjust my position under him, and suddenly, he's hitting the right spot. I moan. Waves of pleasure rumble through my body, and my pussy clenches hard around him. Every muscle in his upper body flexes over me. He closes his eyes and squeezes his lips together, stifling his grunt to barely a whisper.

Slumping over me, he groans once more, flooding my pussy with his cum, pressing his mouth to my neck. I pull him closer as he continues to thrust slowly inside me. He takes a deep breath, kisses my neck once more, then lifts his head up and smiles, exhausted.

"That was"—I struggle to catch my breath and find the words—"amazing."

"I know."

He wipes his mouth and raises his body higher, looking down to take in the sight of our coupling. He pulls back, and I follow his gaze to his still-hard cock buried halfway inside of me.

I say, "You feel so good."

"We're just getting started."

"But I need a break." I tap him on the shoulder. "I need to at least change positions. My legs are starting to ache."

He slips off of me and onto his side. We lie, facing one another, our eyes wandering over each other's bodies—vulnerable, naked—savoring the aftermath of what just happened.

Chapter 30

Most of My Workday Is a Penis-Fest

It's nearly one thirty as Kyle and I lie in his bed, still unabashedly naked and uncovered. I can't recall being this free with my body ever. Not even with David. Not that we had much of a chance with his roommate always popping in and out of their dorm room or even later, when he had his own room. Even on the few occasions when we went away to a hotel, I don't remember ever just lying around this way and having it feel so natural. I mean, I barely know him, but for some reason, I'm not self-conscious.

Out of nowhere, he blurts out, "So, you work with naked men, right?"

"Well, I'm not a *Playgirl* photographer." I chuckle. "You really have no idea what I do, do you?"

"No, I do. You're a urologist."

"Okay, and what does a urologist do?" I ask in a slightly patronizing tone while holding back a laugh.

Shrugging his shoulders, he turns his palms up. "Looks at lots of soft penises and writes tons of prescriptions for Viagra."

"Yes, that's part of it. We do treat erectile dysfunction. We also monitor for and treat prostate cancer, reproductive issues, and other urinary tract disorders."

"But basically, you look at penises all day."

"I do have some female patients, but, yes, most of my workday is a penis-fest."

"Penis-fest. I like that." He laughs. "The reason I ask is, you're pretty much an expert, and I, um ... I want you to give me your honest opinion of him." He points to his groin timidly.

"What? Why?"

"It's silly." He closes his eyes and turns away. "When I was younger—a lot younger—my sister saw it, said it was small, and sorta laughed at me. I've always been a little self-conscious about it."

"Well, that's mean." I frown. "How exactly did she see it?"

"In my defense, it was before I hit puberty, and I think I was just wearing boxer shorts, and the flap opened. She maybe got a glimpse for, like, one second."

"Well, I've seen hundreds over the years. Lots of old ones." I close my eyes and cringe. "Really old ones. And some testicles that would ... let's just say, they weren't that attractive. But in my sensitive position, I've learned to ignore the sights and smells and just focus on treating the patient."

"But it still has to occasionally get to you. Like, I'm sure you've wanted to run out of the room, screaming."

"Maybe once or twice." I concede with a nod.

"I'll bet. Now, back to ..." He motions to his prize.

"I've only seen three erect ones. Yours, John's, and David's." As a memory flows back to me, my eyes widen. "Wait, four ... no, five."

"Who were the other two?"

"Over the years, I've had two patients get sort of ... involuntary erections during digital examinations of the prostate." I wince. "At least, I hope they were involuntary."

"Wow, that must have been awkward."

"Well, it wasn't too bad for the one, but the other gentleman turned around really fast, and it nearly hit me."

"No way." He chuckles. "What happened?"

I bug my eyes out. "Well, I referred him to another urologist."

"That makes sense." He recoils in horror. "I'm not even going to ask what a digital exam is. I mean, I think I have a pretty good idea, but—"

"Oh God, you men and your irrational fear of anything going into your anus. If I had ten dollars for every man I examined who clenched up like they were being violated by a baseball bat, I'd be a very wealthy woman."

"Well, I understand that. Things really shouldn't be going in there." He nods confidently. "Well, I mean, unless you're a gay man. I have a couple of gay friends, and sometimes, they share a little too much, so I hear things."

"Interesting." I cock my head. "What about women?"

"What about them?"

"Should 'things' be going in there?" I ask, using air quotes.

"Things, as in what exactly?" He lifts his brow in question.

"Oh, I don't know. Penises, for example." I shrug.

Frowning, he flaps his hand at me. "Oh, no, that's fine."

I shoot him a withering look.

"What?"

"Okay, you just made my case. Why are men so horrified of this"—I hold up a finger—"going back there for two, maybe three seconds to check for nodules on the prostate, but it's just a day at the beach for something three to four times that big around pounding into a woman's—let's face it—generally much smaller area?"

He shrugs. "It just is."

"Okay." I roll my eyes and chuckle.

"Can we get off my ass and get back to my dick?"

I lose it and let out a rather loud cackle before he covers my mouth with his hand, shooting me a scolding look, whispering, "Hey, keep it down, anti-anal girl."

"I'm not anti-anal. I'm just pointing out the double standard and irrational fear of men with that simple test."

"Oh, so you're pro-anal then?" he asks with a hopeful smile.

"I didn't say that either," I grumble. "I'm ... I'm ... anal neutral."

He grins. "Really? We'll just have to revisit that at a later time."

"No, we probably won't."

"So, back to me." He motions with both hands to his area and holds his head awkwardly up, wearing an odd expression. "I want your honest opinion."

"Stop it. You're going to make me laugh. Jeez, I wish I had my white doctor coat. That would feel more professional. I'm not usually nude when I do these exams."

"Just do it."

"Okay, okay." I climb off the bed and move to the chair.

"Oh, you don't want to do it here?"

"No, I'm always seated." I clear my throat and say in a professional tone, "Mr. Davis, could you please report to me?"

Kyle walks over with both hands covering his groin.

I shake my head, holding back a laugh. "Now, Mr. Davis, there is no need to be shy. I'm a professional."

He stands before me and places his hands on his hips.

Grasping his testicles, I say, "Now, turn your head and cough."

He stares down at me, frowning. "You're not really a doctor, are you?"

"Sorry. I'll actually be serious now." I rub my hands together and clear my throat. "Okay." I've seen much smaller flaccid penises. "I'd say you're in the top ten percent in flaccid size, but what really counts is length and girth when erect. Most men are around six in length and maybe five inches around in girth."

"Huh."

"I don't have my tape measure handy, and I've never really officially measured one, but I think you're seven and a half, maybe eight inches long and maybe five and a half to six inches around."

"And the shape?"

"Well, there, I can comment." I take hold of his penis with one hand and his testicles in the other. I move his manhood around, really taking a good look at it. I push it to his belly and tilt my head, moving closer and squinting. It begins to thicken and lengthen just a bit as I continue, "The head is big and defined. Your circumcision was done perfectly. Your testes are quite large and in nice proportion, complementing your penis. Also, your grooming is very nice. I'm seeing very few stray hairs. I would give you a nine out of ten."

"A nine?" He scoffs.

"All right, nine-point-five."

"I can live with that. Thanks."

"You're welcome." I smile, standing while holding up three fingers. "Now, turn around, bend over, and place your elbows on the bed."

"Hey, what's with the three fingers?" he asks, wearing an expression as if I were holding a gun on him. "Before, you just showed me one!"

Tilting my head, I say in a casual tone, "Yes, most doctors go with just one gloved finger, but I like to be a tad more thorough." Reaching out while putting on a more ominous tone, I add. "Now, *this is* going to happen. It's for your own good."

Backing away and cowering, he covers his backside with his hands, holding back a smile. "I don't feel at all safe right now."

"Come on. I promise you won't feel it … *much*."

I reach again for him, and he smacks my hand away playfully.

He chuckles. "I bet you'd like that, wouldn't you? You get off on violating guys back there, don't you?"

"I do. I do." I nod confidently. "Don't tell anyone, but that's why I went to medical school."

"Ha-ha." He rolls his eyes, then says, "Put your fingers away, and instead, let's do you now."

"What do you mean?"

"I'll be the doctor. Let me examine you and give you my expert opinion."

"What?" I recoil, shaking my head. "I don't think so."

"Come on."

"No way. I don't want you scrutinizing every fold and crevice down there and pointing out every flaw."

"I've got news for you. I already spent quite a bit of time down there, and it's nothing short of perfect."

"Oh, that's sweet." I step to him. Grinning, I place a hand on his lower back, then trail a finger slowly down, just to the edge of his cheeks.

Quickly turning his head, he frantically attempts to see what I'm doing on one side, then the other.

"Stop. Step back," he struggles to say without cracking up.

"All right." Holding my hands up, I say, "Just know that the next time we're in the shower together, I'll drop the soap, and when you go to pick it up, I'll complete my exam."

"Funny." He rolls his eyes. "You know, I'm not on the medical board or anything, but I'm fairly certain you could lose your license for this behavior."

"Oh, you think?"

"I do."

He pulls me into his arms and kisses me. I feel that new but now very familiar stirring in my core. I surrender my mouth to his and can feel his quickly rising erection pressing against my stomach.

He whispers, "Before we get to round two, I have a confession to make."

"What's that?"

He pulls back, pointing downward. "My sister never saw my, you know, or commented on it, and I'm not self-conscious about it at all."

"What?" I punch him in the shoulder. "Then, what the hell was all that stuff for?"

"Oh, I guess I just like hearing nice stuff about him."

"Jerk." I punch him again, but this time, it's a little softer.

"Sorry." He kisses me softly, then pulls back. "Sorry."

"Now, I want you on the edge of the bed."

I guide him there, and after he lies back, I get on my knees between his legs. His cock is semi-hard and flopped on his thigh. Wrapping a hand around it, I cover it with my mouth, then slowly lick and suck until it's standing at full attention.

Lifting my mouth from him, I jerk it slowly up and down. "Do you still not feel safe?"

He cranes his neck to get a look, smirking. "I don't know. Just make sure I can see your hands at all times."

"You mean, like this?" Lifting my hands up, I take his cock into my mouth and widen my eyes, gazing at him while mumbling with my mouth full, "Is. This. Good?"

His mouth drops open, and he gasps, "Uh-huh."

I let him fall from my lips while keeping my hands raised. "I feel like I'm under arrest."

"I know there's a joke there somewhere, but most of the blood has left my brain, so it's escaping me."

I giggle.

He frowns, disappointed. "That was starting to feel really good."

"Was it? Can I use my hands, or are you still *concerned*?"

He gives me a tired look. "Can we stop with all the jokes and just, you know ..."

"What? Do you think we went one joke too far with this whole thing?"

"One?" He scoffs. "Try at least six. Let's just knock it off."

"You're right. You're right." Taking his perfect cock in my hand, I stroke it and whisper, "I will if you will."

"Oh, I will."

I cover him fully with my mouth, and it's on.

* * *

He successfully fulfills the three-to-four-hour claim he so arrogantly voiced during our outdoor shower encounter. I've lost count on which one of us has had more orgasms, although I'd venture to say, he prevails. We've done it on the bed, the floor, in the shower, then back on the bed in any number of positions. I'm sure there were many times where he lost track of exactly where my hands were, but I swear they didn't stray anywhere unwanted. I mean, sure, I might have brushed inadvertently against a forbidden spot once or twice, although no verbal complaints were raised. I'd say, in one night, I've atoned for roughly five years of my ten-year sex sabbatical.

I sneak back to my room and slip into bed, undetected, next to my soundly sleeping husband at just after four. As I lie there, exhausted, but unable to fall asleep, my imagination plays through the scenarios of making up for those remaining lost years and anticipating how soon I can start.

Chapter 31

No Way. She's on OnlyFans?!

"Ally. Ally."

I'm stirred from sleep by a soft voice. Forcing my eyes open slightly, I discover John sitting beside me.

"Hey. What time is it?" I ask groggily while snuggling with my pillow on my side.

"After eleven."

"Jesus." Turning onto my back, I squint at the bright daylight bleeding through the blinds. "I don't think I've slept this late since college."

He chuckles. "Yeah, we were all wondering if you were still breathing."

"I was in and out of sleep pretty much all night." That's not a lie. And I finally cashed in on my side of this semi-bizarre *don't ask, don't tell* marriage arrangement—and in a big, big way.

"Why are you smiling like that?" He gives me a concerned look.

"I'm not smiling," I reply defensively.

"You are."

I wave my hand in the air dismissively. "Um, well, I ... I was just remembering this crazy dream I had."

"Yeah? What happened?"

"What do you mean?"

"In the dream."

"Oh, I barely remember any of it, and what I do remember is too embarrassing to tell."

"Gotcha." He pats me on the hip. "Hey, we all had breakfast earlier, but I didn't want to wake you up. Everyone is heading down to the beach. Do you want to go?"

"No, I'm exhausted. I think I'll just hang around here for a while and maybe come down later."

"Sounds good."

He heads out of the room, and before I know it, I'm back asleep.

* * *

"Ally. Ally."

I grumble, "John, I told you, I don't want to go to the beach."

"I feel so used."

I force my eyes open to find Kyle standing before me, holding a tray. "What time is it? What'd you say?"

Something smells delicious, although I can't quite identify it.

"It's almost twelve thirty, and I said I feel so used. You're calling me by the wrong name." He quivers his lips, as if he were on the verge of tears, and adds in an over-the-top cracking voice, "Did last night mean nothing to you?"

I sit up in bed. "You're a very funny guy. Have you thought of a career in stand-up?"

"No, but that whole *rectal exam* bit from last night was

pretty hilarious. We make a great comedy team. We should go on the road."

"Maybe." I chuckle. "But please, let's not start that again."

"Agreed. It's completely played out."

Craning my neck, I try to get a look at the contents of the tray. "What's this?"

"You'd be surprised to hear that we're all alone in this big, beautiful beach house."

"I would not be surprised."

"Why not?"

"John woke me up, like, an hour ago and told me everyone was going to the beach."

"Not everyone." He raises his eyebrows suggestively. "And you didn't sneak back to my bed when you thought we were all alone? Again, I'm hurt. You're one of those *hit it once and quit it* gals, right?"

I don't bother to reply to his little joke. Instead, I straighten my spine and say in a pouty voice, "First, I assume that tray is for me. Are you going to give it to me, or am I going to starve?"

"Now, I'm not so sure." He smirks, pausing a few moments before he places it over my lap. "I made French toast and scrambled eggs. After this and the egg sandwich yesterday, we've reached the limit of my culinary skills."

We share a laugh as I take in the scrumptious-looking meal.

"I'm starving, and it looks and smells amazing." I take a sip of coffee, then go to work on my plate. "Aren't you eating?"

"I already did, and I figured the both of us having breakfast in bed could be a little risky in case someone pops back home. Somebody could get the wrong idea."

"You mean, like we just spent the night exploring every inch of each other's bodies?"

"Yep, that would be so silly." He flips his hand up. "Who would even think that?"

"Right." After slipping a forkful of eggs into my mouth, I shake my head. "This is really good."

"I'm glad. So, back to my question. Why didn't you come find me for some more fun after they all left?"

"A couple reasons. First, I'm not nineteen." I take a sip of coffee. "Second, I'm exhausted, and third, everything is sore—my mouth, my legs, and my, um ..." I point to my midsection. "All of that is still recovering."

"Wow, you are old."

"Hey!"

"I'm kidding."

I take another bite. "And I take it, you are just raring to go?"

"Well, my tongue hurts. But that's to be expected. I don't think I've ever done *that* for that length of time. The rest of me is fully recharged." He stands and looks down to his groin. "Want to see?"

I scrunch up my nose, holding back a smile. "I'll take your word for it."

"Your loss."

I turn away, closing my eyes as a wave of heat and desire rolls through my body. Just from him suggesting we do it again or even the hint that he might show me *it* again has me reacting like a horny teenager. I think I might just be able to power through and have a repeat of last night's festivities. Sure, it might kill me, but it might just be worth it. I feel a warmth between my thighs and a stirring that is sending tingles through—

"Ally?"

"Huh, what?" Suddenly yanked back to reality, I open my eyes.

"Where'd you go?"

"No place. I'm just tired."

He sits down near my feet as I take another bite. A smile spreads over his lips, and he shakes his head.

"What is it?"

"I was just thinking about your mother. Call me crazy, but I swear she was staring at my crotch the other day. And at one point, she sorta touched that whole area with her hand, and I swear there was ... what's the word? Um, cupping."

"Cupping?" I narrow my eyes.

"Yes, definite cupping. She apologized like it was an accident, but—"

"Like, *she cupped your balls* cupping?"

"Uh-huh."

I say matter-of-factly, "Oh, she's probably just sizing you up for her OnlyFans site."

"What?" His jaw nearly drops into his lap. "No way. She's on OnlyFans?! Doing what?"

"She's, um ..." I swallow hard, closing my eyes momentarily while I find the courage to share.

"She's what?" he asks with way, way too much eagerness.

"She's the, uh, the Ball-Busting Granny," I say slowly, looking like I'm about to be sick.

"You're shitting me." He cackles.

I pause, taken aback by the sheer pleasure on his face. "I'm literally horrified to tell you that I am not shitting you."

"That's so cool." He stares out the window, nodding his head.

"Believe me, it's not cool."

Raising his palms up, he concedes the point. "Well, cool, but in a completely embarrassing and twisted way."

I nod. "Actually, she, um, tried to get me to recruit some of my more, let's call them, well-suited patients to appear with her on her site."

"What do you mean, well-suited?"

"Do I need to say it, or do you think you can figure it out from the name?"

As the realization washes over his face, his smile somehow grows even wider. "So, really big balls."

"Bingo," I acknowledge with a weary nod. "You're enjoying this news too much. It's creeping me out a little."

"Sorry. I mean, if I found out my mother was doing this, I'd probably jump in front of a bus. But since it's yours, it's pretty fucking hilarious."

"Gee, thanks." I enjoy another forkful of eggs, then say, "She must have a sense about you. Yep, she has an eye for talent."

"What do you mean?"

"With your equipment, you might make the perfect addition to her site," I joke.

"Would I have to show my face?"

"I'm going to pretend like you didn't just ask me that and that you're not actually considering it."

"What?" He raises a brow. "I've been looking for a business opportunity."

"Call me crazy, but I wouldn't consider having your balls repeatedly crushed by a senior citizen a 'business opportunity,'" I say, using air quotes.

"Crushed?" He recoils.

"Yes, crushed. What did you think it was?"

He replies weakly, "I don't know. Maybe just some light fondling."

"You're looking past the keyword—*busting*."

"Yikes. No thanks." He cringes. "So, men actually let someone do this to them?"

"They do." I cover my face with my hands as I admit, "I, um, actually witnessed it firsthand."

He raises his hands up in surrender. "I'm not sure I want to know what that means."

"Believe me, you don't."

"And people actually pay to watch this?"

"She says she makes money. I think, like, ten thousand a month so far ... maybe more."

"No way." He runs his fingers through his hair. "This is just beyond crazy."

"Tell me about it." I nod, pushing my plate away. "I think I've lost my appetite."

"So, did you?"

"What?"

"Recruit any of your big-balled patients to work with her?"

I press my lips together in utter humiliation as I refuse to look at him.

"Is that a yes?"

I explain apologetically, "In my defense, he was a new patient, he had extremely large, um, you know"—I widen my eyes—"and he told me he was out of work and on the verge of losing his house."

"Jesus."

"So, I simply made the referral."

"Do you know if he actually contacted her and—"

"He sent me flowers," I admit, gritting my teeth.

"No shit!" He laughs out loud.

"That was the end of it for me. I swear. And I told her to find her own candidates, going forward, which"—I close my eyes and scowl—"is *evidently* what she was attempting to do with you."

"Wow!"

"Yeah, wow." I nod in a daze.

"Can we see?"

"See what?" I ask nervously.

"Her site!"

"Absolutely not." I raise my hands up. "I've never even been on it."

"Come on."

"No way."

He slips off the bed and bounces on his heels. "I'm getting my computer."

By the time I open my mouth to voice another objection, he's already run out of the room.

Chapter 32

Meet the Ball-Busting Granny

After eliminating all evidence of my surprise and very thoughtful breakfast, I'm cleaning up in the kitchen as Kyle sits in the great room, searching the OnlyFans site for the infamous Ball-Busting Granny.

He yells to me, "Hurry up."

"That's okay. I really don't need to see."

He cracks up laughing. "Get this. I found Ball-Busting Marcy. She lists herself as a *twenty-something ball-busting queen.*"

"Oh, she sounds like a peach," I call back while washing a skillet.

"Your mom has a little competition."

Rolling my eyes, I reply with my words dripping with sarcasm, "Hopefully, the market has room for more than one ball-busting queen."

"You would think. Oh, yeah, she must serve a younger demographic," Kyle quips. "Can I read you what she's famous for?"

"Please don't," I reply as I store a dish in the cabinet.

"It says: *I'm a lil' famous in the ball-busting universe for my bustin' videos, including 'Squeeze Me Some More' and 'Squeeze Me Some More 2.' As well as making a busting-virgin blind date literally throw up from a ferocious knee-to-balls encounter, as seen in my video 'Balls Meet My Knee.' "*

Cringing, I head over and sit down next to him on the sofa. "She makes a guy throw up?"

"That's what it says. But I guess you just need to spend forty bucks to find out." He smirks.

"I really don't need to confirm that." Looking at her page, I groan. "I can't believe people make a living doing this stuff."

"You mean, people like your mommy?" he fires back with a grin, desperately fighting back a laugh.

"You're enjoying this a little too much."

"I think I'm enjoying this exactly the right amount." He studies the screen. "Okay, here we go."

"Oh, no, I can't look." I cover my eyes with my hands.

He rubs his hands together and exclaims like he's announcing a WWE bout of wrestling, "WELCOME. TO. THE. BALL. BUSTING. GRAAAANNNNNY."

"Don't tell me anything about it."

"I won't."

Spreading my fingers apart, I try to get a look at the screen, and he catches me.

"Hey, no peeking." He chuckles. "I might even go as far to say, you've been *busted*! Get it?" He turns to me, waiting.

"What?"

"Don't you get it? I said, you're *busted*, and she's a *ball-buster*."

"Ha-ha." I add sarcastically, "Yeah, the best jokes are the ones you need to explain."

"Well, I thought it was clever," he sneers. "You know, you were a hell of a lot more fun last night."

"Are we done?" I put my hand over the laptop screen and

ask, "Can I put my bathing suit on so we can go to the beach already?"

"Keep your pants on." He flashes his eyebrows, grinning.

"Jeez, what now?" I make a face. "Oh, I get it. That's another joke because I want to get out of these pants. That's not bad."

He gently removes my hand from the screen. "So, your mom charges only twenty a month. That's a bargain. I guess she's low*balling* to capture more of the market. Low*balling* ..." He presses his lips together, but a girlie giggle spills out anyway. "Sorry."

I move to the edge of the sofa and say in a tired voice, "I'm going to go. I'll meet you down there."

He pulls me back. "Wait. I'll stop with the puns. Promise."

"Is it that bad?" I lean close to him to study the screen, but get sidetracked by his scent. "Wow, you smell good. What is that?"

"Soap. Okay, so she lists herself as a genuine grandmother who loves to bust balls. Her subscription features exclusive content, including pics, stories, and videos not shown anywhere else. She does scheduled live streams with her either sharing stories, answering questions, interacting directly with fans, or busting balls!"

"I can confirm the live part," I mutter, scowling.

He continues in a casual tone, "Regular topless photos. Unlimited free messages for chitchat and ball-busting talk."

"Holy shit! I can't believe she wrote all that."

"It sounds like you get a whole lot of ball-busting action for your money."

"Okay, now, are we done?"

"Nope. Let's just look at one sample picture."

I exhale a long, slow breath. "One."

"Oh, this is a nice one." He turns the screen to me, and it's a picture of a pale blue high heel, sandwiched between some very large, semi-flattened testicles with an engorged penis over it.

"I bought those for her last year," I boast.

"Nice."

Looking closer at the picture, I narrow my eyes. "I'm going out on a limb here, but I'm fairly confident that's my patient, Mr. Ballentine. The one I referred. I think I'd know those testicles anywhere," I add with pride. "Hopefully, he makes a lot of money for this humiliation."

"Did you say Mr. *BALL*entine?"

"Okay, I'm done." I quickly get to my feet and head toward my room, yelling back, "Meet you out here in two minutes."

* * *

In my room, I mull over my bathing suit collection. I'm choosing between two relatively conservative one-pieces or another skimpier one-piece—one that I look pretty damn good in, if I'm being honest. Then, there are my bikinis—a tiny, skimpy one, which I haven't tried on in a long time, and a more conservative one that I think I can pull off. I think it looks pretty good with my aging but still relatively attractive figure. I'm feeling sexy, of course, from the events of last night, but not like a complete slut, so I go with the safer two-piece option.

When I reach the great room, wearing a cover-up and carrying sunscreen, Kyle is already there, slathering on lotion over his perfect frame. I have to force myself to tear my eyes from him. I slip my cover-up off and open the lotion bottle.

He notices, immediately stopping what he's doing and staring. "Wow."

"What?" I say shyly.

"You look amazing in that."

"Thanks. Would you mind putting some on my back?"

"No problem." He makes his way to me, staring so much that I feel uncomfortable but flattered.

I hand over the lotion. He rubs some into my upper back, then under my bikini strap, and what started as a lotion application is quickly heading into massage territory.

I fight to suppress my moan. I want to reach my hand back and grab his cock out of his trunks. I want to lick it and suck it and then ...

"How does John not come on to you every single night?" He kneads the muscles in my lower back, just above my ass, as he adds, "I just don't understand it."

It feels so good that my head slumps over as I answer, "It's complicated, but he's not really attracted to me."

Kyle cackles loudly. "There is no way he's not attracted to you."

"He's old. He's not interested in all that."

"Keep telling yourself that. I don't care what age a guy is. If I were sleeping next to you, I'd be rolling over to your side nightly."

I moan as he works his strong hands over my skin. "That feels so good."

He squeezes more lotion onto his palms and returns to work on my lower back, slipping his hand into the top of my suit. His finger slides down between my cheeks just barely, sending shivers down my spine and blood to my midsection. I groan in pleasure. I can feel his warm breath on my neck. It's all I can do not to turn around and kiss him—and more.

He moves his hands to my sides, rubbing lotion into my skin before slipping them under my bikini top, directly over my taut nipples.

"Oh ..." I moan, and I feel something hard pressing between the cheeks of my ass.

"Fuck, you're sexy," he whispers into my ear.

I press firmly into him, and he yelps in pain.

I turn around. "Sorry."

My eyes are instantly drawn to the bulge in his trunks. "You should not be hard right now."

"But I am."

"I think you're supposed to be simply putting lotion on me and not performing some sort of sensual massage. You did that to yourself."

"I did that to myself?" He shoots me a sideways glance.

"You did."

"Who strutted out here, wearing that tiny, sexy bikini?" He shimmies his shoulders from side to side with his chest sticking out and continues on in a helpless, whiny, girlie voice, "*Oh, can you please apply lotion to me? I can't reach my back, and I don't want to burn. Here, look at my shapely ass, but don't touch it.*"

"That voice—is that supposed to be me?"

"Well, if the bikini fits." He widens his eyes.

I sneer, "First, I didn't come out here like this to turn you on." *Um, actually, I did.*

"Uh-huh."

"Second, I certainly didn't ask you to apply lotion halfway down my ass, between my cheeks, and all over my nipples." *Although all of those things felt great.*

"Sue me. I didn't want you to burn."

I point to the problem area. "Just look at you. You're still hard. What the hell do we do now?"

"I can think of three"—he places a finger to his lips—"no, four things we could do to relieve the swelling."

Checking the time on my Fitbit, I frown. "They've been gone an awful long time. They'll probably be coming back for lunch soon."

"Well, we'd better hurry then." He moves to me and lays a gentle kiss on my lips.

My knees weaken. "Oh fuck."

I drop down, pulling his trunks down with me, and his engorged cock springs free. Without skipping a beat, I cover him with my mouth, licking and sucking and jerking him with one hand while I massage his balls with the other. If I could reach him with my foot, I'd probably tickle his ass with my pinkie toe.

He's moaning and groaning and rocking his hips back and forth, driving his cock deeper and deeper into my throat. I'm purring in delight as he swells even larger between my lips, rewarding me with drips of his sweet, sweet pre-cum.

Suddenly, I hear movement from downstairs. I push him away, and he tumbles onto the sofa, his trunks down around his ankles and his huge boner sticking straight up.

"Go," I whisper angrily.

As the sound of footfalls on the wood stairs grows louder, he struggles to pull up his trunks while scampering away, down the hall and out of sight. I quickly wipe my mouth, reach for my cover-up, and switch gears, applying lotion to my legs with my heart beating out of my chest. I take a few deep breaths just as John and Kate appear at the top of the stairs.

"Oh, you're up," John says.

"I've been for a while. I was, just, um, heading down there to join you guys. I guess I slept too late."

"Where's Kyle?" Kate asks.

I put on a confused look. "I'm not sure. I think he's putting on his suit." Or, if experience is any indication, I should say, he's struggling to pull his suit up over his still-hard penis.

I think I'm pulling this nonchalant attitude off. I'm fairly certain they have no idea that, just thirty seconds ago, Kyle was a couple of properly timed strokes from finishing.

"We just came up for lunch," John says. "Did you eat?"

"I had breakfast. I'm all lotioned up, so I think I'll just meet you down there." I head toward the steps just as my parents reach the top of the stairs.

"Okay," John replies. "Leave us the one cart. Your parents aren't going back later. There's a cooler full of drinks and chairs already out there."

"Thanks."

"Honey, are you feeling all right?" Candace asks.

"Yes, Mom."

Kyle appears from the hall, looking a little flushed, holding a towel over his shorts. "Are you ready to go?"

"Yep."

"I'm serious." She reaches out to my forehead. "You look all flushed. Are you coming down with something?"

"I'm fine."

"You feel warm."

"Yeah, we're at the beach, and it's hot in here," I snap.

"Okay, well, just stay hydrated."

I escape down the stairs and thankfully don't encounter any of the other lucky travelers along the way as Kyle follows close behind.

When we finally reach outside, I turn to him. "Jesus Christ, she's like a detective. Maybe she can swab me for DNA."

"You're being silly. She's concerned you're getting sick, not suspecting that you're ... you know."

"You think?"

"One hundred percent."

We climb in the golf cart, and he drives out to the main road, then turns onto the cart access. The summer heat and blazing sun bake my skin.

I glance at his groin. "I see you took care of your ... *problem*."

"Well, not exactly. I couldn't finish. I'm not good under pressure."

"So, it just went down on its own?"

"It went down enough to not draw attention."

"Oh." I grimace. "Are you doing okay?"

He glances at my legs, then quickly returns his attention to the sand. "Just stay covered. It's like a volcano that could blow at any second."

"I wish I could take care of it for you."

I place a hand on his arm, and his head slowly lolls back as he moans.

"Please don't touch me." He motions down to a growing lump in his lap. "See? You even just saying something suggestive or touching me like that causes issues."

"Okay, I'll stop." I pull my hand away.

"I'll be fine. When we get to the water, I'll dive in, and it's pretty cold."

I shake my head. "I don't know how you guys walk around with those things."

"It ain't easy. Believe me, it ain't easy."

Chapter 33

If the Tent's a-Rockin'

Kyle parks the golf cart near our tent, and I scan the area, surveying the vast, open, and mostly unpopulated beach. When you're near the water here you can only barely see the houses, which are pretty far away.

There is a group of four or five people maybe one thousand yards to our right and no one else in sight. I poke my head in our tent, then step inside. The door faces the water, and the tent has screened windows on the three other sides, about two and a half feet off the ground. As I assess the logistics of this beach setup, my thoughts journey to places it hasn't since I was a horny young college student, looking for opportunities to get busy with David.

Sitting down on the blanket inside the tent, I slide my bikini bottoms aside, exposing everything. "Kyle, come here."

He appears at the entrance, and his gaze quickly goes to my sexy reveal. *"Mrs. Larson, you are trying to seduce me, aren't you?"*

I smile. "Wait, how does she reply in the movie? Um, I don't think—"

"No, she says something like, 'Well, no, I never thought about it.'"

"That's right. Such a classic scene." Rising to my knees, I turn away from the ocean. "Now, get in here and take a look."

He kneels next to me, and we look out the back of the tent. "I don't see anything."

"Exactly." I grin, then turn to the left and point. "Nothing." Turning right, I point out the screened window. "Nothing." Then, I turn toward the water, reach down, and zip the tent door up the side, then over until the flap closes, leaving the same two-foot blind spot close to the sand and another surveillance window above. I'm beaming now. "As long as one of us stands guard, watching, the other one can, you know, please the other orally."

"Orally?" He gives me a dubious look. "You're serious?"

"Yes, but we have to be quick. I'm sure we have at least twenty minutes, but we have to get moving."

"Okay." He nods, looking all around, and a broad smile spreads over his face. "So, who's going first?"

"I am. I can be super quick. Just do what you did last night, and I'll be done in five minutes. Then, you'll have the rest of the time."

"Wait, why don't I go first? Then, we can get me out of the way, and then you—"

"Look, you're wasting time." I scowl. "Do you want to do this or not?"

"Okay, okay. Where do you want me?"

Motioning down the middle of the tent, I say, "Lie this way with your head right here."

He follows my command, and I squat down over his waiting lips, pulling my bikini bottoms to the side. His tongue slides deep inside me, and I smash down a little too hard, feeling his teeth on my sensitive skin. His moans mix with the waves crashing on the shore. I close my eyes, basking in the heat, the sounds of the ocean, and his talented tongue licking me everywhere.

Suddenly, I remember I need to keep an eye out for anyone coming close. I look left, then right, then toward the houses, and we're still in the clear. I gyrate my hips over his industrious mouth and tongue. I feel the heat rising up in my loins as I move closer and closer to an imminent, earth-shattering orgasm.

My eyelids flutter closed. Reminding myself once again to keep watch, I force them open, grinding harder and harder over him. I run a hand down to my breasts, slipping fingers under my bikini top to squeeze my nipple hard. I groan and move my other hand to my clit, gently rubbing, then harder and harder as he works his tongue all over my pussy.

All at once, I find my release with my leg muscles tingling and my body trembling, and I collapse over his face. My body shudders, my clit pulsates in his mouth, and my loud screams most certainly are drowned out by the roar of the ocean. I look down to see his eyes opened wide, appearing as if he's in some distress. I'm surely suffocating him, but I'm powerless to move. He brings his hands up to my thighs and gently coaxes me off of him.

"Oh my God," I mutter while down on all fours, struggling to recover and breathe.

When I finally turn to him, his trunks are completely down, and his cock is completely up.

I raise a finger. "I think I need a minute."

"Seriously?"

"I need a water too. Could you grab me one?"

"Um, do you think I should leave the tent like this?" He motions to his groin.

"Who told you to take your suit all the way off?"

"I won't be able to come unless I'm fully naked. I think we

saw how that worked in the house. Sometimes, I need to spread my legs wide, and I can't do that if I've—"

"Jeez, you are really high-maintenance."

"Should we be having this discussion now? Remember, this was all your idea."

"I know; I know. I'm really wiped out now. I didn't realize how hot it was going to be out here. Maybe I should have let you go first."

"You think?!" He shoots me a look before nervously looking out all sides of the tent screens. "I think we need to hurry."

"Okay, okay." I slip out of the tent, grab an icy-cold water, and return inside, re-securing the door. I take a big, sloppy sip of water, and much of it flows down my chin and over my chest. I cringe. "That's really cold."

"Uh-huh." He rolls his eyes.

"Almost ready." I hold up a finger. Tilting back the bottle, I swallow a large gulp and am struck with intense pain behind my eyes. I close them, tilt my head forward, and rub my temple. "Ouch. Ouch. Ouch."

"Jesus, what the hell is it now?" He glares at me.

I look up at him. "Brain freeze."

"You've got to be kidding."

"No, I drank too fast."

"And I'm the high-maintenance one." He shakes his head, exasperated. "We're running out of time."

"It still hurts. What do I do?"

"I heard you can put your finger to the roof of your mouth." He demonstrates, mumbling the rest with his finger still lodged in his mouth, "Hld tit thr untl da pan gos avay."

"What?" I bug my eyes out of my head.

"I said to hold it there until the pain goes away."

"Oh." I follow his direction, and after a few seconds, the pain slowly dissipates. "That worked."

"Thank God." He positions himself, kneeling in the center of the tent as he keeps watch.

His manhood has only softened slightly, and I turn on my side at an awkward position and take it in my mouth.

I can't get a great angle on it, and I gag, backing away a moment to cough. "Sorry."

I begin again, and then as I attempt to adjust to a more comfortable position, I slip and inadvertently bite down on him.

"Ouch! Ah! Shit," he cries out.

I pull away from him. "Sorry about that."

He runs his hand over the injured area, tilting it up to examine it. "It's okay. It's okay."

I say, "Stand for a second."

"What? Why?"

"Just do it."

"All right."

Grumbling under his breath, he gets on his feet. I get on my knees to gauge the level of the windows with the position of his groin and frown.

"I really need you to be standing with me kneeling, but then people would be able to see what we're up to. Crap!"

"So, what do we do?"

I shake my hands, biting my lip. "I don't know. I guess I didn't think this through."

"What?"

"The logistics of how you took care of me just don't work with the angle of man parts, I guess."

He glares at me. "I can't believe you. That's why you wanted to go first. You knew this wouldn't work for me."

"That's not true." I sigh, exasperated. "Let's try it anyway," I say as I lie down flat on the blanket. "Here, sort of hover over me and put it in my mouth."

"What?" His forehead scrunches up.

"Like you're doing push-ups over me or something. Hurry up."

"Okay, okay."

"Just make sure you can still keep a lookout."

He slips down to his knees and inadvertently swipes sand over my side and neck. I brush it away.

Rising up on his toes and with his bulging arms locked, he positions himself over me. I take him into my mouth and go to work. It's hot, and I'm sweating, and my jaw is aching. I power through to please him but, at this point, mainly just to get this over with. He groans in pleasure, and I try to see his face, but cannot. His muscles are straining, and his back is arched. Grains of sand and beads of sweat fall onto my face and neck as I struggle to tighten my grip around his flesh and bring him to climax. I would add my hand to the pleasuring mix to assist him, but it's presently covered in sand and would not be good for his sensitive skin or, for that matter, the inside of my mouth.

Humming, licking, and sucking, I try to get him there faster. I tilt my head back, straining my eyes upward to try to get a look at his face. I'm now suddenly concerned he's not keeping a proper lookout. My mind goes to the beach police rolling up in their Jeep and poking their head in the tent. I picture the mugshot of my flushed face, covered in sand, sweat, and semen with my hair a complete mess.

Oh God, how did I get myself into this?

I struggle to speak with my mouth full of him. "Cn u c?"

"What?"

I repeat, "Cn u c?"

He pulls away from me, landing on his hip, causing sand to spray everywhere.

Frowning, I spit out some grains and look at him, shocked. "Did you finish?"

"No!"

"What happened? I was dying, but that was sorta working."

"I couldn't see, and I thought I heard something." He pops his head up to glance out of the tent.

"Yuck." Frowning, I brush sand from my face. "Is anyone out there?"

"No," he grumbles. "This is the worst blow job ever."

"Tell me about it. Try being on the giving end of this disaster."

"Well, the receiving end is no picnic either." He sighs. "Maybe we should just give this up and try it later when we're—"

"No, we've come this far. Let's just get this over with."

"Oh," he says, scowling and shaking his head. "That's exactly what you want to hear when you're getting a BJ."

Exhaling deeply, I take in the sight of his gorgeous and still-hard cock, and my expression quickly morphs from annoyed to sorry and lands on arousal. "I'm sorry. You are so sexy. I want to please you." I place a sandy hand on his knee.

He relaxes his shoulders. "I'm sorry too. So, what do we do? I feel like they're going to be down here any minute."

"Let me think." Suddenly, it comes to me, and my eyes brighten. "Do you see anyone?"

He looks all around. "No."

"Okay, stand up and spread your legs."

He follows my command, and his groin is just below the height of the window, so worst case, anyone might see the top of my head, but wouldn't really be able to tell what I was up to.

"Can you still keep watch?"

He cocks his head. "If I do this."

"Good. Do that." I move in front of him. "Spread your legs a little more."

He does.

"A little more."

He spreads further, and now, he's got them really wide, and his midsection is down pretty low. I'm sitting comfortably now, and the target area is right where I need it. I think he's still in a good position to keep watch. I grab the water bottle and pour some in my hand, then do my best to rinse them. Wrapping my hand around his manhood, I plunge my mouth over him, taking it nearly to the back of my throat.

He groans in pleasure. "Oh God, yes. That's it."

I move faster and faster over him. Sweat drips from my every pore. The heat is nearly unbearable as I lick and suck and jerk him. I reach up with my one free hand and squeeze his balls. He takes hold of my head, guiding me over his length. I can feel him throbbing and his cock pulsating as he nears his climax.

"Jesus fucking Christ." He falls back from me, right on his ass, scrambling to locate his swimsuit.

"What is it?"

"They're coming!"

"Shit."

I unzip the tent door, try to get out, and catch my foot on the bottom fabric. I fall face-first in the sand, my arms and legs akimbo. I'm spitting sand out of my mouth as he runs past me, still pulling up his swimsuit, making a beeline to the water. I attempt to brush myself off, then plop down into a chair just as he dives into the ocean.

My front is basically completely covered in sand due to the combination of lotion and sweat. It's all over my face and in my hair. I must look like a vanilla-frosted doughnut, freshly dipped in fine whiteish-yellow granules. Grabbing a water bottle from the cooler, I open it and shake it violently all over my face and body. In my haste, I've forgotten that it's icy cold and let out this ear-piercing scream when the water hits my chest.

That's when the golf cart pulls up, and John hops out in a panic. "What's wrong? Are you okay?"

"You scared me." I bug my eyes out at him. "I, uh, just spilled a little water, and it was very, very cold."

"It sounded like you were being murdered." He inspects me, horrified. "You're completely covered in sand."

"Well, I, uh ... Kyle thought it would be funny to bury me." I force a laugh.

"It's in your hair. You look like someone hit you in the face with a sandy cream pie." John turns his attention to Kyle in the ocean. "Where was he off too so fast?"

"Um, he, he ... well, we both had a couple of beers, and he really had to pee, so ..."

"Oh." He lays his towel over a chair.

"I'd better go wash off." Rising to my feet, I rush quickly toward the water.

The water is fairly cold, and once I get knee deep, I attempt to splash water up to the rest of my body to rinse the sand. I'm shivering, and it's not working well. Kyle is twenty feet farther out, so I tiptoe my way toward him gingerly, letting my body adapt to the temperature while gritting my teeth.

When I reach Kyle, his mouth drops open. "Your face! What the fuck happened to you?"

"I, uh, had a little mishap." Standing chest deep, I attempt to wash off the *sticky lotion and sand* paste mixture from my shoulders and arms, but it's not coming off easily. "Shit."

"It's in your hair and everything."

"I know; I know."

"Are we okay?"

"I think so."

"What did you tell them?"

"I, um ..." I close my eyes before admitting, "That you buried me in the sand."

"That I buried you?" He twists his face.

"What? No good?"

"Buried you? What are we, eight?"

"Sorry."

"It's not great, but I guess you can't change it now. Why didn't you just say you fell?" He widens his eyes. "You know, the truth."

"I panicked." I raise my shoulders apologetically. "And he asked why you were running."

"Oh my God, what did you say?" he asks, alarmed.

"Um, I said you had to pee really badly."

"Okay."

"Oh, and I told him we'd had a couple beers each."

"What?!" He scoffs.

"What's wrong with that?"

"What if he packed the cooler and looks in there and knows the count?"

"He's not some sort of inventory control freak." I sigh. "I'll take care of it when I get up there."

He cocks his head, frowning. "You know, you're not very good at making up stories."

"I'm sorry. I'm sorry. But you took off and left me there. Again, I panicked."

"Don't worry." He moves to me, picking a large clump of sand from my hair. "You should dunk your head under."

"We've got to stop taking these risks. We're playing with fire."

"I know, but if I don't come soon, my head is going to explode."

"I'm so sorry." I turn toward John and Kate, force a smile, and wave. Luckily, they aren't watching. "Maybe we can slip off to your mother's rental one day."

Kyle grits his teeth with a fake smile toward our tent and

complains, "I'm not going to last one day. I need to take care of this sooner than that."

"Tonight, I promise I'll come to your room and take care of you properly when everyone is asleep."

"Okay, sure, sorry." He dips down in the ocean until the water reaches his chin. "I found out that we can't use the rental. I went by there the other day and saw a couple using it."

"That stinks," I say as a wave rolls past me, lifting me up. When my feet return to the sand, a thought hits me. "Oh, damn."

"What?"

"I just realized how this could have worked better. I needed to be buried in the sand a few feet, and then you could have knelt down and—"

"So, we just needed a shovel and maybe an hour of prep work." He chuckles.

"I guess that's not a practical idea."

We share a laugh, and he says, "I knew I shouldn't have let you go first."

"Sorry again. I will make it up to you."

"Maybe we should stick to the air-conditioned comfort of the house and not try to give ourselves a heart attack or end up on the local news."

I laugh, and he turns away, diving into the water.

Chapter 34

The Storm before the Calm

I stir awake and fight to get my bearings. For a few moments, I'm unsure where I am. It's hot, windy, I feel sandy and just a little tipsy. I'm staring up at the roof of the tent. The sound of the ocean mixes with laughter and chitchat from outside. Did I dream that Kyle and I were doing all sorts of inappropriate things in this hidden yet still dangerously public place? No, crap, that actually happened. The rest is coming back to me now.

***

When I returned from my attempt at cleansing myself in the water, John was heading toward the ocean, and Kate was engrossed in a novel. I grabbed four beers from the cooler and snuck them into the tent.

Now, I'll preface this next part by pointing out that, in my defense, I haven't been thinking all that clearly as of late. Maybe you've noticed. With all the sex, sneaking around, and near misses, plus the horniness, for lack of a better term, I haven't quite been my sane, professional, MD-accredited self. In a manner of speaking, I've let my hair down, and with it, all logic, reason, and good judgment went out the window. Cut me some slack. I've been through a lot in the last two-plus decades. Not to mention that the madness has really heated up recently with my mother, my father, and this hot, sexy young guy I've fallen into lust with. In short, I'm a big, hot mess.

Without fully working out my plan, I twisted open a beer and guzzled it. My thought was that John might be expecting to smell more than just ocean and seaweed on me if he got close. I'm pretty much a lightweight when it comes to drinking, but after some struggle, I was able to finish the entire bottle. Then, I looked out the tent to confirm that Kate was still preoccupied and that John was in the ocean, and I popped open the second beer. Three-quarters through it, I realized I was an idiot and that I had other viable options. After digging a small hole in the sand, I poured the last of my beer and the remaining two beers into it, safely covering my tracks. From there, I just had four beer bottles to deal with. I spotted the recycling bag just outside the tent and stealthily deposited them.

* * *

And now, as I continue to fight my way back from both sleepiness and tipsiness, I get to my feet and spot my three travel companions in chairs outside the tent. Kate is still reading, John appears to be sleeping, and Kyle turns to me, looking cool in his sunglasses with his ridiculously fit body. My heart thumps a bit faster as I flash back to the recent goings-on in the tent. I'd never before ridden a man's face like that. The way I could control the pressure and location of his attention was mind-blowing. I make a mental note to revisit that position again and very soon.

I take the open chair between my sleeping husband and my lover, then slip on my sunglasses. Kyle slides his large foot over to mine and suggestively teases me with his pinkie toe. I'm momentarily concerned as I check John and Kate, but it's safe, as his mother is at the wrong angle to see what we're up to.

Suddenly, it hits me—*his mother.* Holy shit, I'm having sex with her son and under her roof. I mean, I've known that I'm a horrible person for doing this, but it's really shaking me to my core now. I'm just awful. She's one of my good friends, and I'm the worst. I move my foot away from Kyle's, and he turns to me with his lip twisting.

Leaning in, he whispers, "Are you okay?"

"I'm fine," I lie, but I'm not fine. I'm having a mini panic attack, and I'm tipsy, hot, dehydrated, and very quickly losing my mind. "Could you hand me a water?"

Kyle grabs a water from the cooler and a beer for himself. He pops the top and takes a swig.

I sip my water, then lean over and whisper, "Remember, that's your third."

Lifting his sunglasses up, he mouths the word *what* and gives me a look like I'm nuts.

He's right. I am nuts. Why did I just tell him that? Do I think someone is monitoring the exact amount of his alcohol intake? And who would that person be, and why would they do that? Is someone going to hook him up to a polygraph and question him on this? Jeez, I'm losing it.

"Sorry, I-I ..." I rise to my feet and take another large sip from the bottle.

"Are you okay?"

"Yes. I'm just, uh, going for a walk." Turning on my heel, I rush toward the water, fighting to get there through the deep sand. When I reach the edge, a wave laps over my feet, and I look down to the foam hanging on to my ankles as it recedes.

I turn right and head south on this nearly deserted beach for what's called The Point, the tip of the island where the Atlantic meets the Bogue Inlet. It's supposed to have the best views on the island, especially at sunset. However, my mind is elsewhere, and all I can think is that I need to get off this fucking island and back to my practice, where I look at penises all day, every day. Not sexy, large, erect, mouthwatering penises, but wrinkly, veiny, sometimes-smelly, old ones. Ones that aren't hanging deliciously down from godlike frames. Ones attached to middle-aged bodies, where the bulbous stomach sometimes needs to be lifted just to gain proper medical access.

I drain the last of my water just as I reach The Point. Taking a deep breath, I bask in the beauty of it all. It's breathtaking at this time of midday, and if this is any indication of what's to come, I must return to experience the sunset. Slowly, I spin to look at the large and gorgeous houses behind me, then back to the emerald green water of the ocean, mixing and swirling with the blue of the water of the inlet to create gorgeous hues. I see the white foam of waves farther out and the ones crashing on the shore. The soothing sounds of the surf mix with the light breeze as I spot what looks like an island off to the right.

This view and my *just completed irrational, internal* meltdown of penises, both sexy and non-sexy patient ones, have taken the edge off. I feel better about it all. To be clear, I don't feel great, just better. I realize I'm still behaving in an immature and foolish way with my relationship with this much younger man, but I think I deserve this. My marriage is what it is, and I'm not violating the sanctity of it or going against any promises I made to John. I just need to continue to explore this but be a little more careful and not, for example, have sexual intercourse in a fitting room, other public places, or—let's say—a lounge chair by the pool. That seems like a reasonable compromise. I think I can handle this. I take another deep breath, and all at once, a calm washes over me. I realize I'm fine. I'm still here. I'm alive, and I'm just living my life.

A smile spreads over my face as I sit right in the sand at the edge where the waves are barely breaking on the shore. Extending my legs, I lean back with my eyes closed, enjoying the sunshine. I didn't mean to throw my patients' genitalia under the proverbial bus just now. Most of them are fine. I was simply venting. In fact, none of us are perfect, certainly not me, so I have no room to talk. But now that I gaze out at the gorgeous blue water and this incredible view, I realize this beach is perfect, and for that matter, so is Kyle. At least, he's exactly what I need right now.

* * *

I head back to the tent at ease and with a whole new outlook on things. My stress has almost entirely melted away, and I'm fairly certain it's not because I'm still a little tipsy and quite possibly suffering from some mild heatstroke.

When I reach Kyle, John, and Kate, I'm all smiles. "Have you guys seen how beautiful it is where the ocean meets the inlet down there?"

"I haven't," John replies.

Kate says, "It's been a few years, but I have. You should see the sunsets. I can't believe I haven't mentioned that. We should check it out one night."

"Let's all go tonight. We'll take some wine and enjoy the sunset." I bounce on my heels, smiling. "Come on."

"That sounds good," Kyle says.

"You seem to be in a better mood," John comments.

"I am. I really am. That walk did me some good. I feel ... I feel centered for the first time in a long time." I turn to Kate. "I want to thank you again for inviting us all down here. I desperately needed some time away. Living at my mother's condo has been crowded and a little too ... too ..." I search for the right word ... a little too pornographic? No, obscene. No ... how can I describe this without revealing to Kate that my mother is a ball-busting internet porn star? How about crushing? Yes. "Crushing. I mean, soul-crushing."

Kate smiles. "You're welcome, and we should do it again next year."

"We should."

Kate looks at her watch. "It's already getting kinda late. Doing the sunset sounds like a great idea. Why don't we go back, get cleaned up, have dinner, and get everything together to return before sunset?"

Chapter 35

Good Golly, Miss Molly

The first thing I notice when Kate pulls the golf cart under the house into the breezeway is a very tall blond man rubbing his hands together.

I study him curiously as Kate explains, "That must be one of your parents' masseurs. I told them they could do their couples massage down here. It's shaded and cool."

"Huh." I step out of the golf cart and take a few steps toward the shower. From that spot, I can see the very ends of both massage tables while the rest remains mostly hidden behind the lattice wall.

"Hello," the tall man greets me with a smile.

"Hi." I hang my towel on a hook outside the shower just as John and Kyle's golf cart pulls up. From this new vantage point, I see two pairs of legs and the second masseuse—another tall blonde, but this time a woman. She waves and smiles, and I return the gesture.

Looking closer, I discover to my horror that the geriatric clients are completely naked. Thank God they're lying face down on the table. At present, no *parts* whatsoever are in view since the masseurs are blocking my eyeline, now working from the foot of their tables.

I turn to Kate and whisper, "But did you say they could do it naked?"

"Not exactly, but there is a lot of privacy down here so ..." She tilts her head, cringing.

"Not nearly enough," I interject with an eyebrow raised.

We stare, frozen at the spectacle before us, although I'm not sure why. I guess it's like driving past an accident where you simply have to look. John and Kyle join us just as the masseurs move from their positions to the sides of their respective tables. That's when a hint of my father's unmentionable bits come into sight. I turn my attention to my mother instead, although the view is still problematic, as it is the crack of her backside.

Suddenly, we hear very aggressive moaning coming from both clients as their massages grow more intense, but certainly not sexual. To be clear, the masseurs' hands are nowhere near any erogenous zones.

Not even close.

I would think anyone within earshot could only assume there was a couple getting very busy down here.

The moaning somehow swells louder and more intense, and as I take in the faces of my fellow observers, I notice John and Kate's jaws are both hanging open while Kyle is wearing a smile. Sadly, we all need to rinse off in the shower before we return to the house, so we cannot venture too far away. With massage central right in front of where we need to be, we're simply trapped like animals.

"Oh God, yes," my mother groans softly. "Yes. Yes."

"That feels soooo good," says my father.

When I hear this exchange, my eyes widen in alarm, and I whisper, "Am I seeing things, or are these massages the furthest thing from sexual, but ..."

"I don't get it either," John replies.

"They must be really great masseurs," Kate says.

"I guess." John nods.

It's not until we hear the woman say in a thick accent, "Let us turn over now," that all four of us spin on our heel, averting our eyes from the spectacle.

"Um, who wants to rinse off first?" I ask.

In unison both, John and Kate say, "I do."

While shielding his eyes from the goings-on, John holds the shower door for Kate. Then, John and I slip away to stand behind the golf carts and out of danger. Kyle joins us a few seconds later, wearing a wide grin.

"Well, I *was* in a good mood." I frown.

The three of us stand together uncomfortably as Kate showers, the sound of which mostly drowns out—or at the very least masks—the inappropriately sexual noises pouring out from the spa area. When Kate eventually turns off the water, the loud and very peculiar moaning can again be heard.

"Right there. Oh yeah," my father groans with a throaty drawl.

Glancing back to the massage tables, I discover each masseur is simply working on their client's feet. I shake my head. "That must be some foot rub."

"Yeah, I'll have what he's having," John says.

John and I share a look. Then, once I spot Kate emerge from the shower, I rush toward it, shielding my eyes. After a quick rinse, I scurry back toward the men, passing John, who's heading my way. Wearing a subtle smile, I wish him good luck, and I'm out of there.

* * *

After getting showered and changed, John, Kate, and I stand in the great room, each enjoying a very strong gin and tonic. We haven't yet spoken about what we witnessed.

After a healthy sip, I'm the first to break the ice while staring out the window at the ocean. "When I close my eyes, I still see it—the dim lighting, the tall masseuses, the bottoms of their feet, and, uh"—I swallow hard—"other *unmentionable* stuff. Do you think that's what we have to look forward to as we age?"

"There are just some things that you can't unsee." John stares down at his feet.

"I don't think you really ever come back from that." Kate shakes her head. "You just accept that life is different now, and you move on."

"Uh-huh." I nod.

My parents appear at the top of the steps, wearing short robes and bright smiles.

He says in a tranquil voice, "You guys really should get massages. It will be my treat."

"I've never been more relaxed," she adds.

None of us reply. We instead watch as they slowly make their way toward us. Their eyes are heavy, and I don't think I've ever seen anyone so peaceful in all my life.

My father continues in his slow, serene, soothing tone, "I just want to say how happy I am that we are all here together. The house is beautiful. The beach is beautiful. You all are so beautiful."

I cringe. "Dad, are you okay?"

"I've never felt better."

"You sound a little, I don't know, off."

"Oh, that's probably the drugs." He looks to Candace, and they share a smile.

"The drugs?" I notice the tie on my father's robe appears loose and dangerously close to no longer doing its job.

"Yeah, it's the ecstasy. It affects the brain's chemistry by releasing a high level of serotonin, which plays a role in regulating mood."

"So, you're on ecstasy." I nod with my eyes wide. I look to John. "He's on drugs. My father's on drugs. Okay, the weirdness just went up a notch."

"We both are," Candace adds.

"Well, that's just super." I click my tongue, then take in the horrified expressions of John and Kate. "Okay."

Suddenly, my father's robe tie fails, exposing a little too much of him.

Looking down at my feet, I say, "Okay, Dad, a couple things. First, I'd appreciate it if, in the future, you weren't high on Molly in front of my son and the other kids. It doesn't send a great message."

"Well, I am a sexual being," Glenn replies.

"I understand. I understand." I gnaw at my lip, attempting to summon the strength, then finally plow ahead. "And while I can appreciate that and since you mentioned it, that leads me to my second point." While shielding my eyes, I point in the general direction of his groin. "You might want to close that robe."

"What's that?" My father looks down, which causes the robe to open even further.

"Okay!" Rushing over, I guide him to spin around. Just as Kyle reaches the top of the stairs, I say, "I think that's more than enough for today."

Upon noticing the still-wide-open robe, Kyle chuckles. "Mr. Glenn, watch out there. Looks like the weasel's about to escape from his cage."

Mumbling some incoherent obscenity, I tilt my head as far away as humanly possible while I re-secure his robe for him.

"Thank you for noticing, young man." My father turns back. "Oh, Kate ... that second photo shoot we were going to do—why don't we do that later today?"

Kate looks up, horrified. "Okay, um, I'll need to see what's happening later."

"Okay. Whatever works best for you." My father nods, wearing a relaxed smile, then turns to me, wrapping his arms around me. "I love you, honey."

"Love you too," I reply uncomfortably while refusing to return the hug.

He takes a step toward Kyle, opening his arms wide.

Placing my hand on his shoulder, I pull him back. "I think he'll take a rain check."

"Oh, okay." My father sighs. "Your mother and I are going to take a nap."

"Good idea," I grumble, running my hands through my hair as my parents make their way to the other side of the house.

We all share a *what the fuck* look and a few moments of silence.

"As a parent, you do everything you can to keep your kids off drugs, but you never think you'll have to steer your own parents away from them. Sheesh." I exhale deeply, then turn to Kate. "You might want to wait till he comes down off the Molly before you let him see you in lingerie again."

"Definitely." Kate takes a long sip of her cocktail.

"And you two might want to avoid him too." I look pointedly at the men. "There's no telling how touchy-feely he's going to be for the next few hours."

John and Kyle share a meaningful look before we all head out on the deck to enjoy the ocean view.

Chapter 36

The Perfect Sunset

After a takeout meal of burgers, fries, and milkshakes, we sit in the great room, patting our overfilled bellies. We got them from Hwy 55, this little regional fast-food chain right out on the main road. They were absolutely amazing. It's been by far the best restaurant meal we've had since arriving here. We discussed it and all agreed that nothing else compared. We've tried pizza, other takeout places, and even gone to a fancy restaurant out in Morehead City, North Carolina, and that was barely average at best and very expensive. There was something about those burgers and fries that satisfied me. Sometimes, you just need a greasy cheeseburger to feed your soul.

Maybe it's all the sex I've been having lately that has made me ravenous. Before I arrived here, I was starving for some physical attention and to feel attractive again. Kyle has given me that and then some, and now, this meal has made me even more satisfied.

The sun is about an hour from setting, and Kate prepared some fresh fruit, which we plan to take as a healthy snack to pair with a few bottles of wine John had picked up at the liquor store. The disastrous tent adventure and my parents' antics aside, it's turning out to be a near perfect day.

My mind keeps replaying the giant, earth-shattering orgasm I had out in the heat today as I ground myself into Kyle's hungry mouth. I gave serious thought to sneaking down to his room and trying for an encore, but it would have been too great a risk. Not to mention, I owe him something first, and I really want to take my time with it. My mouth has been watering with thoughts of him. It's been a long, long time since I've wanted to do something so intimate with a man. With Kyle, I don't think there is much that I wouldn't do—within reason, of course.

When I see him, I get all warm inside at my core. My knees get weak, and I want to touch him, feel him inside me, and please him. He's brought me back to life. My son is grown and off to college. He barely talks to me, and it seems like he doesn't really need me anymore. Outside of my career and my daughter, there hasn't been any passion in my life, and a life needs passion.

I'll admit that my lack there has all been my fault. John is a stable, attractive, and sexy man, who's always there when I need him, but as I said, I just couldn't let myself be happy. He's everything any woman my age would want in a partner. Although now, in the midst of this affair, I've found myself thinking about John more and more. Maybe when we're in the new house with a fresh start, things will be different. I'll be different. Because I know this affair with my young boy toy will end very soon, simply because it has to. But for now, I'm all in.

Maybe John won't want to get close to me. He won't want to be intimate again. I assume he's seeing another woman, and we don't speak about it. For all I know, they are in love and waiting for our daughter to go off to college so they can be together forever. I guess we'll see.

* * *

As we head out to The Point, I'm riding in one golf cart with John, Dave, and Morgan while Kyle drives the other, carrying his mother, along with the wine and fruit. It takes a good ten minutes to get to the edge of where the ocean meets the inlet, and it's a mildly warm but fairly windy evening. I can't imagine how exhausting it would be to make this journey on foot through the pristine, sandy white dunes. Kyle pulls ahead of us and flashes me a sexy grin, and all I can think about is what's to come later. I can hardly wait.

After laying out the two blankets, we pour the wine and enjoy the fruit as the sun nears the horizon. We all take in the glorious view. The bright reds mix with fiery oranges, vibrant yellows, and subtle blues, along with streaks of gray and white clouds reflecting over the glassy blue-green of the ocean. It's a breathtakingly beautiful symphony of color and undeniably romantic.

Tearing my eyes away from the gorgeous sight, I study John's face and smile. He really is a good man.

When I look at him, it makes me think of Rachel, our perfect daughter, born of this imperfect relationship. I wouldn't trade her or it for anything.

I wipe a tear from my eye. "I wish Rachel were here to see this."

"Me too." John smiles. "We'll bring her out when she gets here."

"She'll love it," I say. "But I understand from your parents that she's having so much fun at Disney that she doesn't want to leave, but hopefully, she will have had enough of the Magic Kingdom and be ready for the beach."

"Nine is a great age. I remember when Morgan was that age.

She actually liked me and would talk to me." Kate tips back her wineglass.

"Mom, jeez," Morgan groans. "That's not true."

"It is so."

"I might have talked to you, but as I recall, I wasn't such a big fan of you, even back then," Morgan says with a sly smile.

Kate scoffs. "I can't believe you would say that."

"Did you like your mother growing up?" Morgan asks pointedly. "From the stories you tell, I doubt it."

"Let's just say, I was a rebellious child, and I didn't exactly see eye to eye with my mother, but as I've aged, I have a new appreciation for parenting and some regrets for how I treated her." Kate cocks her head. "You might give all that some thought."

"Okay, Mom," Morgan grumbles.

"I'm not sure I'm ready for her to become a teenager. That's going to do me in," I say with my voice cracking. I cover my mouth, and more tears slide down my cheeks.

John studies my face. "I don't think I've seen you this emotional since last year. Watching that movie about the girl with the deaf parents. What was that called again?"

"*CODA*," I say. "At the end, when the daughter sings that Joni Mitchell song, 'Both Sides Now,' in front of the panel—oh, wow. Once she starts signing to the parents, I lose it."

"Oh, I know." Kate sips from her glass.

"I enjoyed that too." John asks, "Did that win Best Picture?"

"It did," Kate replies. "Hey, we should watch a movie tonight."

"We should." I take a bite of mango, and it's so juicy and good. It makes me think about kissing Kyle—and even more. I glance at him as he lies back on the blanket and looks skyward.

"Morgan and I are going out tonight, but you guys have fun," Dave says.

"I'm meeting some friends," Kyle begins. "But I should be back around *two*."

When I look over to him, he's staring right at me, and with the way he said *two* and the fact that he mentioned the time at all, I know it's a coded message just for me. It causes my heart to race, and I feel a warmth flood my body.

Wow, the effect he has on me is unlike anything I've felt in a long time.

"You guys be careful. No drinking and driving," Kate says, then holds out her wineglass to John for a refill, wearing a smile. "But I'm not driving."

After taking in the last rays of sunlight over the horizon while draining two bottles of wine, we head back to the house.

Chapter 37

How Long Does Ecstasy Last?

After returning from the most beautiful sunset in the history of sunsets, Kyle, Dave, and Morgan head out for the night. I hadn't seen my parents since the massage and subsequent open-robe incident. I assume they're either sleeping, having sex, or out, trying to score some more drugs. I'm not sure which would be worse, but I'm just glad that I've gotten a little break from them tonight.

Kate, John, and I sit in the great room to select a movie to watch. We land on this odd film called *The Menu*, and I'm a bit preoccupied during most of it, so I can't tell you whether it's good or bad. There is this interesting scene where the chef prepares the perfect cheeseburger, and I find my eyes are glued to the screen.

Maybe I'm so moved by this burger preparation because I am trying to steer my thoughts away from my upcoming night with Kyle. Since he went out, my mind's been wandering to what's to come, and it's been hard to focus on anything else for very long.

At around one a.m., the three of us decide to call it a night as we struggle to remain conscious while watching some home renovation show on HGTV. Dave and Morgan have returned home safely and retired to their rooms while Kyle is still out. John climbs into bed while I take a bath and shave my legs, along with pretty much everything else below my waist for my young lover to enjoy.

I return to the room to find John once again snoring lightly in a deep sleep. I slip into a bra and panties. Sitting on a chair, I watch the clock advance minute by minute as I wait for two o'clock to roll around, and my thoughts are all over the place. I'm missing my daughter and anxious to see her on Sunday. I'm worried about our upcoming malpractice insurance renewal and how much it might go up this year. I'm thinking about John and what a good father he's been to our daughter and the son he sacrificed his own life to help raise. I'm feeling a little guilty, but again, I don't know what John's own situation truly is, and I need to let this affair with Kyle play out at least for the next few days.

When the clock hits four minutes after two, I poke my head out the door, see that it's clear, then make my move toward the stairs and down to the first floor. I open the door to find Kyle lying in bed, wearing only boxer shorts. His hair looks damp, and steam emanates from the bathroom, so I can tell he's prepared himself for me.

I lock the door and turn to him. "How was your night?"

"Not quite as good yet as your father's." Grinning, he motions with a few head nods toward the window.

"What do you mean?"

"Check it out."

Peering through the blinds, I spot two shadowy figures in the hot tub. It's dimly lit, but I can make out exactly who they are and exactly what they're up to.

"Jesus, why did you send me there? And for the love of God, how long does ecstasy stay in your system?"

"I don't know, but do you think he'd hook us up with some?" He flashes me a sexy smile.

"I don't think you need any," I say, and we share a laugh. "I hope Dave and Morgan don't see them."

"Don't worry; their rooms face the front of the house."

"That's true."

"Hey, did your father do another bedroom photo shoot with my mom tonight?"

"No, and with what's going on in the hot tub, I'm glad."

Smiling, he shakes his head.

"What is it?" Sitting on his bed, I place my hand on his knee as my gaze roams over his body.

"Nothing. I was just thinking of something stupid. Forget it."

"No, tell me."

"So, when I was out tonight, I had a weird thought about those two and the bizarre picture taking. It's crazy and silly and—"

"Spit it out." I squeeze his foot playfully.

"Oh my God, so what if those two got together—you know, like fell in love or something?"

"Eww. What? Gross."

"No, hear me out."

"If they started screwing, then there would be some crazy—what would they call it—multigenerational or intergenerational something ... you know, since he'd be screwing her, and you and I are—"

"Wait, you make it sound like incest or something." I cringe. "I don't think those are the right words to use. It's called a May-December romance or an age-gap relationship."

"You're right ... but—but what if they got married?" His eyes brighten. "That would make him my stepfather and you, my stepsister."

"What is wrong with you?"

He takes in my disgusted look. "I told you it was stupid, and I tried to warn you."

"Jeez, why are you telling me these things? I already feel a little weird without you making it even weirder."

"I think the whole stepsister fantasy is pretty hot. It's my go-to porn when I want to, you know ..." He cocks his head and smiles.

"Okay." I raise a hand, holding back a laugh. "I think we've had enough sharing for one night. The way you men think sometimes just floors me."

"I just like the forbidden fantasy type of stuff."

Motioning between the two of us, I cock an eyebrow. "And this isn't forbidden enough for you? I need to be both nearly twice your age *AND*, by some super-bizarre twist of fate, be your stepsister?"

"No, you're right. You're right. This is plenty forbidden." He smiles. "But what about you? Don't you have any fantasies?"

"I do, but they aren't as complicated, involving relatives marrying other relatives and super deranged, like, whatever the hell you just told me."

"Okay, okay." He runs a hand slowly over my back. "Let's forget I told you that and you tell me about yours."

"Some things you can just never unknow." I shake my head, putting on a mock frown.

We share a smile before I pause a moment to get serious as the sexy memory comes flooding back.

Turning to look him in the eye, I moan softly with my eyelids dipping closed. "When I was hovering over your mouth in that tent, it was hot—and not just because it was freaking hot. I mean, I had the biggest orgasm of my life."

"You did?"

"Hmm," I purr.

"My jaw still hurts a little." He rubs his chin. "But we can definitely do that again."

I run my hand slowly up his thigh to the bulge in his boxer shorts. "But first, I believe I promised to take care of you."

"That's right; you did." He leans his head back and exhales.

"And I've been thinking about you all day and all night. Since the tent." I slip off the bed and remove my shirt, revealing my semi-sexy bra.

"Me too."

Devouring him with my eyes, I lick my lips and say softly, "I want to feel it grow in my mouth."

"Uh-huh," he mutters, his eyes never leaving mine.

Pushing my shorts down my legs slowly, I say, "I want to make you come over and over."

I take hold of his boxer shorts, and as he lifts his hips slightly off the bed, I pull them down. His already fully hard erection stands at attention.

I frown, disappointed. "So much for growing in my mouth."

"Please just do it already." He motions to me with his hand. "You look so hot, and I'm dying here."

Wrapping my hand around his cock, I slowly stroke him up and down, swiping a huge drip of pre-cum from the head and smearing it over the tip. "I guess I'll just have to feel him grow in my mouth during round two."

"Oh fuck," he moans.

"Come to the edge of the bed," I command.

He does, then leans back with his hands resting behind him as he watches me without blinking.

I move between his legs, kneeling on the floor with my hands resting on his thighs. His huge cock stands straight, thick and throbbing with every beat of his heart. Leaning forward, I place a soft kiss on the tip, then swirl my tongue around it.

His eyes roll to the back of his head. "That feels so fucking good."

I lick my lips. "You taste so fucking good."

"I can't wait any longer. I'm either going to come in, like, thirty seconds or die."

Grinning, I plunge over him, taking half his length into my mouth.

"Oh God, Ally."

I suck hard, swallowing more of his juice, and purr with delight. Without using my hands, I work him over with my lips, mouth, and tongue as he groans in pleasure. I feel him swell even larger as I move faster and faster over him.

He collects my hair, pushing it to one side, and I tilt my head, sliding my mouth slowly up and down his shaft. His eyes lock with mine as I swipe my tongue over his balls.

I run my tongue to the tip and swipe it again before taking just the head between my lips and sucking hard. He groans. Rising higher, I wrap one hand around the base and stroke him with my other hand while I plunge my mouth up and down on him.

"I'm going to come."

I don't skip a beat as I pick up the pace, tilting my head a bit so I can meet his gaze.

"I'm going to ... come," he repeats while looking me in the eye, as if to warn me.

I stare right back at him, grinning and moaning like I want it. I don't need a warning. I want to feel him throb and swell and explode in my mouth.

Gripping the sheets behind him, he tenses every muscle in his body as he lifts his hips slightly off the bed. I take too much of his length into my mouth and nearly gag but then power through, reaching up to cup his balls with one hand and stroke him with the other. That sends him over the edge. His cock swells, and he explodes.

It's way too much for me. I've never done this before, so I pull away from him with my eyes watering and him leaking from my mouth as I keep running my hand along his length. He lies back, twitching and writhing on the bed until he can no longer take it.

Suddenly, he covers my hand with his and coaxes me to stop. "Oh fuck. That was ... amazing."

I wipe my mouth and place my head on his thigh, studying his slowly shrinking erection. "I guess it does get soft ... eventually."

He cranes his neck off the bed. "After that, yeah."

"Your cock is so sexy."

I grin, then take hold of him and suck his head into my mouth. He flinches and white-knuckle grips the edge of the mattress with both hands.

"Oh, Ally."

He's a bit soft and floppy but still thick as I gently lick, suck, and pleasure him between my lips. He grows bigger and harder as I move faster over him.

He rakes his fingers through my hair. "I have to taste you again. Now."

I ignore his request, redoubling my efforts. Lifting my mouth off of him, I circle the head with my tongue over and over as I stroke him furiously.

"Yes," he groans.

My jaw aches, and my arms are tired, but I keep going and going. Finally, he places his fingers on my chin, coaxing me off. He stands before me, extending a hand to get me to my feet. Leaning down, he moves his lips to mine, sliding his tongue into my mouth and kissing me hard as he runs his fingers through my hair.

He pulls back, looking me in the eye. "You are amazing."

"Gee, thanks." I smile bashfully.

"I'm serious."

Reaching behind me, he expertly unclasps my bra, and it slides to the floor. He kneels before me, taking hold of my panties and slipping them down my legs, and I kick them aside. He slides back on the bed and lies flat with his hand extended to mine. I take hold of it, and he guides me to straddle his chest, where he reaches up and gently massages my breasts.

Leaning back, I groan as his fingers work their magic on my chest, over my nipples, then slowly down to my core. He slides his hands under my bottom, gently lifts me up, and slips further under me before slowly depositing me right over his waiting mouth.

The moment his tongue slips inside of me, I groan in pleasure. "Mmm."

I watch, enchanted, as his lips and tongue explore my every inch and fold. Circling my hips, I grind them slowly over his face, adjusting my pressure and location as he works me into a frenzy. His hands cup the cheeks of my ass, and I feel him brush a finger under me, then slide it into my pussy. He takes to sucking my clit and sliding his finger deeper inside of me, and suddenly, my orgasm washes over me.

Biting a knuckle to suppress my screams, I writhe over him, bucking up and down as wave after wave rolls through my core. I try to pull away from him, but he grips my thighs, making it impossible for me to move. He presses his tongue deep into me and swirls it all around. The pain mixes with pleasure, as my skin is much too sensitive from all the attention. He places one last kiss on my pussy, then releases his grip on my body. I slip away from him to safety.

He reaches for me, and I gently slap him away. "Just wait."

"Your pussy tastes so good."

"I just had the biggest orgasm," I say breathlessly.

"Let me know when you're ready for another."

After catching my breath, I straddle him once again, positioning my center over his stomach, and grind my body slowly into his. Reaching behind me, I grasp his soft cock and run my fingers over the head. The feel of his silky-smooth thickness has me longing to once again take it in my mouth. I flip over and maneuver back with my hips over his face and quickly suck his cock between my lips. He's fully hard in no time, and he pulls my hips down firmly to his waiting mouth and begins slowly devouring my pussy as I do the same to his gorgeous cock. Soon, we're both coming hard again, and this time, I keep working my mouth over him. He's twitching and writhing under me until he can no longer take it, and he gently guides me away. I slip off of him, exhausted, panting, and struggling to catch my breath.

* * *

Resting my head on his chest, I run my hand softly over his skin while drifting in and out of sleep. He's lightly brushing the back of my neck, and it's sending tingles down my spine. I twirl the trail of hair down his stomach between my fingers.

Suddenly, my eyes pop open wide. My thoughts are on Rachel and not this torrid affair. I lift up from him, exhaling sharply.

"What is it?"

"My daughter's going to be here on Sunday."

"Yeah, I heard you mention that." He slides his hand down my lower back to the cleft of my ass and massages my cheeks.

"When she gets here, this is going to have to stop. She sometimes climbs into bed with John and me in the middle of the night."

"I understand."

"We'll have two more nights together if you want them," I say as our eyes meet.

"Oh, I want them."

I turn to look at the clock. "I should get back."

"I wish you could stay."

"Me too." I pull up from him and slip off the bed, letting my eyes roam once more over his sexy, naked body. "Yeah, me too."

Chapter 38

Good Talk, Dad

After washing away all the evidence of my encounter with Kyle from my body, I slip into bed next to John. It's just before four a.m. I've been running on six hours of sleep or less for the last few days, but I've never felt more alive or more full of energy.

I wake around ten and make my way down to the kitchen, where I find my father sitting out on the deck. Grabbing a cup of coffee, I join him outside. "Morning, Dad."

"Hey, Ally."

I narrow my eyes, holding back a smile. "So, how are you feeling?"

"You know, coming off that ecstasy is not fun." He blows out a long, slow breath. "I gotta say that being on it is enjoyable, but the other side ain't so great. I feel a bit anxious and have a headache."

I cock an eyebrow and say in a mocking tone, "I wonder if that's why it's illegal."

"Could be. Could be."

"You know, Dad, that's part of what I wanted to talk to you about. I tried to be supportive when you started your sexy photography business and didn't really object when you put on some sort of erotic massage workshop below the house."

"I appreciate that."

"But Rachel's going to be here soon, and we've got other young people in the house. I don't think it sets a good example for you to be doing illegal drugs in front of everyone. If you want to experiment when you're home, that's one thing, but not in front of the kids, okay?"

"You're right. That was a little too much."

"Yeah, just a tad." I take a sip from my mug, and then my eyes widen. "There is one other thing."

"What's that?"

"Oh, and banging Mom in the middle of the night in the hot tub is probably not a great idea either."

"You saw that? I thought we were quiet."

"We did see that—I mean, I saw that," I correct myself.

He sips from his coffee cup, then gives me a curious look. "How did you? Your room doesn't face the pool, and it was late."

"Oh, um, I was up. I couldn't sleep. I heard some noise and spotted you from the back door."

"Ah, yeah, sorry about that. I promise, no more of that. The drug can make you do some crazy things."

"I can imagine."

"I'm going in, and I think I'll take an aspirin."

"I hope you feel better."

"Thanks."

"Good talk, Dad."

"I'm glad we had it too." Rising to his feet, he smiles and gives my shoulder a squeeze before heading into the house.

* * *

Kyle is spending the day with friends, and John is taking a break from golf, as the temperature is forecasted to reach one hundred degrees. We head to the beach with Kate, Morgan, and Dave, packing the cooler with lots of water to drink, leaving the beer and wine at home for a change.

John and I drag our chairs down to the water, and the waves lap at our feet. That, along with the slightly cool breeze off the ocean, brings us some much-needed relief from the blazing sun.

John says, "Maybe we should have bought a beach place instead of building the dream house."

"This is nice." I splash the cool ocean water onto my legs. "So relaxing."

"Yeah." He turns to look at me. "You seem really happy down here."

I shrug. "I haven't thought about work much in a few days. I miss Rachel terribly, but I know she's in good hands and having a blast."

"And Izzie?"

"Yes, I miss her too. I FaceTimed with Laurie the other day, and baby girl was running around like a lunatic with the other dogs. She didn't seem to miss us at all."

"I'm sure she'll be crying and wiggling like crazy when she sees you again."

"I know."

"I'm so tired today," he says.

"So am I."

Our feet are brushing against one another in the water, and I watch as his pinkie toe slips over my foot and slides down between my toes. It feels nice. I can't recall us ever playing footsie like this before. I lean back and close my eyes, enjoying the feel of his big, thick toes invading mine. It's sorta sexual, and I find myself feeling aroused. Lifting my foot up, I slide it over his, performing the same move on him. My head bobs forward, and I catch myself from falling asleep. In that moment, I'm not sure if I'm sitting next to John or Kyle.

Opening my eyes, I spot his hand moving closer to mine with his pinkie reaching out. When it finally brushes my skin, he pulls it away, along with his foot. "Sorry, I'm falling asleep out here."

"Yeah, me too."

He rises to his feet. "I feel like I'm starting to burn. I think I need some more lotion."

After a long day at the beach, we return to the house. We shower and change and then relax before heading out to dinner. My parents decide to have a date night, and with Kyle still out, the rest of us go out for a meal. When we return home, it's such a nice night that we sit down by the pool, drinking and talking, while Dave and Morgan alternate between the hot tub and the pool. I receive a text message from Kyle that he's definitely going to be home by two and that he's been thinking of me all day. This sends a chill down my spine and butterflies in my belly as I fantasize of what the night might bring.

I drink maybe two more glasses of wine, and John and I retire up to our room around one o'clock. After a bath, I lounge in bed, surfing Facebook and Netflix. I glance at the clock every five minutes or so in anticipation. I don't find anything that holds my attention, so I switch to my reading app and start a new novel.

I nod off to sleep a couple times and will myself to stay awake, sitting up straighter in bed. That's the last thing I remember.

I'm trapped in a dream—or at least, I think it's a dream. I'm straddling Kyle, and he's deep inside me. Rising up and down, I gyrate my hips slowly over him as he gently cups my breasts. It's wonderful, and I'm nearing climax. He slides his hand down to my clit and brushes a finger over me.

"Oh God," I groan.

Leaning back, I place my hands on his T-shirt-covered stomach and increase my rhythm over him.

"Oh, Ally," he moans.

"Oh fuck," I mutter, but it's an *oh no* fuck, not an *oh, yes* fuck, as I realize I'm actually awake, and I'm riding John and not Kyle.

He's not looking at me, but I don't think he's asleep or dreaming. He must be awake. I, on the other hand, must have been dreaming when I climbed on top of my husband. At least, that's my story, and I'm sticking to it. Although now that I'm fully awake and still gyrating my hips over him, what's my excuse?

I look to the clock, and it's past three. I'm not sure if I should stop or keep going, but he's moaning and groaning under me and grabbing my ass with his eyes still closed. He's definitely close. I feel him swell, his thickness throbbing inside me. I'm close, too, and it feels way too good to stop.

Suddenly, he stiffens, and his whole body tenses under me as he takes hold of my hips, pulling me closer. I feel the gush inside, then one last thrust, and that sends me over the edge.

"Oh," I groan and collapse over him, my head resting on his chest.

He rakes his fingers through my hair, and we lie there, motionless and silent, but still connected at our cores.

When he slips from me, I fall over to my side of the bed, curling up with my pillow. Lying there, I try to process that I missed my night with Kyle and instead had sex with John for the first time in more than ten years. John and I don't speak or touch, but he shifts positions on his side of the bed. I feel his warm breath on my neck, and his fingers brush the skin of my lower back for only a second before he pulls away.

After a few minutes with my head spinning, I roll onto my

back and look out of the corner of my eye at my husband who's now turned fully away from me and breathing in a soft, steady rhythm. I attempt to recall how exactly this happened and whether John or I initiated. Since I was on top and I'm not wearing anything while he's still in his T-shirt, I think the evidence is clear. Any court would find me guilty.

Grabbing my phone, I discover four texts from Kyle, starting at one fifty, each spaced about five minutes apart.

Kyle:
I'm back.
Where are you?
I guess you fell asleep.
My door is always open.

I consider going down to see him or texting him back, but I know I shouldn't dare do either.

Chapter 39

I'd Settle for PG-13

When I wake, John is still asleep next to me. I quietly get out of bed and get dressed in some sweats, then slip out of the room. The house is silent, and it seems like no one is up. It's a little before eight, and when I reach the second floor, I spot my father outside on the deck, but he doesn't see me. I head down to the first floor and tiptoe my way to Kyle's room.

At the door, I press my ear to it and don't hear a thing. Cringing, I turn the knob and slowly push it open, stepping inside until I'm able to crane my neck around the interior wall to find him sleeping. I'm actually glad since I haven't really thought of what to say. The truth seems like the best option, which is that I fell asleep, but should I share the entire truth about what happened after?

I think I'll need a second opinion. Retracing my steps, I slip out of his room, then open the door to the pool area, where a cool breeze washes over me. Stopping at the outdoor refrigerator, I grab a water bottle, then head down the wooden trail toward the dunes. I slip off my shoes and leave them there before walking through the sand toward the ocean, taking sips along the way. When I finally make it past the dunes, I sit down in the sand and can barely hear the waves breaking on the shore. Pulling out my phone, I FaceTime Laurie.

Her grinning face appears on the screen. "You're up early."

"I have to tell you something. I had sex last night."

"So, you called to brag." She chuckles.

"No, I had sex last night with ... with John."

"No way."

"Yes." I close my eyes and sigh.

"Correct me if I'm wrong, but didn't you do it the night before and the night before that with Kyle?"

"Can I plead the Fifth on that?"

"You slut, you!" she squeals.

"I'm the worst." I rub a hand over my face.

Laurie pauses a moment, then asks, "Was it at least not the same calendar day when you slept with them both?"

"What?" I ask, puzzled.

"I'm asking if it happened in the same day."

"I don't know. I'm—"

"So, last night, did you do it with John before or after midnight?"

"Definitely after."

"Whew." She wipes a pretend bead of sweat from her forehead.

"Why does that matter?"

"It matters, my friend, because if you'd slept with John before midnight, it would have been in the same calendar day as Kyle, and you would have slept with two guys in one day and officially become a whore and not just a slut."

"Oh, is that how it works, huh?" I glare at the screen, then take a drink.

"I'm kidding, but don't you think it's a little better that you didn't bang them both out on the same Friday?"

"I guess, but I still feel like shit."

"How was it?" she asks, eyes twinkling.

"I'm not sure. I was sorta dreaming at first, I think. I mean, I didn't mean to do it. It just happened." I scrunch my nose up. "The worst part is that I think I initiated it."

"So, you fucked your husband." She shrugs. "Shit's bound to happen once in a while when you sleep in the same bed with the same guy for ten years."

"And I think I thought I was with Kyle while it was happening, so that makes it, like, ten times worse. Don't you think?" I drain the rest of my bottle, then wipe my mouth with my hand.

"Maybe." She grins with her eyebrows raised. "Tell me. Which one is better?"

"What?"

"Which one is better in bed?"

My jaw drops open. "I'm not telling you that. I don't think I—"

"Fine, so which one is bigger?"

"I'm going to ignore that question."

"You're no fun."

After giving her a withering look, I ask, "So, how's Izzie?"

"So, we're changing the subject, are we?"

"For now, until you get your mind out of the gutter and actually try to help me?"

"She's perfect. She's actually curled up with all her friends right now. They exhausted themselves, running around the yard yesterday." Laurie swings the camera around to the four dogs of varying sizes sleeping all around her in the bed.

"Oh my God, they are so cute."

"They are." Laurie's face returns to the screen. "I think I need a bigger bed though."

"Probably," I say, and we share a laugh.

We stare at one another in silence for a few seconds until I sigh and finally say, "I don't know what to do."

"Okay, so we're back on your harem of men."

"Really? Are you going to keep making jokes?"

She cocks her head. "Actually, I think you need a minimum of three to be a harem."

"That's funny," I say in a tired voice.

"Look, I have very few people to talk to in my life. You want to see what my life is? Here, look ..." She flips the phone around, and the screen fills with the mugs of four scruffy, adorable dogs sitting upright, panting with their tongues hanging out of their adorable little mouths. "This is my life. They start this crap as soon as they get up, and they won't stop staring at me until I take them for a ..." She mouths the word *walk*.

"They're so cute." I place a hand over my heart. "You're so lucky you have all of them."

Laurie's face reappears on the screen. "Lucky? Yeah, you try bringing eight poop bags with you on a ..." She mouths *walk* again. "Yes, eight because, sometimes, they each need two. Then, trying to corral four dogs while you pick up their mess is an adventure. It's not easy, and it's not fun."

"I can imagine."

"But they're perfect, and I love them," she says.

"I know."

She flips her hair out of her face. "So, what the hell was my point? Oh, I know. I mostly interact with dogs. There are no decent men in my life, and you are currently blessed with two. So, shoot me for having the nerve to ask for a few little spicy details."

"All right. I'm sorry."

"Give me one interesting nugget about either one of them. It doesn't have to be X-rated. I'd prefer R. Hell, I'd settle for PG-13. That would be more than you've shared so far."

"Okay. Okay, let me think." Looking toward the ocean, I spot the area where we set up the tent a few days back, and the memory comes rushing back to me. I close my eyes, and my lips part as I exhale slowly.

"What's that look?" Laurie asks.

"What look?"

"That look and sigh you just gave ... that feels more like an X than an R. Share."

A smile spreads over my face. "It's definitely an X."

She rubs her hands together and flashes her brows up. "I'm waiting."

"Two days ago, Kyle and I were"—I flip my camera around to show her the beach—"in a tent down there on this empty beach and—"

"God, it's gorgeous there," she interrupts.

I flip my camera back. "I know. So, we were in a tent alone after being interrupted in the house. We saw that no one was around, and—this was my idea—I had him lay on a towel and I ... I ..."

"What? Jesus, what?"

"I sorta sat down on his face, and he ... he went to town, you know."

"He ate you out. Nice!"

"Eww." I frown. "Do people really call it that?"

"What the hell do you call it?" She continues in a deep, nerdy voice, "*Cunnilingus?*"

"Well, no," I reply defensively.

"Good, because no guy wants to hear, *Please perform cunnilingus on me.* They want to hear stuff like, *Come eat my pussy,* or, *Lick my pussy,* or *Eat me out.*"

"It's the *eating* part that doesn't sit right with me. I'm also not a big fan of the word *out*." I scrunch up my face, and after pausing to think, I add, "Let's go with *lick my pussy*."

"I can live with that." She smiles. "You actually asked him to do this?"

"Well, not so much asked as just put it right out there on his ..." I hold my hand in front of my face.

"Gotcha. God knows men have been doing that to us for, like, forever."

"They do that?" I recoil.

"Some do."

"Huh? So, how do you handle that?"

"Well"—she tilts her head to the side—"you either slap it away or enjoy a little snack."

I give her an uneasy look. "See, you're back to the eating-related sex terms. I don't like that either. Food should have no place in the bedroom."

"It's just semantics." She flaps a hand at the screen. "Regardless, I'm so proud of you."

"Thanks."

She presses her lips together and squints like she might just burst into tears. "Aww, our little girl is growing up."

"Stop making fun of me."

"I'm not. I'm genuinely proud." She cocks her head. "So, was he good at it? Some guys get lost down there and are clueless."

"He was not lost." I shake my head slowly. "Not for one minute."

"Wow. See, you can sorta tell a sex story. Now, that wasn't so terrible, was it?"

"Not really, no."

"Are you going to tell him about John?"

"Who's him, and what is this about John that you need to tell him?" Kyle says, standing beside me.

Startled, I drop the phone in the sand, then scramble to pick it up.

"Is that Kyle?" Laurie asks.

"Got to go." I end the call.

Chapter 40

The Doctrine of Promissory Estoppel

"Kyle!" I look up at him, shielding my eyes from the sun.

"Hey there." Grinning cockily, he sits next to me in the sand and says in an over-the-top-curious voice, "So, who was that?"

"Um, just my friend Laurie."

"You obviously told her about me. Didn't you?"

"What? No," I lie with as much conviction as I can.

He narrows his eyes. "Then, why did she just say, 'Is that Kyle?' before you hung up on her?"

"What? Um, no, she ... no, she didn't say Kyle. She said, 'Is that *Carl?*' *Carl* with a C."

"Oh, Carl. Who's Carl?" He stares at me, waiting. "Another boyfriend?"

"No. No. Well, Carl, um, he's just the guy down here who looks for beach treasure. In fact, you just missed him." I point to some random guy a thousand feet away. "Actually, if you look way down there, you can see him with his little metal-detector thingy."

"Uh-huh." He eyes me skeptically. "And she was asking

about him, why? Was she hoping for some beach metal-detecting tips?"

"Would you buy that?" I ask with a hopeful smile.

"No, not really." He shakes his head.

"I didn't think so." I sigh, then whine a bit as I explain, "I needed someone to talk to about all this, and I might have mentioned your name."

"And what was that again that you needed to tell me about John?"

"Wait, how did you find me?" I ask.

"No." Shaking his head, he clicks his tongue. "Don't change the subject."

"I'm not. I was just wondering."

"Your father said he saw you heading down the path to the beach."

Suddenly, alarmed that the entire group is watching us, I turn back toward the house, but can barely see the roof behind the dunes. I breathe a sigh of relief.

"Don't worry. I took the long way. He didn't see me."

"Good." I tilt my head back, blowing out a raspberry.

"Let's put a pin in the *what you need to tell me* thing. I'd like to start with a different question first."

"Okay."

"I missed you last night. What happened?"

"Sorry. I fell asleep."

"Did you get my messages."

"Not until way after three."

"You still could have popped down for a little fun." He shoots me a sly smile.

"Look, I want to be honest with you." I turn to him, placing my hand on his arm. "I'm not sure exactly how it happened, but I fell asleep, and I think I was dreaming I was in bed with you because … because …" I cringe. "When I woke up, I was, um … I was having sex with John."

"Seriously?!"

I nod. "I'm sorry. Those nights I was with you, we were in and out of sleep and doing it around the clock. It was sorta like that."

He gives me a puzzled look. "But at some point, you realized it wasn't me, right?"

"Well, yes."

"So, then did you stop it or …"

I draw in my lower lip with my teeth, then say, "I want to be honest with you."

"Okay, that sounds like a no."

"I didn't. I couldn't. By the time I was fully awake and realized what was happening, it was too late."

He turns away and runs his hands through his hair. "I'm not mad or anything. I mean, I have no right to be. I get it; we're just having a little fun here. But it feels a little weird that you were with him last night, you know?"

"Yeah, I understand."

"I really like you. I mean, like, I'm just … words can't even—"

"I really like you too." My lip quivers a bit as my emotions try to get the best of me.

"This feels …" He turns to look me in the eye. "This is the end, right?"

Pausing, I suck in a deep breath, then close my eyes. "I think that's best. We're playing with fire here, and after last night and some other things that have happened between me and John, I think there's a chance that we might … things might be different between us. I'm not sure what's going to happen, but I think I want to talk to him about it."

"I'm just going to throw this out there." He takes my hand. "Just give me one more night. You promised and—"

"What?" I chuckle. "You're serious?"

"I am." He grins. "I hate to throw the law at you again, but I feel this situation calls for it."

"Oh God, here we go." I roll my eyes.

"You see, I had this business law class my junior year, and there's this one thing we learned, called the doctrine of promissory estoppel, that's always stuck with me."

"I'm very scared to ask, but what is that?"

"It has to do with oral contracts and when a promise is made and not kept, and there are damages then—"

"You're making this up."

"No, just google it."

"Okay. I will." I sit up a little straighter. "How do you spell that?"

"E-S-T-O-P-P-E-L—"

Grabbing, my phone, I type it in. "Wow, it already knows what I'm after."

"I told you, it's a thing."

Google returns a ton of results on the subject.

I turn to him. "Okay, so it's real. Now, how exactly does it apply to our situation?"

"Well, there are four components to the doctrine. You're the promisor, and I'm the promisee. That's one and two." He clears his throat. "And you made a promise to come to my room last night and broke the promise. That's three."

"I'll give you that. So, this fourth thing..." I read from my phone. "It says it needs to be that the promisee suffered an actual, substantial detriment in the form of an economic loss or loss of well-being, which is a result of the promisor failing to deliver on their promise."

Holding his head high, he manages to say with a straight

face, "Exactly. I suffered a substantial detriment in a loss of well-being."

"By not having sex with me?" I ask, my words drenched with sarcasm.

"Yes."

"You're joking, right?"

"Not at all." Taking hold of my hips, he slides me a few inches closer to him and says softly, "Permission to speak frankly?"

I laugh in his face. "Did you just downshift from legal to military speak?"

"I'm versatile." He flashes me a grin.

"You're crazy." I bug my eyes out of my head. "But I'm curious to see where you're going with this."

"Okay, I'm serious here." Leaning forward, he begins in the softest, sexiest voice imaginable, "I just love eating your pussy."

The color drains from my face. "I just had this conversation with Laurie."

"What?" he asks, wearing a look of concern, mixed with a bit of intrigue. "She loves eating your pussy too?"

"No, jeez." I sigh, exasperated. "We were just discussing what phrase is acceptable for that ... that, uh, activity."

"I won't ask how you ended up on that topic."

"Please don't." I raise a shoulder. "Long story short. I landed on *lick my pussy*. It's not as formal as some options and not as crude as others."

"I see." He twirls a finger around counterclockwise. "So, I'll just back up and rephrase."

"Please do." I hold back a smile.

"I really love"—he pauses, tilting his head for effect—"*licking* your pussy."

"Wow, I just got chills when you said that, and I want to hear more."

"Good. Then, I'll keep going." Leaning his head back, he closes his eyes, seemingly reliving it. "I mean, you taste so good, and I felt like the last time we were together, my tongue got tired, and I think I sorta shortchanged you."

"I didn't feel that way at all. It was wonderful. I came, like, three times. What more could I ask for?"

"I think I can do better. I really do. Yesterday, I googled it and got some tips, and actually, there are some new things I want to try. I was planning on doing this all last night, and then it didn't happen."

I point a finger skyward. "And hence the substantial detriment."

"Exactly."

Leaning forward, he whispers in my ear some of the filthiest, sexiest things I've ever heard, and my mouth falls open. I listen intently as he describes in explicit detail all the ways and places he is proposing to please me orally. My pulse is literally quickening, and I feel the heat rising in my core.

I swallow hard, and all I can mutter is, "Okay."

When he pulls back from my ear, I stare into his gorgeous eyes with my mouth hanging open. He turns toward the ocean, and I simply look straight ahead with my eyes glazing over.

"It's so nice here, isn't it?"

"What?" I shake myself out of my trance.

He waves his hand toward the shore. "It's beautiful. I haven't been out this early before."

"Yeah, it's really nice," I reply breathlessly.

He turns back to me, and we once again lock eyes.

"I can see you're taking this under advisement." He grins from ear to ear. "Sorry. Another legal term."

"Uh-huh."

"I'll just throw in one other wrinkle if it helps get you there. I mean, don't feel like you have to answer now."

"Wrinkle? What wrinkle?"

"You wouldn't even need to touch me if you didn't want to. You could think of it like ... like you're doing a public service for the potential other women in my far, far, far out future."

"A public service, huh?"

"If it helps you get there." His eyes brighten, and he touches my hand. "It would be like you're a CPR mannequin, and it would be more of a ... of a training workshop."

"A workshop?" I cock my head. "Okay."

"Just think about it."

I say in a monotone, trance-like state, "Okay, I will definitely think about it." *Frankly, I don't think I'll ever think of anything else for as long as I live.*

"That's all I ask." He rises to his feet. "You sit here for a few minutes while I go back first."

"Good idea."

Leaning down, be places his hand on my chin, lifting it up until our eyes meet. "You look a little pale. Did you eat?"

"Eat?"

"Breakfast."

"No."

"I can see you're empty. Take my water bottle." He hands it over. "I'm going to be out most of the day, but if you have any follow-up questions or concerns, text me."

"I will." I nod slowly.

"Get something to eat. Mull it over, and we can chat about it later."

"Sounds good."

I watch as he heads off toward the cart entrance. I feel weak and dizzy. Maybe I do just need something to eat. Opening the bottle, I take a big sip, then shake my head. I start babbling to myself, "Wait, did he just make oral sex sound like an interactive webinar, and I bought it? He's good. He's really good. He would make a great lawyer."

Tilting the bottle back again, I inadvertently spill some down my chest. It's getting hotter out here, and it feels good. After another sip, I splash what's left over my face and chest. I needed that.

Suddenly, my phone chimes with a text message.

John:

Where are you? Can we please talk?

Chapter 41

Tell Carlos Her Pussy Looks Ridiculous

I make the trek back to the house as the sun and heat intensify. My thoughts are whirling a mile a minute. I'm not thinking clearly at all as I head with purpose up to the third floor. I think I pass my father and possibly Morgan along the way, but honestly, I could not say for sure.

Opening the door to our bedroom, I hear the water running and head into the bathroom to find John inside the glass-enclosed shower. A phone on the counter chimes.

He spots me. "There you are."

I move to the glass and take in the sight of his nakedness, looking him over from head to toe. "I just went for a walk on the beach."

"What?" He squints through the glass.

I repeat louder so he can hear over the spray of the shower, "I went for a walk on the beach."

"Is it raining?"

"No."

"Why are you all wet?"

"I spilled some water."

The phone chimes behind me again as he turns away and rinses his hair. He looks pretty damn good for a guy in his early forties. He's attractive and in great shape. No beer belly. He's very sexy. What the hell have I been thinking all these years? Suddenly, Kyle and his oral sex training session proposition are the furthest thing from my mind.

He asks, "When I get out of here, can we go somewhere and talk?"

The phone chimes three more times, back-to-back-to-back, and I glare at it, annoyed. When it chimes once more, I head over to it.

"I want to talk too," I mutter, lifting his phone to discover eight notifications from someone named Carlos rolling up on the screen. While I'm holding the phone, two more messages appear.

"Who's Carlos?"

"Oh, that's, um, just a guy from work. I'll get it when I get out."

"You've got, like, ten messages here. It sounds like it could be urgent."

"No, I, uh ... ahhh, ouch. Damn shampoo." Out of the corner of my eye, I see John rinsing his face and grimacing in pain. "Hold on."

I punch in his passcode and bring up his messages, where I'm smacked in the face with an extreme close-up of what looks like an underage and very thin girl's hairless vagina.

"What the hell?" I glance between the phone and John.

He's at the glass now, staring at me with his jaw hanging open.

"Are you ..." I cringe so hard that my head might explode. "Are you a pedophile?"

"What?"

I step to the glass and press the phone to it with a loud thump. "What the fuck is this? Are you in some child porn ring with this Carlos character?"

"No! God, no." He lifts his hands up defensively. "That woman is an adult. I swear. I would never—"

"Can't be." I look again, cocking my head. "That's an adult? There's not a stitch of hair."

He grips the back of his neck. "Some women ... they, uh, they shave it all."

"Yeah, I get that, but this looks really, really young."

"Believe me, it's not," he pleads. After turning off the shower, he opens the glass door and stands there, dripping wet. "I forgot my towel. Could you hand me one?"

I eye him with suspicion. "We don't have any secrets, do we?"

"No, not really." He extends his hand and says softly, "A towel, please."

"So, you don't mind if I look at more of these messages to prove that this is not some child sex thing, right?"

"Well, yeah, but I wouldn't. Could you please just hand me a towel? I'm ..."

I scroll up the screen to the previous picture. It's the same bald vagina but attached to a rather large set of breasts on a faceless picture. I turn the screen toward him. "Okay, so it's either the youngest breast-implant recipient in the world, who's spent way too much time in the sun, or that's an overly thin middle-aged woman with an imperfect boob job."

He laughs nervously. "See, I told you."

I scroll up and am horrified by the text and pictures these two have been sharing. I skim intimate questions that seem to be about me and things he's revealed about me. I don't read them fully because I just can't. I land on a picture of this woman using some sort of giant purple sex toy on herself.

"Jesus," I groan, wincing.

I place the phone on the counter, then turn to look at my *still dripping wet and naked* husband. "Carlos has got some big tits."

"Look, I just ... we ... you and I have this odd relationship. I didn't ask for it. You sorta forced me into th—"

"I forced you?!" I glare at him. "I forced you. Really?"

"Well, I mean ..." He kneels down on the floor, sadness clouding his features, and whines, "Could you just throw me a damn towel, please?"

I grab a towel from the rack and heave it at him hard. He stands, dries his legs quickly, then wraps it around his waist.

I glance at the phone and notice it's still displaying the sex toy picture. I hold it up for his benefit, cringing. "Is this what you and Carlos are into?"

"No, it's just ..." He exhales, fatigued. "Could you please stop calling her Carlos?"

"So, what's Carlos's real name then?" I wait for a response with my head tilted back, looking down my nose at him.

"That's not important."

"Fine then. As far as I'm concerned, she's Carlos." I hold up the phone and point to the name on the screen. "What does that say?"

"Carlos," he replies, defeated.

Placing his phone on the counter, I turn back to him, wearing a satisfied smile.

He blows out a long, slow breath. "I thought we'd be having a very different conversation now. What about last night?"

"What about it?" I fold my arms over my chest.

"It was amazing. Wonderful. You seem so different on this trip. You seem happier and—"

"Did you tell Carlos about last night?"

"No."

"She seems to have a number of opinions about me from the messages I skimmed. Why don't we share last night with her and get her thoughts?"

Sitting down on the edge of the bathtub, he gives me a withered look. "Come on. Can't we talk about this like adults?"

"Next time you text Carlos, could you tell her that her nipple-to-breast ratio is a bit off?"

"Please stop."

"Stop what? If Carlos can have and share her opinions about me to you, why can't I have feelings and opinions about her that I share with you also? And feel free to share those feelings with her and get her thoughts on what you share that I shared," I mutter, the sheer circularly frantic logic making me a little dizzy.

"What?" He looks at me like I'm from another planet.

I point an angry finger at him. "You know what I mean."

He opens his mouth to reply, but I've obviously left him speechless.

After a long and awkward silence, he finally sucks in a sharp breath. "So, what now?"

"Where are your car keys?"

"Why?" He narrows his eyes.

"I'm going out."

"Where?"

"Shopping," I snap.

He points out the door. "On the dresser, I think."

"I'm going to shop a little, and when I return later, I'm going to sleep on the pullout in the game room. Don't come down there, looking for me or wanting to talk. I'm sure you'll enjoy the alone time so you can spend the night sexting with *Carlos*."

"So, you're coming back then, right?"

"Tonight at least. Rachel gets here tomorrow, and I want to see her."

"Good." Leaning forward, he rests his elbows on his knees and exhales deeply.

I walk into the bedroom, grab the car keys, then yell back, "Tell *Carlos* her pussy looks ridiculous. Maybe she should go with a landing strip instead."

Chapter 42

Do You Think My Ass Looks Fat?

After slamming the bedroom door a little harder than I intended, I lean back against it and close my eyes. I don't really feel like shopping. I don't know where to go, but I don't want to stay here either. I take a deep, cleansing breath, then force a smile and head toward the stairs. The door to Kate's room opens, and my father rushes out.

"I'm sure I brought the fireman suspenders. They must be in the van."

I peek into Kate's room and find her sitting on her faux fur blanket–covered bed, wearing a fireman's jacket. Pretty much everything I saw in the back of my father's van is now in her room. The fur stool, the egg chair thing, along with all the props I desperately tried to forget. A large fan blows her hair back while bright freestanding lights illuminate the bed.

My mouth falls open as I stare, mesmerized, at her side profile. She has yet to see me, as she's admiring herself in the mirror.

Turning, I take a step to slip away, and she calls out, "Oh, Ally, come here."

I stop in my tracks, close my eyes, and sigh.

"Ally?"

"Yes, Kate?" I take a steadying breath before heading into the room.

"What do you think?" She stands, wearing a bright smile and nothing more than the large, open fireman's jacket and a tiny pair of panties. Luckily, the jacket is covering most of her large breasts, leaving visible just a bit of inside cleavage.

"Looks, um, good."

"Your father went to look for the suspenders."

"I heard," I mutter, avoiding eye contact.

Looking down at her chest, she beams proudly. "He says I can wear those over my nipples, open up the jacket more, and really get some great shots. They'll be very sexy, but still classy."

"That's fantastic," I reply with as much enthusiasm as I can fake. I click my teeth and nod my head toward the door. "I was just on my way out, so you ... you stay classy."

"Where are you off to?" she asks, clearly preoccupied, as she turns to check herself out in the mirror again. She opens up the jacket more and extends her exposed leg like one of those red-carpet celebrities.

"Oh, I'm going to drive John's car onto the pier we saw the other day and leap out just before it falls into the ocean," I reply matter-of-factly.

"Okay, have fun."

I stare at her, waiting for any tiny little indication that she actually heard what I said, but none comes.

Instead, she turns to me and lifts up the jacket in the back, flashing her thong-covered backside. "Do you think my ass looks fat?"

I open my mouth to speak, but nothing comes out. Dumbfounded, I point to the door, then slip outside.

As I reach the top step, I hear her say, "Don't be too late.

Dinner's at six, and then we're doing karaoke and having another game night."

* * *

I climb into John's SUV and start the engine, pondering my options. While I would like to put his car into the sea, I'm not sure I could pull off the stuntman maneuver of jumping out at the last minute. Not to mention the possibility of getting arrested for driving on the pier. Call me crazy, but Kyle's proposal is starting to sound better and better. Pulling out my phone, I type a simple two-worded text message that says it all.

Ally:
I'm in.

Upon seeing Kyle's three dots, a smile spreads over my face.
Kyle:
OMG, I just got a little hard.

Ally:
And I don't plan to just be a spectator,
so prepare yourself ...

Kyle:
Okay, now, I'm hard as a rock.

Ally:
Buying lingerie too. :)

Kyle:
I just came ...
But I recover quickly, as you know. :)

Ally:
Please be home before midnight.

Kyle:
Definitely!

I set the GPS for the nearest store selling sexy unmentionables, and I'm off. I realize that I've never purchased lingerie in my life. Not even once. Sure, I've bought bras and panties, but never anything sexy that one might put on in advance of a romantic night. I have to be one of only a handful of near middle-aged women capable of making that claim. It's more than just a little sad. I'm both terrified and excited by the prospect, although I don't have the first clue what's fashionable or sexy or just plain lame. I plan to ask for assistance.

I arrive at the Emerald Isle Boutique and am quickly over-whelmed by the wide variety and styles of lingerie. The sales associate pulls the most popular bestsellers and shows me to a fitting room. I try on six items, of which I like three. A red tied-with-a-bow teddy, which is a peekaboo bodysuit, high-lighted with a trio of satin bows, three cutouts in the front, and accented with a cheeky mesh back. A lacy black lace-up, crotchless teddy, which features a plunging neckline with an alluring lace-up detail over the crotch. And finally, an embroi-dered lavender push-up corset top with floral embroidery, lace-up detail, and sheer mesh, which includes a matching panty.

While in the fitting room, I snap a suggestive picture in the embroidered corset top, framing the shot to showcase just a hint of my cleavage and down to my belly button. I send it to Kyle, along with the caption, *A preview of tonight's lingerie show, featuring three costume changes.*

He replies in seconds that I'm literally killing him. I send back a smiling emoji.

The damage comes to over two hundred dollars on my Visa card.

Next, I head to Emerald Isle Day Spa, where I purchase their flexible day of beauty package. I get a deep-tissue massage, manicure and pedicure, and their most popular body treatment —the buttermilk and honey wrap. It is described as a rich body-butter mask, infused with buttermilk and honey, which is applied, then wrapped in place. It's hyped to soften and moisturize your entire body while you relax and drift away.

Looking for a hair removal option, it's suggested that I go with the Nufree Nudesse. It boasts to be a wax-free, pain-free, swelling-free, healing-time-free alternative to traditional waxing. It is said to be completely botanical and safe for the entire body. Most importantly, with no redness or swelling, it gets me game ready in time for tonight's festivities. I select the full Brazilian, going full Carlos on top as well, but at the last minute, I decide I just can't do it and opt for a thin landing strip instead.

As I'm lounging in my body wrap, I snap a picture of my beautifully manicured and painted toes and send it off to Kyle with the caption, *Full day of beauty at the spa. Later, see if you can guess what I've had done, just for you.*

He replies that his friends just had to give him chest compressions, but not to worry because he didn't show them any of the pictures or messages.

The spa day total comes to a little under five hundred dollars with tip. I leave, feeling relaxed, energized, and with my skin never softer.

I head back to the house, and it's just before four. I slip into the laundry room and wash and dry my newly purchased unmentionables on the machine's delicate cycle. I do so while reading a steamy novel and without leaving the room in order to guard my secret purchases before surreptitiously carrying them to the third floor, where I hide them in my luggage.

I come down to dinner at six. Everyone is in attendance, except for Kyle. John and I are civil but say very few words to one another. I suspect no one can sense the chill between us or is aware that we're in the middle of this current standoff. I skip out on the family fun events, using my standard migraine excuse. I ask John if he'll kindly give me privacy in our bedroom from nine to eleven, and he agrees. I plan to use the time to bathe and primp.

I soak in the tub, then use this scented body wash I picked up at the spa. After styling my hair, I apply a little makeup and stand before the mirror in the bathroom, admiring my new hairstyle down below. Running my fingers over my most private of areas, I'm pleased with the look and feel of the smooth, hairless skin and this newfound sensitivity, which sends chills through my body. I dress in some sweats and pack my new lingerie items in a small bag.

When I reach the second floor, I spot my parents, Kate, and John sitting out on the deck and move to the first floor, where I discover that Kyle is still out. I pull open the sleep sofa and make it up with a fresh set of sheets I found in the closet. I lounge in bed, picking up where I left off in my book.

Just after eleven thirty, Kyle returns home, spots me in the game room, and tells me he needs fifteen minutes to get ready. My pulse quickens, as I know our night is now imminent, and I spring into action, arranging towels and pillows under my blanket to make it look like a body is lying there. It definitely wouldn't fool a curious detective, but it's good enough to send a polite passerby scurrying away. At this point, I'm less concerned with covering my tracks and more focused on having the most incredibly intimate night of my life.

I enter Kyle's room while he's still in the shower. I lay out my three lingerie purchases on the bed for his benefit, then lounge against the headboard. When he turns off the water, I remember I was supposed to give him a show instead, so I collect the outfits and hide them under my sweat top, clutching them to my belly.

He emerges from the bathroom, a towel wrapped around his perfect waist, with beads of water on his neck and shoulders. I suppress the desire to collect them with my lips.

He gives me a cocky smile. "Is this one of your new lingerie outfits?"

"Yes, it's the latest from the Shaquille O'Neal line." I get to my feet and strike a pose. "Do you like?"

"I do."

Patting my bulging stomach, I say, "I've got the fashion show right here."

"Can't wait."

He tosses his towel over a chair and heads, bare-assed, toward the bed. I can't tear my eyes off of him until he slips under the sheet, concealing most of the parts that were distracting me.

When he's finally settled and my wits partially return, I do another slow spin in my sweats, then smile. "Take a good look at this one so you can remember it when you see the others."

"Please tell me that the rest weren't also designed by Shaq." He laughs. "Not that you don't look incredible in them."

"You'll see." I flash him a smile before slipping off to the bathroom and closing the door.

I return, wearing the lavender corset and matching panties, and stand before him with my hands on my hips.

"Wow," is all he says.

"Okay, that's number one—or two, if you're still considering the sweats." Grinning, I head back to the bathroom.

When I return, I'm wearing the red teddy with three bows.

His eyes light up. "Wow ... you ... look, uh, amazing. I like that one. Let's go with that."

I put a finger up. "Wait, I need to try them all on. They were expensive."

"I am going to die here." He pushes the sheet off his midsection, exposing his huge erection.

My gaze immediately goes there, and I gasp. "Wow."

"I might have to start without you."

"Just one more, I promise," I plead, but my feet don't seem to want to take me away.

"Well ..." He shoots me a tired look. "Are you going or staying?"

"I'm thinking." I bounce on my heels, then head toward the bathroom. "This next one is my favorite, so I have to show you."

He calls out, "Okay, but there isn't much point to it since you won't be wearing it long."

I slip on the lacy black crotchless teddy and stand before the mirror, taking it in. I look good. Damn good. I saunter out in front of him, initially hiding my sexy, bare, and explicit front from his view.

"I like this one."

I turn to face him, standing tall for his pleasure. His gaze travels down my body, briefly stopping at my lace-covered breasts before landing on my exposed crotch.

His jaw drops open. "I think we have a winner." He leans forward, squinting. "Did you change something down there?"

"I changed a lot down there. The spa sort of got rid of all of it."

"Me *likey*." He flashes me a grin.

"I thought it might be helpful for what you said you had planned." Spreading my legs slightly, I push my hips forward. Then, I slowly slide my hand down my body and make a V with my fingers on either side of my newly hairless lips. "It feels sorta nice. Do you want to feel?"

He nods quickly.

"Plus, with this teddy, there is a lot of access to things."

"I see," he says while gripping his package.

"Which one do you want me to wear?" I ask coyly.

"I don't know ..." He taps his chin, looking away. "Can I see number two again?"

Playing along, I take a step toward the bathroom.

"Get over here now," he commands with a smile.

I move to him, and he gently pulls me down on top of him.

Our lips meet, and he kisses me tenderly, then says, "I have been looking forward to this all day."

"So have I."

Curling a hand around my neck, he guides my lips back to his, and we make out like teenagers in the backseat of a car. He rolls to his right, leaving me on my side, then slides down, in line with my chest. Slipping the lacy fabric off my breasts, he takes to pleasing them one by one with his lips, mouth, and tongue. I thrust my head back and moan.

He nibbles his way down my body until he reaches my crotchless area and places featherlight kisses all over my sensitive skin. He moves off the bed, and taking gentle hold of my hips, he guides me up to kneel on the edge with my head and elbows resting on the mattress. Now, with my rear sticking up high, I crane my neck back to watch him. I feel his hot breath on my thighs and pussy.

"You have the sexiest ass I've ever seen."

The cutouts in my teddy give him open access to all of me. He swipes his tongue over my core, and it sends tingles down my spine.

He smooths his hands over my cheeks, then down my thighs. I spread my legs a bit, lifting my ass higher in the air. He presses his mouth fully on me, and I groan in pleasure, my hands curling into fists as I collect the sheets in my grip.

"Oh fuck, lick me."

My words must register, as he swipes his tongue directly on my clit, pressing his face firmly into me.

I mutter in delight, "Yes, right there."

He licks me enthusiastically from my clit up past my pussy and beyond, over and over with his thick tongue.

It's driving me wild, and I groan. "That feels so good."

I want to touch him.

I want to feel his cock in my hand and taste it.

I want it inside me.

My eyes roll back in my head as he takes hold of my thighs, spreads them, and extends his tongue deep inside of me. He slips lower and gently sucks on my clit.

"Your pussy tastes so good." He rises to his feet, and I feel his hardness brush against my skin.

Pushing up on my elbows, I tuck my head down and watch as he stands behind me, his thick, hard erection waving between my legs. Suddenly, I feel his cockhead pushing just barely inside me, spreading me open and teasing me.

I whisper breathlessly, "Fuck me."

Slowly, he drives it inside, deeper and deeper, and my eyes close. Reaching back, I grab his balls and gently tug on them as he thrusts in and almost all the way out, filling me fully with his length.

He slides his fingers under me and rubs them on my clit, pressing harder and harder as he drives his cock inside me. I'm so fucking close. My heart thumps in my chest as I struggle to breathe.

"Your pussy is so wet."

He moves faster now. He gathers my hair in his hand, and I straighten my arms, pushing my upper body higher. He pulls my hair gently with one hand as he strokes my clit with the other. He pushes into me fully, and when I press back against him, my orgasm sweeps through me, starting at my core. My eyes slam closed, and I throw my head back as my climax hits me fast and hard. I moan and writhe, pressing against him while reaching back to massage his balls.

He releases my hair, and I slump forward, returning to my elbows, along with my head to the mattress. Moving in a smooth, steady rhythm, he thrusts into me, clutching my hips and pulling me harder into him with each downward stroke. He cries out, and I feel him throb and gush inside of me. He collapses over me, thrusting slowly, and I feel his warm breath on my back. "You are incredible."

He falls to the mattress, breathing heavily, and I lie beside him. We turn to one another and gaze into each other's eyes as we slowly recover.

Reaching out, I run my fingers through the trail of hair leading from his belly button to lower and say, "I'm still pulsating."

He smiles and places a hand on my hip, cupping my ass as we both close our eyes.

* * *

When I wake, I find him breathing softly and watch him for a few minutes, simply admiring the view as he sleeps. Running a hand down his lean, strong body, I wrap my fingers around his soft cock and slowly stroke it.

He opens his eyes and says, "Hey there."

"Hi." I smile. "Are you too tired?"

"No."

"Good."

I pull gently on his shaft, and he quickly responds, thickening and lengthening with my touch. I kiss my way down his body, and he slides back a bit then flips around the other way, pulling my hips over his face and sliding his tongue inside me.

"Oh." I groan, throwing my head back before taking him into my mouth.

He grabs my ass cheeks and pulls me down to him, licking me everywhere he can reach. Cupping a hand around his swollen balls, I grip the base with my other hand and work my mouth over him, matching his enthusiasm.

I purr in delight, sucking harder on his cock, licking down the shaft and returning to the head, swirling my tongue over him. Lifting up, I stroke him firmly before plunging down and taking half of his length into my mouth. I work his cock up and down as he moans with his lips and tongue pressed firmly into my core.

Suddenly, he throbs and swells between my lips. I take too much of him, too deep. I gag, and then he reaches under me, as if he's trying to get away, but I'm pressing down too hard on him. Without warning, he explodes, filling my mouth, and I pull back from him quickly, more surprised than bothered as I wipe my lips.

"Sorry. Sorry." He slips free of me and kneels on the bed, gasping for breath. "I didn't mean to do that. I just ... lost control."

"It's okay."

He wipes something from my chin, then slips the straps of my teddy off my shoulders. "This is nice, but I want to see all of you."

He slides it down my body and over my hips. I sit on my backside and push the teddy off my legs. He kneels on the floor next to the bed and coaxes me to the edge. Placing his hands under my knees, he curls my legs back toward my stomach and devours me. I grip the sheets, staring up at the spinning ceiling fan as he explores my every crevice, and soon, I feel my climax is nearing. He laps at me furiously from below my pussy to my clit, and it's driving me wild.

I moan softly, "Make me come."

He moves faster over me, redoubling his efforts, licking me and pushing my knees back further toward my chest, spreading me open. Grabbing his hair, I pull him closer, and he pushes his tongue deep inside, and that does me in. I cry out as wave after wave of pleasure rolls through me. He slides lower and places tiny kisses on my skin, which sends electrical pulses through me.

I pant and moan, then finally push back from him when he rises up to lick my sensitive clit. "No, stop."

I slide away from him, and we curl up together under the covers, panting and catching our breath.

I place my hand on his cheek. "You're incredible."

He pulls me close to him and presses his lips to my hair. When he turns onto his back, I settle on his chest, and soon, we both fall asleep. Over the next few hours, we're in and out of consciousness while doing it in all manner of positions. I'm on top. He's on top. I'm on all fours, then on my stomach. I also have a distinct memory that we were lying on our sides, doing sixty-nine in some contorted position—of which, I didn't know I was capable. Basically, it's an all-night acrobatic sexual marathon of epic proportions. There's also a hazy recollection of me putting on one of the other two outfits, although that might have just been a dream.

When I wake again, I notice the clock shows seven past five, and I tell myself I'll lie there for a few more minutes before returning to the pullout sofa. That's the last thing I remember.

Chapter 43

For the Love of God, Would You Put That Away?!

I'm awakened from a dream to find John standing at the foot of the bed, and for a moment, I've forgotten our fight and the fact that I'm not in my room.

I give him a groggy smile. "Good morning."

"Is it?" he snarls.

It takes me a few beats before my faculties return, but when they do, my eyes widen in alarm. "Shit!" I'm in Kyle's room!

I sit up quickly, the sheet falling to expose my naked breasts, which, in turn, uncovers more of a shirtless Kyle, who is sleeping next to me.

I pull the sheet over my chest. "It's not what it looks like."

"Really? Then, what is it? Because to me, it looks like you're fucking your friend's son!" John's face turns a bright crimson.

Kyle stirs, turning toward me. He slides his hand up to my right breast, uncovering it again as he massages it sensually. "I'm tired. Maybe we can do it in, like, an hour."

Turning my attention to John, I shrug. "Well, maybe it is what it looks like." I'm not sure where I was going with that *it's not what it looks like* bit. Like I mentioned, I'm still a little groggy.

"Get up, you little shit!" John rushes to Kyle's side of the bed, and like a young mother lifting a car off her child in an emergency, he somehow garners the strength to pull the two-hundred-plus-pound athlete up to his feet by his arm.

"What the fuck?" Kyle mutters. Upon realizing the situation, he raises his hands up. "Oh shit. Look, I, uh—"

"Let me guess," John begins in a sarcastic tone, then continues in a put-on innocent one, "It's not what it looks like."

"That works for me if it does for you," the naked young Adonis replies with a grin.

Still holding Kyle's one arm, John makes a fist with his other hand and pulls it back, ready to strike. Instead of making a fist, Kyle opens his large hand and spreads his fingers, as if he'd simply catch the punch. When he does this, the muscles in his arm flex and look very impressive, if not completely sexy.

From my vantage point, I see the tall, bare-ass-naked Kyle with broad shoulders somehow being manhandled by a middle-aged guy who must surrender sixty pounds and four inches to him. It's not even close to being a fair fight, and it's reminiscent of the movie *Rocky III*, where Hulk Hogan towers over Sylvester Stallone. In that movie, Rocky won the fight, but I doubt that would be the result here.

"Guys, now hold—" I lose my train of thought upon noticing that Kyle is sporting a massive hard-on, which I'd venture to say has somehow escaped my husband.

John's gaze travels from Kyle's face to linger briefly on his bulging bicep. At that point, he seems to lose his nerve, thereby releasing his grip on Kyle's arm.

When John's attention is directed lower, his eyes bulge out of his head, and he says with disdain, "You put *that thing* in my wife?"

Kyle notices his manhood and shrugs. "Um, what would you have me put in her?"

John returns a confused look, stepping away from Kyle. He turns his attention to me, disgusted. "Jesus Christ, Ally."

I open my mouth to speak, but have nothing.

Bending down, John picks up the red bow teddy and holds it up. Spotting something else on the floor, he grabs that, too, and finally, in another location, he picks up yet another item. Holding up all four pieces of lace and satin, he glares at me. "This wasn't something that just happened after our fight, was it? I've never seen you wear lingerie. Hell, you don't own any. And three outfits ... you guys have been screwing all week. You planned this. You bought these all for him!" He balls up the fistful of sexy items and chucks them, smacking Kyle in the chest, before heading for the door.

"John, wait," I call out, but he doesn't stop. Upon noticing Kyle is still hard, I glare at him and snap, "For the love of God, would you put that away?!"

Chapter 44

Would You Stop Calling Me Carlos?

When I reach the great room, in my T-shirt and shorts, I discover John sitting at the breakfast bar, wearing a solemn look, while Kate cooks in the kitchen. The aromas of pancakes and bacon sizzling mixes in the air. Morgan and Dave both lounge on the sofa, immersed and smiling at something on their phones, while my parents sit at the large dining table, reading the newspaper and sipping coffee. I'm so glad we're all here to see the shit hit the fan. I stand at the top of the stairs, trying to figure out what to do or say.

My mother spots me first and says, "Good morning, sleepyhead."

"Morning," I reply, and John turns to look at me.

He shakes his head and mumbles something inaudible.

Kate leans close to him and says quietly, "What's wrong?"

"Morning, Mom," Dave says without taking his eyes from his phone.

"Morning." I give my son a half wave as I make my way to John. I softly say, "Can we go somewhere private and talk about this?"

He simply returns a stare.

"Please," I plead.

"No."

Covering my face with my hands, I sigh.

After a few moments of silence, John stands and points at Kate, announcing loudly, "Do you want to tell her what her son's been doing, sneaking around here every night, or should I?"

My eyes widen in a panic, and then suddenly, there is rustling, followed by a crash behind us. We discover Dave face down on the floor, lying next to a fallen side table among a sea of magazines. All eyes go to him. Dave quickly gets to his feet and looks nervously from Morgan to Kate before finally landing on John.

John turns back to me. "Last chance."

"Well, um, I—"

"Wait," Dave interrupts, flapping his hands in the air. "All right. All right. I've been having sex with Morgan."

"What the hell, Dave?!" Morgan drops her head into her hands.

"What are you talking about?" John looks to Dave, obviously perplexed.

"What do you mean? I thought ... wait." Dave looks at me. "Did you say YOUR son, as in Mom, or HER son, as in ..." He motions with a couple head nods toward Kate.

"Her son." John points to Kate.

"Oh." Dave slumps down on the sofa. "Shit. Never mind."

Morgan punches him in the arm. "You stupid idiot."

"This is just ... I can't even ..." I stammer, then narrow my eyes at my son. "Are you using protection? I sure hope you are."

"Jesus, Mom." Dave pulls his legs up on the sofa. Turning to Morgan, he says softly, "Sorry."

I continue with my subject-changing safe-sex cautionary

tale, "You know, all it takes is one slipup. Sometimes, *just the tip* and *just for a minute* turn into *more* than just the tip and *more* than just a minute. And sometimes, someone gets you pregnant, and sometimes, someone just up and dies on you and leaves you all alone."

Kate steps into the great room and points a spatula at her daughter. "Morgan Ashley Davis, you go to your room right now."

"No." Morgan rolls her eyes. "I'm not a kid."

Kyle suddenly appears at the top of the stairs and says, "Look, I can explain."

"Explain what?" Kate asks.

"Wait, what's going on?" Kyle wears a confused stare as he studies the room.

"Your sister is sleeping with Dave."

Pointing at his sister, Kyle looks to me. "So, this is about her, not …"

Kate shakes her head. "Hold on. I haven't had my coffee yet, so I'm a little slow today. Not to mention, I'm still processing the news that my baby has lost her virginity to a boy who might as well be her cousin."

"Eww, Mom. He's not my cousin, and I wasn't a virgin!"

Kate appears to exaggerate a fake dizzy spell, grabbing the counter to steady herself with one hand and clutching her heart with the other. "We'll talk about that later." She looks to John. "So, you're saying that Kyle has been sneaking around, sleeping with someone in this house, right?"

"Uh-huh." John bugs out his eyes, like he cannot believe she hasn't put two and two together yet.

Kate scans the room, using her spatula as a pointing device, briefly stopping at my mother and shaking her head before training it on me. Suddenly, her jaw drops open as the lights come on. "So, that must mean ... she ... is sleeping with"—she points it at her son—"him."

"So, are we all caught up now?" John says sarcastically before spinning angrily toward me. "Based on the sheer volume of the extensive lingerie collection I found in his room, it's been going on all week."

I raise a finger. "If it's any consolation, all that lingerie is new. I bought it last night, and I have the receipt to prove it."

"Oh my God, that makes it even worse. You wore that all in one night? How many times ... Jesus ... I can't even." John steps away and stares out at the ocean, folding his arms over his chest. Suddenly, he turns, wearing a deadly serious expression, and points an angry finger right at me. "That day we surprised you two down on the beach and he was running from the tent ..." He scoffs. "He buried you in the sand, my ass."

Dave, Morgan, and my parents are all on the edge of their seats, taking in the scene with their mouths hanging open.

"You've been sneaking around here, having sex with my son!" Kate scoffs. "I invite you to my house, and this ... this is how you repay me?"

"Look, it just happened. I didn't plan on it," I plead with my hands raised, "There was this note I found and thought was written to me by him, but it wasn't, and then I ... I don't know."

"Oh, that's where my note went," Glenn chimes in. "We've been looking for that."

"Yeah, I eventually figured out it was yours." I add with an edge to my voice, "Why the hell are you guys starting this up again? It didn't work the first time around."

My parents both shrug without bothering to answer.

After pausing a moment to collect my thoughts, I turn to Kate and exhale. "Look, I tried to fight my attraction to him, but it just happened, okay?"

"Oh, it just happened. Okay. Okay ..." Kate sighs. "And here I thought, we were good friends."

"We are. I just—"

"Good friends don't have sex with each other's sons."

Kyle scoffs. "Mom, don't you think that's just a tad hypocritical?"

Kate looks to her son, alarmed. "So, now, you're accusing me of sleeping with Dave."

"Eww! Gross," Morgan shrieks.

I look at my son, who's got his hands raised high in the air as he faces Morgan. "I swear I'm not banging your mom. Jeez, she's old as crap." After taking in Kate's jaw-dropping, horrified expression, he adds, "Sorry, I didn't mean that. Not that you're not a MILF. I mean, I wouldn't go there, not because you're old, just because—"

"What?!" Morgan glares at him. "What the hell are you even saying right now?"

"I'm just saying that I didn't have sex with your mother and that she's not too old." Dave sighs, exhausted. "I'm just going to shut up now."

I point to Kyle. "What are you talking about?"

He begins, "I didn't want to be the one to tell you this, but—"

"You're wrong," Kate interrupts.

"Oh, really? How was 'golf' the other day?" Kyle says, using air quotes. "Did you get any holes in one? You know, I saw you two coming out of the condo. I knew it was odd that it wasn't rented in the two most popular weeks of the summer. How many times have you guys been *playing golf* since you've been here and prior to getting here? Huh?"

"We're in love." Kate puts her hand on John's arm.

"No, we're not." John pulls away.

"What the hell?" I glare at my husband.

John begins, "Wait, I can explain. We—"

"Jesus Christ!" I boom. "Is there anyone in this house not sneaking around and having sex with someone?" I scan the faces of all the sex maniacs, waiting.

Glenn raises his hand. "I haven't been sneaking around."

"What! You've been screwing her since the first day we got here." I point to my mother.

"Well, yes, but I haven't been sneaking around, doing it. Remember, you saw us in the hot tub then—"

"Dad, please shut up." I rub my hands over my eyes. "Is there something in the water here? I mean, what the hell is going on? Has he"—I point to my father—"been slipping ecstasy in the iced tea or something?"

"I swear I have not. I'm all out." Glenn raises his hands in the air.

I direct my wrath to Kyle. "And you knew about this?"

"Um ..." Kyle grimaces, raising his shoulders. "I did."

"Why didn't you tell me?"

"I ..." He exhales deeply. "I didn't want our relationship to be some sort of revenge thing. Plus, you told me you had that wacky arrangement with your husband, so I just thought—"

"Yes, we have an arrangement, but one of the main rules was that he was not supposed to be with anyone I knew."

Kyle scoffs. "Sorry I'm not up to speed on all the crazy rules of your wacked-out marriage."

I return my attention to John and Kate standing together. "And you two. You hypocritical, self-righteous, lying, cheating bastards. How dare you call me out for this when you have obviously been fucking around behind my back for what, like, nine years?!"

"And you ..." I point to Kate. "For years, you've been asking me intimate details about my marriage. Pretending to be my friend, and the whole time, you've been sleeping with him." Suddenly, it hits me, and my jaw falls open. "Holy shit!"

"What?" John asks.

My gaze roams from John to Kate as I raise my palms up. "How did I not ..." I turn my attention to Kate. "She's Carlos. You're Carlos!"

"What?" Kate wears a perplexed expression. "Who's Carlos?"

"You are!" I choke out a laugh, pacing around frantically and flailing my hands. "I saw your dirty pictures, Carlos. And I have a question for you, Carlos. Did—"

"John, why does she keep calling me that?"

"She's Carlos," I repeat, chuckling to myself and shaking my head.

"Because ..." John sighs, looking like he wants to crawl into a hole. "Because I have you in my phone listed under the name Carlos."

"What? Why?"

"It was just a name," he explains wearily. "A random name I picked. Just to keep us secret. I don't know."

"Well, that worked out well," Kate fires back sarcastically.

"Thank you for pointing that out," John says before turning his attention to me. "Ally, look—"

"But why did you make me Latina?"

"What?" He spins back toward Kate.

"Why did you make me Latina?" Placing her hands on her hips, Kate shoots him a deadly look.

"I didn't make you anything." He raises his palms up, and they are literally shaking in frustration. "Look ... I ..." His mouth hangs open as he seemingly tries to find the words. "I was on a Zoom meeting, and one of the guys was named Carlos. He had this cool accent, and I just really liked the name, okay?" He locks eyes with Kate, who appears to relax her shoulders a bit. He sighs, then rakes his fingers through his hair. "Ally, can we—"

"Because I think it sounds a little like cultural appropriation," Kate blurts out. "And I don't want to ever be accused of—"

"What?" John spins back to her, dumbfounded, and presses his palm to his forehead with a loud smack. "What the hell is it now?"

Kate powers on, "You see, this thing happened with Alec Baldwin's wife, Hillary. She's white, and she's been going by the name *Hilaria*. She's really Hillary from Boston, not Hilaria, with a silent H, from Spain. She changed her name out of the blue, and she's been accused of—"

"What are you even talking about right now?" John looks at her like she's got three heads.

"Cultural appropriation."

"Cultural appropriation?"

She nods, standing taller, and her jaw grows tight. "Yes."

"I believe I understand the term correctly, and you haven't *appropriated* anything." He sighs wearily. "For you to *appropriate* something, you would have to be out and about, announcing yourself as Carlos and speaking Spanish and maybe wearing a fucking sombrero! Have you done any of those things?" He stares at her impatiently. "Have you?"

Her shoulders slump. "Well, no."

"And I haven't either so ..." He bugs his eyes out at her. "It's just a name I picked out of my ass, okay?!" Clutching the back of his neck with both hands, John takes a deep breath. "Where the hell was I?"

Kate says, "John, I can show you a way to shut off message preview and to mute the notifications on your phone. That way—"

"Carlos!" John spins back to her one more damn time. "Would you please shut the fuck up?!"

Kate's cheeks flush a bright red. Her jaw falls open, and she's left speechless—at least for a moment.

He lifts his hands in the air and shakes them, on the verge of a stroke or nervous breakdown. "Where was I?"

"I don't think you were the one speaking last." Glenn stands and points to me. "She had just realized that Kate was Carlos. And I think she was about to ask Carlos a question when she was interrupted."

"That's right. Thank you, Dad." I smile wickedly. "Carlos, did John tell you that we had sex two nights ago? Did he share that little nugget?"

Kate glares at him. "Is that true, John?"

"Yes, but ..." John closes his eyes and sighs. When he opens them, he finds both Kate and me right in his face. If looks could kill, his head would be a mushroom cloud. His gaze starts on me, then goes to Kate before he says. "Jesus, I don't know who to try to explain myself to first."

Glenn says, "I'd go with Ally since you've been married for over twenty years. Start there."

"Thank you, Glenn," John mutters, his words dripping with scorn. "Helpful, as always."

John turns to me, then says, "Listen, Kate and I just started as friends. After Rachel was born, you pulled away from me, and, I-I ... Kate had just lost her husband, and we just ... we simply comforted one another as friends. At some point, it became something more. I've loved you since I met you, and you—"

"We both agreed that was best," I say. "You knew I couldn't ... since David died, I—just ... every time I looked at you, it brought up so many memories of him."

"I didn't want that agreement. I went along for you."

I wipe a tear from my face. "Look, I told you, you could do whatever you wanted. I knew you needed some passion in your life, and all I asked was for two things—that you keep it quiet and that it wasn't with anyone I knew. I didn't want there to be some big, embarrassing scandal."

"What about you?" John scoffs. "I guess it's fine for you to be screwing the teenage son of our friend. Call me crazy, but isn't he someone we know?"

"Hey, I'm not a teenager," Kyle says.

"You stay out of this," John says pointedly, gritting his teeth.

"Oh yeah, you motherfucker—and I'm using that term literally!" Kyle takes an aggressive step toward John.

I move between them. "Wait. Let's all just calm down." I blow out a long, slow breath before looking to John. "I never agreed to that. You did."

"What?" John looks at me like I'm crazy.

"I never agreed to not have a relationship with someone we knew."

"Yes, you did." John raises his palms up. "We both did."

"No, I didn't."

"So, you remember our conversation word for word from, like, a decade ago?"

"Yes, I ... I do." I pause, thinking, my expression softening a bit. "Maybe. I don't know."

"Uh-huh." He shakes his head, frowning.

"Well, I never acted on it," I reply defiantly.

"Until now." John looks down his nose at me.

"So, how many women have there been? Ten, twenty, what?" I stare at him, waiting.

"No, not ten or twenty."

"Are you screwing Laurie too?"

"No!" John snaps. He closes his eyes for a moment before pleading, "Can we not do this in front of everyone?"

"We're obviously all adults here. *Sick. Twisted. Insane* adults, but still adults." I scoff. "Why not do this in front of everyone? Both my father and mother are naked in front of everyone. Kate is posing in nothing but fireman suspenders and possibly even less for my father." I turn to Kate. "So, Carlos, are those *classy* pictures for my husband?" I don't wait for an answer. Instead, I wave my arms around willy-nilly for effect. "Everyone here is screwing everyone else here like there's an asteroid about to destroy the planet."

"Stop calling me Carlos!" Kate's eyes harden and narrow into slits. "I'm warning you."

"Yeah?" I click my teeth, looking down at her. "What are you going to do?"

"You'll find out." She clenches her fist.

"That's enough." John steps in front of Kate, placing a hand on her shoulder. "I think we all need to calm down."

"Don't touch me." Kate shoves his arm away.

I spin toward John, my nostrils flaring. "How could I not have seen this coming? I must be an idiot. I guess when you tell your husband he can sleep with every other woman on the fucking planet, except for just *two*, you sorta let your guard down. I mean, that leaves, like, four billion other—"

"Three," a voice calls out faintly.

"What?" I angrily scan the room for the source.

"I said, three." My mother adds self-consciously, "I would hope I'm also on that excluded list since you know me, and that would be, um, a total of three women that—"

"Thank you." I sigh and say in a weary, sarcastic tone, "Yes, Mom, I stand corrected. Three."

"Sorry you were sort of on a roll there, and I ..." She hangs her head. "I'll just shut up now."

I direct my anger back to Kate. "And you ... you ... my. Good. Friend. At that dinner we went to, you did nothing but pump me for information you could use against me. When I told you that I was maybe starting to miss being intimate with him, you talked me out of it. You're a monster."

"I was just trying to help."

"Right." I shoot her a deadly look. "You and those big fake tits. You told me they were for you, not some man in your life. Yeah, right! They're clearly for him."

John turns to Kate. "She told you that, and you didn't tell me?"

"I, um, I didn't want you to get hurt," Kate says.

"We're done." John glares at her before returning his attention to me with his expression softening. "You really told her you missed me? You said that?"

I dismiss him with a flip of my hand, then get right in Kate's face. "Oh, and one last thing. I'm not sure if your boyfriend told you, but I saw the beaver shot you sent him, and your pussy looks ridiculous, shaved like that. Why don't you try a landing strip instead ... *Carlos?*"

Kate shoves me hard. I tumble onto the sofa next to Morgan, who jumps to her feet just before her mother leaps on top of me. We flip to the floor, rolling several times over each other with our arms flailing about. I'm sure it looks like one of the lamest girl fights ever. Kyle pulls his mother upright and holds her back as John helps me to my feet. He slides behind me, wrapping his arms around my body, keeping my arms at bay.

Kate and I glare at one other, both breathing heavily.

"You're so lucky he saved you," Kate says.

"You are." I struggle to try to break free. "Let me go."

John sighs. "I will once you're calm."

"I'm calm." I take a breath, relaxing my shoulders, and a bit of my anger dissipates. "I'm calm. I am."

"Okay, okay."

When he releases his grip, I look him in the eye. "After all I've been through, you do this. How could you?"

Sighing, he thrusts his head back before leveling his gaze with mine. "Ally, I—"

"Don't waste your breath." I walk swiftly toward the staircase, down to the first floor, and out the door.

Chapter 45

It Happened to Us

John calls out, "Ally ... Ally, wait for me."

I break into a sprint as I step off the wooden deck, where it leads to the path through the dunes. "I don't want to talk about it!" Looking back, I spot him gaining on me, so I run faster. "Leave me alone."

He catches up to me, grabbing my arm, and when I pull away, our legs get tangled. I topple into the sand, where he falls next to me. We lie there, catching our breath, him gazing at me, and I turn away, refusing to give him the satisfaction.

"Ally, please look at me." He scoots closer, placing a hand on my arm, and I face him. "That night we made love was amazing. I can't stop thinking about it."

"Yeah, it was a mistake. A big mistake."

"It wasn't. I love you."

He leans in, pressing his lips to mine. I kiss him back. I'm not sure if I want to or if I'm simply taken by surprise, but I do.

After a few seconds, I come to my senses and push him away. "Stop. Just stop."

"Ally, I don't know how we got here." He sits up, brushing the sand from his clothes.

"I do. Do we really need to go over it again?" I ask, kneeling in the sand.

"I'm not talking about here, here. I'm talking about the last twenty-two years of our marriage." He pauses with his bottom lip quivering. "I could never compete with the memory of David."

"No one asked you to."

"You've been walking around all these years like this just happened to you, but it happened to us."

A single tear slips down my cheek, and my mouth falls open. "He was going to be my husband."

"I get that. It's different for you. Very different, but he was like a brother to me."

A silence falls over us as we wallow in our own thoughts. The only sound is the waves crashing nearby.

Finally, he says, "I always felt like I was in his shadow."

I wipe my face. "Well, if you felt that way, that's on you. I didn't put that on you."

"Ally, I do love you. I've always—"

"You don't love me. You only married me because you felt guilty, like what happened to David was your fault. I never should have agreed."

He stares into the sand. "I thought you blamed me for his death all these years."

"I never blamed you."

"I know you've said that many times, but I wasn't sure if, deep down, you ever really believed that."

I exhale and shake my head. "Look, I don't know how else to say it. Either you believe me or you don't."

Reaching out, he places a hand on my arm. "You seemed so different once we got here. Like you were your old self again. Almost like when we first met in college. Was it all because you were having sex with him?"

"No." I gaze out to the ocean for a few moments, then turn to face him. "I mean, at first, I guess the flirting made me feel alive again. It awakened something in me that I hadn't known was still there. Passions I never thought I'd ever feel again. I fought it, and then once I gave in to it, I was ... I don't even know how to describe it."

"I wish I could have been the one to bring that out of you again, like when we were in Key West."

"I just couldn't with you." I place a hand on his arm. "I'm not sure why. Maybe, subconsciously, you're right ... part of me could never let go of him."

"Well, I'm here, and he's not. I've been here all along. I'm sorry, but I've tried to love you all these years, and you just shut me out."

"You mean, in bed." I glare at him.

"Yes, in bed. But that's not the entire story. You're the one who pushed me into this crazy arrangement."

I grumble, "You were constantly moping and in a bad mood because we didn't have a physical relationship. That's why I suggested the arrangement."

"That's not true. It's not all about sex. There was a lot of stuff going on at that time with my job and you being pregnant. It was a difficult time."

"Well, it seemed like it was all about sex."

"I swear it wasn't. I love you. I've been in love with you since I first saw you." He exhales deeply, pausing to look out at the water. "David was crazy about you. That first night we all met, he told me, 'That's the girl I'm going to marry.' It crushed me. What was I supposed to do with that information, except let it all play out and see what happened? You guys started dating and were inseparable. I had to stand by and watch." He leans back. "Does that make any sense?"

"I guess." I look down to the sand. "You know, sometimes, a

great memory of David will come to me. It's usually something small, like when he bought me that teddy bear or surprised me with some candy that I liked, and … and it would make me feel bad, like it was so horrible to be here without him." I wipe my face, turn to him, and our eyes lock. "I wanted to stop feeling that way."

"I know."

"I was starting to break out of that pattern here. I would remember things about him and not want to cry." I lower my chin and sigh. "But now … I don't know … I feel like I'm right back there again, feeling bad and—"

"Don't." He places his fingers under my chin and coaxes me to level my gaze with him. He smiles and swipes a tear off my face with this thumb. "What if we start over? We'll move into the new house and—"

"And what?" I pull away from him. "Pretend that you weren't lying to me for the last ten plus years, going around behind my back, screwing my friend?"

"Technically, it wasn't behind your back."

I look at him like he's out of his mind. "It was, and if you can't see that, then it's all the more reason that we should not be together."

Neither of us says a word for what seems like an eternity until, finally, I turn to him. "John, I really think I'm done. I think we both need to move on. You know as well as I do that we were staying together just for Dave. Then, when Rachel happened, we made that stupid arrangement. You're not happy. I'm not happy. We started as friends, and we'll always be. We get along. We'll both be there for Rachel. Maybe everyone will be better off if we just go our separate ways."

"Don't say that." He appears to come apart a bit. His eyes cloud as he fights to breathe. "You can't mean that."

"I do." I exhale sharply, fighting back my own emotions. "I think, in time, you'll see it's the best thing too."

Placing his elbows on his knees, he rests his chin on his hands and stares down at his feet. "Fuck."

"Your parents will be dropping off Rachel in a few hours. I'd like to use your car and take her on a trip, just the two of us. You can either stay here with your girlfriend, Carlos, or ..." My lips curl up into a smile.

"Don't call her Carlos." He gives me an evil look and pinches his lips together, desperate to kill his smile. "And she's not my girlfriend."

"Well, probably not anymore." I make a face.

"No, probably not."

"But you never know. Women can be forgiving. Stay here for the rest of the week, if she'll let you, or get a ride home with your parents."

"Kate and I are done. I swear."

"Whatever." I shake my head. "It's up to you. When we return home, we'll figure out what to do with the house. I'm sure that it's appreciated in price in this crazy real estate market, so we'll do fine." I stand and brush the sand off of my shorts. Placing a hand on his shoulder, I say, "It's nobody's fault, really. It just wasn't meant to be."

He exhales deeply, shaking his head. "I don't know. Maybe you're right."

"I think I am."

He stands and looks me in the eye. "You were right about something else too."

"What's that?"

"The *completely hairless vagina* thing. It's a bit much."

Smiles form on both of our faces until we're giggling like schoolchildren.

When we finally collect ourselves, he gives me a serious

look. "We were always so good at the friend stuff and joking around."

"I know." I place a hand on his shoulder.

"If we could have only figured out the rest, this could have been a great love story."

"Yeah." My eyes fill with tears, and I turn away.

When I look back, he's already walking away.

He calls back with his voice cracking, "I'm going to take a walk on the beach. Just take the car. Take whatever. I'll see you back home. We'll figure it out."

I fall to pieces inside with tears streaming down my face, simply watching him go.

Chapter 46

Please Put on Some Pants

Opening the door to the house, I peer inside for any sign of the artist formerly known as Carlos and discover the coast is clear. I quietly close the door, then head down the hall to Kyle's room, where I find the door shut. After knocking and not hearing a reply, I go inside. The shower is running, and once again, I'm catching him naked.

Jeez, he takes a lot of showers. I'm not complaining, mind you, because he always smells good, but it seems like a lot. File that away under unsolved mysteries. I have more pressing matters to discuss.

Standing at the doorway, I take a moment to enjoy what will probably be my last view of him this way. And what a view it is as he rinses off his hair with his muscular and shapely rear end on display for my pleasure. I tiptoe into the room and smash my nose up against the glass, waiting for him to notice me.

He turns and nearly loses his balance, crying out, "Holy shit!"

"Sorry. Sorry." I step back, giggling. "I didn't mean to scare you—well, maybe just a little."

"I was wondering where you ran off to."

"I'm back now, but I'm leaving soon."

"Oh crap. I guess it's not unexpected." Taking a step back, he motions with his hand. "Can I interest you in a shower? Plenty of room for two."

"Um, as appealing as that sounds, I'm going to have to say no."

"Okay, it's a limited-time offer." Placing his hand on the valve, he gives me a naughty look. "Because once I turn this water off, it expires."

"Again, it's a no, but you don't know how badly I want to say yes."

He hangs his head as he turns off the water. Opening the glass door, I hand him a towel. Water beads and drips from him everywhere—and I mean, everywhere—and I'd like to lick off every last drop.

I take a few steps back and lean against the sink as he steps out and proceeds to dry himself. He's bending over and rubbing the towel here and there, and it's probably the most erotic thing I've ever seen. I could watch him do this for a long, long time and never get bored.

I must look like a lost puppy or something because he takes in my expression and says, "Are you okay?"

"No. Yes, I'm fine." I wave a finger behind me. "Just had a conversation with John on the beach."

He cringes. "And how'd that go?"

"Not great. I think this is the end for us."

"I am sorry to hear that. I've got to tell you though, I'm not sure how he could let you go. I would have been doing everything in my power to make you happy. I wouldn't have been going along with any weird open-marriage thing."

"It's more complicated than that. Don't blame him. It was all my fault."

Kyle wraps the towel around his neck and stands before

me with nothing on and everything hanging out. He looks fucking delicious. I'm glad I'm still leaning back on this sink because, otherwise, I might faint. I haven't eaten or had anything to drink all day, and I just spent twenty minutes getting emotional and baking in the sun on the beach. I'm exhausted.

I cock my head. "Do you want to put something on?"

"Do you *want* me to put something on?"

I raise a shoulder. "I'm good, just enjoying the show a little longer."

He motions from his abs to his chest, up and down. "You're sure this isn't too much for you?"

"No, actually, it's not too much. It's just the perfect amount."

"I'm going to fucking miss you." He shakes his head slowly. "You are something."

"I can't tell you what this week has meant to me." I choke back my emotions. "I was just losing it on the beach, and I refuse to cry in here, especially in front of a naked man. That would be weird."

"That would be. If you start crying, I'm definitely getting dressed."

We share a laugh, and when his smile morphs into something serious, he says, "I could see how easy it would be to fall in love with you. If I wasn't a young idiot athlete who plans to be a semi-sleazy attorney and—"

"What?" My eyes brighten. "You're going to law school! You decided?"

He shrugs. "Yep, all that sexy legal banter we tossed around sorta got to me."

"That's wonderful. You are going to be a great lawyer."

"Maybe." He scowls. "Hey, you interrupted my closing argument I had prepared here."

"Oh, this is something you worked on." I straighten my back, extending my palm to him. "Sorry, please continue."

He pauses a moment, looking up and mouthing some words silently, then says, "Okay, yeah ... any other guy with half a heart would be begging you to run away with him. We'd have some torrid six-month affair, and you'd eventually grow tired of me. Luckily for you, I'm sort of an asshole." His lips quiver. He presses a knuckle to his mouth and forces a crooked smile.

"Yeah, luckily." I take a few steps toward him. "If I were fifteen years younger, you'd need a restraining order to keep me away."

He smiles. "I wish I had another legal argument to quote to get you back in my bed, but sadly, I only have the one, and I spent it."

"I did enjoy that." I chuckle. "Wait, be honest. Have you used that before?"

"Um, I plead the Fifth."

"Oh my God." I turn away from him. "You totally played me."

He lifts his hands in surrender. "I swear it was only one other time. The first time I thought of it, it didn't work."

"Oh, that makes me feel better," I grumble, turning back to him.

"What I'm trying to say is, this time, I really had my argument thought out, and if it's any consolation, that girl didn't mean anything to me, but you ... I mean, I can't even begin—"

"You're right." I move to within a few inches of him and say softly, "You are an asshole."

"Told you," he says, gazing into my eyes. "What if I promise to never use that again? I'll retire—"

I put my fingers to his lips. He kisses them, then pulls back slightly, scrunching his face all up.

"Is that sand?"

"Oh, sorry. Yes, I sorta took a tumble out there."

"They smell a little like seaweed too. Here's a tip." He raises a brow. "Maybe wash when you come inside before you put your fingers to someone's mouth."

"I'll try to remember that."

He gives me a sweet smile. "Should we hug or ..."

"We should." Suddenly, my attention is seized lower to something between his legs. Something that's growing quite a bit. I shake my head, laughing. "My God, it's ... it's ... please put on some pants so we can hug and say goodbye without the possibility of penetration."

"You're no fun." Grinning, he cocks his head, then heads for the door.

I follow him out, enjoying my last glimpses of his perfect body as he pulls on underwear, shorts, and a T-shirt.

He turns to look at me. "Better?"

I nod, and a tear streams down my face.

His eyes look red as he opens his arms, and I step inside. He wraps them around me, and I hug him back. We squeeze each other so tightly, and I swear I feel him trembling.

He whispers in my ear, "I will fucking miss you."

"Me too."

When I pull away with tears streaming down my face, I refuse to look at him. I don't want him to see me, nor do I want to embarrass him if he's overcome with emotion too.

"Bye," is all I say before I walk out of the room.

Chapter 47

Girls-Only Trip

I'm able to walk up two flights of steps without seeing another person. All the doors are closed, and I can only assume everyone is hiding away in their rooms, traumatized after all the fireworks. I slip into my bedroom and quickly pack all my things.

In less than thirty minutes, I'm in John's car, heading north up the coast on Emerald Drive. Prior to leaving, I had quick conversations with my parents, who both seemed to be very understanding of my situation. I also had an extensive conversation with my son, where I apologized for my inappropriate behavior with Kyle and my unwarranted reaction to his relationship with Morgan. He gave me a hug, and I'm pretty sure no permanent damage was done, but that remains to be seen.

Pulling into a shopping center, I park under the shade of a tree and take out my phone. Looking at a map, I read the names of the nearby coastal towns, settling on Atlantic Beach, which is about a thirty-minute drive north. It's far enough away that I can steer clear of anyone who might want to kill me, but not so far that I can't return to collect Rachel after John and I invent a story that doesn't potentially scar her for life.

I contact a local real estate company and tell them what I'm looking for—oceanfront with at least two bedrooms and within walking distance of some shops and restaurants. They tell me I'm in luck, that they just had a last-minute cancellation. With five bedrooms and a pool, it's much more than I need and more than I wanted to spend, but I give them my credit card information, and they give me the address and the code.

I make the beautiful drive through the green forest of the aptly named Pine Knoll Shores to sunny Atlantic Beach, and the house is even nicer than the one I was just evicted from. The pool is large, and the landscaping is gorgeous. The bedrooms are big, and the place actually looks clean for a rental. I'm more than pleasantly surprised. The best part is that it's much closer to the ocean, so I won't go into cardiac arrest, simply walking to the surf.

Sitting in the great room, I glance out at the breathtaking view while I call John. We have a nice chat, where we settle on a story that Daddy needs to get back home to take care of some things with the new house we're building, which actually turns out to be true. And while all that is happening, Rachel and Mommy will have a girls' week at the beach. He tells me he's just heard from his parents, who are about an hour away. I tell him I'll gladly come pick her up.

We instead come up with a plan to invite his parents to stay in Atlantic Beach for the night to rest up before the long drive home. John is invited as well, and I have more than enough bedrooms to accommodate them all.

About two hours later, they arrive, and Rachel runs out of the car and gives me a big hug. Soon, she'll be ten, and she won't want to have much to do with me—or at the very least, our relationship will change as she gains more independence. I'm looking forward to these next seven days alone with her.

I show everyone to their rooms. John has his own, but we

don't let Rachel know this. After his parents get cleaned up, we walk to a waterfront restaurant just up the street, and it's fabulous. We spend the rest of the night out by the pool, enjoying the view and the sounds of the crashing waves. We laugh and talk as we reminisce about so many things.

That night, alone in bed, part of me wishes John would slip into my room and hold me, but it doesn't happen. I don't sleep well. Maybe I'm right that too much has happened for us to be a couple.

The next morning, Rachel and I stand in the driveway as John climbs in the backseat of his parents' car and waves goodbye to us. Rachel comments that he looks like a little boy, sitting there, and he does, and it almost makes me cry.

The rest of the week is an absolute blast with just us girls, getting our hair done, visiting the day spa, eating junk food, and spending every waking moment together. We swim in the pool and the ocean, build sand castles on the beach, and take about three million pictures of it all.

One day, while standing in the waves, Rachel and I both comment on how we miss Daddy and little Izzie as well. On Saturday, when we finally head home, she sleeps most of the way. While I drive, I think about everything that's been happening in my life since I met John and David. A couple of times, I openly cry, but luckily, Rachel is sleeping, and I escape from having to explain what's wrong.

Chapter 48

Funny Running into You Here

The day after we return to my mother's condo, I swap cars with John since he was driving mine while we were away. I'm so backed up at work that we don't have much time to discuss where we go from here. The house is still a few days from completion, and in this hot real estate market, the longer we procrastinate, the higher the prices are likely to go. Basically, we're in no hurry.

I end up working an eighty-hour week. As it turns out, having a new doctor in the practice isn't the solution that I thought it might be. There are a few stubborn patients who don't want to see anyone else. I also seem to be the only one with the knowledge of the quirks of our computer system or have the ability to navigate certain challenging insurance issues. It's fine with me because it makes me feel needed and a tad irreplaceable, and it's so much better than the alternative.

On Friday afternoons, I normally take a longer lunch around two at this restaurant I like since we don't schedule anything later in the day. The staff appreciates it, as most Fridays, barring an emergency appointment, they can start their weekends early.

When I walk into the restaurant, I hear my name being called and am surprised to see David's parents, Jane and Ben, waving me over.

Jane smiles. "Funny running into you here."

"I know."

Ben stands and gives me a hug. "Are you meeting someone, or would you like to join us?"

"I'd love to. How have you both been?"

"We're fine," Jane replies. "You look good. You're all tan."

"Just got back from two weeks at the beach. It was a little hectic the first week, then very relaxing after that."

"I know. John told us," Ben says.

"Oh, you spoke to him?"

"We had dinner the other night. We spoke to Dave too. We're glad he's doing well. He told us he had a great time at the beach."

"I bet he did," I grumble under my breath.

"What's that, dear?" Jane asks.

"I think it's safe to say that everyone in that house had a great time."

Ben says, "That's what vacations are for."

I nod, fighting back my urge to smile. *If they only knew the entire story.* "Do you guys come here a lot?"

"First time." Jane looks over the menu. "What do you recommend?"

"I always get the Bistro Club. I love it. It's chicken with avocado, and the bacon is, like, out of this world." I narrow my eyes. "Mmm ... and the bread ... it's on this rustic, toasted bread. It's just fantastic."

"Well, you sold me." Ben closes his menu.

"Me too."

After the waiter takes our order, Jane puts her hand on my arm. "John tells us that you guys are thinking of splitting up."

"Well, yes. Nothing is official yet, but sadly, I think it would be best for everyone."

She gives me a sympathetic look. "He didn't give us any details, but he made it sound like you guys have been struggling since Rachel was born."

"We have, and it's very complicated."

"I understand if you don't want to talk about it, but I have to say that you guys hid it well. I never would have guessed you were anything other than a happy couple."

"Yeah."

"Had I known, I would have shown this to you a long time ago." Jane pulls a rather large vintage cell phone out of her purse and places it on the table in front of me. "Do you know what this is?"

"An old cell phone?" I shrug.

"It was David's."

"It does sorta look familiar. Why do you have it?"

"Well, you remember the day of the accident, he was texting everyone because he was intubated."

"I remember." I squeeze the side of the table to help quell my emotions. "I, uh, still have his messages on my phone. I look at them sometimes."

"Well, we didn't have cell phones back then. So, when it happened, David typed messages to us and handed us the phone so we could read them. I keep it charged and look at the messages sometimes too."

I pick up the old Nokia and look it over, wiping away a tear. "I forgot how heavy they were."

"Did John ever show you the messages David had sent him that day?"

"No, I think he lost his phone and changed services, so they were all gone."

Jane points to the phone. "They're on there, and I think you should read them. I don't think David would mind. He loved you both so much. He just wanted you to be happy and have a good life."

"Can I?" I'm literally falling apart in front of their eyes as tears stream down my face. I sniffle back my emotions. "If I do it here, they'll be picking me up off the floor."

Ben says, "Why don't you take it out to your car and read them? When you're ready, come back, and we'll have a nice lunch."

"Okay." I wipe my face.

I place the phone in my purse and head toward the entrance of the restaurant. When I open the door, the sun blinds me. I shield my eyes from it while tears cloud my vision as I make my way to the car. I pull the car door closed, and it's boiling hot on this July afternoon. I drop my purse on the passenger seat, start the engine, and turn the air-conditioning on full blast.

Holding the steering wheel with both hands, I rest my head on it before turning to look at my bag as it sits there mocking me. I grab a tissue and blow my nose, then take a deep breath and pull out the phone.

The interface is clunky compared to modern phones, but I'm soon navigating the texts. I spot my name and skip it, then locate John's and press the large middle gray button to bring up the last text conversation between my fiancé and husband.

John:
You're going to make it.

David:
*If I don't,
take care of her.
She's amazing.*

John:

You're not going anywhere.

David:
*But if something happens, you
promise me you'll take care of her.*

John:
I will.

David:
*And don't you dare blame yourself
for this for one second.
It's not your fault.*

John:
I won't.

David:
I'm serious.

John:
I swear I won't.

David:
*I'm sorry I stole her from you.
I knew you liked her, but I just
couldn't resist. I'm an asshole.*

John:
You won't hear me argue that.

．　．　．

I read this and nearly choke from laughing. I'm flooded with emotion with tears streaming down my face and my sinuses going into overdrive.

David:
I know you're in love with her.

John:
She's your girl.

David:
You're in love with her, aren't you???

John:
Okay, I fucking love her.
You stole her from me, you dick.
Is that what you want to hear???

David:
Yes, you dick!!!

John:
You're going to get better.
If you don't, I'm going to be pissed.

That is the end of the messages. I'm partially smiling over their stupid college-boy banter and name-calling, but I'm mostly a big fucking crying mess. I turn off the phone and sit in the car for a few minutes, weeping my eyes out. When I finally pull myself together enough to leave the car, I return to the restaurant. I find Jane and Ben sitting at the table with three untouched sandwiches.

Jane takes in my expression. "Are you okay?"

I nod and hand her the phone. "Thank you for letting me see these."

"I'm sorry I kept them from you."

"I think I'm going to go." I open up my purse. "Let me pay for your lunch."

"Not a chance." Ben stands and puts his hand under my elbow. "Do you want us to drive you anywhere?"

"No, I'll be fine."

"Are you sure?"

"Yes."

"At least let me walk you to your car."

"Thanks." I turn to Jane. "Goodbye."

"Goodbye."

Ben walks me to my car and again asks if I'm okay to drive. I assure him I am, and he gives me a hug. As I drive away, I see him in the rearview mirror, crying right along with me.

Chapter 49

We Should Do This More Than Once Every Decade

With Rachel at John's parents' house, I spend a night thinking about all of it. Recalling some of the messages between John and David, I'm at times laughing and at times crying. I don't remember falling asleep, but when I finally wake, it's after ten, and I must have slept pretty well because I feel refreshed.

I'm supposed to meet John at the house today to talk about staging it for the sale. I'm starving because I haven't eaten in more than twenty-four hours.

After breakfast, I shower, then get in my car. Pulling into the driveway of the new house, I spot John's SUV parked with the liftgate open. It's filled with shopping bags, but he's not around. The front door is wide open, and I head inside. The house looks perfect, but completely empty. It has that new-house smell but not overly, so my mind doesn't wander elsewhere. There don't seem to be any ghosts or old memories haunting me, like the last time I was here.

The faint sounds of what I think is the clothes dryer spinning echo through the furniture-less house, so I head back through the kitchen to the laundry room. There, I find the brand-new washing machine sloshing through a load. My curiosity is now piqued since John doesn't normally do laundry.

Doubling back, I head to our primary bedroom to discover John struggling to get the last corner of the fitted sheet over a thick mattress on a new king-sized bed. A bed I recognize from a store we were shopping in months ago. The room is full of matching furniture and looks professionally decorated with pictures hung, flowers on the dresser, and a white shiplap accent wall behind the headboard.

Upon seeing me, he's startled, then slips, losing his grip on the sheet and smashing his hand in the process. "Shit!" He stands upright. "You're here."

"Shit, I'm here?" I give him a look.

"No, I didn't mean shit, *you're* here. I meant, shit, my hand hurts, and I'm pleasantly surprised you're here."

"Ah." I smile.

"I didn't want you to see it until I was done."

"Looks great."

Grimacing, he rubs his banged-up hand. "Jesus, God. Why do they make these so damn tight?"

"I don't know." I chuckle, then spin, taking in the entire room. "You remembered that bedroom set we saw."

"I did. I know how you always wanted a king-sized bed, but we could never fit it in our old room." He joins me near the foot of the bed, looking it over. "You don't think it's too big, do you?"

"I think it's perfect. How did you do all this?"

"I had a little help from a decorator."

"So, is this your idea of staging the house for sale?" I shoot him a dubious look.

"Well, it wouldn't hurt, I don't think, but I was sorta hoping I might be able to sell you on another idea."

"What's that?"

"Moving in here and sharing this bed with me for real this time."

"Okay," I say casually.

"Just like that?" he asks with trepidation.

"Why? Do you want to argue about it instead?"

"No." He puts up his hands, shaking his head. "Definitely not."

Turning to look me in the eye, he begins, "Look, Ally, I'm so sorry about—"

"I don't want to talk." Placing my hands on his chest, I push him gently back toward the mattress.

"You don't?" He looks at me, confused.

I shake my head. "Lift your arms."

He does, and I pull the shirt over his head and say, "I've been an idiot."

"You have?"

He seems a bit frightened now as I take hold of his shorts, unbutton them, and pull them down his legs. I push him back, and he falls onto the mattress with his shorts around his ankles.

"I've been stupid and wasting too many years with you."

"Well, we've both done things—"

"Can I finish?" I glare at him.

"Sorry."

I pull the shoes, socks, and the shorts off of him. Stepping back, I remove my shirt and bra. "Something's been missing from our otherwise perfect relationship."

"Yeah, what's that?" His mouth drops open, and he's visibly aroused in his boxer shorts.

"I think you know. We've got a lot to make up for, so I figure we should get started ASAP."

"We really should."

After kicking off my shoes, I slip out of my shorts and underwear and stand before him with nothing on. He looks me up and down with his eyes glazing over and his mouth handing open.

"But we, um, we probably need to talk."

"Talk?" Moving to him, I lean in close to his face. "Haven't we spent the last twenty years talking? I think there are other parts of this relationship that have been sorely neglected."

I grab hold of his underwear. He lifts his hips up, and I slip them down his legs. His strong erection stands at full attention.

I motion to it with a couple of head nods. "He doesn't seem to want to talk. Looks like he'd prefer to focus on something else."

He laughs self-consciously. "Well, he does have a mind of his own."

I gesture with both hands for him to move back. "Scoot."

He complies, and I climb on the bed, straddling his hips. His erection, now standing taller, throbs and pokes against my stomach. He gasps as I gyrate slightly over him as the sensitive skin of his shaft rubs against my core. Reaching down, I take hold of him. He breathes out with a shudder, and his eyes close.

I say, "Still want to talk?"

Craning his neck, he watches as I slowly massage his length. "Maybe later."

"I'm glad you're on board." Rising up, I move forward and position his thick head at my entrance. After slipping just the tip in, I hover over it, staying perfectly still. I gnaw at my lip with my eyes closed, moaning.

"Oh fuck." He grabs my hips and groans, "Ally, that feels so good."

Slowly, I slide down on him inch by inch until there's no more space between us. His thickness fills me completely. We lock eyes and stare at one another with our mouths slightly open.

I rise up a few inches, then back down, slowly at first, then begin to pick up speed. His face contorts, and his eyes close.

"Oh fuck. Stop, or I'm ..." He grabs my hips to keep me from moving over him. "I need a minute."

"You can come." I cock my head. "I'd prefer I did first, but—"

"I don't want to yet. Just give me a minute." He massages my ass as he breathes deeply. "You feel so good."

Leaning forward, I place my hands on his chest.

He says, "Maybe we can have a little chat while I take a short break. Just don't move much."

"I can do that."

"Look, I'm sorry about everything. I dated a few women, like you'd sorta asked me to, many years ago, and they all seemed crazy. You don't know what it's like out there. It just happened with Kate. I didn't mean for it to, but she seemed almost normal and safe. You know, I didn't picture her breaking into our house and boiling up our bunny."

"But we don't have a bunny."

"You know what I mean. In some weird way, I thought I was doing us a favor. I'm an idiot."

"I do forgive you. I'm sorry about Kyle. I got caught up in it."

"I understand." He reaches up to my breasts and caresses them gently.

I gyrate my hips over him, and it feels amazing. "Why is it so much easier to forgive someone when they're inside of you?"

"I don't know, but it does seem oddly easy for me too. Maybe we're not thinking clearly."

"I feel pretty clear. Do you?"

"Uh-huh."

"Oh, I had lunch with Jane and Ben yesterday. I was surprised to see them at the place where I go to lunch every Friday, right at the time I normally go." I raise my eyebrows and ask, "You wouldn't happen to know anything about that, would you?"

He shakes his head and says sarcastically, "Really? You have lunch at the same place every week? I didn't know that."

"Uh-huh." I begin thrusting over him. "Is this okay?"

"Yes, but slowly." He nods, breathing heavily.

Sliding his hands back down to my ass, he lifts my hips up slightly and thrusts.

It feels fucking amazing, and I groan. "So, you're good now to start again?"

"I am."

"Good ..." Picking up the pace, I bounce over him with more purpose. "Because ... I'm ... just ..."

He grasps my thighs tightly, controlling my movements over him as he drives his hips up and down into me. I'm so close.

"Oh God," I moan.

He pulls me down tightly over him, and all it takes is for me to rotate my hips, and I'm done. My orgasm flows through me, my body quivers, and my core convulses around him. I can feel him thicken and throb inside me, and then he explodes. I collapse over him with my heart thumping while fighting to breathe.

He runs his hands softly over my back as we lie there, still connected, recovering for a long, long time.

He kisses me, then says, "Oh my God, that was ..."

"I know ..."

I slip off of him on my side and lay my head on his chest, running a finger lightly up and down his stomach. "I've missed you."

"I've missed you too."

I say, "We should do this more than once every decade."

"We should."

We share a smile as he caresses my lower back. "I was wondering if we might try something new at some point?"

"What's that?"

"This ball-crushing thing that your mother's into. Does that run in the family or ..."

I lift my head. "You want your balls crushed, really?"

"Maybe not crushed, but massaged might be kinda nice. You know, I'm getting older, and I'll probably need a little more stimulation in the future in order to, you know ..."

"I think I can do that." Reaching down, I massage them gently.

His eyes roll to the back of his head. "That feels so good."

"I can tell."

He's breathing heavy and moaning as I use both hands on all his parts, and soon, he's rock hard.

He climbs over me, his arms suspending his body over mine as he gazes into my eyes. "I never ever wanted anyone else."

"I'm all yours."

Leaning down, he presses his lips to mine. "We certainly have a lot of lost time to make up for."

I feel his erection poking into my stomach as I say, "That we do."

I adjust my position under him, lining up our parts the way they should be. Suddenly, I feel him pressing slightly inside me, and I say, "Let's start now."

"Let's."

Wrapping my legs around him, I pull his hips into mine, and he sinks fully inside me. I groan in pleasure, and it's nothing short of perfect.

Epilogue - Three Hundred Fifty Days Later

John, Dave, Rachel, and I stand at the foot of David's grave on his birthday. We decided to visit as a family. It's been almost a year since the disastrous and eventful Emerald Isle trip, and as I think about David and quietly reflect on everything that happened, I'm both sad and content. The trip was a shit show in every sense of the phrase, yet I wouldn't trade it for anything. Had it not been for that gorgeous house on that beautiful beach with that manipulative woman, I'm almost certain that we would not all be as happy as we are today.

It turned out that it wasn't as easy as John and I had thought to forgive each other for all that had transpired in Emerald Isle and the decade or so that had led up to that trip. Sure, it seemed like a piece of cake when we were, well, you know ... but it should be no surprise that we had a tad more work to do.

To be clear, we went to therapy.

A lot of therapy.

The sex sorta complicated and clouded things, as it has been known to sometimes do. I think I was riding a high—no pun intended—from reading the text messages David had written to

John, along with the following emotional night that I'd spent alone. And I think it bears repeating that those two earth-shattering climaxes that we shared—in the new house, in that gorgeously decorated bedroom—resulted in some not-so-clear thinking on both our parts.

At least, that's the excuse we both landed on when, shortly after moving back in together, the resentment and unresolved issues began bubbling up to the surface. I guess it was too much to hope for that one amazing afternoon of sex, combined with a couple of quick apologies, would put everything safely behind us.

We found this great couples therapist and started out by going twice a week. About a month later, we scaled back to weekly sessions and finally stopped "working on us" just after the end of the year. I can honestly say we're in a good place. It took some work to get there, but we're here now, and I think we're here to stay.

I believe I'm in a good headspace as far as David is concerned as well. I think I've grieved way more than my fair share. I know he would want me to move on with my life, and I'm finally ready to actually get on with it. Proof of this is that I switched to a new cell phone carrier, and with it, I left my old texts, some painful memories from my past, and my old phone in the recycle bin.

You might be happy to know—God knows I am—that my mother retired her high heels for good. Not for walking—just for crushing things that are much better left uncrushed. And it wasn't just because she loved suede and a number of her favorites were collateral damage, ruined in the wake of her profitable yet cringeworthy venture.

We all know suede is a bitch to clean, but what she experienced took it to a whole other level.

She and my dad fell in love—again. They've decided against

making it official, but they are now living together. His boudoir photography business is thriving, and she's partnering with him on that. I have my fingers crossed that it all works out for those two this second time around.

Izzie is healthy and as adorable as ever. Rachel is doing fine and has no idea that her parents were ever anything other than blissfully happy. I want to keep it that way.

Dave doesn't seem to have any permanent damage related to learning his mother had a very brief yet torrid affair with a man only a few years older than himself. At least, he hasn't mentioned it. I think he's been too busy finishing up his first year of law school, and he's now slaving away sixty hours a week at this internship he landed at a great firm.

John and I have a destination vow renewal booked in Key West in early December. It's going to be a small, family-only affair. The weather should be gorgeous, and we're all looking forward to it. My parents have agreed to leave the illegal drugs, camera, and other boudoir equipment behind.

They've promised to be on their best behavior. We'll see how that goes.

All in all, things are good and Emerald Isle is to blame. John and I are happy, and it only took us a couple of decades to get it right. Getting it right, no matter how long it takes, is really what it's all about.

* * *

Never miss a Luke Young release, announcement or sale by signing up for my NEWSLETTER.

I hope you enjoyed this story. Please help spread the word about my books by posting a review where you bought it and/or on

Goodreads and telling friends and sharing about it on social media. It's not easy to find readers and I would really appreciate it. Please find an excerpt, after my Author's Note below, for the first novel in my Friends with Benefits series. It's called Friends with Partial Benefits and it's another reverse age-gap, but this time a Rom Com without the heaviness of this story. I think you'll really enjoy it.

Hang out with me on social media: **Website Facebook**

More Books by Luke

Friends with Benefits Series

Follow the sexy and hilarious adventures of Jillian and Brian as they navigate the tricky waters of their reverse age gap romance in the seven-book complete series.

FRIENDS WITH PARTIAL BENEFITS

FRIENDS WITH FULL BENEFITS

FRIENDS WITH MORE BENEFITS

FRIENDS WITH EXTRA BENEFITS

FRIENDS WITH TOO MANY BENEFITS

FRIENDS WITH MULTIPLE BENEFITS

FRIENDS WITH REAL BENEFITS

The Friends with Benefits Prequel

FRIENDS WANTING BENEFITS

Discover the hilarious backstory of how Victoria and Jillian meet. When two very different couples, one who's just getting started and one who's apparently just getting finished... meet on a cruise, the better halves become fast friends.

The Friends with Benefits Bonus Book:

FRIENDS WITH BENEFITS BONUS BOOK - VOLUME ONE

Four stand-alone stories featuring your favorite "Friends With Benefits" characters. Some laugh-out-loud funny, some sexy and some, well, both...

Erotica by Luke Young under his Ian Dalton Pen Name

DESPERATE THOUGHTS

Uncover Victoria's secret in, Desperate Thoughts, the erotic prequel the Friends with Benefits Series! It's a dark and sexy tale of love, loss and letting go...

It's been fourteen months since Victoria's husband died and she's struggling to move on with her life. As the attractive widow tumbles into a clandestine sexual encounter with a much younger man, she's re-awakened sexually and motivated to pursue her desperately unfulfilled desires. With each new encounter the risk grows, along with the passion, until events spiral out of control and she's forced to choose between continuing down a path of self-destruction and finally letting go of the past.

Stand Alone Novels

BLAME IT ON EMERALD ISLE

Falling for a younger guy wasn't in the cards, but might be just what she needs.

Never quite getting over the loss of her college soul mate, and settled into a marriage of safety and convenience, Doctor Ally Larson fights a forbidden attraction during a much-needed beach vacation. If battling her own desires isn't disrupting enough from her getaway, dealing with her divorced, oversexed and quirky parents might just send her over the edge.

Torn between the memory of a man she lost, the young sexy man she desperately desires and her near-perfect husband who she just can't get out of her own way to love, she's teetering on the edge of disaster. Who will she choose and will anyone survive the fallout?

Blame it on Emerald Isle is a guaranteed HEA reverse age-gap romance with an overworked heroine, sexy younger man, zany parents and the cutest dog ever. It's a vacation destination read filled with laughter, a full range of emotions, and heat so hot you will need SPF-5000.

SERIOUSLY MESSED UP

Eli Stevens has everything going for him. Married and successful, he's moving in the right direction, when suddenly his world shifts on its axis and he desperately needs to escape... After saving a pop star's life, he's given every man's fantasy as a thank you--a beach house and two incredibly hot women. From there, of course, nothing goes as planned...

CHANCES AREN'T

How far would you go for a second chance? Stunned by an impending divorce, Ben Hunter's life, which was barely working to begin with, suddenly takes a turn for the worse. After a series of extraordinary events, he's given a chance to fix all of it and in the process comes face to face with the last person he ever expected to see — himself...

CHOCOLATE COVERED BILLIONAIRE NAVY SEAL

Roll on the floor laughing while enjoying this contemporary romance parody. Heir to a chocolate empire, Brock Fullman joins the elite Navy SEAL team in order to avenge the death of his high school sweetheart. With his billionaire family one bad day in the stock market away from the dreaded "Mm Mm Mm..." word (Yes Millionaire... he's the only family member who can actually say it), he's torn between the woman he must marry to guarantee his family's future and the new woman he secretly loves. Out for revenge, will he destroy the company, his family, himself and all those around him in the process?

SO FAR GONE, GIRL: A GONE GIRL PARODY

You think you hated Amazing Amy... just wait until you meet Wonderful Winnie! Read the hilarious parody of Gone Girl. Get the ending you were hoping for and laugh out loud along the way.

What do you get when you take the amazing GONE GIRL story, replace the lame anniversary treasure hunts with deadly SAW movie-esque traps and have all the craziness investigated by lunatic detectives channeling the ones from the television show THE KILLING? You get an unputdownable and hilarious parody of EPIC proportions. Don't miss it!

SHRINKAGE

Be careful what you wish for because sometimes you might just get way too much of it!

Is it in yet? It's the phrase that no man ever wants to hear. Luckily, Tim Garrett has never heard those words. At least he has never heard them out loud despite being on the wrong side of the bell curve in the male endowment department.

Author's Note

Let's just say it's been a few years since my last novel—seven, but who's counting...

So, here's a long winded story about how this novel came together. Feel free to skip over it to the excerpt from Friends with Partial Benefits. If you're still with me, here goes ...

I have this folder of files on my computer—short documents with thrown together mish mashes of "what if this" and "what if that" sentences that are not fully fleshed out ideas for potential books. I had this one called "Becoming my mother's wing woman" which was supposed to be about a recently divorced woman who's forced to move in with her now single sixty-plus-year-old mother, and her mother is having an incredible dating/sex life while the daughter is really struggling with her own dating life. I'd written two paragraphs five years ago about her waking up sorta depressed on her birthday and that was it. That was the seed of an idea that started this story.

To me, there is something about forbidden romance that makes for interesting situations between people. Situations where you need to hide the romance from the person who would not approve—generally, that is, the rest of the damn world. And, of course, with these types of things everyone finds out—because if they didn't, it wouldn't be a story. Then when all hell breaks loose, big, hopefully really funny interactions result. (like the Carlos scene ...) That's what I want to capture with this book.

Earlier this year I re-watched the movie, *Blame it on Rio*, a story about an older man falling into an affair with his best-friend's teenaged daughter on a trip to Rio. I thought turning the tables on that premise might make for a good addition to my wing woman story.

Plus, there is this movie called *The Love Letter* about an older woman who ends up having an affair with a man half her age partially because she discovers this love letter she thinks that he wrote for her. Of course, he didn't, and the young man discovers the letter too and he thinks she wrote it for him. This same letter keeps floating around the entire town and everyone who reads it thinks it was written for them. It's a good story and a pretty good movie too.

I sorta combined shades of those two ideas into one and added them to my move-in-with-mom idea.

I knew I wanted Ally's parents to be off the wall. I'm not sure how exactly I came up with the idea for having the mother be an OnlyFans star, but once I did, I googled "what are the strangest pages on OnlyFans" and sure enough some woman is on there crushing guy's testicles. It doesn't do anything for me, but whatever floats your boat ... I needed the mom to be doing something embarrassing and that certainly more than fit the bill. Of course, if Ally's mother is going to be crushing balls, it makes perfect sense that Ally would have a job involving that same general area and hence she became a urologist. Now for the father—my sister actually has a boudoir photography business with her husband, and I thought it might be funny if Ally's father had one as well. I loved writing about when he pulls up to the vacation house with a van full of all his props.

I wanted Ally to be in this unusual marriage and that's where the tragedy comes in. It might not be perfectly plausible for Ally and John to have the relationship that they have, but I think I pulled it off fairly well.

I did struggle with one part – I knew I needed David to ask John to marry and take care of Ally, and I wanted some way for it to be captured in writing, somehow, so they could look at it years later. The only way to really pull that off is if David is on his death bed and for some reason cannot speak. Here is where you have actor Jeremy Renner to thank. In January of this year, Jeremy did something really dangerous with a giant snowplow that he owns. He stepped out of it while it was still running and got caught under the giant thing nearly getting himself killed. He's still recovering and will probably never be fully healed.

I watched the Diane Sawyer interview with him and learned that he wrote notes, to his family on his phone, in the hospital before going into surgery. He did this since he was intubated and could not speak to them. This solved my problem and thankfully cell phone texting was just taking off in the time frame where my story is set.

Okay, so maybe my text messages are a little long for that time period with those old phones where you need to press the key three freaking times for some letters, but cut me some slack —it's a freaking novel ... :)

Now on to Emerald Isle—my family and I took a trip there last summer and when I visited the area called The Point, I discovered this wide, beautiful and nearly empty beach. As I stood out there baking in the sun, it felt like the perfect setting for a novel.

This beach is lined with large homes in this upscale community where the Atlantic Ocean meets the Bogue Sound. The area is known for its breathtaking sunsets although I didn't get to experience one, nor did we stay at one of the large homes on The Point. Instead, we were in a small, mostly dirty, rental house, miles away that sorta smelled like mold, but with a great view of the ocean. Let's just say the place had its plusses and minuses...

Two years ago, my family got the same type of dog I write about in the book and she acts the same adorable way as the one does in my story. Her name is Pippa and she's the cutest, cuddliest, quirkiest, dog on the planet. We lost our beagle, Brody, when he was eight about four years ago to cancer and I was really devastated when he died. I was nowhere near as close to Brody as I am now with Pippa. I've been working from home since the pandemic and this dog is as attached to me as I am to her. I cannot imagine the mess I'll be when she's gone. I hope she lives a long, long life.

And I almost forgot—the only other part of this story that is sorta based on something in my life is the Doctrine of Promissory Estoppel thing that Kyle uses with Ally. In college, I was working as a waiter at this ice cream place (gee that sounds like an 80s song lyric) and was dating this amazing girl who worked behind the counter. We went out a few times over a few weeks and I thought things were going well. I believe she may have been dating someone else or had just met someone else and we were suddenly having the "talk"—things were coming to an end.

We agreed to go out one more time, and at the last minute she was having second thoughts. Well, I was taking a summer business law class and we had recently gone over this Estoppel thing. Somehow, I pulled it out of my bag of tricks (empty bag as it was) and believe me when I tell you I had zero game in college —I was not a player. I barely dated anyone. I explained that I was in that class and told her all about the Doctrine thing in a funny way. I told her how I was suffering a substantial detriment due to her wanting to cancel our date. Long story short, I made her laugh, and our date was back on.

I guess it's true that women want a guy who can make them laugh, at least for one more date... This was the time of my life and the girl I write about in my novel, Chances Aren't. If you get a chance you might want to check out that novel. I think it's very funny.

I had a ball, no pun intended, writing this story. I hope you enjoyed it, laughed a little and maybe got a tad emotional too. I do hope you'll continue on with some of my other books. Please help spread the word about my books by posting a review where you bought it and on Goodreads and telling friends and sharing about it on social media. It's not easy to find readers and I would really appreciate it.

So, I think that's all I wanted to say. Stay safe and I'll be sure to get my next book out slightly more quickly than this one.

Luke

Excerpt Of Friends With Partial Benefits

Jillian Grayson sat up in bed, typing away on the keyboard of her laptop computer. She wore a nightshirt that wasn't all that sexy, but what she was typing was... or at least it started out that way...

Dallas lay in bed, unable to sleep and wondering if Katrina was suffering the same fate—and for the very same reason. Did she want him as much as he wanted her? Katrina was but a few steps away, yet he dare not go to her, for he was a guest, and then there was Katrina's mother, who was just across the hall. For Dallas, sleep came minutes later, but it would be short-lived, for soon Katrina stood over him, completely nude and pondering how to proceed...

Dallas must have been in a deep sleep, since he didn't feel it when Katrina peeled the sheet carefully off him, exposing his muscular body, six-pack abs, and sizeable manhood. She quivered when his impressiveness sprang into view. For a long time, she kneeled next to the bed, just studying his body and savoring his scent. Taking his sex into her hand, Katrina worked it until it was rigid while she watched him sleep. When Dallas woke, he looked into her eyes, swallowed hard, and whispered, "I've been waiting for you."

Just as fast as his sex expanded, it lost its firmness and flopped against his leg. Katrina looked down at it in disappointment and then moaned in frustration. "What's wrong?"

Dallas said sheepishly, "Sometimes that happens to me. Sorry. Ever since I cheated on my wife with that whore in the pool, I haven't been able to—"

Jillian stopped typing and thought she might be heading in the wrong direction with this. How did her ex-husband get into the story? Then again, most men are assholes, she thought.

Picking up the glass of wine from her nightstand, she took a long sip and then replaced it. She highlighted the last paragraph about Dallas's problem, hit one key, and it was gone. Just like his boner. She laughed out loud.

She wasn't exactly in the correct frame of mind to write at the moment, especially on this particular subject. She stared straight ahead and wondered about the likelihood of Dallas slipping in the shower, striking his head, and dying instantly. Or maybe an earthquake could strike, and Dallas's amazingly perfect body would be trapped under a giant beam.

What the hell kind of name was Dallas anyway? She thought she might want to give her character a real name like Stewart but figured no one would believe that a guy named Stewart could give you six consecutive orgasms in one night.

What was she doing, anyway, writing novels about people having amazing sex when she'd never had any? Okay, maybe once or twice twenty years ago, but none since then. She had no right. If people knew that she was the one writing these books, they wouldn't buy them. She was a fraud.

Jillian picked up her wineglass and took another long drink.

She grinned, wiped those unhelpful thoughts from her mind, and started typing again...

Katrina took his sex in her hand and worked it until it was rigid. As she studied it closely, Katrina noticed two red bumps on the underside of his pathetic excuse for a penis. She recoiled in horror—

Jillian hit the backspace key to erase everything after Dallas's "sex" started expanding. Romance novels about erectile dysfunction and STDs weren't exactly big sellers. She closed the lid on the laptop and tossed it gently onto a pillow at the foot of the bed. After emptying her wineglass with one last sip, she turned on the television.

Jillian Grayson wrote under the pen name of Jaclyn West. She'd written fourteen bestsellers so far and had more money than she needed flowing in, so her next novel could wait. The book royalties had paid for her large, beautiful house in Miami. She still had plenty of money, even after the divorce, which forced her to part with nearly half of her earnings to her bastard ex-husband.

She'd never forget the day she came home early from a book tour and found George performing oral sex on that slut in the pool, the pool she had paid for and an act he rarely, if ever, did for her. Jillian always thought he hated oral sex or, more specifically, he hated the giving part. But there he was, naked, standing in the shallow end of the pool, and going to work on some other woman as she floated in the pool on a ring, which Jillian had also paid for. The pool oral sex thing actually looked like it might be kind of fun, and she often wondered why George had never once tried that on her.

That day, when she spotted them from the second-floor balcony off their bedroom, she had watched for a little longer than she'd care to admit. Maybe that was because all her erotic romance writing had left her desensitized to sex, at least a little. At first, it didn't seem real; it was as if she was visualizing a scene for a book, not watching her husband cheat on her.

When she finally came back to earth, Jillian left the house and went to the side of the pool. She snuck up on the adulterous couple and stood there until the woman noticed they had an audience. The woman tapped George on the shoulder to get his attention. When George turned around, he had a guilty look on his face that Jillian would never forget. Jillian wouldn't let the naked woman back in the house to get her clothes. She simply threw the clothes out the door and forced the woman to get dressed outside, shamefully leaving through the back gate. George went into the house, dressed, and left through the front door. It was the last time he ever set foot inside the house.

Jillian didn't cry that day; instead, she put on a pair of kitchen gloves and retrieved the ring float from the pool. When her attempts to drain the float of air through the valve seemed to be taking too long, she stabbed it ten times with scissors. That could possibly have been overkill, but it did the trick and gave her a much-needed outlet for her rage. She called a company to have the pool drained, scrubbed, and refilled at the cost of fifteen hundred dollars. It was worth it, she thought, because she would never have been able to dip a toe in the pool until she replaced every last drop of that contaminated water.

She imagined what George had been up to all those times she was traveling. What types of women had he explored in and out of the pool? How long had he been screwing around and with how many women? Although Jillian was out of town quite a bit, she had never suspected anything. George never seemed to be sneaking around, nor was he ever evasive about where he was going or what he had planned. Their sex life was certainly not great or very active, but he seemed to be an attentive and loyal husband—at least, most of the time.

Once she discovered the infidelity, she wanted to know if George had left her with any other little surprises. She went to her doctor for a complete STD panel of tests, and luckily for him, she came back clean. Had George left her with something, she would have cut off his balls, or worse.

Jillian could always come up with stories and had never suffered from long bouts of writer's block in the past. But lately, her male characters ended up mangled in some horrible accident, diseased, or unable to perform. Although she had no personal interest in the lifestyle, she even pitched an idea for an all-female, lesbian romance novel, but her publisher declined. She could not focus. Maybe she would try to write in another genre, she thought, but this romance stuff used to come so easily to her.

She was sitting on four unfinished manuscripts. Once Jillian found a story heading down the wrong path, she would start another, but that technique didn't seem to be working for her, either. Since the divorce, she found herself unable to finish a novel, and she was beginning to think that maybe what she needed was a complete break from writing.

She couldn't blame George completely. Ever since her first bestseller, she definitely was less attentive to him than she needed to be. It was probably at least ten percent her fault, although she never admitted that to him. Even so, did he really need to screw other women in their house, especially in their pool? Couldn't he have gotten a divorce first or at the very least done it in a hotel or something? What if their son, Rob, had come home to catch his father with another woman in broad daylight? Rob, currently attending college in Georgia, would have been devastated.

He'd be home for Spring Break in about six weeks, although

Jillian was sure he'd spend nearly all his time with his girlfriend, Laura, who was going to school in Miami. They'd been dating since their junior year of high school, and it looked like these two kids were in love and would be married once they graduated from college.

Even though she knew she wouldn't see him much while he was home, Jillian looked forward to his visit. She knew her son was the only truly good thing to come out of the marriage.

Jillian grabbed the remote control and changed the channel just in time to catch the Super Bowl as it was ending. She had forgotten it was on. Not that she would have tuned in anyway. She used the Packers' victory celebration as a distraction from thinking about romance novels, ex-husbands, or even men in general. Although, she did like the way Green Bay's quarterback filled out his tight football pants. She might be bitter, but she wasn't dead.

Staring up at the ceiling, she wondered what had brought her to this place in her life. How had she ended up all alone in this big house? What had she done wrong? She glanced back to the screen. When she saw an image of the Steelers locker room filled with nearly naked men, she thought about her best friend, Victoria Wilde. Jillian wondered what she was doing. She checked the time and saw it was still early. Grinning, she wondered why she bothered checking, since two in the morning would be early for Victoria. She grabbed the phone and dialed. The phone rang three times and just as Jillian was about to hang up, she heard the click. After five seconds of complete silence, the sound of soft moaning spilled through the phone.

Jillian listened for a moment. "Victoria?"

"Hello?" Victoria finally replied in a throaty drawl.

"Hey, what are you doing?"

"Oh, uh... not much. I just have a friend over."

"Sorry, I'll let you go then."

"No, don't worry about it. I can talk for a few minutes."

Only two blocks away, Victoria sat on the sofa in her living room, wearing a skintight cleavage-featuring top. She had just turned thirty-nine but looked much younger. She was in spectacular shape and dressed like a woman in her late twenties. Her 'friend' wasn't currently visible at her eye level, but he was nearby.

"So, what's going on?" Victoria asked.

Jillian sighed and began, "I tried to do some writing tonight, but I'm struggling again. I'm just not in a very sexual mood."

"Why don't you try watching some porn? That always gets me in the mood."

"I don't have any... porn," Jillian replied, in a voice clearly indicating to anyone paying the least bit of attention that she was taken aback by the suggestion.

Victoria, however, was preoccupied and slumped down low on the sofa, her miniskirt pulled up to her waist with her twenty-six-year-old friend Austin's head buried between her legs. He was extremely busy.

Victoria moaned slightly, "Yeah," in a low voice.

Back in the Grayson home, Jillian narrowed her eyes and asked pointedly, "You sure this is a good time?"

"I think the ice melted," Victoria said.

"What?" Jillian asked.

"Sorry, I was speaking to my friend."

"Oh. You sure you can talk?"

"I have at least five minutes."

"Okay..." Jillian said, a little confused.

"You have no porn? Really? Check Rob's room. I'm sure he has a stash."

"I will not go searching my son's room for porn," Jillian replied, horrified.

Victoria said a little curtly, "Ice."

"What?"

"Again, sorry I was talking to my, uh, oh..." Victoria exhaled deeply. "Come over here, and you can borrow some of mine or I could send you a link to great website that has—"

"No thanks. I think I'll just go to sleep."

Jillian heard rustling over the phone as if it had fallen then she could make out a voice say, "Oh, yeah... that feels good."

"Victoria?" She widened her eyes. "Victoria, are you sure I'm not interrupting anything?"

There was no reply.

"Victoria, are you there?"

"Sorry about that," Victoria finally answered.

"Who's over there? What are you—"

"Oh, yeah. Keep doing exactly that." Victoria moaned. "Jillian, have you ever had anyone perform oral sex on you while sucking an ice cube?"

"What?" Wrinkling her nose, Jillian shook her head. "Ice? No!"

"Well, that would certainly help you write. Oh, my..." After breathing in deeply, Victoria moaned again.

Jillian made a face. "I'm almost afraid to ask. Are you, uh, doing that... right now?"

Victoria exhaled slowly and said languidly, "Yeah, and it's... amazing!"

"And you're talking to me?"

"I can multi-task," Victoria replied, casually.

Jillian's mouth flew open as she thought about how to proceed.

"So, what else is up?" Victoria asked.

"Should you really be talking to me with some guy doing that to you?"

"Well, I figured I'd be returning the favor soon, and..." Victoria paused to exhale deeply again and continued, "I certainly wouldn't be able to talk to you then."

After Jillian nodded, her face registered mild agreement. "Oh, that makes sense... Wait, no it doesn't... I'm going to go."

"Oh... yeah, Austin." Victoria paused for a moment. "Jillian, what I meant was when my mouth is full, it'll be really hard to hold a conver—"

"No, no. That part I got," Jillian interrupted. "I think I'm going to go and let you—"

"You should... totally try this. It would clear up that writer's block issue immediately. When's the last time someone went down on you?"

Jillian made a sour face. "I'm just going to—"

"I mean, like, really got in there and did a good job with it?"

"Okay, I'm really going to hang up now."

As Jillian hung up the phone, her sick expression morphed into a smile. However, it didn't take long for the smile to fade—replaced by something resembling more of a sad longing. She could go for some good oral sex right about now. She stared blankly ahead as she tried to recall the last time anyone did that to her, much less if he did a good job while doing it. She couldn't remember exactly, but she knew it'd been a long, long, long time.

Friends with Partial Benefits **is available now.**

About the Author

Hey everyone! I'm romantic comedy, contemporary romance and comic fiction author Luke Young. I've written over sixteen books, including one Amazon number one in comic fiction and five Amazon and iBooks Rom Com Bestsellers. The best way to stay in touch with me for news and new releases is to sign up for my email list here: https://lukeyoungbooks.com.

You can email me at authorlukeyoung@gmail.com or on Facebook at https://www.facebook.com/LukeYoungAuthor. Please reach out and let me know what you think about my books! I love hearing from readers.